Praise for
Hilma Wolitzer
and

H E A R T S

"A fictional success . . . so rich in well-realized characters [that] it raises ordinary people and everyday occurrences to a new height . . . very funny and very sad at the same time, gentle and humane in mood, fully believable in its parts and in its whole, *Hearts* is a novel of our time and, I feel quite certain, for some time to come."   —*The Washington Post Book World*

"Splendid . . . Wolitzer's ear is flawless; her dialogue has perfect pitch. . . . This is a comedy about the heart-wrenching process of growth; it is written with great skill. . . . Few readers will fail to be moved."
                                                  —*The New Republic*

"Hilma Wolitzer has the extraordinary ability to make the ordinary into something rare and meaningful. She is a novelist whose central concern is our domestic lives, and she may well be the best such novelist we have."   —JONATHAN YARDLEY, *The Miami Herald*

"Apt details of contemporary American life [and] an encompassing joie de vivre . . . delightful reading."
                                                  —*Library Journal*

HEARTS

HEARTS

A NOVEL

Hilma Wolitzer

BALLANTINE BOOKS   NEW YORK

2006 Ballantine Books Trade Paperback Edition

Copyright © 1980 by Hilma Wolitzer
Reading group guide copyright © 2006 by
Random House, Inc.

Excerpt from *The Doctor's Daughter* copyright © 2006
by Hilma Wolitzer

Published in the United States by Ballantine Books,
an imprint of The Random House Publishing Group,
a division of Random House, Inc., New York.

BALLANTINE and colophon are registered trademarks
of Random House, Inc.
READER'S CIRCLE and colophon are trademarks
of Random House, Inc.

Originally published in hardcover in the United States
by Farrar, Straus & Giroux, New York, in 1980.

This book contains an excerpt from the forthcoming book
The Doctor's Daughter by Hilma Wolitzer. This excerpt has
been set for this edition only and may not reflect the final
content of the forthcoming edition.

ISBN 0-345-48751-6

Printed in the United States of America

www.thereaderscircle.com

9 8 7 6 5 4 3 2 1

WITH GRATITUDE for the generous support of
the National Endowment for the Arts
and the Corporation of Yaddo

FOR MY MOTHER, Rose Liebman,
and for Danny Arnold—
two brave hearts

HEARTS

IN THE IDEALIZED VISION OF MAPMAKERS, New Jersey is tinted a delicate pink that has nothing to do with the industrial darkness of its larger cities. Linda Reismann, nee Camisko, drove her husband's green Maverick from the hospital parking lot in downtown Newark into the gloomy evening landscape. She was a new driver; Wright had taught her with touching patience on the six Sunday afternoons of their marriage, while she sat rigidly upright and held the wheel in an uncompromising grasp, as if it were an enemy who might make a sudden hostile move.

Wright had just died of a massive coronary seizure on the fourth floor of that hospital, shortly after the doctor left the room. "Well, he's stabilized now," the doctor said, bouncing a little on his heels. The stethoscope hanging from his pocket danced like a rubber snake. "And I'm really happy with our findings so far. It looks good—all systems go!" He gave a thumbs-up sign and went whistling down the corridor. Wright, who had been nodding and even smiling during the doctor's pronouncement, nodded again, at Linda, released his weak grip on her hand, and shut his eyes forever.

She was only twenty-six and there had already been three important deaths, with Linda the only one watching: her father's, her mother's, and now Wright's. Maybe it was a kind of divine test, with the miraculous reward of personal immunity. To never have to die or be old! And with a couple of bonuses thrown in: to be as famous in the world as one is to oneself, to be thrillingly in love, and loved back, always.

Wright died in the quiet modest way he'd lived. He collapsed at the surgical-instruments plant where he was

HEARTS

an assistant foreman, and was taken to the hospital by ambulance. Between fainting spells, he protested about the fuss, saying it was only gas, only some junk he must have eaten, maybe that chicken hash, until they pressed an oxygen mask over his face and he was still.

It was Linda's day off from the Fred Astaire Dance Studios in Bayonne, and she was at home trying to feel at home when the telephone rang. Wright's supervisor cautiously played down the seriousness of his call. "Listen," he said. "It could be anything, right? Or it could be nothing." A range too wide for her to contemplate. "So don't worry," he added, but his voice was as grave as a newscaster's about to deliver an important bulletin.

The trip to the hospital was the first one she'd ever made alone in heavy traffic. She went very slowly, braking every few hundred yards whether she had to or not, and honking warnings at cars and trucks that approached in the adjacent lanes. The Maverick's horn made a silly, high-pitched squeal, like the sound of a whoopee cushion. Other drivers honked back, their horns deep and aggressive, and they made profane gestures from behind their rolled-up windows. Was she supposed to return them as part of some unwritten code of the road? But she was afraid that if she removed one hand from the wheel, even for an instant, the car would careen out of control and charge like a guard dog over the divider.

By the time she reached the hospital she was exhausted, and the parking lot was filled. It was right in the middle of visiting hours. Linda finally found one stingy space, recently vacated by a motorcyclist, a space that required parallel parking, her major shortcoming as a driver.

But she did it, with the contemptuous encouragement of two male kitchen workers who came from a side door of the hospital wearing white hats and carrying knives and spatulas. One of them stood directly behind the car, with the daring of a toreador, waving his knife like a sword. One false move on her part and he would probably slash her tires.

"Come on, lady," he said. "Turn her to the right. To the *right*, I said! Come on, come on, you have plenty of room, now cut it, cut it! Jesus H. Christ. Now straighten her out . . ."

She was in perfectly, although she had no memory of the series of motions that put her there. And God only knew how she'd ever get out; the car in front and the one in back were only inches away. But she was manic with success for the moment, and then with terror because she had been summoned to this place.

Upstairs, she found Wright asleep, the only occupant, except for a nurse, of the six-bed unit. The nurse looked at her watch. "Ten minutes only," she said sternly, as if she had recognized Linda at once as a waster of valuable time.

Wright was hooked up to leave for the moon. She stood in the doorway and stared. What would she say to him when he woke? She kept thinking the word "husband" as if that would give her a clue. But its private meaning eluded her, and was as mysterious and alien as it had been on the day they'd married. Husband? He was someone she barely knew, a dancing partner, an older man with a leftover child from another marriage, and with a sad, submissive heart. She closed her eyes briefly and tried to remember precisely how he looked, and could not.

His illness frightened and embarrassed her. But she

HEARTS

hardly ever knew what to say to people, even in ordinary circumstances. This was one of the reasons she had married so impulsively, as if the state of wifehood could mystically bestow instant experience and social ease. Other wives she'd seen, in supermarkets and movie theaters, had it, a smug radiance that demanded the best cuts of meat, that brought butchers and husbands alike to their knees.

Her lack of confidence was also one of the reasons Linda envied actors and actresses. No matter what anyone said about how hard their profession was, all the words were written out plainly for them to say, and how to say them, and where to stand. She'd read recently in a movie magazine that even the kissing, which appears so convincingly spontaneous on the screen, doesn't just happen. The actors are told exactly where their lips have to meet, so the light will be perfect, and the camera angle. They have to do it over and over, and when their lips become dry and chapped from the effort and the frustration, a makeup artist comes by with a little plant atomizer and sprays them back to moist sensuality.

She tiptoed in and put her purse and sweater on a chair near one of the other beds. Wright's eyes had opened and they explored the room for her like those tower search beams in movies about prison breaks. He spoke in a disguised voice, hushed and sedated. "Linda?"

If this were a movie instead of her real life, there would have been a director across the room, slouched in one of those canvas chairs they use, who would say, "Go to him now, Linda. Slowly. Sit by his side, with your head tilted this way a little. Ahhh, that's good, that's fine. Now take his hand and say, 'I'm here, sweetheart.

It's all right.' " Or something like that. At least she would know what to do. But she was definitely on her own. The nurse, with another significant glance at her watch, had turned her back.

When Wright said Linda's name again, she dreamwalked to imagined instructions. She sat carefully at the edge of the bed so as not to jar him or the fantastic machinery to which he was secured. Without thinking, she looked directly into his face, and it *was* a known face, despite its astonishing pallor. Comically rugged, like a fist, but kindly. She couldn't deny knowledge of its sometimes greedy, sometimes apologetic mouth, of the reddish chin bristles that had sprouted since his early-morning shave, and of the brown eyes as gentle and undemanding as a domestic animal's. And she heard him sigh and breathe deeply, the way he often did in troubled sleep. Husband. She looked across the room again and only her red sweater was there, neatly folded on the molded plastic visitor's chair. Even the nurse had disappeared into a closet, where she could be heard rustling among supplies.

Lights. Camera. Linda thought of taking Wright's hand, but before she could he took hers, which looked unnaturally ruddy and durable, and tried to squeeze it. She squeezed back, willing the transfer of some of her own unfair portion of health. Before she could speak, the door swung open and, powered by the excitement of his own optimism, the doctor came into the room.

HEARTS

2

ROBIN WAS LISTENING TO THE RADIO AND finishing the fine details on her social studies project—a diorama of the French Revolution.
Dr. Fox and his stupid assignments. She had cut his class a lot this marking period and he'd threatened to fail her if she didn't turn this thing in on time. What a total asshole. On the wall in the girl's room at school, someone had written: *Do you know Dr. Fox's wife? Yeah, every night,* someone else had scrawled.

The scene in Robin's diorama was fixed in a shoebox her father had given her. He always saved stuff like that: shoeboxes, shirt cardboards, frozen-juice cans, in case she'd ever need them for something. Robin had painted in the backdrop of spectators at the beheading of Marie Antoinette. She worried now that they looked too modern, too American, like fans in the bleachers at a Mets game. Any moment they might rise as one and yell, "Play ball!" The rest was wonderful, though. Her father had helped her the night before with the construction of a miniature working guillotine. In fact, he became so excited and so involved that he practically did the whole thing himself. After a demonstration, using a raw carrot that fell in precise golden circles, he insisted on inserting the sharp edge of the razor blade into the wood, for safety's sake. Too bad. Robin would have loved to see sly old Fox try it out—ca-chunk!—his finger falling like a carrot slice into the provided basket. Now it only contained Marie's tiny molded clay head. Robin had reluctantly used yellow Plasticine for that, after eliminating the other available colors. Green and blue were out of the question and the red was too blushingly healthy. Marie looked as if she had been strangled first; her clay eyes popped and her tongue protruded. The rest of her body, dressed in a tattered Kleenex, still knelt in a belated attitude of prayer. Linda the Wimp had said it was certainly a very unusual and creative project, but she'd turned pale when she looked at it and wouldn't eat any of the carrot slices later.

The Bee Gees were singing "How Deep Is Your Love," and Robin kept peering quickly into the shoebox, and squinting, to see if a sudden glimpse gave the whole thing more historical reality, if the cotton balls pasted onto the sky-blue sky could easily pass for clouds.

At least Linda wasn't here now, breathing down her neck, offering dumb advice that nobody asked for. Last night she'd tried to get Robin to put a small purse mirror somewhere in the scene as a frozen lake, with the rest of the cotton fluffed around it for snow. She said that she'd always used a mirror when she made a diorama for school. If you put little cardboard skaters on it, Linda said, they'd be reflected in the mirror. Skaters! While the queen was telling them to go eat cake, and getting her head chopped off for it.

Something was missing, though. Robin stepped back from the kitchen table to get a new perspective, and noticed the printing on the side of the box: *Cordovan Stroller 11D 19.95.* She'd have to cover that with masking tape later. The thing that was missing, she realized, was blood. There had to be plenty of blood. She thought of using ketchup, the way they did in the movies, but from some of the permanent stains on her clothing, she knew it would dry too dark. She could prick her own finger for the real thing. That idea made her feel a little queasy and would bring the same eventual results as the ketchup. This blood was supposed to be freshly spilled, freshly red. Nail polish! That was it. Linda wore it all the time, even on her toenails; twenty spots of lacquered blood.

Robin went into their bedroom, trying to avoid notice of the bed itself. This was almost impossible to do, since it was king-sized and took up most of the modest room. It was better not to think of what probably went on in here. She looked away to the dresser top, where a few items of Linda's makeup were scattered: mascara, lip gloss, blusher. No nail polish in sight.

Robin opened the night-table drawer on Linda's side of the bed, her interest quickening despite her disgust. Who knew what she'd find? Last year, when she and her friend Ginger were sitting for the Firestones, a young couple on the next street, they'd discovered a circular plastic case in the bedroom, with Mrs. Firestone's diaphragm inside. Robin had only a vague idea of what it was, but it looked shockingly clinical and was the same color and texture as the rubber gloves she'd once seen in the doctor's office. As she stared at the diaphragm, she thought of cows' udders and unspeakable examinations, and was confused by the innocent sprinkling of talc across its surface. She and Ginger searched after that for more evidence of the Firestones' secret nights, but they didn't find anything else.

Linda had lots of junk in her bedside drawer, but nothing that could ever be construed as sexual. There were check stubs, a single brown shoelace, a stick of gum, and supermarket coupons for room deodorant and dog food. They didn't even have a dog. The drawer had a pungent domestic smell, like camphor or laundry bleach.

Robin's mother must have kept other, more exotic things here. Robin wasn't sure what they were, but she knew they had to have been intimate and delicate, the small private treasures of a beautiful woman. She slammed the drawer shut and went into the bathroom. The nail polish was right there, next to the spare roll of tissue, on top of the toilet tank. The color was Frosted Fire, and it was perfect.

Robin carried the bottle back to the kitchen, where, humming with concentration, she dipped the little brush over and over again, and applied the final scarifying details to the diorama. It was a veritable bloodbath when she was done. There were generous drops of red polish on the divided sections of the queen's neck, more on her dress and on the guillotine's dull blade. There was a thick, glazed puddle at the bottom of the basket and, after Robin's hand faltered, a few splatters on the cotton clouds and across the faces of the cheering crowd in the backdrop.

She was thrilled with the dramatic results, and as she moved back to admire them from a distance, a car door slammed outside. Wait till her father saw *this!* She ran to the window, but it was only Linda, walking slowly from the Maverick toward the front stairs.

Robin quickly covered the polish and shoved the bottle into one of the cabinets. She turned the volume up on the radio to drown out the blood rushing in her ears, and looked around for something to eat.

HEARTS

3

LINDA OPENED THE DOOR TO THEIR GARDEN apartment, using Wright's keys. They were heavier than hers, and the ring was attached to a thick leather strap. She sniffed at it and thought she detected his own particular smell, something like machine oil and bread. There were other, unfamiliar keys on the ring and she wondered what doors they opened. Maybe they were to another apartment, somewhere he had once lived with his first wife.

Robin, the product of that marriage, was doing something at the sink, with her narrow, hunched back to the door. It was Linda's responsibility to tell her that her father was dead. There should have been someone closer to the girl to give her such terrible and personal news. But the only one truly close to her had been Wright. Despite all of Linda's efforts at friendship these past weeks, Robin had hardly talked to her, or looked right at her, for that matter.

The radio on top of the refrigerator was tuned to a rock station, and playing loudly. If Linda spoke she might not be heard. She coughed for attention and Robin started and turned, as if she'd been caught in some forbidden act. But she had only been eating chocolate cake. A few crumbs were scattered on the drainboard and others clung to her fuzzy, pale yellow shirt. Her blondness, everything matching—skin, hair, shirt—gave her a hazy, unfocused look. The white lashes, as usual, were lowered, so that it was difficult to read her mood. For the first time, Linda recognized that Robin had noticeable breasts, and hips that flared in her jeans like a bell. Unwatched, she'd emerged suddenly and strikingly female from that other small neuter figure. Stepdaughter. Orphan.

They looked at one another in the din of music, and Linda hoped the message could somehow be transmitted this way, with just an exchange of allusive glances, or that a telephone call from the hospital had preceded her arrival home, and that Robin already knew. But that was stupid. Would she be eating cake, *enjoying* it, if she'd just heard of her father's death? Linda waited until the girl finished chewing and swallowing. Then she said, "I have to tell you something, Robin. Something bad."

After she said that, Linda's gaze wandered anxiously, and for the first time since she'd come in, she noticed the diorama and its latest gory embellishments. "Oh, God," she whispered, and turned back to Robin, who only squinted and appeared puzzled. She didn't even bother to lower the volume on the radio.

Linda raised her voice. "Your daddy!" she shouted, and the title was heartbreaking to her, with far more tragic meaning than "husband" could ever have.

Fortunately, she didn't have to go any further. A rapid series of expressions moved across Robin's face, and then she swallowed deeply, as if one crumb of cake had not gone down properly. "He died," she said, at last, "didn't he?"

Linda nodded, relieved. "Yes. That's what happened."

A frantic frog pulse leaped in Robin's throat. She went haltingly to the table and sat down. Her movements jostled the shoebox and the little clay head rolled in its basket and settled.

Linda shut her eyes, but she was compelled by Robin's silence to open them and go on. "Heart," she said, and heard in her own enunciation of the word derision for the easy mortal surrender of that organ.

HEARTS

The girl continued to sit, her hands opened palms-up on the table, as if she expected to have her fortune read. Well, that wouldn't be hard to do. There was definitely a long journey in her near future. She'd have to be sent, or taken, to her father's people in Iowa, or Idaho, wherever it was that they lived. But this wasn't the time to discuss that. This was a time for grieving. If only Robin would say something, express her grief, or her anger. Then Linda would be able to quit talking. But Robin didn't, and Linda said, flushing, "He went to sleep and that's all." Oh, shut up, she told herself, and continued, "He didn't wake up or get scared." An instant picture of Wright's dying came into her head, followed by a wake of tenderness for his child. She felt an urge to embrace Robin, even though they had never touched one another before, even if it would be awkward. But Robin had to indicate that she would accept an embrace. Robin had to make the first move, and it was hard to tell if she was even breathing.

Maybe she was in shock. And what was it you were supposed to do about that? Slap her? Raise her feet and lower her head? Throw on warm blankets, or was it cold water? Why did they give that first-aid course in high school, anyway? No one had ever drowned in Linda's presence, or broken a leg, or bled recklessly and needed a tourniquet made from a shoelace and a ball-point pen. Except for her father, they had all died in bed, quietly, irrevocably.

Almost everything you were taught turned out to be useless: capitals of foreign countries, major crops and imports, climate, population. All that information and Linda had become a teacher of social dancing for adults, a purveyor of the newest craze—the Hustle, the Worm, the Vegetable, and the Freak.

Still, facts stuck and once in a while, in the nervous clutch of some Freaking fool, she'd suddenly and unaccountably think of the monsoons of Jakarta, or about the thin mountain air of Machu Picchu that made visitors giddy and necessitated longer baking schedules for breads and cakes. And sometimes she imagined the wonderful breathkiss of resuscitation given or received on a moonlit beach.

"I was right *there*," she told Robin, desperately. What was wrong with this girl that she didn't cry for her father, who loved her and whom she loved? When Linda's father died sixteen years ago, she'd quickly become hysterical. Neighbors had to shake her and force her to drink burning whiskey. They begged her to stop crying before she made herself sick. She'd wailed and rocked all night, although she had secretly and fiercely wished for a long time that he would die, and in agony, if possible. Of course the circumstances of her father's death were different, were bizarre, and the agony far more extravagant than Linda's worst imaginings, yet seemingly there at her own bidding.

But she had wept for Wright, too, albeit more calmly. After the dreadful frenzy of activity in the hospital room, the nurses took her to a small alcove behind their station, patted her shoulder, and then went off to do whatever it is they do to the dead. A little while before, Linda had been unable to concentrate on being married, and now, perversely, she felt utterly forsaken. The tears that came first were for herself.

Very soon she remembered Wright, who had been

HEARTS

taken by surprise like that, actually ambushed by death, and was even more forsaken than she the moment his spirit rose like a turncoat from his body. And the thought of the body itself brought fresh weeping: that thinning blond crown checked so often for recent losses, the small paunch he quickly inhaled when he caught her looking, and his penis that once led him, rosy and exuberant, to their bed, and was now doomed to an eternity of melancholy decline. Poor Wright. Only forty-two years old, an age that had seemed biblically ancient only weeks ago, and was obviously an outrageous gyp as a whole lifetime.

She thought, too, of his Sunday hobby, those earnestly realistic landscapes he painted indoors, of lavish streams and mountains, without even looking once through the window at the miserable clump of birch in the courtyard, or the perpetually overcast patch of Newark sky.

This time she wept only for him, and when she was finished she went out to the parking lot and found everything there new and shimmering in her tear-dazzled vision. The car in front of the Maverick was gone, giving her plenty of room to maneuver. It was evening and the windows of the hospital were cool rectangles of light. But where was the light switch on the dashboard? She turned on the windshield wipers and the emergency blinkers and the radio before she found it. Then she gunned the motor and backed up by mistake, hitting the car behind her. After drying her eyes on the sleeve of her sweater, Linda looked through the rearview mirror; there was no visible damage. With determination and a grinding of gears, she went forward this time, out into traffic and the world.

Linda handled widowhood with surprising efficiency. It had taken her much
longer to adjust to marriage. Each day she
performed another new task that would lead her back
toward single society. She even arranged for the funeral
all by herself. How could she ask that poor zombie
kid to decide on a service or help to pick her father's
coffin?

The funeral director was a young man who seemed to
have centuries of experience. His dark eyes were extraor-
dinarily expressive, and she wondered how he managed
to convey so much without actually saying it. It was as
if she could read his very thoughts: *You can put him in
a plastic lawn bag for all I care, lady. The poor stiff
won't know the difference, even if he did work his balls
off for you. It's between you and God.*

To Linda, who had so much trouble expressing herself aloud, it was a stellar performance. And when he
finally did speak, his voice was freighted with judgment.
"You know," he said, with a self-deprecating little
chuckle, "it may seem like a strange notion to you, but
this is, in a way, the last thing you and your husband
will be doing together."

It certainly did seem like a strange notion. It was
only Wright's last thing to do. And he was going to do
it alone.

The choices she was offered were dizzying. It was
something like trying to buy an airline ticket, with all
the confusing options they gave you these days: Sunday
Freedom Fare, Midweek Supersaver Special. Finally,
Linda took a package deal, including cremation, that
was a little cheaper than the others, and she suffered

HEARTS

only a slight afterthought of guilt. She was convinced that cremation was the right thing to do. It eliminated all those terrible and illogical words—corpse, cadaver, remains—for what was so recently a warm and animated presence. When she could bear to think about it, she imagined she'd want to be cremated, too.

And money was going to matter. She'd gone to the Social Security Office, and the Veterans Administration, and the headquarters of Wright's union, where she was grilled by clerks who were either indifferent or in a homicidal rage. In the end there weren't too many benefits. Wright had let his V.A. life-insurance policy lapse after his first wife left him. There was one for fifteen hundred dollars from the union, though, and with unfathomable trust, he had made Linda his sole beneficiary on their wedding day. She intended to split everything with Robin, as Wright must have known she would do: the insurance, their meager savings, and the money received from the couple who were going to take over the apartment with its furniture. It would be a kind of orphan's dowry to make Robin more attractive to her father's people in Iowa.

Linda was going to give her door-to-door service there. She was doing it for Wright, seeing that his only daughter was safely situated with blood relatives. Besides, the arrangements with his family were not firmly established. Linda had sent a long telegram explaining everything to Wright's father and older sister, after finding an address for them among Wright's papers. She offered to delay the funeral for a few days in case either of them was able to attend. Before they were married, Wright told her he'd had a falling-out with his family years ago and had lost touch with them. Surely, Linda thought, this tragedy would erase old grudges and hard feelings. But there was no response to her message.

She'd never known any farmers personally, but in books and movies they were practical and taciturn (that's where Robin probably got it) yet scrupulous about family duty. Maybe they never answered telegrams and letters because they were backbreakingly busy from sunrise to sunset with farm chores. Maybe it was just understood that Robin would come to them, that they were bound to her through some rural code of ethics. Linda did consider telephoning one night. She checked their number and address with the long-distance operator to make sure they had not moved. But at the last minute she was nervous about calling—didn't farmers go to bed as early as children?—and she hung up without dialing.

Anyway, Iowa was on the way to California, Linda's ultimate destination. Her mother had spoken of going to California during her last years, "to get away from all this," with a vague gesture that might have included the house on Roper Street, the harshness of Northeastern winters, and the inexorable downward path of her life.

Everybody wanted to go to California. Linda believed it was a migratory instinct, apart from the rational arguments for its good weather, geographical beauty, and glamorous movie industry. Yet she was excited by the idea of seeing palm trees and redwoods, the Pacific Ocean, and famous stars pushing shopping carts in those all-night supermarkets. And if happiness is to be found somewhere, isn't it likely to be at the furthest distance? She imagined herself driving in bluish evening light to

HEARTS

the very edge of the coast, stopping short at a place where small waves would break at the Maverick's fenders.

On the morning of the funeral, Linda woke thinking she had forgotten something critical. Whatever it was rose almost to the surface of consciousness and then sank, like the content of a dream. She had to wake Robin by shaking her, and the girl sprang up in bed gasping as if she'd been attacked. They dressed in silence and sat down to breakfast in continuing silence. Linda was forced into chattiness and an explosion of platitudes in order to break it. Did Robin want orange juice, grapefruit juice, tomato juice, or V-8? At least it wasn't raining; rain made everything more depressing, didn't it? How about Raisin Bran? Total? Cocoa Puffs? She was treated to that now familiar little shrug, as automatic as a tic. How would they ride all the way to Iowa together, only the two of them alone in the car?

Even at the mortuary, Robin was impassive, except when the furnace door was opened to receive the coffin, releasing a rushing sound like the very winds of Hell, and her eyes widened and her hands jerked to her face.

Several men from the surgical-instruments plant were there to pay last respects, and they watched and listened with solemn faces in which Linda thought she detected a faint underglow of relief. Not me! Not me! Hallelujah, not me!

The organ was played with crashing fervor and then an unbearable softness, and whoosh! it was over, and everyone hurried into sunlight.

and more frequently as the term went on.
After her father died, she hardly went to any
at all.

One morning, Linda announced that she would drive
Robin to school every day from now on, on her way to
work. It was actually *out* of her way, as Robin pointed
out, but Linda insisted she needed all the driving practice she could get before the big trip. They wouldn't
leave for almost another month, until late in June, because she wanted Robin to finish the term with her
classmates.

What a pain. As soon as Linda let her off on the
school corner, and waved and zigzagged back down the
street, Robin started walking home. It was a mile and
a half away. She put her thumb out whenever a car
approached, but no one stopped for her. By the time
she got to the apartment, she was flushed with heat and
very thirsty. She drank two Cokes and then sat on the
front step to wait for the mailman.

As she expected, there was another letter from the
principal of the junior high school, for her father, urgently requesting that he come in for a conference about
Robin's truancy. The language was a little stronger than
in the last letter, and there was an undercurrent of
sarcasm. "I know you are a busy man," the principal
wrote, "but the time taken now to deal with our young-
sters' 'small' problems will work as insurance against
future large ones." Robin ripped the letter into tiny
pieces and dropped them down a sewer grating on the
way to Ginger and Ray Smith's.

"What took you so long?" Ginger asked. Her breasts

---

looked enormous, even under her pajamas, and Robin glanced away before answering.

"Asshole made me ride to school with her, and I had to walk all the way back."

Ginger laughed. "Oh, shit, that's good. Well, come on in."

Robin could hear the usual whine of the vacuum cleaner from another part of the split-level house. The Smiths' maid, a grizzled old woman, seemed always to be vacuuming. She vacuumed everything: walls, windows, ceilings, bathroom. Robin believed she left the machine on whether she was using it or not. The good thing was that she minded her own business, even when they took the second family car, a cream-colored Camaro, out of the garage for a neighborhood spin. And she never went near Ginger's room when they were in there.

Ray, his sister's elder by less than a year, was propped against the floral pillows, surrounded by Ginger's stuffed animals and her doll collection, sipping a glass of gin. He raised it in languid greeting.

The elder Smiths suspected the maid of drinking and watering their gin, so Ray devised an ingenious network of very fine thread around the liquor bottles in the bar server, a booby trap that his father bragged about at the office, and that Ray had to snip off with his mother's manicuring scissors and replace each time he drank.

With the door shut behind them, and the stereo blasting Aerosmith's "Come Together," the vacuum sounded as distant as the traffic on the turnpike a half mile away.

Ginger sat cross-legged next to Ray, and they joggled and nudged each other until some of the gin spilled.

"Pig," she said, but without animosity. Then she rolled a joint from materials stashed in the pouch of a gingham kangaroo, and handed it to Robin. "Let Ray know when you start to feel good, Rob," she said, "so we can do it."

Robin hit and passed it on to Ray. "I don't know if I want to . . ." she began.

"You're not chickenshit, are you?" Ginger asked, and Ray smirked and rolled his eyes.

"Ze doctor has performed zis operation many time," he said.

"Listen, I bought the pen already," Ginger said. "It cost a buck. And I got my mother's ink. She probably measures it like they do the gin."

It had seemed like such a terrific idea yesterday when she and Ginger looked at the photographs in that magazine. The tattoos on the models were delicate and pretty: tiny birds, teardrops, flowers, hearts. She and Ginger chose favorite designs, and Robin's was the heart.

Why was she so hesitant now? It wasn't the thought of pain. She even welcomed that idea a little; it would be another test of her endurance. For days, weepy Linda had been urging Robin to cry, too, to "get it all out and go on with life." Another one of her brilliant sayings. Well, one of the many things Linda didn't know about Robin was that she *never* cried. It was her greatest pride, and she would lie in bed at night and devise brutal tortures and sorrows to see how much she could stand without cracking. Often, these inventions involved dark, oiled men in loincloths who tied her to a bedpost and took turns beating her. They promised to do worse things, later, if she didn't break down. Of course she didn't.

HEARTS

Once or twice, while her father was still alive, she had even imagined his death. She saw the waxy color of his skin, and the black dirt filling the hole in the ground, and the worms lying curled in the dirt ready to do their dirty job. These morbid fantasies made her tremble feverishly, but she remained dry-eyed. And when they proved insufficient, she reviewed the hard facts of eternal separation. She had plenty of experience with that, ever since her mother, Miriam, left home when Robin was five years old.

Now Robin lay on her side on Ginger's shag rug and thought about her mother. She forgot about testing herself and simply reached back in time, wanting only to improvise on memory and be comforted. Her mother had dark hair and was gorgeous. Well, very pretty, any-way. She had a purple dress and a watch with a small, round face. The instant Robin was born, she saw her mother smile.

"Hey, Robin," Ginger said. "What's happening?"

"Shhh," Robin said, severely. "I'm doing something."

This made Ginger and Ray laugh. "Oh, shit, she's *doing* something," Ginger said, and they collapsed against each other.

Her mother left on a Friday, and for months and months all Fridays were terrible anniversaries. Even if he had been cheerful on Thursday, Robin's father would be freshly abandoned on Friday and come home from work stunned with despair.

No one really explained anything to Robin. She was very young, and when she whined for her mother and asked her father when she was coming back, his tough-guy face would crumble and he would moan and crush

Robin to him. When she questioned her various baby-sitters, she was told, "Mommy went away for a while," or "You must have been a very naughty girl," or "Don't you want to watch television?"

A frequent sitter was an elderly, palsied neighbor who watched a particular soap opera every afternoon and talked aloud to the characters, advising them in their conflicts. In one episode a woman awoke in a hospital room suffering from amnesia. Her eyelids fluttered and she murmured, "Where am I?" The babysitter said, "Where are you? You're in Central General Hospital, suffering from amnesia. You got knocked on the head and everybody thinks you was killed."

Robin, whose attention had wavered between the screen and a toy she'd been playing with on the floor, was alerted, as if she'd been given a private signal.

The woman in the soap opera had been hit by a car and now she couldn't remember who she was or where she lived or the fact that she had two children whom she had once loved dearly. Her head ached every time she tried to think of their names.

So for a while Robin's mother, too, wandered dazed and headachy with amnesia. It was only a matter of time before everything came back in a thunderbolt of recollection, the way it happened on *Our Precious Days*.

When Robin was almost nine, she heard about the man for the first time.

The Aerosmith record ended and Ginger got up to go to the bathroom. She didn't close the door all the way and they could hear the dreamy flow of her urine. Ray smiled at Robin and she attempted to smile back. She didn't feel high in a good way and wondered if

HEARTS

there was something wrong with the stuff. Ray seemed happy, though, and when Ginger came back into the room, still hiking up her pajama bottoms, he looked at her with a kind of dopey, but more than casual, interest. She'd once told Robin that they undressed in front of each other sometimes, and Robin suspected they did even more than that when she wasn't around. It was disgusting between a brother and a sister. It was disgusting between anybody.

Now Ray went into the bathroom and came out with a bottle of rubbing alcohol and a roll of absorbent cotton. "Is ze patient ready for ze operation?" he asked, and he and Ginger laughed again.

"Sure," Robin said, pushing up the sleeve of her T-shirt, and thinking, My father used to do it with asshole Linda. Probably a hundred times a night.

"Ze heart," Ray said, "is not belong on ze arm."

"*She'll* see it there and give you a hard time," Ginger said.

Who cares? Who cares? "So do it on my leg," Robin told them.

"But then you won't be able to wear shorts," Ginger said, with exasperating logic.

They finally decided on a spot slightly to the left of her spine, and just above the waist. The skin there was smooth and hairless. Ginger swabbed the designated place with alcohol; it was shockingly cold and it stank. Then she took a red Magic Marker and carefully drew the outline of a heart. Robin could feel Ginger's soft breath on her back as she worked, and the light, pleasant pressure of the marker.

"There!" Ginger said in triumph, and Robin moved

backward to the mirror, holding her shirt up behind her so she could see. The drawing seemed insignificant, not much larger than the tiny raspberry birthmark she had inside her right thigh, that proof of herself. And the heart was neatly and symmetrically made, with the innocent charm of a valentine.

She sat down near the center of the bed with her knees raised and her arms folded across them. Then she put her head down, too, letting her hair fall forward in a pale, translucent screen. She felt so relaxed now, yet powerful with resistance and control. Even if it hurt terribly, she would not cry. Other girls she knew cried at everything, cried with a kind of delirious joy at stupid movies, sad books, lost football games, and bad grades. Robin amazed them all by failing to be moved even by the television rerun of Ali MacGraw's death in *Love Story*.

"I'm gonna start," Ray said in a serious voice, and Robin nodded assent.

She jumped at the first puncture and cried out.

"Oh, shit, does it hurt a lot, Robbie?" Ginger asked. She raised the curtain of Robin's hair and poked a new joint inside.

Robin toked and shook her head. The moment the pain subsided, leaving only a mild residual sting, she felt peaceful again. The vacuum whined and Ginger and Ray quarreled in loud whispers behind her. "Look what you did, fuckup. You smeared the whole outline."

"Well, it was *bleeding*, prick. Do you want to get it all over my bed?"

They were her friends, and they were funny, and good. Even the thought of her own blood, something

HEARTS

that usually made Robin uneasy, didn't bother her now. It was possible to hypnotize yourself, she knew with sudden wisdom. You could do that, go outside your own body and give orders. In India, or somewhere, they could walk on fire or razor blades! Robin made tight fists and let the stubs of her fingernails bite into her palms, manufacturing new pain to distract from the old one.

This hurt all right; each jab of the pen brought a fresh surprise of pain. Ginger murmured sympathy and stroked Robin's hair. But she was in no danger of crying. She had not cried when her father died, either. And she had loved him, although that love was tempered by intolerable pity. She pitied him in his long loneliness, which was like her own, and again in his brief foolish happiness with Linda.

Ow! The pen point piercing her skin hurt. The pain radiated up the curve of her back and traveled around to her chest, where her real heart thumped.

His heart had killed him all right, but not in the way that Linda said. He died of a *broken* heart that had suffered its fatal fracture eight years before and never healed. It just cracked slowly, slowly, the way the crust of the earth does. He was murdered.

She could hear her own breath, and it was a harsh sound, like the wind at night after her mother was gone. Like the wind that blew Dorothy and Toto from Kansas. Like the wind when that door opened and took him inside.

those weeks before their departure for Iowa.
It was due partly to experience and partly to
an extreme mustering of will. After parallel parking,
entering major highways was the greatest challenge; to
come suddenly abreast of all those other vehicles moving
at suicidal speed, and to have to find one's place without
breaking stride!

She tried to think of it in terms of dancing, how she
always managed to place her foot between her partner's
feet for the briefest moment, without hesitation or loss
of beat. But that didn't work. Driving was not like
dancing.

Yet there seemed to be a kind of music that everyone
else heard and drove to. If she could only relax a little,
she might hear it also. Real, car-radio music didn't help.
Everyone could be tuned to a different station. It was
more like an inner song, like those rounds you sang in
school. Row, row, row your boat, gently down the . . .
And you had to enter at the precise moment . . . *merrily*,
merrily . . . so that the rhythm was flawless and the
music endless.

Other drivers honked and cursed at her less, she
thought, and her own physical responses were less dramatic. She wasn't always sweaty anymore, and she didn't
feel like throwing up or have tachycardia after a fifteen-
minute ride on the Jersey Turnpike, or a round trip
through the Holland Tunnel. But she knew that none of
these minor excursions really prepared her for the long-
distance journey. How about endurance? And what about
consistency?

One morning, after she dropped Robin at school,

Linda headed for the highway and drove more than one hundred miles to Slatesville, Pennsylvania, where she'd been born and where she had lived until she was eighteen. She had not been back there since 1974, when her mother died. There was no reason to go back, no family or friendly attachments. It was the sort of place you left right after high school, so that the population slowly diminished, even during the post-World War II baby boom. And among those who stayed, Linda couldn't think of anyone now with whom she'd had more than a glancing relationship. Slatesville was simply an arbitrary choice for this trial run.

The trip was eventless, except for a close call with a tractor trailer near the Interstate entrance at Lebanon, and she arrived in the center of town before eleven o'clock. It looked the same, yet somewhat altered in a tricky way. Had they moved the railroad tracks slightly to the north? Of course, some of the signs over the double row of shops showed change of ownership, and the face of the bank had been sandblasted to a snowy brilliance.

Linda parked in front of the Station Diner and went inside for coffee. She didn't know anyone there, not the middle-aged woman behind the counter, who was carefully building a pyramid of pastries, or the two men bent in conversation at the only occupied booth. She was relieved. What if someone said, "Linda Marie Camisko! What in the world are you doing back here?"

She drank her coffee and got into the car again. Then, just to test her memory and her sense of direction, she drove down Sweetwater Avenue, past the high school, past the mills, to Roper Street, in search of her old house. It was a gray wooden structure, built in the late twenties, with a circular wooden porch and a monumental tree in the yard that used to cast all the front rooms in darkness and keep the porch railings sticky with sap and bird droppings.

There it was, just as remembered, except for a sign on a pole that announced it as The Maple Inn. Guests. TV. Meals.

The landlady had been a practical nurse, like Linda's mother, and they had rented four rooms on the second floor from her. Her name was Piner, Mrs. Loretta, and her husband, like Linda's father, worked at the asbestos spinning mill a mile away. They had no children, but there used to be a frenetic white dog they kept chained outdoors. Mrs. Piner did her practical nursing at home, taking in the elderly and giving them dinner and baths and all the other things they could no longer manage for themselves. Linda recalled those frightened and frightening wraiths in bathrobes, encountered on the stairs, and the moans that came from the large hall bathroom, where Mrs. Piner was cutting someone's toenails. She would have gone right to the quick.

She wore white uniforms and nurse's shoes even though she worked in her own home. A long time before that, though, she'd been a baby nurse, like Linda's mother, who stayed for a few weeks at a time in the homes of wealthy Harrisburg families to care for newborn infants.

Linda parked the car and went up the porch steps, sounding herself for nostalgia. There wasn't any. Of course she had been miserably unhappy much of the time here: that sad parade of displaced persons, her

HEARTS

mother's frequent absences, her father's constant raging presence after the emphysema kept him housebound. And then his terrible death. There had been some private moments of ecstasy, but they had occurred in the palace of the imagination rather than in the narrow perimeters of the house. She had only dreamed here.

No one was sitting on the green-painted porch chairs, and peering through the rippled panel of yellow glass in the door, she saw a dim distortion of the front hall, unbroken by human shadow. As a child, she'd had a habit of scaring herself. What if it was Frankenstein who *really* had the room next to the downstairs kitchen instead of poor Mr. Botts, who was so frail and confused? What if those heavy footsteps on the stairs were not Mr. Piner's but the monster's, whose unholy mission was to get her, Linda, where she shivered exquisitely in bed?

Now, after she'd banged the boar's-head knocker twice, she felt some of the old chilling expectancy. What if it was her father who came to the door, breathing his furious dragon's breath, or the tired ghost of her mother, uniformly white, satchel in hand, ready to leave once more for a job?

Then there was movement inside—someone broke the wavy still-life of her view—and the door opened. It was Mrs. Piner, wearing a green print housedress. Her shoes were white and rubber-soled.

She had aged remarkably in those few years, and was wearing eyeglasses as dense as paperweights. She didn't recognize Linda at first and thought she had come about a room. But even after Linda prodded her memory— "Alma and George Camisko's daughter? My hair was longer? Upstairs?"—Mrs. Piner's expression didn't alter.

It's her bad vision, Linda thought. She's probably almost blind.

Linda explained that she was driving through and just dropped in to say hello. It was the most unlikely thing she'd ever said in her life. No one drove through Slatesville. It didn't lead anywhere else. But Mrs. Piner didn't take notice of the lie.

Linda looked past her into the parlor, where Mr. Piner was sitting in an armchair, watching television. He was wearing a cardigan sweater over his blue work shirt, and corduroy slippers on his feet. He must have retired from the mill.

At last, Mrs. Piner gestured Linda inside, and she found herself on the sofa, facing the screen. It was the only source of light in the long, tree-darkened room. She received a grunted acknowledgment of her greeting to Mr. Piner. He was busy with the remote-control panel for the television set, pushing the button with a steady click, so that cartoons, commercials, and movies went by with the speed of an express train. He finally settled on a quiz program that was in progress.

Mrs. Piner sat next to Linda and folded her hands in her lap. Nobody said anything. A contestant on the quiz program had to decide if she was going to risk an accumulation of prizes valued at over three thousand dollars for the possible win of a brand-new Cadillac Coupe de Ville. "Oh, wow," she kept saying, and the emcee moved the microphone under her chin each time she said it. The audience was screaming as if the studio were on fire and they were all trapped inside.

What am I doing here, Linda wondered, but she also felt oddly comfortable, even sleepy. The Piners didn't ask her to explain herself. They hardly paid any attention to her at all. She could have been their grown child enjoying a cozy daily ritual. "Oh, wow," the contestant said again, and Linda slumped a little and yawned. She might have stayed there, forgetting Iowa and Robin and everything in their recent past, if Mr. Piner had not suddenly pushed his button one more time, throwing the room into darkness and silence.

"Well," Linda said. She decided to forgo asking about the rooming-house business, if it was profitable and pleasant. There wasn't a sign of a tenant anywhere, and it might be an indelicate subject. Instead, she said, "It's been over five years since my mother died."

Mrs. Piner came to life. She moved conspiratorially close on the sofa and said, "She died from the babies, you know."

"Pardon?" Linda said, although she had heard perfectly. Her mother had died of a stroke, of a rapid series of strokes, each one taking another faculty, another measure of hope. Linda looked to old Mr. Piner for help, but he appeared to be fast asleep. Old people dropped off like that.

"From those tiny rooms they gave you," Mrs. Piner continued, "and the babies used up all the air."

"Nursing is a difficult profession," Linda said, and bit her tongue so she would not add, "but a rewarding one."

"The families sat around eating lamb chops," Mrs. Piner said with bitter intensity, "and you got this tainted luncheon meat."

"It was a long drive just to drop in like this," Linda said, forgetting her original story. "And I really have to get going." She stood and walked to the doorway. "Say so long to Mr. Piner for me, please. I'd hate to disturb him; he looks so peaceful."

Mrs. Piner walked behind her, soundlessly. "They gave you a corner in the closet to hang your clothes," she said. "Next to the folding bridge chairs and the ironing board."

Linda walked rapidly to the front door. As she did, it opened and a man carrying two shopping bags hurried past her and up the stairs. Did he live in one of their old rooms? Mrs. Piner didn't seem to see him. She took Linda's arm with the grasp of an arresting officer, and her voice fell into an ominous whisper. "And do you think those young couples ever waited six weeks, postpartum? You could hear them going at it all night, through the walls."

Linda fled.

HEARTS

"WE'RE GONNA MISS YOUR SMILING FACE around here, kiddo," Simonetti said, looking everywhere but at her face. Linda had come to the studio for her last paycheck and he held it in one hand and slapped it against the other while he talked to her, but he didn't hand it over. She had a memory flash of her father doing something like that with a piece of candy; withholding, teasing. Did she ever get it?

"I'm going to miss you, too," Linda said with sweet insincerity. She had hated Simonetti from her first day at the Bayonne Fred Astaire's. He was the one who hired her, on the recommendation of a mutual friend in the midtown New York City branch where she'd worked before. She lost that job when the building went residential and the studio folded.

Simonetti had looked her over then, too, with the same kind of cruel scrutiny that made her feel graceless and conscious of all her physical flaws. "You're too tall," he said, and she slouched and shrank. He wanted to know if she could do something with her hair, go blonde maybe. They already had Iola, who was brunette. When she hesitated he took her on unchanged, indicating that they were desperate.

Linda wasn't beautiful. She had good skin and a cleft chin, but her nose was too short and a little broad, and she had an overbite. A favorite two-stepping client often pointed out that her eyes were her best feature and that her smile was nice. Ah, whose smile wasn't nice?

Once, when she'd turned down the advances of a drunk who'd wandered in during a get-acquainted open house, he told her that girls like her were a dime a dozen. "You have a cute ass; I'll give you that," he said. "But you're nothing special. What's your name?" he demanded, even though it was right there on the name badge pinned to her sweater. "Donna? Rhonda?" He was perilously close. "They're all called Donna or Rhonda," he said. "They all look like you."

When he became noisy and abusive and shouted that he didn't have to crawl for pussy, Simonetti, convinced that he was not a likely prospect for even the one-month trial offer, threw him out.

Iola, who was frugging with a sailor from the Naval Station, waved to Linda and rolled her eyes in sympathy. Later she said, "Creeps. Jesus. How do they all find us? We must be in the Yellow Pages under Victims."

He was drunk, of course, and he *was* a creep, but Linda couldn't help feeling diminished by his account of her. It confirmed what she had always suspected, that she was ordinary in a frightening, anonymous way. Even the word "victim" that Iola had used ironically was accurate. Whenever Linda read an article in the newspaper about the unidentified body of a young woman found in the woods somewhere, or dragged from a river, she felt a disturbing affinity.

The check had disappeared and Simonetti had his arm around her. "Your regulars will be heartsick," he said. She wondered which pocket held the check. But she wasn't going to beg for it; she'd just wait it out. At least he wasn't dangerous in a sexual sense. When she'd first started working there, she guessed she'd be fighting him off constantly, and would probably get fired for not giving in. But it was all innuendo with Simonetti, and no real action. He leered, patted, threatened, and made funny sucking noises, and that was it.

HEARTS

Iola tried to figure him out. "I don't think he's queer," she said, "but maybe he's one of those weirdos that can only get it off against the side of a building or in his mother's pocketbook."

Whatever the reason, they were relieved. There was enough trouble with some of the clients. One of them they'd nicknamed Supercreep, but it was like whistling in the dark. They were really afraid of him. He always came to the studio well-dressed, with slicked-down hair and heavily scented aftershave, and he was polite to the point of formality. He danced like a mechanical man with too few gears for a variety of movement. And he made the same stiff conversation with his instructor during each lesson, as if they had just met for the first time. Sometimes, not always, he spoke with a foreign accent no one could place. If anyone asked where he was from, he only smiled and shut his eyes in a peculiar way, like a lizard.

Simonetti said that he couldn't act on their complaints. So the guy wasn't Robert Redford. As far as he could see, he was still a perfect gent.

"Maybe you'd better get your eyes checked," Iola told him.

"Okay, what does he do?" he asked. "Does he cop feels? Does he use rough language?"

"You," Iola said, disgusted. "If the Boston Strangler boogied in here, you'd think it was Prince Charles." She convinced Simonetti to at least spread Supercreep's lessons around, so he wouldn't get a fix on any one of the girls.

But he did, anyway, on Linda. He hung around the building for hours until she left, and walked just behind her to the bus stop, saying some more inane things in his robot's voice. "I believe we are in for bad weather," he'd say. "Do you enjoy living in New Jersey?"

After a few days, his conversation became more personal. "I admired your blouse today. Did your boyfriend buy it for you? You must have plenty of boyfriends." From there it was only a skip and a jump to: "Does your boyfriend put it in you when you are wearing that blouse? I would like to put it in you." Etc. etc. etc.

Sometimes, when he wasn't there, she suspected that he was close by but not making himself known to her. And she began to get telephone calls in the middle of the night. At first there was the usual breathing, and then . . . *humming.* Not a tune or anything, just the menacing humming sound an insect might make before diving for the kill. Linda was terrified.

Simonetti said she read too many books. The guy was harmless, all talk. Iola suspected Simonetti had signed him up for a Lifetime Membership. "Maybe even with a clause for the afterlife," she said.

Linda believed she was going to be killed. Unidentified body of young woman between the ages of . . . Mutilated beyond . . . Dental charts necessary for . . . She realized that she had not been to a dentist for over two years.

Instead of being murdered, she ended up getting married. Not to Supercreep, of course, but to Wright, who was walking past the bus stop one evening when she was sure she was being followed. It was raining and the visibility was very poor. Headlights appeared occasionally in the foggy distance, with the eerie glow of UFO's. But the bus didn't come. Did she only imagine she heard a humming sound? Oh, God, were those *footsteps?* The footsteps grew stronger and closer, and Wright

HEARTS

appeared under the streetlight, a reasonable-looking man with his hands in the pockets of his bomber jacket. She rushed over to him and touched his sleeve. "Please," she said. "Could I walk with you?"

What she remembers best is that, as she took his arm, he tensed the muscles in it. She thought it was to show off a little, and to assure her of his protection, and that it was a lovely and primitive thing to do.

Later, in bed one night, he confessed that it had been from the joy of being touched that way. And he reviewed the scene with obvious pleasure. "How did you know *I* wasn't a killer, too?" he said, smiling.

"Well, I've got to go," she told Simonetti. "I have a lot of packing to do."

"Am I stopping you?" he asked.

"Come *on*," Linda said, trying to sound equally playful.

"You know," Simonetti said. "It's too bad that you and me never, you know, got together."

"Uh-huh."

"Listen, drop me a line when you get there. I'll send you a letter of recommendation. We got a lot of branches on the Coast. Hey, you'll probably meet producers, directors, all the stars of stage and screen! Our little Linda."

Just as she was about to break down, to ask outright for her money, he lost interest. His eyes went blank and sorrowful, and he put his hand absently into his breast pocket and removed the check.

Iola hugged Linda and gave her a going-away present. "Open it later," she said. "It's only a little something. Just don't forget to use it."

At suppertime, Linda remembered the present and

brought it to the kitchen table. There was a box of note-paper inside, each page imprinted with a floral border and a different saying. *Thinkin' of ya. Better late than never! Just a little love note. I'm blue for you.*

Dear Iola.

Hi! I really *am* thinking of you, and I'm glad for a chance to use this adorable stationery. So far we are having a lovely trip, with many side visits to places of interest. Robin and I are enjoying . . .

Slowly Linda became aware again of Robin sitting opposite her at the table, stony with contempt. So she picked up her fork and began to eat.

HEARTS

IOWA, WHICH IS HEAVILY AGRICULTURAL, was appropriately colored green on the map in Robin's old geography book. Linda was pleased to note that California was blue.

8

On the Exxon road maps, all the states had been neutralized to a noncommittal white. The mechanic, a stocky man in coveralls, wiped his grease-coated hands on a greasy rag. "You picked *this* summer to drive to the Coast?" he said. "Oh, lady. What are you, an Arab?"

"I didn't pick it, actually," Linda said. "It just worked out that way."

"Oh, yeah? Well, good luck to you, then. You may have to sell a pint of blood to get a gallon of gas on the way. You may end up living in Timbuktu."

"Oh, no. I have to—"

"So, why don't you fly?"

"I guess I'll need a car once I get there, won't I? And as long as I'm going, I thought I ought to see America on the way. Maybe this will be my last chance."

"Yeah, well, don't be disappointed. An awful lot of it looks like Jersey," he said. Then he bent to the maps opened across the desk in the station office and pointed with one blackened finger to the route she would take.

Linda had a notebook and pen ready. She was prepared for an onslaught of highway numbers and city names she would have to scribble quickly in a makeshift shorthand.

The mechanic picked up a yellow highlighting marker and began to trace a crawling line across the states. "You pick up Interstate 80 right here, and you take it all the way through," he said. "If you don't get off, you can't get lost. You could drive this baby blindfolded."

43

Was that it? Linda looked at him and then back at her notebook. She had written the number 80 at the top of the page, and nothing else under it. The road he'd indicated was practically a straight horizontal line. They would shoot across America like a guided missile, without seeing anything of beauty or interest. She felt very disappointed, and wondered if this was the *best* way to go, or simply the fastest. But she was too shy to ask him. Outside, another man pumped gas, and behind him, in the garage, two cars were elevated on pneumatic lifts. She was probably keeping the mechanic from his real work. She wrote a series of diminishing 80's down the whole page. Finally she closed the notebook and, looking over his shoulder again, read the wonderful names of cities she'd never visited: Sandusky, Toledo, Elkhart . . . They *were* going to see the country. They'd only travel by daylight, and as soon as she was tired of driving they'd stop at a motel and rest for the night. While she was packing that morning, she'd asked Robin if there was anything special she'd like to see en route. Blink. Shrug.

Linda had never taken any trips when she was a child, but a few people she knew did, and other children came to school with accordion folders that opened at a finger flip into a cascade of picture postcards that reached the floor. Lake views, mountain views, historical battle sites, and museum villages. Wineries, breweries, glass-blowing plants, and caverns. The last intrigued Linda the most. Those stalagmites and stalactites, and the little boat you traveled in underground, like the one in the Tunnel of Love at the Slatesville amusement park. She'd get a guidebook or two to places of interest and see if she and Robin could visit any caverns on their way west.

HEARTS

"Say, Interstate 8o goes through Davenport," the mechanic said. "I have a brother-in-law there with a Gulf station. Stop in, why don't you, and say hello from Don and Mickey."

She was opening her notebook again to write it down, but he had gone back to marking her route and she realized that he'd only been kidding.

But now she knew his name was Don, and Mickey was probably his wife. At night he went home and made love to her, leaving indelible hand prints all over her body and the sheets.

Linda often imagined the intimacy that took place between people she hardly knew. She wondered if they fell on each other with joyous shouts or only ground out a sad little spiral of desire. This was not mere curiosity, or the restlessness of her own unsatisfied lust, although that was part of it. Wright had been ardent, and she had responded. Afterward he often said, "That was good, wasn't it?" She always answered, "Yes," without thinking. Was there another possible answer to that question? She suspected that there was much more to sex, though, or should be, some glorious epiphany she had never experienced with Wright, or the few lovers she'd had before him. Maybe it was a rare privilege, like beauty or great wealth, and given only to certain chosen people. Once, she read a novel in which the heroine cried out in the throes of passion, "Oh, dear God! Oh, love, oh, *murder* me!" Linda believed instantly in such extremes of ardor; no one could have made that up.

The mechanic folded the road maps and gave her the bill for the tuneup on the Maverick. He said it was shipshape now, with new sparks and brake linings, and he wished her a good trip, if she ever got there, and a nice day.

Robin packed her things in a tan imitation-leather suitcase that had belonged to her father. It was frayed white at all its corners. He might have used this same suitcase on the honeymoon he'd taken with her mother. They went to Niagara Falls, where it had rained all the time.

She was packing as little as possible, in preparation for the other, *real* trip. She had no intention of staying too long with her father's family in Iowa. They had not spoken to him for years. It had something to do with her mother and herself, but he was unable or unwilling to discuss the details with her, and referred to the situation as a falling-out.

When she was a little younger, Robin wondered if the estrangement came about because she had been born a girl. Her father's family were farmers who raised corn and oats, and farmers counted on male children to work the fields. She guessed they were like those Spartans in her social studies book last year, who were bitterly disappointed at the births of females. But at least the farm country was low and flat, without mountain peaks from which men in overalls and straw hats could hurl helpless baby girls.

Once they got to Iowa, she'd have to get Linda to give *her* some of that money she kept talking about leaving in trust for Robin with her grandfather and aunt. Then she would be able to start out on her mission to find her mother, and avenge her father.

While Robin was still packing, Linda came home

H E A R T S

from the gas station, foaming at the mouth about reconstructed Quaker villages and underground caves, and how it was really important to see America first. What an asshole.

A few minutes later Ginger and Ray came over to take what they wanted from the stuff Robin was going to leave behind. Ray brought her some of the antibiotic capsules he'd been given by a dermatologist because of his acne. The place where he'd tattooed her had become infected, despite their careful prophylactic use of alcohol. At night she felt slightly feverish and the heart oozed and festered. It was so misshapen now, it might have been drawn by a very little kid with an unsteady hand, and it appeared to be much larger than the day they'd done it.

Linda went to the door to let them in. "Your friends are here, Robin!" she called out cheerfully, as if they were all characters on *The Brady Bunch*.

Robin didn't answer. She had made two piles of discards at the foot of her bed. They were mostly records and clothing that she still liked but could not bring with her if she intended to travel light later on. Now she looked at them and tried to harden herself against forfeiture.

Ginger and Ray came in and went right to the booty. Ray began shuffling through the albums as if this was Disco Discounts, and Ginger moved to the mirror, holding a pink plaid shirt against her ample chest. When she smiled at her own reflection, Robin felt instant remorse. It was a nice shirt, and in good condition. It was probably her *favorite* shirt. But Ginger was already stuffing it into a paper sack she had brought with her. Then she

took off her own blouse to try on another one of
Robin's. She was wearing a deeply cut, flesh-colored
bra.

Robin was glad that she didn't have breasts like
Ginger's. Her own development had been much slower
and less ambitious, and she regretted even that modest
growth, and mourned her old flat and uncomplicated
body.

Ray took all the records for himself, and Ginger
most of the clothing, and they quarreled over a strange
electrical sculpture Linda had bought for Robin as a
thirteenth-birthday present a couple of months before.
It looked like a little tree of limp plastic spaghetti, but
when you plugged it in, it lit up and colored liquid
light moved through the branches in theatrical spasms.

Ray teased Robin about going to Iowa. He kept
calling it I-o-way, with an inflection and twang that got
on her nerves. She finally said, "Just shut up about it,
okay? I'm not staying there. I'm not staying with them."

"So what will you do?" Ginger asked, combing her
hair with her fingers. She had put her own blouse into
the sack and was wearing Robin's.

"I don't know," Robin said, her secret plan as bright
and burning inside her as the liquid in the tree lamp.
For the first time she felt desperately eager to share it
with someone. But wisdom quickly overcame impulse.
Saying it aloud might diminish it, turn it into melodrama
or simple childish fantasy. And she didn't trust Ray very
much, or Ginger either, for that matter. In dumb-eyed
reverence, she always told him everything.

"I'll go somewhere," Robin said. "I'll get a job."

Ray hooted. "Who'd hire you?" he said, and she

HEARTS

wished she could take her records back. They were worth plenty of money. Her father had been generous with money; he gave her anything she wanted.

Ginger tried to soothe things. "When she wears her hair back," she told Ray, "she looks much older. Doesn't she? You could be a waitress or something, Robin. You'd have to get a fake ID. And maybe stuff your bazooms," she added, with a sly glance at her brother. "Say, Rob, are you taking your radio?"

How could she have been friends with them? She thought of all the days of stoned giddiness in Ginger's floral, smoke-clouded room. She tried to remember what they'd talked about and why they had laughed so much. Had it really been fun? Is it ever fun if you can see yourself working so hard to have it?

Now they both seemed selfish and unattractive to her. Ray's neck was flushed with acne and with greed, and his eyes were small and mean-spirited.

As for Ginger, she was a sex-crazed moron.

With a plunging sense of loss, Robin realized that they were also her best friends, her only friends. Nothing ever stayed the same for a minute. Everything in the world changed and disappeared. "*Yes*," she told Ginger, her voice pitched to a spiteful shriek. "I *am* taking it." And she threw the little white portable radio into the suitcase.

Ginger grabbed her sack and took one last pleased look in the mirror. "Well, I guess we better go, Ray," she said. Then she hugged Robin and made kissing sounds near her ear. "Oh, shit, I'm gonna miss you, miss you, miss you!"

Ray gathered everything else up under one arm and

walked over to Robin. If he was going to kiss her, too, she would kill him. Instead, he reached into his shirt pocket and removed two crooked, shredding joints. "Here," he said. "Freebies. Take them with you for the road. Go ahead." Then he put his free hand firmly on her behind and said, "Keep your sweet ass out of trouble." And when she merely gaped at him, he added, "And don't forget to send me a card from I-o-way."

Linda heard the murmur of the kids' voices through the bedroom wall. At least Robin spoke to *somebody*.

The girl had only wanted one suitcase for her own use, which surprised Linda. People of Robin's age usually have a firm attachment to the sentimental trash of childhood. She herself struggled with the choices that had to be made: what to take with them, what to leave behind. There wasn't that much room in the trunk of the car, but they could put a few things on the floor in back. Something that would take up very little space was the box containing Wright's ashes. The ashes were a residual Linda hadn't considered when she decided on cremation. But the day after the services for Wright, the young man from the mortuary telephoned, insinuating himself once more into Linda's life. And once more there were choices. A plastic box or an Everlasting Urn? The remains could be delivered, picked up by a member of the family, or arrangements could be made for burial. "Burial!" Linda cried. That was exactly what she thought she had so efficiently avoided, and she was ashamed of her own dismay at learning that there *were* remains, after all, that death and prayer and even fire

---

HEARTS

don't release you from certain obligations. She chose the plastic box and promised to come by and pick it up. Later she wondered fleetingly what they could do if she left town without keeping her promise. Would she be followed and dunned forever like someone skipping out on car payments? These thoughts produced further shame.

The next day Linda went down to the mortuary and was given, after signing a receipt, a brown lucite container that resembled a book in its size and shape. Its weight was not significant. She sat in the car for several minutes with the container on her lap, like a magician who has forgotten the magical restorative words. Then she put it into the trunk and drove home. On the way, she decided that this development was too morbid to share with Robin; in fact, too morbid for Linda herself to contemplate right away.

For weeks, the box of ashes remained in the trunk of the Maverick and Linda only wondered occasionally what she would do with them. She thought of scattering them in one of Wright's favorite places, the beach for instance, with its constant surf and infinite distance. But she didn't get around to doing it right away. By the time she thought of it again, and actually drove to the shore, the season had started. It was a hot day and the lifeguards were whistling from their perches. Sun worshippers were tearing off their clothes, and the music from transistor radios was so loud the ocean might have been merely a backup group. Linda stood next to an overflowing trash basket, her shoes filling with sand, and decided that the beach wasn't the best place for eternal rest, after all.

She felt it was wrong, even irreverent, to keep Wright's ashes in the trunk of the car, like a mobster's hostage, and she knew that she'd have to make a decision about them eventually. When she began to pack for the trip, it occurred to her that she might take the ashes to Iowa, too, and scatter them near Wright's place of birth, maybe in the cornfields, and her heart was eased.

Linda also decided to keep a carton of Wright's smaller paintings. She didn't know whether they were good or not, in a critical sense, but they contained his particular vision of things. Perhaps art, even bad art, was the only thing you could leave after death that would continue your consciousness in the living world.

Iola once said she was going to have a talking head-stone installed on her own grave. Anyone who wanted to know what she was like could step on a little switch that would activate a taped recording of her voice. "Hi, there! Thanks for stopping by. My name was Iola Behnke . . ."

A few days before, Linda went through Wright's belongings while Robin was in school. She packed his clothing in two big cartons for a Goodwill pickup: shirts, suits, underwear, even the bomber jacket he was wearing the day they'd met. For some reason the sight of his shoes touched her the most. Maybe because they took on the particular shape of each human foot, or because shoes without feet inside to move them were so poignantly inanimate. She gave his bowling ball to a co-worker at the plant, who thanked her with tears in his eyes and said he'd have to have the finger holes enlarged, if she didn't mind.

Still, there was plenty of junk, and she had to hurry before Robin came home. In the very back of the bed-

HEARTS

room closet, behind a box of barbells, she found a smaller box, and it was sealed with heavy gummed tape and tied with rope. Linda opened it with a straight-edged razor and the fearsome instinct that she had found treasure.

She wasn't really wrong. Inside were things Wright's first wife, Miriam, had left behind when she abandoned him and Robin. Maybe he'd kept them at first because he had hopes she would return, and then later because their disposal would have required a ceremony he couldn't bear. Sealed up like that, and hidden, they were obviously not relics he browsed through and brooded over on solitary evenings. There was a hairbrush with a silver-plated back and nylon bristles that still held long strands of brown hair. There was a much-folded note, and as she opened it, Linda knew this was an invasion of unguarded privacy, but that didn't stop her.

It wasn't even a love letter. It just told Wright that there was some cold chicken for dinner in a blue bowl in the refrigerator, and that the cleaners didn't have his slacks ready. "See you later. Love, M.," it said, so it wasn't the farewell note, either, if there had ever been one. He'd probably saved it because it was written in her hand.

There was a pharmacist's vial of small pink pills prescribed for Mrs. W. Reismann (that was herself now!) by Dr. Victor Klein. One tablet after meals and before bedtime. There was a deck of Tarot cards bound with a rubber band. Did Miriam lay out her own future and discover the other man in the cards? Finally, there were two manila envelopes, one large and one small, and they were both as thoroughly sealed as the carton had been. The smaller one felt as if it might have photographs in it. Linda thought of wedding pictures, and she wondered if there would be anything suitable for Robin. But when she opened the envelope, only a half-dozen faded brown Polaroid prints fell out. Someone had forgotten to put that stuff on them to fix the images. Five of them were of the same woman, nude, in various poses. Her face had faded the most, but, because of dark lipstick, it was clear she had been smiling. Two dark smudges of hair, above and below. She was lounging across a bed, surrounded by rumpled bedclothes and other things. Peering closely, Linda could make out magazines and cigarettes and what was probably the case of the camera. Then she began to recognize other, unfocused details. It was *this* bedroom, the same bed, night table, lamp. In the last photo, Wright, blurred, but obviously clothed, appeared beside the woman. He must have had one of those timers. He was smiling, too, his arm around her waist, and Linda thought he looked breathless and happy, like a man who has boarded a train just as it was pulling out of the station.

She tore open the larger envelope. There was a stapled sheaf of papers inside. The top one read: *Report on Mrs. Miriam Reismann, nee Diamond—April 2 thru April 11, 1971. Albert J. Lapozzi Agency, Detection and Protection.* There was an address in downtown Newark.

Linda sat down on the bed and read quickly through the pages. It was like reading the outline for a detective novel about a missing person. All the characters, major and minor, had been sketched in; the plot was implied.

Miriam's Newark friends claimed they had no knowledge of her whereabouts, but hinted at her friendship with a man named Tony.

H E A R T S

Lapozzi had gone to the ex-wife of the man, Anthony Bernard Hausner. Mrs. Hausner had not seen her husband for more than a year, but he called his children on the telephone occasionally, and sent them birthday gifts. He had not been in touch with them since March 15, the suspected time of his departure with Mrs. Reismann. Mrs. Hausner gave the names of two male friends of her ex-husband's who might have knowledge of his whereabouts. They didn't, but one of them remembered Tony mentioning the possibility of a good job with an electronics firm in Sarasota, Florida. A check with a Florida agency contact proved negative. No Hausner or anyone fitting his description had applied for employment at any of the large electronics firms in that area. April 5 to 9 was a dead end. Hausner's mother in Milwaukee said she didn't know where he was, and what's more, she didn't care. He had not tried to contact his brothers or old army buddies. Mrs. Reismann had not visited her hometown of Shaker Heights, Ohio, since 1964. Both parents dead, no siblings. Then, on April 10, Mrs. Hausner's twelve-year-old son received a postcard from his father postmarked Glendale, Arizona. It was stapled to the last page of the report. There was a picture of a giant saguaro cactus on the front. "Hello," Hausner had written. "Here I am in the wild, wild west. There are lots of Indians here. It is 108 in the shade. Take care. Love, Dad."

On April 11, Lapozzi had an address.

Linda threw it all out, after she'd reduced to shreds everything shreddable: note, photos, postcard, everything. But first she'd copied the address onto a scrap of paper, without knowing why she did it. She wondered if Wright

2

had acted on the report, had tried to contact his wife and beg her to come back to him and his child. It was something she'd never know.

Robin's friends were leaving. Linda poked her head out and said, "Bye, bye!" Robin saw her look at the lamp sculpture Ray was carting off, with a mixture of bewilderment and pain.

HEARTS

THEY WERE A FEW MILES OUT OF JACKSON-
ville, Pennsylvania, when Linda realized she
might be pregnant. "Oh!" she said, and the
car swerved, almost changing lanes before she righted it.

9

"Whuzzat?" Robin sat up in the back seat, jolted
from a nap.

"Nothing," Linda told her. "Just a little bump in the
road," and Robin lay down again. Then Linda's memory
gathered the clues to her revelation. The nausea she had
blamed on the anxiety of driving, the sudden sleepy
peace of late afternoons, and the pressing knowledge that
would not rise into her consciousness on the morning of
Wright's funeral, or any time since, until now. It was
something only her body knew, and wasn't broadcasting.

Her periods had always been irregular. It wasn't unusual for her to skip one or even two months. Since her
late teens, Linda had kept a careful record of her own
cycle, but in the turmoil of the past weeks she'd forgotten about it. When was her last period? She hadn't been
careless about contraception, though, and she tried to
recall a magazine chart that evaluated the success rate
of different methods. Wasn't an IUD right up there
with the best of them?

A doctor she'd consulted when she was twenty prescribed birth-control pills to establish an artificial regu-
larity her system might adopt. But she began to throw
up and have violent headaches, and the pills were dis-
continued. She remembered how the doctor said not to
worry, it would probably straighten itself out in a few
years and that her only problem might be in conceiving
a baby, since it would be difficult to pinpoint ovulation.
Had ovulation somehow been pinpointed, without her
knowledge or her consent?

For the first time, Linda found herself driving without thinking about driving, without that fierce concentration that left her hands almost arthritically cramped when she stopped to rest. She knew she had better pay attention or they'd wander onto Highway 144; she had recently seen signs warning of its impending junction with I-80. And pretty soon she'd have to start looking for a motel for the night. One with a drugstore close by.

Of course she might be mistaken; she wasn't *married* any more, wasn't even sleeping with anybody. Just yesterday she had contemplated Wright's paintings in terms of his immortality, and now there might be this other, further proof that he'd been here, and recently. Please, don't let it be, she thought, and I promise I'll be good. Although she had no idea in what direction sacrificial goodness lay.

Robin didn't wake up again until they pulled in at the office of the Dutchboy Motel. As Linda had guessed, the rates were reasonable, and they had a vacancy. The place was close to the main road, and it didn't have a restaurant or a coffee shop. It had a look of slight disrepair—the V and N weren't lit on the vacancy sign—but small things like that probably held the price down.

Once inside their room, Linda knew that other factors contributed to the low rates, too. The room was tiny, and except for a mammoth color television set, the furniture seemed scaled to children or dwarfs. Well, thank goodness for the television set, anyway. It would give Robin something to do, and introduce the variety of other human voices. She offered the girl first choice of beds, although they were exactly the same. Linda lay back on hers and massaged her hands. They were still curled from steering, and looked like the hands of Snow

White's stepmother when she was cackling over the poisoned apple. In the other bed, Snow White herself lay, pale and bored.

Robin was very upset, but with her gift for self-control, Linda would never know about it. It hadn't occurred to Robin that they would have to share a room on the road. Now she was worried about having to undress in front of Linda. She would sleep in her clothes, if necessary. But she supposed she could use the bathroom or do it under the covers, and she hoped Linda would do the same. Robin's other fear was that she might talk in her sleep and give away secret thoughts. Once, when Ginger slept over, she said that Robin had not shut up all night. "What did I say?" Robin asked anxiously, and Ginger only smiled and said, "Oh, lots of things. Wouldn't you like to know?" Of course, she was well known for her lying and exaggerating.

She could feel Linda's eyes on her. Linda was *always* looking at her and talking at her, even in the car, pointing out everything as if Robin had never seen a tree or a cow before. And she was such a rotten driver. A few times, Robin was sure they were going to be killed. Linda sighed and Robin knew she was about to speak again. She often gave little warnings like that: sighs, throat clearing, an introductory cough.

"Are you hungry?"

Robin shrugged.

"Me, too," Linda said. "Let's wash up and find a nice place for supper."

In the tiny bathroom, Linda shut her eyes as she sat down on the toilet. "Please," she whispered, but when she opened her eyes again, her peach-colored bikini panties were still unsoiled.

In the diner, they sat in a booth that had an individual selector of taped music mounted to the wall. Robin kept turning the wheel that flipped the song titles, click, click, until Linda wanted to grab her hand to make her stop. Linda's need to talk, so as not to have to think about herself, was enormous. Questions demanded answers, and she was determined to provoke some of them and begin a volley of conversation. "Have you ever stayed on a farm before, Robin?" she asked.

"No."

"I haven't either," Linda confessed, "but it sounds nice and healthy, doesn't it?"

That was definitely a wrong move. She could tell by Robin's little curling sneer. Health is of no interest to teenagers, anyway. Most of the time they seem bent on *destroying* their health. Right now, Robin was eating a meal almost entirely composed of starches: spaghetti, french fries, and a buttered soft roll. An accompanying salad lay untouched. Well, she wouldn't compound her error by saying anything about that. She wasn't the girl's mother, she wasn't anyone's mother. "Ohhhh," she moaned, remembering, and Robin was so startled she said, "What's the matter?"

"I don't know," Linda said. "I guess I must be full." She looked down at her plate, at the revolting pink edge of her half-eaten hamburger.

Linda excused herself to go to the bathroom. As soon as she left the table, Robin went right to the local telephone books on a stand near the rest rooms. She turned quickly to the R's: Reich, Reilly, Reinhart. But

HEARTS

there was no Miriam Reismann listed. She slammed the book shut and hurried back to the booth as Linda came through the door marked with the silhouette of a woman.

They walked a short distance to a small shopping center that reminded Linda of the one in Slatesville. She pointed out the five-and-dime next door to the drugstore, and she gave Robin two dollars in case she wanted to buy something. But Robin trailed just behind her into the drugstore.

There was a lot of junk on the counters, but not what Linda wanted. "Look at this!" she cried, at a display of soap miniatures she hoped would distract Robin while she made discreet inquiries. Robin ignored the soaps and tailed Linda as if she were suddenly scared of being separated. Linda pretended to browse. She even took off her shoes and tried on six pairs of those Japanese rubber beach thongs. The Child's Large, the Man's Small, and the Woman's Medium all fit her. The pharmacist called from behind his counter: "May I help someone?" Linda looked around; they were the only customers in the store. She fixed a smile and ambled up to him, sensing Robin right behind her.

Linda thought that if she were a shy young man buying condoms for the first time, there would probably have been a forbidding matron, the twin of her high-school health teacher, behind the counter.

The pharmacist wore a pristine white coat, and he had gray hair parted in the middle, giving him a paternal/professional aura that confused her. She felt she wanted his approval, which didn't make any sense. He was a complete stranger; she would never see him again.

Linda leaned toward him, clutching the counter's edge. She had removed her wedding band on the day of Wright's funeral, and now she wondered if she should be wearing it, the way women used to wear borrowed or dime-store rings when they checked into quickie motels.

Behind her, Robin had paused at a magazine rack against the wall, and was standing there, turning pages.

"Do you have those pregnancy-test kits?" Linda hissed.

The pharmacist reached between them and handed her a small blue box from a prominent pile of small blue boxes. They had been right there all the time, in plain sight, under a sign that said *Family Planning Center*. And the pharmacist didn't even seem curious. She might have asked for aspirin or Band-Aids for all he cared. His indifference gave her a rush of courage. She paid for her purchase and marched away, forgetting completely about Robin for the moment. At the doorway, she remembered and turned to see Robin buying something, too. Linda waited for her with concealed impatience.

The kid stayed in the bathroom for what seemed like hours. What was she doing in there? As soon as the door was shut, Linda had pulled the blue box from her purse and scanned the instructions. They were not complicated at all. How civilized life had become when such torturous suspense could be shortened, and when no middleman was necessary to obtain this internal information.

According to the literature, she'd have her answer in two hours. If Robin ever came out of the bathroom. The toilet flushed once, then again; water ran into the sink for the millionth time, and the door opened. Robin, in blue pajamas, was barefoot and pink-faced. Linda rushed past her, closed the door, and locked it.

Robin dropped her discarded clothing on the floor next to the bed that was hers for the night. If she woke first in the morning, which was her intention, she would probably have everything back on again before Linda even stirred. The tattooed place on her back was tender when she lay on it. It was probably still infected. The antibiotic capsules Ray had given her were huge, and she'd always had trouble swallowing pills. When she was little and became ill, her father would crush the baby aspirins and hide them in applesauce.

Asshole Linda had knocked on the door, asking if everything was okay, just when she almost had it down, and she had to spit it out and start all over again. Her belly was bloated with all the water she drank, trying. The capsule kept rising into her mouth no matter how far back she pushed it, no matter how fast she gulped the water. She turned both faucets on all the way so Linda wouldn't hear her gagging. Robin had to throw two capsules down the toilet because they had become such a gelatinous mess. The third one went down her throat on the first try.

After that, she took two short tokes on one of the joints Ray had given her, and then carefully put it out. She opened the window and waved at the smoke while Linda kept banging on the door.

Now Robin pulled the covers up and lay on her side to think about her mother. Once Robin learned about the man, she had to give up all those soothing fantasies of amnesia and kidnapping by pirates or gypsies. Gradually, since her father's death, her mind's image of her mother changed, too. The beauty she believed she remembered became shallow and ordinary. Yet Robin clung to an old idea that the man in the case was handsome and rich, maybe even famous. One day Robin might open a newspaper and find her mother in the act of dining at the White House or attending the Academy Awards. She could only think of Miriam in extravagant circumstances, wealthy in every respect except for peace of mind and true happiness. All the furs and jewels in the world were unable to console her in her regret. And she would be almost unrecognizable now because of the rapid and savage aging process that had left her ruined and undesirable.

When Robin found her, truly ugly and deserted by *him*, she would tell her how Wright had died. Her mother would cry out in grief and lay apologies like roses at Robin's feet, too late, too late. Then joy would overtake her at rediscovering her lost child and she would open her arms. Robin would go into them, but only to exact her revenge. Then all of Miriam's money, and the horrified screams of her servants, couldn't save her.

The pot was finally starting to take. Robin felt good now, easy. Her thoughts became random and before long she allowed herself to dissolve into sleep. What! She jerked awake and sat up, confused. She was in a dim room, lighted briefly by passing cars. It was a motel room, somewhere in Pennsylvania. Linda was in the bathroom doing something in absolute silence, and Robin's father was dead.

She lay down again and under the covers her hands came together between her thighs in irreverent prayer.

HEARTS

She clenched her teeth until they ground against each other, forbidding the escape of careless speech, and then she gave herself up again to sleep.

There were two glasses on the shelf above the sink. Linda took the one still wrapped in a bag marked *Sanitized For Your Protection*, unwrapped it, and urinated into it. The diagrammed instructions were unfolded and propped against the faucet. After she glanced at them once more, she took an eyedropper from the kit and put just three drops of urine into the provided test tube. Soon this magical fluid from her own body would reveal its mystery.

She removed a plastic vial from the kit and added its contents to the test tube and then shook it. There was a little stand in the box and she placed it on the edge of the sink and balanced the test tube in it. A mad scientist in the bathroom laboratory of a third-rate motel.

Linda stared as the frothy liquid settled and grew still. If a dark ring formed near the bottom in two hours, the test was positive and she was pregnant. If nothing happened, she was not. It was nine o'clock. At eleven, the results would be in. Watched pots. She couldn't simply sit in that claustrophobic space and wait. Linda wished she had someone there to share the time and suspense with. She thought of Iola back in Bayonne shaking her hips right now to amplified music.

After Wright died, Iola visited Linda and said that they *all* die, one way or another. Every relationship she'd ever had ended in pain. Now her body was beginning to retreat from men, a little at a time. She didn't regret the loss of muscle tone, the sagging. Soon she'd retire from the arena completely, with a vibrator and some mood-inducing music. "That sounds so lonely," Linda had said. "Yeah, I suppose," Iola agreed. "But at least you don't have to worry about getting involved." She would probably have something cheering to say now, too, something to make Linda smile and relieve her of this feeling of isolation.

Yet it wasn't Iola Linda wanted. It was her own mother, with a wanting so strong it surprised her. In that common error of childhood, Linda used to think her mother delivered babies in her nurse's satchel. What else could make her departures so urgent? A family was always waiting eagerly for its new child. Once Linda held on to her at the door, suspending her weight from the starched skirt. "I wish you didn't have to go!" she cried. Her mother pried open the clinging hands, first one and then the other. "If wishes were horses," she said sadly, which confused and distracted Linda long enough for her mother to make her getaway at a steady trot, the newest baby wailing in the satchel.

Even after Linda understood her mother's real function in those other households, there was a stubborn authority about her connection with human reproduction that stayed. Her mother used to say that she could look into a woman's eyes and tell immediately if she was pregnant and, if the pregnancy was advanced enough, the sex of the unborn child, too. "What do you see?" a woman once asked, and Linda's mother said, "The truth," and would not elaborate. But it was not only for this thrilling authority that Linda missed her now. It was for that staple of early existence, for which she once waited hungrily at windows and doors, the mothering itself.

The contents of the test tube remained the same, a

HEARTS

clear and silent sea. Linda, sitting on the closed toilet and staring, found herself dozing off. She stood and stretched and, glancing into the wastebasket under the sink, saw a bloody sanitary napkin clumsily swathed in an excess of toilet paper. At first she thought it had been left by a former tenant of the room, and she blamed bad housekeeping and ironic coincidence. Then she realized it was Robin's, a part of *her* secret purchase in the drugstore. Going by in her pajamas before, the girl had seemed half her true age, disaffected and immature. Yet she menstruated, ready or not, more evidence of life's mindless eternal chain.

Linda opened the door as slowly and quietly as she could. Robin was asleep, with the unguarded innocent face only sleep allowed her. Linda longed to get into the other bed but was afraid she'd fall asleep also, before the two hours were up. Instead, she sat in the one chair in the room, an armless wooden construction with a thin loose pad on its seat. She pulled it over to the wall first, so she could rest her head. All that driving; she was dizzy with fatigue. Haphazard thoughts almost became dreams. A parade of people, in irrelevant order, filed past: Iola, Wright, her father, Simonetti, her mother. She imagined the first man and the first woman ever to recognize the connection between sex and procreation. It was probably before the discovery of fire, the invention of the wheel, maybe even before the achievement of language. Lovemaking was the one mute comfort they could take without danger in a dark and beginning world. Oh, what a rotten trick!

Linda looked at her watch. It was only 9:20. When she was very young she thought about love a great deal of the time. She drew hearts pierced by arrows on the pages of her school notebooks, and the beautiful profiles of women and men who were destined to fall in love with one another. She wrote names for them in her best script under their portraits: Diana, Glenda, Jonathan, Brent. The men had cigarettes or pipes clenched between their teeth, and no one existed from the waist down.

She thought about the possibilities of men's bodies, none of which she had ever seen. Her father had kept himself from her unclothed, as he had clothed. Linda had witnessed her future in her mother's large, soft shape, and looked forward to her own pendulousness, her own private forests of hair. But of course she wasn't satisfied; word was out.

There was that dog, Prince, that Mrs. Piner kept chained in the yard. He greeted Linda wildly whenever she came home from school, and one afternoon she sat down next to him on the grass and pulled him onto her lap. His thick white coat ruffled under her fingers, and then shed in an airborne drift, like blown dandelion puffs. As she stroked his ears and belly, his black tongue lolled, he sighed in surrender to pleasure, and a thin red tube emerged from that hair-tipped pinch of flesh with the startling clarity of Linda's mother's lipstick.

Mrs. Piner, who had been sweeping the porch steps, flew down them, a white fury, and beat the dog on the rump and head with the broom. "Bad dog!" she cried, and Prince growled at her.

When a friend's baby brother was diapered, Linda saw his miniature parts, still wrinkled from passage, as they were quickly powdered and covered again from view. And sometimes she watched from the stairs as old Mr. Botts came from the bathroom, his pajamas askew, for a glimpse of his poor, broken-necked sex.

It was almost ten o'clock and she was tempted to look at the test tube in advance, but suffered a superstitious fear of disobeying those printed instructions. In her sleep, Robin made unintelligible sounds that were almost words, and Linda said, "Shhh. Shhh." Then she took a flashlight from her purse and opened one of the Exxon maps across her bed. With her finger she found their approximate location and then traced the continuation of their journey over the yellow line. The next state was Ohio, the state of Presidents. Linda couldn't remember where she had heard that. Or why she thought of it now. She was so tired. Maybe if she slept for a few minutes. You could set yourself like an alarm clock to wake at a particular time if you wanted to. She could lie down on the covers, not get too comfortable or settled. Under her arm, the map crackled and she pushed it away, gently, so as not to tear it. Her flash of intuition in the car that morning could have been nothing, a false alarm. She didn't feel different, really. There were supposed to be other signs, weren't there? Breast soreness and swelling, weight gain, and whatever her mother saw in other women's eyes. Cars went by on the road outside. There were people who traveled all night to get someplace. Trucks carried milk and eggs into Ohio for the breakfasts of future Presidents. In her mind's eye, Linda followed them down the real double line of the highway until they disappeared into the darkness.

When she woke, she was conscious first of the continuing traffic. She peered and squinted until her eyes adjusted, and she saw that it was almost two o'clock. Robin had flung off the covers and was lying spread-eagled and open-mouthed. Linda went into the bathroom and put on the light. A roach ran crazily for cover behind the toilet. Even before she saw the ring in the test tube, she felt the stunning blow of truth.

HEARTS

THE HITCHHIKERS WERE EVERYWHERE. **10**
You'd never know it was against the law.
There was at least one contender at each entrance to the parkway, arm raised like the starter's in a
demolition derby.

They were mostly young people, probably recently
sprung from college, and setting out to see the world
on this glorious June day. Some of them held signs:
Chicago. Phoenix. Anywhere! Maybe the state troopers
were looking the other way, given the gasoline shortage.
Linda knew better than to pick anyone up, no matter
how innocent he might seem. In their newspaper photos,
captured murderers and rapists didn't always appear
sinister or different, either. When a criminal was hand-
cuffed to a detective, Linda often had to read the
caption to see who was who. Not that she worried so
much about her own safety; she was too miserable by
now to care. In some respects, the worst had already
happened. But she was still responsible for Robin, who
sat or lay in the backseat as if Linda were the chauffeur
and there was a wall of glass between them.

There was a new joyless refrain in Linda's head:
What will I do? What will I do? When they crossed
the border into Ohio and were welcomed by the gover-
nor's sign, she could not work up the enthusiasm to
share it with Robin, who was looking the other way.

As they approached Youngstown, Linda felt a slight
change in the car's movement that she ignored, and even
when it seemed to limp and there was a strange plopping
noise, she attributed it to the uneven surface of the
road. When a trucker passed to her left and blasted his
horn and gestured downward, she finally understood that

she had a flat tire. She signaled and pulled over too quickly onto the graveled shoulder, and stopped at the end of a skid. Before she could open the door, a bearded man in a khaki T-shirt and chinos ran up to the car and yelled breathlessly, "Hey, thanks!"

Linda stepped out, clutching the keys in her fist. "For what?" she asked, and saw that he had a backpack with a bedroll attached, and knew that he was the last hitch-hiker she'd watched to the diminishing point in the rear-view mirror. "Oh," she said. "I didn't stop for . . . I wasn't . . ." Her hands fluttered, but the man was already squatting at the deflated tire, his backpack flung to one side.

He changed the tire for them in relentless sunlight, after urging Linda and Robin into the sparse, dappled shade of a single young oak just off the shoulder. By the time he was done, the khaki shirt was dark with per-spiration and he had wrapped his forehead in a gypsy's bandanna. He came over and collapsed at their feet, the backpack under his head. "Now that flat is your spare," he told Linda. "You'd better get it fixed soon. You might need it."

"I will," she promised, and opened her purse.

He held up his hand. "No, no, it's okay," he said. "I'm independently wealthy." When she fumbled with her wallet, he said, "Listen, outdoor work is terrific for the health. I try to do a couple of these a day. I'm lucky you came along."

"Thank you, then," Linda said, her hands at a loss. "Thanks a lot."

"Yeah, thanks," Robin echoed, her first voluntary civility of the trip. Linda wanted to shake her and per-

HEARTS

haps loosen other pleasant contained words, like change stuck in a slot machine.

They walked back to the car, Robin lagging and turning to look back at the man under the tree. Linda turned, too, and his arm was half raised in a lazy farewell salute. "Well, come on!" she yelled.

How could she not offer him a ride? It would have to be premeditated murder for him to go through all that work first just to do them in later. Besides, he looked as if he would no longer have the energy, if he ever had the inclination.

He was handsome, in the current way that young men were handsome: Christlike and sinful at once, just down from the cross or out of a neighbor's warm bed. He put his pack beside Robin in the back and got into the front passenger seat. When he did, there was the sudden heady fragrance of sweat and sunlight. His thigh, resting at least six inches from Linda's, seemed swollen and confined by the chinos, and she felt an erotic impulse that shocked and appalled her. Now, of all times. It could have something to do with a hormonal imbalance; so many things were going on inside her that she could not discern or control.

In the meantime, the hitchhiker turned to smile at Robin, who *smiled back!* Maybe he was a hypnotist, or a magician. Maybe a flock of doves would rise from his bedroll and fill the car with the beating of wings.

He asked their names and told them that his was John Wolfe Blaise, usually known as Wolfie, and that he was on his way to a wedding in New Mexico. Linda said his name to herself a few times, trying it out.

"Jesus," he said softly when she pulled onto the road

again, with a hairsbreadth between the Maverick and a roaring semi. When they were in the mainstream of traffic, he looked from one of them to the other. "Are you two sisters?" he asked. "I think I see a family resemblance. Something about the eyes."

Linda began to suspect that he was only a con man. She and Robin might be considered physical *opposites*, if anything. She said, "Related by marriage," and left it at that.

"You married?" he asked Robin, a question guaranteed to win her disdain. Ho-ho, Linda thought, but Robin only smiled again and shook her head.

"Ah," Wolfie said. "Me, neither," as if they shared a conspiracy of wisdom.

Me, neither, Linda wanted to shout. "Whose wedding?" she asked, pretending it wasn't unusual for guests to hitchhike to one.

"A friend's," Wolfie answered, in a way that closed the subject. Then he turned his attention to the landscape. He observed it hungrily and began to point things out to Robin. She usually ignored Linda's shared observations, but she listened carefully to his, and even asked questions. What did they call those clouds, and those trees? What caused the pools of "water" on the highway that disappeared as you approached them? He named the white, blooming clouds cumulus, and those small fringed trees they saw everywhere ailanthus, or trees of heaven. They just come up, he told them, even in the sidewalk cracks of big cities. Light waves bouncing off the hot air near the pavement give the illusion of water from a distance. The angle changes as you approach and the mirage vanishes.

HEARTS

Linda listened, too, and when she tailgated the car in front of them and had to stop short, Wolfie's foot braced against an imaginary brake, and he apologized for taking her mind off the road. Later, when he asked where they were heading, she wanted to tell him everything, and ask what he thought she should do, and what states had legalized abortion, and if she might die of one simply because no one would be waiting for her not to.

"Our next real destination is Valeria, Iowa," she said, "where Robin's grandfather and aunt live," and she knew she sounded as carefree as one of the Bobbsey Twins on the way to Grandpa's farm. After that, she told him, she would continue on alone to California, to Los Angeles maybe, or San Francisco, she wasn't sure. He asked what route she planned to take from Iowa, and she showed him the map with its prescribed yellow line. "That's the fastest, I guess," he said. "But the southern route's prettier, I think, if you're not in a big hurry to get there." She asked if he would write it down, and he drew a new penciled line across the country.

Linda said that she and Robin were going to look for a place to stay overnight pretty soon. They were close to some caverns she'd promised they would visit.

"Wherever you want to let me out will be fine," Wolfie said. "I'll probably be able to pick up another ride today, from there. So far I've been pretty lucky. I've made it down from Montreal in five days. I'm moving, but there's still time to look around, to see everything."

"What were you doing up there?" Linda asked.

"Staying out of Vietnam, in the first place. Then, longing for America for a while."

It was the war she had grown up with. When did it

finally end? Five, six years ago? The draft was over even before that.

Slatesville had enjoyed a modest boom of government contracts at the asbestos mills during the war. Much too late, though, for her father to share in the rewards of overtime. She felt that he would have loved the escalation of the war. He'd always hated and feared Communists, unions, pacifists. Like Mr. Piner, he would have raged about Johnson, and then Nixon, who forfeited a hero's potential by not dropping the big one and bringing our boys home. Our boys included anyone not afraid of dying in distant places for uncertain causes. If Linda had been a man of draft age when her father was still alive, she believed she would have gone off without protest to whatever war they happened to be waging, in a last-ditch effort to please him. And she would have been killed, probably, because nothing less would really have done it.

Now she felt a lovely satisfaction in riding next to this beautiful and peaceful man whom her father would have excluded forever from that doomed fraternity of "our boys."

"Do you like Canada?" she asked.

"That first winter was murder," he said, "after New Mexico. I thought I was never going to get warm, and I was unemployed besides. I did odd jobs, mostly, while I slowly turned blue. Then I found work with a silversmith in Montreal. That's what I did before, in Santa Fe." He pulled a chain from the neck of his T-shirt and Linda saw a silver bird in flight across his hand.

"Then I did begin to like Canada, except for the cold. I never really got used to it—guess I'm a desert boy by nature. Anyway, when Jerry sort of pardoned us, I decided to stay. Most of the guys I knew did. Hell, we weren't going to come home and get our hands slapped. Anyway, I was happy with my job by then, with my woman, with my life."

Linda's heart stumbled. But what did she think? Of *course* he'd have a woman. Everybody had somebody. Glancing to either side as she drove, she saw other cars with couples in front and goggle-eyed children in back. Their bumpers were plastered with proof of family vacations. They had gone together to Wigwam Village, Santa's Toyland, and the Parrot Jungle. The Maverick wobbled halfway over the broken line and then back again.

"Hey," Wolfie said. "Are you tired? Here I am, telling you my life story. I can drive for a while if you want me to. I'm licensed, ma'am, reliable, sober."

Oh, she wanted him to, all right. She wanted to see his hands on the wheel, for one thing, and to lay her head in his lap and dive into a deep dreamless sleep. "No, I'm fine," she said. "Really." She asked him how he'd gotten into the country. Wasn't he still kind of "wanted"?

He laughed and said it wasn't hard. The border check was pretty casual these days and he had a friend's ID. Staying in the U.S. might be more complicated.

"Are you going to stay?" Robin asked, Linda's unspoken question.

"I'll see," Wolfie answered. "I'll see how things work out."

While the deflated tire was being repaired, they all went into the Howard Johnson's next door. There was a short wait for tables, and Muzak was playing an orchestrated version of "Love Me Tender," heavy on the strings. Without a word, Wolfie put his arm around Linda's waist and danced her gently around the hostess and the candy counter and back to their place on line, before she could resist. Linda felt exhilarated and oddly unembarrassed, as if ballroom dancing at Howard Johnson's was a usual occurrence. The hostess, who was still smiling, held up three fingers and they were seated. Other diners sitting near them smiled, too. He was obviously the sort of man who got away with things.

When they went back to the gas station, Linda was thinking of saying that they would skip the caverns this trip, and continue driving at least until it was dark. If he wanted to go along, that would be fine with her. She was going in that direction, anyway.

While she paid for the tire, he picked up a ride in a VW van full of teenagers who were heading west nonstop. Linda tried to set her face so that she would not appear abandoned, or even concerned. "Oh, good," she said. "We were going to have to let you out soon, anyway." She pulled the car into a line of cars waiting for gas, and Wolfie leaned his head into the window to say goodbye. She could see the multicolored tangle of hairs that made up his beard, and the starry irises of his eyes. She suffered the kind of vertigo she'd have when she sat too close to the screen at the movies. Con man, she told herself. But what if he kissed her?

He didn't, though. He said, "Bonne chance, Linda," and he touched his hand to hers, sealing it eternally to the steering wheel.

Robin was using the rest room. When she came out,

HEARTS

the van was raising dust in the distance. "Wolfie said to say goodbye," Linda told her.

Robin stared down the road for a long time, shading her eyes with one hand, and she didn't answer. When they were ready to leave again, she climbed into the front seat next to Linda, for the first time since they'd left New Jersey.

THEY WENT DOWN TO THE CAVERNS IN AN *11*
elevator that moved so slowly it seemed reluctant to make the journey. It was crowded
and nobody spoke for at least a hundred feet of their
descent. Then someone farted, the first manifestation
of a developing group anxiety, and everyone laughed and
blamed the small children, who denied it in a round of
protests. "It wasn't me! It musta been Kenny." "Not
me, dumbbell. Judy did it. She does it all the time." "I
did not. It musta been Kenny."

At last they were at the bottom. Of course it was
dark. What did she expect? It was underground, wasn't
it? But the unforgiving quality of the darkness surprised her, and a dampness that seemed to permeate
her clothing, her flesh, to enter her very bones, made
Linda shudder. She looked at Robin, who didn't seem
overjoyed to be there, either.

The group, forced into physical closeness in the
elevator, still huddled, behind the guide now, whose
voice was so automatically cheerful she might easily
have been doing sums in her head at the same time.
"Ladies and gentlemen, welcome to our speleological
tour. Anyone who can spell 'speleological' will win a free
pass to our next scheduled tour in one hour. Okay. It is
believed that Indians penetrated further into Hidden
River Caverns than into any other Ohio caves. Evidence
of ceremonial rites has been found in its deepest recesses:
arrowheads, remnants of torches, and the wrappers from
Big Macs."

The laughter ricocheted. A tall, gray-haired woman
near Linda said, "What in heaven's name would we do

---

if that elevator broke down?" Her breath was sour with fear.

"Oh, they have to have others," Linda said. "Don't they?"

"Okay. The stalagmites and stalactites in Hidden River Caverns are noted for their unusual pink coloration due to the large percentage of quartz in their formation. Ladies and gentlemen, if you'll step through here and watch your heads, please."

The passage they walked through was so narrow they had to go single-file. Robin was in front of Linda, the tall woman behind. "I can never remember," the woman whispered loudly, "which ones go up and which ones come down, can you?"

A man behind her said, "It's easy. There's a little trick I learned in school. Stalac*tites* are on *top*. Get it? Tites and top. They both start with 't.' "

His wife didn't agree. "We were told to remember the mighty mites," she said.

"What the hell is that supposed to mean?" he asked.

"It means that if you're mighty, you're upright, and you've got both feet on the ground."

"That's the stupidest thing I ever heard," he told her.

"See?" the tall woman said. "I've forgotten it already."

"Okay. It is believed that Hidden River Caverns were also used by the Indians as an escape route during the frontier days," the guide said. "The entire length of the passage is ten miles and is on three levels."

Linda wished they'd worn heavier sweaters. It was really chilly. She also wished they had not come here in the first place, and she wondered how long the tour was, and if there was any possible way to leave before it was over. What would happen if a man had a heart attack, or a woman went into labor? Could a cave catch on fire?

"How are you doing?" she asked Robin.

"All right," Robin said.

"Me, too."

The book she'd bought was called *Alice in Underland: A Guide to Our Nation's Caves*. The photographs showed relaxed and happy tourists measuring themselves against giant rock formations, and clowning in front of one shaped like a bear.

Judy and Kenny tested their lung power by screaming in the passageway, and the woman behind Linda said, "People should not bring small children who are too young to appreciate places like this."

"Everybody still with me? We didn't lose anybody? Okay. I'm going to deactivate the lights for a moment to show you the absolute darkness in the caverns. Lovers, beware, I'm going to turn them on again in fifteen seconds!"

It had to be much longer than that, although time isn't really measurable in certain circumstances. Linda knew that this was what it was like to have consciousness after death, to feel the earth all around you, and the darkness, with only a fading memory of light, like an old longing. This is what it was like to be buried for dead and to come alive again later, too late. She had a moment's gratitude for having had Wright cremated, and thought, not without irony, about the ashes being aboveground in the actual world, and Robin and herself being here beneath it.

Somebody made loud kissing noises, evoking weak

laughter. "Oh, God," someone else said, the voice seeming to seep through the walls. "Oh, God."

The lights came on again and they walked into a huge vaulted room. There was the sound of moving water close by.

"Okay," the guide said. "This is the main ceremonial auditorium, and the noise you hear is not because someone left the tap on in the ladies' room."

Was there really a ladies' room? Were there stalactites hanging over the toilets? Stalagmites?

"It is the Hidden River Caverns River, a body of water that is twenty feet at its widest place and less than six feet at its narrowest, and is a half mile long. If you will all step this way, we'll be going on a little boat ride."

"Hurray!" one of the children yelled, and Linda remembered a classmate bragging about just such a boat ride years ago. Had he actually been terrified then? Would he go down here again as a grown man?

They went in two by two, she and Robin partners, and it *was* a little like the Tunnel of Love in the Slatesville amusement park, except you moved out into sunlight again at the end of that ride. This one only led you to the Crystal Altar, where they all disembarked. Linda noticed a few flash cubes scattered on the floor.

The guide explained that Marryin' Sam, a local preacher, performed wedding ceremonies on this spot, out of the regular tourist season. She showed them a heart-shaped rock on which the bride and groom stood, and said that there had been 632 such marriages begun here, so far. Some of the sentimental couples even came back for anniversaries.

Linda and Wright had been married in the back

room of a Chinese restaurant in Jersey City. Iola and Simonetti were there, along with a few other guests. Simonetti asked the waiter for more "flied lice" about forty times. Robin ordered spaghetti from the American menu. When they were ready to leave, Iola asked the manager for some rice to throw at the newlyweds, and was given steamed rice in one of those little cardboard takeout containers.

In the trunk of the Maverick, Linda had a picture of her parents taken on their wedding day twenty-seven years before. Her father was frowning and her mother looked solemn, yet hopeful. She continued to wear white for the rest of her life.

It was hot outside. The group dispersed as if they couldn't wait to get away from one another. Children ran from parents, who didn't call them back. Couples separated and moved around alone near the souvenir stand and the restaurant. Linda and Robin looked at the postcards, and the little paperweights with replicas of the caverns inside them, and the added puzzling element of snowflakes when you shook them. Everything was overpriced and ugly, but Linda asked Robin if she'd like something as a memento of the day. Robin shook her head and then walked behind Linda back to the motel. They passed the Maverick and saw that a sticker had been affixed to the rear bumper. *We Visited Hidden River Caverns. Home of the Crystal Altar.*

This was one of the most expensive rooms they'd had so far, because it was so close to the caverns, and a winery, and something called Donnie's Adventureland. They were told they were lucky to get the last room in the place, even if it did have only one double bed, and the lights from Adventureland playing all over the walls when the drapes were open.

After dinner in the Hidden River Café, which was just another diner, despite the door shaped like the opening to a grotto, they went back to their room again. The air conditioner droned and it seemed as cold in there as it had been underground. Linda was sleepy, and for once she claimed the bathroom first. She turned the shower on and began to pull off her shirt when she remembered a teen magazine she'd bought that morning as a little surprise for Robin, and had left in the car.

Robin was tearing off her clothes as if they were on fire. Linda noticed that the nightstand drawer was open and that the telephone book was on the floor. "Robin," she said. "I forgot to tell you—"

Robin whirled away from her, pulling the just discarded T-shirt against her chest.

"My God," Linda said. "What's that thing on your back?"

"It's nothing. Leave me alone," Robin said.

"But it's *blue!* Let me look at it, Robin, please!"

Robin evaded Linda's reaching arm and ran around the bed yelling, "Leave me alone, leave me alone!"

"I have to see that," Linda said, chasing her. "I'm responsible for you, damn it!"

Robin ducked and dodged and went the other way. "Don't be. Don't be, you asshole!"

Linda stood still. She could hear the shower running behind her. "What did you say? What did you call me?"

They were on opposite sides of the bed, panting.

"I didn't call you anything," Robin said, her voice disappearing on the last syllable.

"You did," Linda insisted. "You called me an asshole. That's a terrible word to call somebody. I haven't done anything to you, Robin. Somebody else might have left you flat, not cared what happened to you."

The girl's eyes were feverish, and her voice had come back, hoarse and dry. "I don't care," she said.

"I mean you don't even *talk* to me, and I'm dragging you all the way across the country. We were only married six measly weeks. That's hardly anything. We were practically strangers. And do you know what I paid for that lamp you gave away without a second thought, miss? Twelve ninety-eight! I shopped for two days to get the right thing. Any other teenager in America would have been thrilled to death to have it. What's the *matter* with you?"

Robin's teeth were bared, the way Prince's had been that day Mrs. Piner beat him with the broom, and her mouth was quivering. "I didn't ask you to," she said evenly. "I didn't ask you to do anything."

Linda became aware of her own mouth's hard and trembling set. Slowly she relaxed it. "You didn't," she admitted. She sat down at the edge of the bed, weary. "Okay, I take that part back. But not the other. Just human decency is all I'm talking about. Why can't you be pleasant to me? What did I ever do to you?"

Robin didn't answer. She turned away again to put on her pajama top. Linda saw what the thing on her back was.

"Who did that?" she asked. "Was it like a secret initiation? It's not infected, is it?"

"No. It's better."

Linda said, "All right, then. Okay." She went back to the bathroom, which was filled with steam, and she

HEARTS

shut off the shower. Her nightgown was damp, but she put it on anyway, and it clung to her breasts and between her legs. She didn't even brush her teeth. It would have required energy she could not call up.

When she came into the bedroom, Robin was already under the green blankets. "Do you mind if I shut off the air conditioner?" Linda asked. "I don't know why, but I'm cold." Robin mumbled something and Linda pushed the switch. The quiet was profound. She turned off the lamp and got into bed. The drapes were open a little and colored lights from Donnie's Adventureland were reflected on the wall behind their heads. They lay cautiously apart, acutely aware of one another, like lovers who have quarreled and are still burdened by unused passion.

It was the caverns that had upset them both, Linda thought. They would probably have been better off going to the winery. In her own interior darkness, cells divided silently and without permission. It was the caverns and their lousy coming attractions of death, their promise of consummate loneliness. Then why did we have to be so lonely while we were still here? Restless, she turned from side to side, but with exquisite care not to touch or jostle Robin, who did not move at all.

"WHAT DO WE HAVE TO STOP HERE FOR?" *12*
Robin asked, as they pulled up to the curb.

"Because these are my friends," Linda said.
"And I want to visit them. I'd think you'd be glad for
a change of scene yourself, glad to be in someone's home
for once, after all this time on the road."

"They're not *my* friends," Robin said.

True enough, Linda supposed, and for that matter,
they weren't actually hers, either. Or hadn't been for
years. She'd first had the idea of looking them up while
she and Robin were having lunch in New Carlisle, Indiana. Linda was sipping iced tea and trying to remember
if she had packed her high-school yearbook, when she
suddenly thought of Sally McKenna, who had graduated
with her, and who had married a boy named Rod. They
were married on Prom night and then went directly to
Indiana, where Rod had a job waiting for him with the
telephone company. His uncle, who was a personnel
supervisor, had arranged it.

Linda remembered them mainly because the town
they had moved to in Indiana was called La Porte, the
same name as the assistant principal's at Slatesville High.
And here Linda was, in Indiana, too. But what was
Rod's last name? Jergen? Justin? Something like that. It
started with a J anyway. She opened the Exxon map
and found that La Porte wasn't very far from where
they were, less than fifteen miles away. "I'll be right
back," she told Robin, and went to the telephone books
in the rear of the diner. She flipped through the pages.
Jaeckel, that was it! The kids used to call him Dr. Jekyll,
and his best friend, Bobby Masterson, Mr. Hyde. They
did a little routine where Rod pretended to drink a

HEARTS

potion and Bobby slowly turned into a monster. Linda never thought it was very funny, but they used to crack everyone else up, including the teachers.

Sure enough, there he was in the telephone book—Rodney A. Jaeckel, living at 2119 Skylark Lane. Robin was staring at her, so Linda waved and pantomimed that she was going to make a telephone call. The line was busy—it was busy for almost ten minutes. Linda didn't give up; it would be interesting to see what had happened to Sally and Rod.

For one thing, they'd had children. When Linda got through at last, a child answered the phone, screaming hello, and a baby could be heard, too. A woman yelled, "Ask who it is, Candy!" Maybe she said Sandy. Or Andy. It was hard to tell because the child was breathing harder than Supercreep used to, right into the receiver.

"Who is it?" the child shrieked.

"Linda. Linda Reis—Linda Camisko."

"Who is it *now?*" the woman called from a distance.

"Nabisco!" the child answered, again at glass-shattering volume, and then dropped or threw the phone to the floor.

Sally picked it up. She sounded angry. "Who is this?" she demanded.

At first she didn't remember Linda. How could she, after all these years? And Linda had been pretty quiet in high school, not very outgoing. But after a while Sally said, "Wait a minute. Did you have reddish hair?"

"No," Linda said. "Sort of a medium brown."

"I think I know who you are," Sally insisted. "Did you have Pearsall for Home Ec?"

"Yes!" Linda said. "I did!"

Sally laughed. "Do you remember when that jerk, Laura Hopewell, set fire to the dish towel?"

Linda didn't—she could hardly place Laura Hopewell —but she laughed also and said, "I think so."

They talked for a while after that about other kids who'd graduated with them, finding no common ground. There was an uneasy pause and then Sally asked what Linda was doing in Indiana.

"Driving through, actually," Linda said. "The amazing thing is, I'm not very far away right now."

There was another pause, and finally Sally said, "I guess you can come over for a little while, if you want to."

Linda thanked her for the invitation, and accepted.

When she came back to the table, she saw that Robin had made confetti out of several paper napkins. She had also been lighting matches in Linda's absence. About ten burnt ones were lying in the ashtray and there was a hovering stench of sulphur. "Are you playing with matches, Robin?" Linda asked.

"No," Robin answered, avoiding eye contact. "They were here from before."

Since one match was still smoking, Linda knew she had a strong argument, but decided not to use it. She was looking forward to visiting Sally and wanted to persuade Robin into some degree of conviviality. It would be marvelous to talk to someone her own age again. Although she and Sally had not had an intimate friendship in high school, there was a natural intimacy among all women these days, and Linda eagerly considered the luxury of having a confidante. Sally was married, and had a family, the experience that Linda

HEARTS

always imagined would confer automatic wisdom. She herself had not been married long enough to find out. Maybe Sally could tell her what to do. At least she would listen with a sympathetic ear.

Skylark Lane was a street of identical hi-ranch houses. There was a Chevy station wagon in the driveway at 2119, and the front lawn was littered with toys.

Linda would not have recognized Sally. She had gained thirty or forty pounds during the last eight years. She greeted Linda speculatively, as if she had never seen her before. Linda wondered if she had changed radically, too.

There were more toys in the living room, in direct counterpoint to the three rifles mounted on the wall above the fireplace. Were they loaded? Linda remembered that Rod had been a moody, short-tempered boy.

The baby had a cold. It lay in a playpen in the middle of the room, inhaling and exhaling the same green globule of snot, and stared at the strangers. It was bald and naked, except for a diaper and rubber pants. There was a faint rash across its tiny tapered chest, and the visible ribs pulsed as steadily as a digital clock. Linda couldn't decide if the baby was a boy or a girl. She suspected that Sally would be insulted if she asked. People usually were if you didn't recognize the sex of their children. "Don't you just love them when they're little like that?" Linda said to Robin, who snorted and went to the fireplace to gaze up at the rifles. "Well, hello there," Linda said to the baby. "What's *your* name?" hoping someone else would answer and give her a clue.

"It's *my* baby," the older child said from the doorway. She was a girl and her name was Bambi. Her piercing voice on the telephone had not prepared Linda for her astonishing beauty. Her eyes were huge and so heavily fringed she appeared drugged. Her face was small, even for that delicate neck, and it had the sweet, soft-chinned shape of a cat's. Who did she look like? Linda pictured Rod, a kind of bird-faced teenager, with ears like a loving cup's. And Sally wasn't pretty, not now, or back in high school when she was younger and slim. "*My* baby," Bambi said again, coming closer. She pinched Linda's leg and ran out of the room.

"That kid needs to be murdered," Sally said. Then she sat on the couch and lit a cigarette. Linda sat next to her, and Robin collapsed into a chair. "Do you want some coffee or anything?" Sally asked.

Linda would have liked a cup of coffee, but she felt the offer was perfunctory, so she said, "No, thank you, we just had lunch. We're stuffed to the gills." After that she sat there, searching her head for something casual to say, something that would lead them into a mood of familiarity. Robin, slumped and sullen, was certainly not going to help. "How's Rod?" Linda asked.

"He's okay," Sally said.

"Still with the telephone company?"

"Uh-huh."

"Do you ever hear from Bobby Masterson, Sally? He and Rod were such a riot when they did that routine. You would have loved it, Robin. Dr. Jekyll and Mr. Hyde. Rod swallowed the potion and Bobby turned into the monster." Linda did a fast takeoff on Bobby's part of the act.

"He was killed in Vietnam," Sally said, when Linda was all fangs and claws.

HEARTS

"Oh," Linda said, and sat back on the couch. She felt guilty for never having really thought Bobby was funny. And compounding her guilt, she thought longingly at that moment of the hitchhiker, of Wolfie.

Sally relieved the silence by asking if Linda was married. She had introduced Robin by name only. Stepdaughter sounded like a wicked designation, and didn't even seem true. When Linda said that she was a widow, Sally was awestruck. She said that Linda was the first widow from their graduating class as far as she knew, although a couple of people besides Bobby were dead. Linda tried to change the subject, looking significantly at Robin, but Sally was into a roll call of fatalities: "Joan Kowalski, leukemia, Artie Hammond, auto wreck, Catherine Johnson, illegal abortion. The family let out that it was pneumonia," Sally said. "But nobody dies of pneumonia any more."

Linda felt weak. She could see no real potential for intimacy here, and she wanted to leave. Before she could say anything, the baby began to cry, and Sally looked at her watch. "Oh, terrific," she said. "What timing. Look, could you do me a favor and feed it? I have to make a few phone calls." She stood and swooped over the playpen, coming up with the baby, who had worked itself into a screaming rage by then. Sally dumped it into Linda's lap and went to get the bottle. Bambi appeared suddenly and dug her little fingers into Linda's arm, and then more fiercely into the baby's. The screaming elevated in pitch as Sally came back. "I'll break your neck, Bambi," she said wearily, without affect, and gave the bottle to Linda, who offered it to the baby.

It was as abrupt and easy as shutting off a radio. The

baby stopped crying instantly. It pulled at the nipple with savage concentration and made a frantic effort to breathe through its clogged nose at the same time. Bambi made faces and jeering noises and went out again. Linda could hear Sally dialing in the next room. "Hello," she said. "Is this Mrs. Alexander? Hi! I'm doing a survey for the Best Brand Home Improvement Corporation? We're calling people in your area to see if they have proper insul—" Sally dialed again. "Hello. Is this Mrs. Allman? Hi! I'm doing a survey for the Best—" She slammed the phone down. "And the same to you, bitch!" she said, and started dialing again. No wonder the line had been so busy when Linda tried to call from New Carlisle.

The baby's head wobbled against Linda's arm. She couldn't believe how heavy it was, compared to the rest of the body; like the surprising weight of a beanbag. This one looked like Rod, poor thing. Still, it had a kind of beauty. The clarity of eye, the poreless texture of skin. It squirmed in her lap and siphoned the milk with a steady hard sucking. It was amazing and terrible.

Linda pulled the front of the diaper away and tried to peer inside. There was a dark smelly mess in there and she replaced the diaper quickly without determining the baby's sex. Whatever it was, she was glad it wasn't hers.

Sally came back into the room and took the baby from Linda's arms. She handled it roughly, distractedly, as if it wasn't hers, either.

Linda and Robin stood at the same time. "This was really great, Sally," Linda said. "Like old times."

"Wait till I tell Rod about you dropping in like this," Sally said. "He'll get a real kick out of it."

H E A R T S

He'll probably shoot you, Linda thought.

"Listen, take care," Sally said. "And keep in touch."

Robin and Linda got into the car. "Cat got your tongue?" Linda asked. As she drove away, a handful of small pebbles scattered against the windshield, making her flinch. Bambi could be seen racing across the lawn and into the house.

I'm blue for you

I'm blue for you   *13*

Dear Iola,

I CERTAINLY AM BLUE FOR YOU. WE HAVE BEEN ON the road for several days now. You won't believe all the crazy things that have happened . . .

Just a little love note

Dear Iola,

As it says above, this is just a little love note to let you know that yours truly has not forgotten her old friends. So much has happened since I saw you last that I don't know where to begin . . .

Better late than never!

Dear Iola,

Remember me? This letter certainly is late! I can't believe we're in Illinois! There is so much I have to tell you . . .

Linda let the paper and pen, and the Bible she was leaning on, slip down the side of the bed to the floor. She had started several letters to Iola during the trip, using the stationery Iola had given her, but she never finished writing any of them. She would fall asleep in the middle, or put the page aside to watch television

HEARTS

with Robin, or go out to supper and forget about it. The longer she put off writing, the more difficult a chore it seemed. Her adventures were getting too complicated to convey on a mere piece of paper. It made her tired just to think about it. Yet Linda often thought of Iola herself and how much she missed her, missed that ironic good humor, her special wisdom, and her tough and enduring attitude toward almost everything. Linda wished now that she could be something like that, too—sophisticated and worldly, if not world-weary. Iola could always make her laugh, could always make her see the funny side of even grim or embarrassing situations.

Once, when they'd gone together for lunch at the sandwich shop next door to the studio, they were invited to a Tupperware party, by Rosalie, the cashier. What she had said was, "I'm having a Tupperware party at my house Friday night. Are you girls into that stuff?"

Linda had been married only two weeks and was trying very hard to ease into domesticity. It wasn't that simple. There was Robin, of course, acting sullen and hostile all the time. And Linda had not replaced any of the household items Wright had shared with Miriam, despite his encouragement to do so. Another woman's touch and taste were everywhere, and Linda began to long for things of her own. Why not start with Tupperware, with those little plastic containers in which she could begin ordering the details of her new life? The party itself would be enjoyable, and she would be in the company she craved, those other wives who might take her in as a member of their secret society. "Yes," she told Rosalie. "I'm definitely into it. And I'd love to go."

Iola had glanced at Linda quizzically, and then she said, "Count me in, too. I'll try anything once."

Wright was pleased with her plans. "Spend as much as you like, honey," he said. "And have a good time." He was going to take Robin bowling, and he kissed Linda goodbye the way he always did, as if they might be separated for years.

Rosalie lived in an apartment house in Bayonne, and when Iola and Linda arrived, the other women, about a dozen of them, were already there. The Tupperware people, a man and his wife, had set up their samples on a bridge table in the living room, and covered them with a drop cloth. They were going to make a grand presentation, Linda realized, the way car manufacturers do with the new models each year. She thought it was a pretty silly and dramatic fuss over small kitchen goods, but she tried to withhold judgment and get into the proper spirit of things. Rosalie's husband wasn't home, but her two small children were there, running wildly through the house in their pajamas. Rosalie kept shouting, "Bedtime! Bedtime!" which only appeared to excite the children to a greater frenzy. Finally they were threatened and bribed into submission, and were sent off to bed. Rosalie put out some Cokes and beer and a bowl of onion dip surrounded by potato chips.

The Tupperware woman, Beverly, introduced herself and her husband, Al, who hobbled around with a serious limp. She explained that they had only recently gone into the house-party business, after Al suffered an on-the-job accident that left him permanently disabled. He had to leave construction work for good, just when their financial needs were at a peak. They had one child with a congenital kidney ailment and another with severe emotional problems. But—hey!—they wanted everyone to relax and have fun—this was a *party*, remember? And nobody had to feel obligated to buy anything, either. Then Beverly said that Al was going to leave now because he believed they would have a better time, *this* time, without a man around. That brought a little laughter, and although Linda wasn't sure why, she joined in.

Al left, his limp seemingly worsened, and Beverly had each guest write her name on a slip of paper. These were gathered and placed into a bowl, for a door-prize drawing to be held at the end of the evening. A blond woman sitting near Linda lit one cigarette from another and said bitterly, "I never won anything in my life."

"Oh, me neither," Linda said, coughing into the smoke screen and trying to smile in empathy at the same time.

Beverly placed a pile of order blanks on the coffee table, next to the onion dip, and then walked over to the bridge table, where she stood holding one end of the drop cloth, like a politician about to unveil a war monument. She waited, and the noise in the room rose a little before it died away. "This is a truly amazing line of merchandise," Beverly announced into the silence. "And I'm really proud to be associated with it. I'm really proud to be a woman, too, an *American* woman, who is modern enough to want to make my marriage an exciting and lasting relationship. Things have changed since our mother's and grandmother's day. Women are equal with men in many ways. We hold high-paying jobs; we are actively involved in politics and sports, science and industry. Don't get me wrong; I'm no libber, but I am for equal rights, for freedom of choice in *certain* areas of life." There was a murmur among the other women that sounded half nervous, half approving. What in the world was she talking about?

"Your grandmother was chained to a hot stove all day," Beverly continued. "Now you can choose to be chained to your bed, instead, ha-ha. Seriously, it gives me great pleasure to introduce you to these marvelous products, and to say that I hope they change your life as happily as they've changed mine!" With that, she yanked off the drop cloth, and there was a unified gasp. Linda, who had just dipped a chip into the sour-cream mixture, let it drip onto her blouse as she stared at the bridge table. At first she wasn't certain what she was seeing, but then everything came into sudden and sharp focus. There were a few dozen penises on the table, in a variety of shapes and sizes and colors, and they were all as erect as soldiers called to attention.

A couple of the women cheered. Some of them giggled. "No need to get up for *me*, boys," Iola said, her inflection like Mae West's. And she poked Linda so hard that the dip-laden potato chip dropped into her lap.

Beverly was talking as smoothly and quickly as a sideshow barker now. "Battery-operated, safe, waterproof, rubber, plastic, lifelike, purse-size, expandable." It was impossible to really follow her, and soon she was leaning down to pull a couple of large cartons out from under the table. "Feel free," she said, from her kneeling position. "Examine, touch, guaranteed, batteries not included."

One by one, the women were slowly rising and walking to the display. They were shy and giddy at first, but soon they were holding the samples with critical and solemn interest, turning them over and hefting them,

HEARTS

like wives at the market choosing the best fruits and vegetables for their families.

Linda stood up, too, to avoid being conspicuous by her solitary presence on the sofa. She was something like a wallflower, she realized. What was going on around here? Where was the Tupperware, those handy storage containers with the famous vacuum seal? Where were the colanders and Jell-O molds, the butter keepers and the ice-cube trays?

Beverly was adding new merchandise to the table, still maintaining her non-stop spiel: "Three-inch extenders, stud buds, Spanish fly, massage creams, pussy cushions." Or did she say cushy push-ins? Linda saw an inflatable Playgal, "Great for gifts!"; Big-Potency Vitamins, "Move him up to *four* a day!" And on and on until the bridge table wobbled and Beverly was out of breath.

Iola picked up a plastic dildo. It was both bigger and more real than life, with a ruddy flexible tip and an incredible network of swollen blue veins. "Get a load of this," she said. "The guy they cut this off probably bled to death in a second."

After a while, everyone was reseated and the order slips were distributed. "Think of birthdays," Beverly advised. "Think of Christmas." It was early April. "There's a ten-percent discount on all bulk orders," she told them.

Some of the women were starting to write on their order slips. Linda felt the way she used to during essay tests in high school, when her mind and paper were still blank and the students around her were scribbling away. She supposed she would have to order something, despite

Beverly's earlier admonition not to feel obligated. She had eaten some of the potato chips, and contributed to taking up Beverly and Al's time. And all those handicapped people in one family. But what would she buy? She glanced at the order blank in her hand. *Free Rubber Penis With Every Purchase!* it said across the top. But the prices were so high. Sexual freedom was really expensive. Finally, Linda checked off the Big-Potency Vitamins. She was somewhat reassured by a printed promise of plain brown wrappers, but she wrote in the studio address, anyway.

Beverly collected the order slips and then drew from the bowl for the door prize. Linda prayed fervently that her own bad luck would hold. It didn't, though. Her name was announced, and the chain-smoking blonde said, "I *knew* it," as Linda rose, blushing madly, to receive her prize.

Beverly handed her a gift-wrapped package. At least it was small, and a conventional square shape. "Congratulations, Wanda," Beverly said. "You've won a valuable set of Chinese bells." There was some grudging applause, and Linda held the box to her ear and shook it, but there was no answering ring.

On the way home, she offered the prize to Iola, unopened. "Whatever it is," Linda said, "I don't think I want it."

"You looked close to death all night," Iola said, and Linda confessed that she had been, that some of the sexual equipment seemed lethal to her, and that the whole experience was very embarrassing.

"Well, why did you go in the first place?" Iola asked.

"Because," Linda said. She hesitated. "Because," she

H E A R T S

began again, "I thought Rosalie said it was a Tupperware party."

"Oh, no," Iola said. "Oh, no. Oh, you poor little dummy. That was Rosalie's idea of a joke. And she said, *Shtup*perware, didn't you hear her?"

Linda shook her burning head. She had never even heard of Shtupperware, but there was something about the word that immediately conveyed its meaning.

When she got home that night, Wright nuzzled her neck in welcome. "You feel like a furnace," he said. "Did you have fun?" He and Robin had had a great time at the bowling alley. She had beaten him by fifteen points. "Did you get what you need?" Wright asked, setting up new flares in her bloodstream. She assured him that she had. The stuff had to be ordered and would be sent to her in about two weeks. At least that part was the truth. And it would be easy to pick up some refrigerator jars at the store in a couple of weeks and pass them off as genuine Tupperware.

Linda watched anxiously for the arrival of the mail at the studio each day. She did so for a week or two, anyway. Then she forgot all about it. One day, Simonetti called her into his office. "This came for you, sweet-heart," he said, and handed her a small brown package. "Got a secret admirer?"

When the ladies' room was free, Linda took the package there and opened it. The Big-Potency Vitamins looked just like the regular ones she and Wright took every morning with their orange juice. That was a relief. But there was something else in the package. It was the free rubber penis promised with every purchase. It was a ghastly violet color, and it flopped in her hand like a wilted flower. Iola came into the ladies' room. "What's *that?*" she asked, and when Linda told her, she said, "The guy they cut that off probably won't even miss it."

On a sudden impulse to economize, Linda mixed the Big-Potency Vitamins in with the regular ones at home. She observed Wright nervously for a few days, but their sexual routine never altered.

Now Linda picked the paper, the pen, and the Bible up from the floor, and arranged them all in her lap again. She reread what she had written before, and then she added, "and so much I wish I could ask you . . ." She tapped her raised knee with the cap of the pen, lay back to think, and was quickly asleep.

HEARTS

THEY WOULD REACH VALERIA BY LATE   *14*
afternoon, if there were no unforeseen problems. When she watched Robin climb into
the car, Linda began to feel an anxiety she couldn't
identify. As she drove, she kept thinking ahead to the
time when she'd be traveling alone. She had been alone
before. And Robin had become slightly more human,
but was still not a sparkling companion. So it wasn't a
separation anxiety in the usual sense.

Of course each day, each mile, brought her closer
to the abortion. Her decision to have one, once she'd left
Robin, had become firm, irrevocable. She couldn't have
a baby, didn't *want* a baby. She was all alone and had
to support herself and have freedom of movement.
Sometimes, in moments of extreme self-pity, she would
reason that she was too *young* to be a mother, knowing
that, biologically at least, she was in her prime. For a
few days she thought about having the baby and then
giving it up for adoption, but that seemed impossible,
like the romantic conclusion of a teenage novel that tries
to deal with real-life problems.

There was the persistent irrational terror that she
would die during an abortion. They were thoroughly
safe and legal now, she knew, not the way they were in
the old days when she'd overhear her mother and Mrs.
Piner discussing girls who were condemned by ambitious
druggists and rusty hangers. Clinics were popping up all
over the country, like those trees of heaven Wolfie had
pointed out alongside the highway, and there would be
sympathetic and strictly hygienic care. Her funds would
be depleted a little and the goal of reaching California
somewhat delayed, but that wasn't so important.

It began to rain, and the windshield wipers established their rhythm and repeated it resolutely. There must have been an electrical storm close by, because when Robin turned the radio on, static crackled on every station. She turned it off and they listened to the wipers and the run of rain on the Maverick's roof.

"Well, this is really farm country," Linda said, as if all the fields of wheat and corn, and all the barns and pigs and cows they'd passed for hundreds of miles were only a rehearsal for this, the genuine article. She wished they could have driven this last stretch in the gorgeous weather in which they had started out. There wasn't a cow in sight now, and the fields were flattened and dismal with rain.

"Maybe they'll give you an attic room with a slanted ceiling," she said. "You'll hear sounds you won't believe —goat bells, and roosters crowing in the morning. There'll be mooing and neighing! You'll be able to pour your own milk right from the cow."

"That's not pasteurized," Robin said. "You could get sick and die."

"Oh. Right, right. But you could gather some eggs for breakfast, still warm from the hen."

"I hate eggs," Robin said, which Linda remembered was true. Still, the girl sounded childishly petulant, and Linda could not promise her a garden where Sugar Pops and Cocoa Puffs could be picked fresh daily. What she had tried to convey, but could not articulate, was the illusion of safety in the countryside, in the perfect order of nature, that she'd held since childhood when she read *Heidi* for the first time. There was much human cruelty in the story, the way there was in life, but goodness and justice had triumphed in the end.

The storm was getting closer. The sky was brilliantly

HEARTS

lit by a sizzling wire of lightning, and the rain was drumming down now. The atmosphere was more like that in a mystery novel than in a wholesome children's book. Linda's anxiety increased, the way it had in the caverns, and she began to feel faint. "I think," she said, "that we shouldn't be driving in this." Her armpits and forehead were wet and her heartbeat was erratic. She knew it was dangerous to pull off the road when visibility was so poor, but there was hardly any traffic, and the other, intangible danger she sensed was far worse, inescapable.

They were away from the main highway, on a paved, two-lane road with a narrow dirt shoulder. We'll get stuck in the mud, Linda thought. And we're under trees, the most treacherous place during an electrical storm—one more unshakable fact from her early education. She shut off the engine, turned the emergency blinkers on, and leaned back against the headrest. "What's the matter with you?" Robin asked. "You're all white."

"I am?" Linda peered into the rearview mirror at her floury complexion, her frightened eyes. She fell back again. "I'm sick," she told Robin.

"What should I do?" Robin whispered. She was on her knees, hovering. Her hand grazed Linda's shoulder, and then her forehead, with a touch that was tentative with inexperience. Linda was washed with tenderness before she passed out.

When she came to, they were in motion. The sun was out, cruelly bright after that darkness, the way it is after you leave a movie theater in the afternoon. Linda was in the front passenger seat, slumped against the door, with a pillow doubled behind her head. Her neck was stiff and she had a headache, but otherwise she felt much better. Robin was driving.

After Linda took the wheel again, she asked, "Did your father teach you?"

"No," Robin said. "My friend Ray did. Ginger's brother. He taught both of us."

"When? *Where?*"

"Oh, sometimes. Just around."

"But he's only . . ." Linda's voice trailed off. What was the use? Of *course* he was only fourteen, and the girls even younger. Of course it was illegal, and outrageous, but she really drove quite well, although a little fast. And if they had stayed there much longer, they might have been mired in the mud. They were going to separate very soon, anyway, and Robin's discipline would become the responsibility of her real family.

They stopped at a general store to ask directions and discovered they were very close, less than two miles away. "I'm getting a little excited," Linda said. "Aren't you?"

Shrug.

The house was set far back from the road, like most of the farmhouses they had passed. There was a barn a few hundred yards to the west and acres and acres of land, but nothing seemed to be growing in them. It had not rained here, apparently, and everything had a parched and barren look. Linda tried to remember some of the main causes of crop failure. Drought? Locusts? No wonder they hadn't answered her telegram. Maybe she'd have to turn over all the money, except what she needed for the abortion and the rest of her journey, out of simple charity. Maybe she and Robin would discover skeletons in overalls huddled around a dead fireplace.

They went through a gate marked Reismann, and again Linda experienced the surprise of that shared

HEARTS

name. It was Robin's too, she reminded herself, their last fragile connection.

There was no neighing or mooing here; whatever animals they had must have been killed off by whatever took the crops. And there was no sign of house occupancy, either. "Wait a minute, Robin," Linda said, after they got out of the car. Robin hadn't moved. Linda opened the trunk. She looked at the plastic container that held Wright's ashes and silently promised imminent release. Then she selected one of Wright's paintings, a peace offering from beyond this world, she thought, and tucked it under her arm.

They walked up the front steps together and Linda rang the bell. The door was solid and the shades were drawn. She remembered standing on the porch of the house on Roper Street and this same sensation of suspense. Robin's fingers worked against one another, as if she were knitting.

Suddenly the door opened and dreaming Linda almost fell inside. The woman standing there looked familiar. Like James Cagney, Linda decided at last, and realized that Wright had also, only not so distinctly. This had to be his older sister, Verna, although she did not look like a farmer's daughter, especially like the unmarried drudge on an impoverished farm. She was dressed smartly in a beige linen suit, was heavily made up, and her arms jangled with gold bracelets, a cacophony that could never be mistaken for goat's bells.

"Yes?"

"I'm Linda," Linda said. "Your . . .? I sent the telegram. And this is Robin." She tried to push the girl forward, but she had rooted herself to the porch, like a weed. Linda wished that Robin would step out of character for once, just this time, and make some attempt to charm, to be ingratiating. Her presence alone should speak for her, of course. She and this woman, her aunt, shared genes, ancestors, history.

"Well, come in, I guess," Verna said. It was not the warmest of receptions, and when Robin continued to stand there, Linda yanked her arm, and they were inside.

Some of the furniture looked new, and shockingly modern in the old house. A ruddy, heavy-lidded man in a gray suit was sitting on a low sofa, part of a modular grouping, and drinking a martini. He was much too young to be Wright's father. Linda peeked through a rear window behind him to see if any surviving livestock were out back, but only two cars, a Continental and a long silver Buick, grazed there, nose to nose.

Wright's sister said, "Lewis, this is my brother's wife, and his daughter." She didn't go any further, didn't say their names, or who the man was.

Linda sank to the armless unit opposite him. Her knees almost brushed her chin, and she tried to arrange herself to look comfortable and relaxed. Robin stood in the doorway.

"You know, it's not really what I expected," Linda said.

Verna raised an eyebrow; the man, Lewis, his glass to his lips.

"I had a kind of romantic fairy-tale vision of farms. I guess I didn't account for modern technology." Yet where was the corn growing? Underground?

"The place is sold," Verna said. "They fought with us to put I-80 through here for years. I wanted to, but my father held out. Now it's all going for housing development. The whole area's being rezoned for half-acre tracts. Lewis is the builder."

The glass went up again. That wasn't all Lewis was to Verna. Linda would have bet on it. She saw them lying locked together in one of those burnt-out fields, and the noise of the bracelets was deafening.

"But where will you go?" Linda asked.

"I've taken a condo in Dubuque. I'm going to travel. And I'm thinking of writing a book."

Linda turned to see how Robin was taking all this news, but she wasn't there, had probably gone off to find a bathroom.

"And Mr. . . . your father? Doesn't he mind, about this?"

"That's right," Verna said. "You don't know."

"Know what?"

"Upstairs," Verna said, walking.

Robin was coming from the other side of the stairway. Linda beckoned and she followed them.

The old man was in the bedroom Linda had imagined as Robin's. It was small and cozy; the ceiling slanted, and blue floral paper was fading on the walls. It stank in there, the unmistakable odor of prolonged illness. The old man had had a stroke; the diagnosis was easy. His features were in crazy disorder, like a child's drawing of a face, like her mother's had been. One pale eye was fixed on them, and wept.

Linda heard a small, breathless sound behind her, from Robin. "It's okay," she said, and then walked to the bedside, her hands clasped at her waist. "I'm Linda," she said. "Wright's wife? I'm the one who sent you—"

"Oh, for heaven's sake!" Verna said. "He can't hear a word you're saying. He's in a *coma*."

"But his eye . . ."

"It got stuck like that when it happened. Three months ago."

A toilet flushed nearby and a fat woman in a white uniform and brown Space Shoes came into the room and took her place in a bedside chair. "Well, visitors!" she said. "How do," and picked up a magazine and began to read.

"You kept him at home," Linda said, touched by that.

"No private insurance," Verna said briskly. "And his Medicare days ran out. If he's still alive when the bulldozers come, Lewis's company will pay for a nursing home."

While Verna was speaking, Linda thought she perceived a flicker of response in that staring eye. What if he could hear everything, and was only unable to respond? If the other women were not in the room, she would have spoken to him, introduced Robin, explained about Wright. Just in case. Verna led the way out. There was to be no deathbed reconciliation, no chance for last-minute repentance.

This was her father's house. Robin wandered into the kitchen after Linda went off to the living room with that woman. Maybe he had sat at this table to do his homework when he was a boy. It looked new, though, so she supposed it must have been at a different table. But he had looked out through those windows, dreaming about becoming a husband and a father someday.

HEARTS

The remains of dinner were on the table and the countertop: the bones of a well-picked chicken, a salad limp and drenched with dressing. She opened a drawer in a cabinet next to the stove and saw the usual chaos of kitchen utensils. The silverware looked old, with its heavily carved and curved handles. She picked up a fork and put it into her mouth, tasting the metal. There were footsteps overhead, creaking, and Robin panicked, shoving the fork into the pocket of her jeans. This place gave her the creeps. She would stay here about three minutes after Linda left. She had to get the money first, though.

There was a telephone on the wall, and under it, the local directory. Reismann, Wright Sr., was listed, making her heart stutter. She shut the book and went into the hallway just as Linda and that woman came from the living room. Linda curled her finger at Robin, indicating she wanted her to follow them upstairs.

An old man was lying in a child's bed, staring at them with one terrible eye. It smelled like a laundry hamper in there and Robin sucked in her breath and held it. Linda and the woman spoke and then they went downstairs again. The other man was in the hallway. At a signal from the woman, he took Robin back into the kitchen. Had they discovered the fork was missing? She felt its cold presence against her thigh. He poured more whiskey into his glass and said, "Want an apple? Want some ginger ale?"

"I'm not hungry," Robin said.

"Go to school, do you?" he asked, leaning against the refrigerator, his eyes almost closed, and Robin knew this asshole's purpose was merely to distract her while the women spoke. Well, she didn't care what they said to each other. She felt supremely calm, superior, armed.

"She doesn't look like Wright," Verna said.

"Yes, the coloring. And around the eyes. There's a definite family resemblance." Who had said that before?

"She's half and half, you know."

Linda was confused. She thought of the cream mixture they used in their morning coffee and cereal. "Pardon?"

Her confusion amused Verna, who looked even more like James Cagney when she smiled and her eyes narrowed. "The chosen people," she said.

"What?" Linda asked, but it was only reflex; she understood. "Was *that* what the falling-out was about? Between you and Wright and your father? Does it go back that far?"

"That one was in the oven when he married her. My father used to say he wouldn't crossbreed cows, even to get a better milker."

Linda felt ill again, the way she had in the car. And beyond the malaise, anger was building. She wanted to tell Verna how Miriam had left him, how he had raised Robin so valiantly by himself, but she wouldn't give her the satisfaction. And of course she couldn't leave Robin here, even if Verna was willing to take her. She could not leave Wright's ashes in this hostile atmosphere, either. Linda had imagined scattering them over cornfields within a playful wind's distance from his first home. But the home itself would be gone soon, and although he'd never told her this, she knew now that his childhood had been miserable.

HEARTS

"What's that?" Verna asked, pointing to the painting Linda held close to her breast.

"It's a painting," Linda said, and she flashed it like a crucifix in the face of a vampire. "By a friend of mine!"

"I could use a painting for my new place," Verna said, ready to strike a compromise.

"Not for sale!" Linda shouted. "Not for sale!" She lurched to the hallway, to the kitchen door. "Come on!" she bellowed at Robin. "Let's go! Do you think we have all night?"

They ran to the Maverick holding hands.

MOST OF THE LARGE HOUSES IN THE AREA
had been converted for other purposes. Driving along slowly, looking for the address, Linda
saw lawyers' offices and insurance offices, a group dental
practice and a travel agency.

Then there it was—511 S. Allison Street. This one
could have been a VFW hall, had there been a flag
flying out front, or an Elks lodge, if there'd been a
BPOE sign on the porch. Instead, there was a small,
discreet shingle: *May F. Livingston Women's Center*,
and a parade of demonstrators pounding their sidewalk
beat.

Linda had to park a block away. As she walked toward the clinic, she saw there were actually two parades,
both composed almost entirely of women. The group
closer to the house was marching clockwise, and they
chanted and carried signs that proclaimed them *Mothers
Against Death*. Other signs said: *Abortion is Homicide.
Life is a Gift. Save Our Future Presidents*. A couple of
marchers pushed strollers festooned with banners, and
with fat, gorgeous babies inside. One woman held a huge
photograph of a human finger. When Linda came closer
she saw the photo also showed a shrimp-curled fetus, its
oddly shaped head no bigger than the finger's nail. And
the chanting became clearer. "Stamp out death! Stamp
out murder!" God.

Across the street, moving counterclockwise, the op-
position held their signs: *Our Bodies—Our Choice. The
Right to Decide. Stamp Out Stampers*. They had a
blown-up photograph, too, this one of a horribly battered
infant. *Born to Die Like This!* the caption read. They
were singing "We Shall Overcome" in sweet, high-
pitched voices, slightly off-key.

HEARTS

A few hecklers loitered on the sidelines, including some small boys who threw pebbles alternately at each group. A police car was parked against the curb in front of the house, its call box squawking, and two policemen lounged against the hood, their arms folded. One of them was smiling.

Linda stared at them and had her first conscious feminist thought. This was a civil war, women against women, and the policemen were out of it, non-partisan, merely keepers of the law. But they were men and therefore, in their own language, the alleged perpetrators.

She walked quickly through an opening in the line of demonstrators in front of the house. "Don't be a killer," someone hissed, intimately, almost in her ear. One of the thrown pebbles glanced off her shoulder. "Hey," the smiling policeman called to the small boys.

The vestibule was cool and dim. The venetian blinds were drawn tightly against the action outside, and the air conditioner was going at top speed, to block the noise as much as the heat, probably.

Almost all the chairs in the waiting room were taken. A receptionist was typing at an old oak desk. "I'll be with you in a sec," she said, without looking up.

Linda waited, clearing her throat in preparation for speech.

When the woman did look up, her face was encouraging, friendly. "Hello. May I help you?" she said.

"Linda Reismann, I called last night?"

"Oh, yes, Ms. Reismann. You have a ten o'clock with Dr. Lamb. We're a little behind schedule this morning, so will you have a seat, please, and we'll call you as soon as we're ready. You can fill out this card for me while you're waiting."

The other people were not all women. An elderly couple flanked an adolescent girl, as if they were her armed guards. A young man held the hand of a young woman, and two women who seemed to be in their thirties had babies on their laps. Linda noticed a playpen and a little jump seat in the opposite corner.

The receptionist's phone kept ringing. She made appointments with callers for Tuesday, Wednesday, Thursday. It was a pleasant room, shabbily genteel, with a few landscapes, like Wright's, hanging on the walls. In what kind of rooms had all the loving taken place?

Linda tried to picture their apartment bedroom in Newark, but it was already dissipating in memory, replaced by that recent series of motel rooms, so vivid in all their plastic glory. You remember best what happened last. And what happened first. When she was a very little girl she'd found a box of wooden matches and spilled them onto the kitchen table. They were lovely, uniform, the heads a white-tipped brilliant blue. She pushed them around, experimenting, and began to make the rudimentary outline of a house, when her father came into the room. "See?" she said, pride overwhelming timidity. He picked her up swiftly, and she was astonished by the anticipation of an embrace, until he carried her to the stove. There he opened a gas jet and held each finger over it briefly to teach her the dangers of playing with fire.

The two women chatted, and the lovers whispered urgently. The elderly couple did not speak to one another or to the girl braced between them, who couldn't have been much older than Robin.

I'll remember this, too, Linda promised, committing to memory a ceiling stain, the pattern of bluebirds on the

HEARTS

girl's blouse, the ping of the typewriter's carriage bell, and the refrain of the ringing telephone.

She took a pen from her purse and began to fill out the card. There was the usual stuff: name, address, age, occupation, allergies. And the more pertinent items: number of pregnancies, number of living children, date of last menstrual period. She had still not been able to recall that, and put in a carefully drawn question mark.

Other particulars stumped her as well. Who to contact in an emergency, for instance. Certainly not Robin, a mile away in the Marriott Motor Inn, which Linda had given as her address. And to Robin she'd said, not untruthfully, that morning, "We need some time away from each other, I think. Everybody needs privacy once in a while. Why don't you stay here and I'll go out for a couple of hours and go shopping, and do some other things."

She had especially chosen the Marriott for this pause in their journey because it had a swimming pool and a coffee shop; and they were given a large room, where Robin would not feel trapped while Linda was away. First there had been the call to the local medical society to get the name of a registered abortion clinic that would treat non-residents. It would be ironic and awful if she had to go all the way back to New Jersey to undo what had been done there in the first place.

What kind of emergency did they have in mind? Just the word on the page implied danger. She tried to assess if she could ask without humiliation if there actually was any danger, say even a tiny incidence of death. They'd have to cart the bodies out through a secret passageway, or the demonstrators would be on them like vultures.

She finally wrote Iola's name and distant address in the provided space.

The receptionist called the young girl, and her parents hesitated, then leaned away a little, releasing her. After a few minutes, one of the women went in, depositing her baby in the jump seat first. The baby began to cry and the other woman walked over and rattled keys in its face until it stopped.

Finally it was Linda's turn. The room she was taken to was an ordinary examining room. It had a table with stirrups, a little curtained enclosure for undressing, and a sink with the usual medical paraphernalia alongside it. A nurse came in and gave her a specimen bottle. "You can go in there," she said, indicating an adjoining bathroom. "And leave it on the counter. I'll get it later."

Linda wondered if they ever mixed up the specimens, giving the wrong people the good/bad news. She undressed from the waist down, as instructed, and put on the yellow paper gown.

Dr. Lamb, a sturdy middle-aged woman, came into the room. She shook hands with Linda and then she scrubbed her own.

Then Linda was in the stirrups, the gown billowed at her waist, and Dr. Lamb was saying, "Oh, yes. Oh, *yes, indeed*. When was your last period?"

"I'm not sure," Linda said. "They've always been irregular . . . And then my husband died, and I really lost track . . . I've been traveling with his daughter . . ." She thought she sounded like a nitwit or a liar.

"I'd say twelve weeks, maybe thirteen."

"It's not too late, is it?"

"To abort? No, not at all. It can be legally done until the twenty-fourth week. Do you use contraception?"

HEARTS

"An IUD," Linda said.

The doctor's hand disappeared again and she probed and poked. "When was it checked last?" she asked.

"I can't remember."

"Well, you may have passed it."

"Does that happen?"

"Sometimes. Do you wear contact lenses?"

What had she found in there? "No, I don't. Why?"

"Try and relax, please. It's just that this reminds me a little of searching for one that's lost. You know, a blind exploration." She washed her hands again and told Linda to sit up. "The IUD isn't there any more. No pain? Bleeding? So we can suppose it hasn't wandered off and lodged itself where it doesn't belong. And you certainly are pregnant. But we'll test your urine anyway. Do you want to terminate this pregnancy?"

"Yes."

"Well then, get dressed and Mrs. LeRoy will set up an appointment."

"Will I be asleep?" Linda asked. Will I die?

"You'll get an injection of a light anesthetic, so you'll be asleep during the actual procedure, which will be a vacuum aspiration. But you'll come back very quickly and you can rest here until you're ready to go home."

"Why did it fall out?" Linda asked.

The doctor shrugged. "It happens. The body rejects it, just as the IUD rejects the sperm. The bouncer is bounced." She opened the door and then turned back. "Did you know that in ancient Egypt, camel drivers setting out on long journeys would insert pebbles in the vaginas of their animals to create an unwelcome atmosphere for the sperm. That's probably the earliest predecessor of the IUD."

"Why didn't they just keep the camels apart?"

"Ahhhh," said the doctor. "*Why?*" And she left the room.

They had a cancellation for the following morning at nine-thirty. "A light supper," the receptionist said. "Nothing by mouth after 10 p.m. The fee is two hundred dollars, payable before surgery."

The marchers crowded her when she stepped outside. "Thou shalt not kill," they said, and then opened ranks to let her pass.

H E A R T S

ROBIN FLOATED ON HER BACK IN THE **16**
turquoise-tinted Marriott pool. Just ahead at
all times was the subtle topography of her own
body: new breasts peaking gently in the blue bra of her
bathing suit, and past them the small white field of her
belly with its silly puffed button. "Ring-a-ling, anybody
home?" her father used to ask when she was little, pushing it in with one finger. You were once attached to
your mother there. If the cord was never cut and tied,
you could not be lost from one another. But then everybody would be attached, wouldn't they? And what about
all the dead people? Only Adam in the whole universe
would ever have been truly alone, while Eve strolled in
Paradise strung to her children, and to their children,
and to their children . . . Robin tried to keep her gaze
skyward, but the glare was brilliant, and there was so
much activity near her in the water. Small children
splashed and screamed hoarsely for the attention of
parents who lay on webbed lounges and frowned into
the sunlight, while water from their dripping suits darkened the shadows beneath them. "Look at me! Look at
me!" the children insisted. "Watch me dive, Dad! Are
you watching? Here I go!"

"Very good, Seth," the parents said. "I'm watching,
Roger. Betsy. Dougie. Felice. Don't scream like that.
Don't get chilled. Are your lips blue?" And they never
looked at all, never moved their forearms or towels or
straw hats from across their eyes.

Robin wished they'd all be quiet, that they'd disappear, so she could think without distraction. She had
never behaved like these kids herself, even when she was
their age. She certainly never shouted, "Look at me!"

to her father, mainly because he usually *was* looking at her. When he took her to the town pool in Newark, he expected her to demonstrate everything she had learned that morning in the Minnows Club. "Show me how you kick," he would say. "Show Daddy the breathing." His interest was anxious and it encumbered her. She wished he'd stay with the other adults and have adult conversation that couldn't be interrupted unless you pretended to be drowning.

Later he always wanted to know if she'd had fun, and she learned to say yes, even on the days she'd been ducked and tortured by bullies, even when her throat was raw from the chlorinated water she swallowed. Then he would sigh, with a kind of sad satisfaction, and finally leave her alone.

But he rarely went into the pool himself, and when he did, he'd hang around the shin-deep kiddies' end, looking pink-skinned and oversized, offering Robin rides on his back, wanting to be her whale, her sailing ship. He called her his fishie or his mermaid. "Had enough, little fishie?" he'd say, as if she had been clamoring for more, and then he'd rise, like Gulliver, from the water. "Had fun?"

These children in the Marriott pool demanded more attention than they would ever get. But at least they had one another, and the harmless illusion of a parental audience. Robin let the water carry her and she stared directly into the sun, wondering dreamily if you could really go blind this way.

She wanted to concentrate, to make plans. Somehow she'd have to get Linda to give her some of the insurance money. As soon as they'd checked into the motel the

HEARTS

day before, Robin had suggested to Linda that she be allowed to carry half their fortune. Linda had looked puzzled. "Why?" she asked. "For safekeeping," Robin answered. "You know, in case of crooks or pickpockets." Linda had smiled. "Oh, Robin," she said. "This isn't Newark. They don't have pickpockets in Iowa. Besides, I want you to just relax and have a good time. Let me worry about things." But Linda seemed unable to contemplate the future. Since their visit to the farm, she hadn't mentioned a word about alternate plans. All she had said afterward was that she had to think things over, that she needed a few days to clear her brain. She told Robin they were both entitled to a little fun, anyway, after all they'd been through. That's why they were staying at this place, which was kind of expensive, but look at the terrific pool, the attractive and convenient coffee shop. "There is nothing better in this world than a big, hearty breakfast while you're on the road," Linda said two days ago. Since then she'd hardly eaten anything at all, and never went near the pool. She spent most of her time in the bathroom, running water into the tub. Once Robin put her ear against the door and heard Linda talking to herself, but she couldn't make out the words.

Everything appeared lighter now, faded, and there were drifting dots of colored confetti in the cumulus clouds. Robin shut her eyes, but the colors remained, trapped inside her lids. When she opened them again, she found she was in the very center of the pool, looking toward the diving board through the vee of her feet. Then there was a great splashing, and a figure went swiftly past her, its wake making her bob and rock in the water. When he surfaced, she saw it was the redheaded boy who'd been at breakfast earlier that morning, sitting across the room with his family.

Robin had come into the coffee shop alone because Linda said she wasn't hungry yet and would probably get something later in town after she went shopping. She'd gone shopping the day before, too, but came back to the motel without any packages. Today she gave Robin a five-dollar bill and repeated that thing about big hearty breakfasts before she drove away. Robin decided to have just orange juice and pocket the rest of the money, her first step toward freedom. She was excited about the prospect of time to herself, too, until she entered the coffee shop, where she felt terribly visible, and shy.

"Only one today?" the hostess asked, as if it were some tragic failure on Robin's part not to have found a breakfast companion.

Once she was seated, Robin had the place mat to stare at, with its pattern of illustrated riddles, and inverted answers. Yesterday there had been different ones, with Presidential facts and figures. Linda had played with her food and shifted the dishes so she could read aloud. " 'Which U.S. President served two terms, but not consecutively?' " When Robin didn't say anything, Linda turned the place mat around and read the answer. " 'Grover Cleveland. Elected in 1884 and again in 1892.' I think I actually knew that one." Then she said, "Listen to this, Robin. 'Until 1825, all U.S. Presidents, except for John Adams, came from Virginia. And the state became known as the mother of Presidents . . .' Oh. Why did I always think it was Ohio?"

Robin looked down. What has four wheels and flies? She was never any good at things like this, and she tilted her head to glance at the answer. A garbage truck. Dumb. She turned her attention to the menu but was aware of the redheaded boy, who was the eldest of five children and was taller than his parents. He stared at Robin above the stack of wheat cakes in front of him and poured syrup until it dripped over the sides of the plate. Robin heard his mother say, "Watch what you're doing, dreamer."

When the waitress came to Robin's table and said, "Oh, is it all by its wonesome iss morning?" Robin didn't answer, but she forgot her decision to economize, and ordered the Old MacDonald Special. When is a door not a door? The redheaded boy chewed, and stared rudely, and Robin felt her whole body bloom with sensation. She wondered if she'd broken out in a rash, and she looked down at her arms, which were still that unbroken white, paler than the paper napkin she was destroying in her lap. She felt furious with Linda, whose absence made her, Robin, so conspicuous. No one else was eating alone, except for a man in a business suit, and he was reading a newspaper.

The family across the room was lively and noisy. The small children sloshed their cocoa and clanged silverware against china. Their voices played against one another without pause. The redheaded boy's was deeper even than his father's, and he sounded like a bass instrument in an orchestra of violins. He smiled at his mother, or past her at Robin, whose face went up in flames. What goes up a chimney down or down a chimney down, but never goes up the chimney up or down the chimney up? The answer had been shredded by the moisture under her orange juice.

She looked across the room again and he did this
asshole thing, lifted a glass of milk as if he were toasting
her with it. She couldn't eat anything, couldn't even
finish drinking the juice. She spilled it a little in her
hurry to get up, and a spoon clattered to the floor behind
her.

Robin continued to float in the subsiding wake,
but her peacefulness had been broken. And now he
circled, swimming underwater like a shark, shimmering
and quick in the wobbly light. When he came up alongside her he was all energy and motion, shaking his
streaming head, churning his arms and legs. "Hi!" he
said once, and went under again. She thought he touched
her foot, and her balance, that easy buoyancy, was instantly lost and she sank like a stone. This time he
definitely touched her, pulled at one of her arms to yank
her upward. "Don't! I can swim!" she said, and water
entered her mouth, making the words come out strangled,
in bubbles.

He was laughing, and his wet eyelashes and freckled
skin were golden. "Don't," Robin said again, above the
surface of the water now, but she did not struggle as
his arms held her aloft. She felt languid, sleepy. Men,
boys were so much more naked in their bathing suits.
She looked at the glittering expanse of his chest, at the
tiny useless nipples, and became excruciatingly aware of
her own, as if all feeling had drained from the rest of
her body to enter those two essential points. "Don't,"
she said, yet a third time, but it was whispered now and
said only to comfort herself.

They hung by their wrinkled fingers from the diving

HEARTS

board. He told her his name was Steve and that he was on his way to Texas to visit his grandparents and a million aunts and uncles and cousins.

"That's funny," Robin said. "We just visited mine, here in Iowa, on their farm."

Steve's family traveled in that big yellow camper trailer. She must have seen it in the parking lot. Most of the time they slept in it, but every once in a while they stayed at a motel. "The old folks gotta have their privacy. You know," he said, and she nodded, offhand and wise.

She told him her name and said that Linda was her aunt and that they were on vacation, too, just seeing the country while Robin's parents were on a cruise.

Had she been to the Hidden River Caverns, he wanted to know. Weren't they neat?

Yes, neat. *Lovely.*

Was she going to Texas?

Maybe, she didn't know. Theirs was a kind of unplanned, casual trip. Like they went anywhere they felt like going. Linda was more like a sister than an aunt. They had lots of fun together.

"Neat," he said.

Yes, neat.

They climbed out of the pool and he borrowed a piece of paper and a pen from his father. His red hair dripped onto the paper, onto her, as he wrote the address of his relatives in Texas.

"Lubbock," she said. "1224 Macon Street," as if she had asked him for directions and was trying to memorize them.

"We'll be there two weeks," he told her. "Until the

fourteenth or fifteenth, and then we'll head back." He wrote his home address, in Michigan, and wanted hers, too.

She was dismayed. Her father was a pilot in the army, she said. They didn't have a permanent address right now.

"In the Air Force?" he asked.

"Yes," she said.

There were gestures from his parents. "We're leaving in a little while," he said. "I have to round up the kids, help to pack. But, hey, we'll write to each other, Robin, okay? You'll have to write first."

Robin's skin, which was like her father's, was burning. The water from her bathing suit and hair formed a warm puddle at her feet. His mother and father were watching them, smiling, talking. She felt humiliated and full of pleasure. Steve turned and waved.

She meant to go right back to the room, number 24 on the second level. The sunburn was bothering her. Her shoulders ached and the backs of her knees were pulled taut. The room key was on an elastic band around her wrist. Steve had worn his on his ankle; she would wear hers there the next time she went swimming.

Her wet feet left clear imprints on the paved walk. She looked behind her and saw them disappear rapidly in order. She was almost at the coffee shop. After that was the game room. This morning, before breakfast, she'd looked inside. There were pinball machines, a little electronic shooting gallery, and a bowling game where you knocked down the pins with a heavy metal disk. A few kids had been in there, punching the coin returns, hoping to loosen some change.

_____

H E A R T S

As she approached now, Robin heard various pinging sounds and the Muzak that was piped in everywhere. She stopped in the welcome shade of the doorway and saw that only one man was there. He was wearing black bathing trunks and he was playing the baseball game. He gripped the sides of the machine with both hands and held a cigarette between two fingers. His player had two strikes, one ball, and there were already two outs against his team. He looked up, even though she had not made a sound. "Bringing me a little luck?" he said. There was a glass on the surface of the machine and ice rattled as the silver ball shot around, ringing bells. "Come on in," the man said in a lazy voice. "The water's fine."

It was much cooler inside, and darker. After the brightness, Robin's vision was dim. Looking down, she could just see inside her top where the sunburn ended and that other whiteness began. She raised the straps gingerly and then tugged at the bottom of her suit where it rose over her buttocks.

The game ended abruptly and the lights on the machine went out. He shook the machine hard and the glass slid toward him. His drink was clear and a lime peel floated in it. "Look at you," he said. "Like a sunset in Hawaii. You're sure going to feel that tonight."

"I feel it already," Robin said, surprised at her own ease in answering him.

The man's body was heavily furred, but the longish dark hair on his head was thinning. His toes were narrow and bent, like fingers. The black trunks were brief and tight and hinted at their secret weight. Robin felt slightly dizzy.

"Want to play?" he asked, and before she could reply

he pushed coins into the machine. Colored lights flashed and Robin could hear the steel balls roll down into playing position. Her father had liked pinball, too, and once he took her to an amusement place downtown where only men went, each one facing his own game intently, like the captain at the helm of a ship. She had leaned her chest against her father's machine while it shuddered and rang, and all the vibrations seemed to happen inside her.

The man fixed it so they could play against each other. His cigarette smelled wonderful; its smoke was slow and blue. "Puff?" he offered, holding it out to her, and she shook her head, blushing. Was he some kind of mind reader?

Her team was up first and he released the ball so quickly it skidded past the batter before she could act. She flapped the lever, too late, and the little metal bat fluttered frantically.

The man laughed. "Easy," he said. "Ea-sy does it."

Her first batter struck out. The second one hit a pop fly, the third a single.

"Nice going . . . er . . . let me guess—is it Debbie?"

Robin shook her head.

"You look like a Debbie I know," he said. "Blond like you."

She had a strange intuition that he was talking about his own daughter. "Ginger," she told him, and he said, "Yeah, that fits, too. That's cute." He finished his drink and chewed a piece of ice. Her next player struck out.

Then he played and the machine rattled against her hipbone. "That's some sunburn you got," he said. He put the glass against her back.

HEARTS

"Oh! Don't do that!"

"Did I hurt you?" he asked. "I didn't mean to hurt you. I thought it would feel good, you know, cool."

She didn't answer.

"You know you're all pink, like a little rabbit."

"Rabbits aren't pink."

"Oh, yeah, you're right. Only their eyes." He laughed. "So who are you here with?"

"Friends," Robin said.

"What are you, fifteen, sixteen?"

She hesitated. "Sixteen," she said. "Sixteen and a half."

"Jailbait in almost any state," he said, seemingly to himself.

"Well, I've got to go now," Robin murmured.

"Hey, before we even finish our game? It's all paid for. Do you want a drink, a Coke or something?"

She shook her head. He went to the doorway, threw his cigarette out and then came back, shutting the door behind him. The room was even darker now. Robin could smell the chlorine rising from her own flesh. A Muzak waltz ended and a Spanish number began. "Qué bonita! Nita! Nita!" a chorus of men sang. The pinball machine glowed; there was no score yet for either side.

He released another ball. "Go ahead. Shoot," he said. "Hit it."

"It's not my turn," Robin said.

"Take my turn. It's okay. Why not? You took the part that once was my heart."

"Somebody—my friends—are waiting for me," she said. "You could play both teams at the same time, if you want to. You could just—"

He threw up his arms. "Would you please . . ." he began, and then stopped for a moment and inhaled deeply. "Oh, Christ. Oh, Jesus. Look," he said, disarmingly serious. "I didn't have a whole courtship in mind. Okay? What I want is just one little thing and that's all. I just want you to suck me off."

She walked around him and opened the door. The sunlight began again right after she crossed the threshold. He didn't follow her or do anything to stop her, but she started to run and kept running until she reached room 24. On the way, she pulled the key from her wrist so it was ready, aimed at the keyhole, when she got there.

HEARTS

LINDA WONDERED IF SHE'D BE INVOLVED IN a wreck on the way to the clinic. Fate often made a mockery of people's foolproof plans.

17

The week before, there had been an article in the newspaper about a woman from Sparks, Nevada, who had saved for years for a trip to Hawaii, her life's dream. The minute she got there a coconut fell from a palm tree, hitting her on the head and killing her instantly.

But there was hardly any traffic this morning—only a few law-abiding citizens moseying smoothly along, well within the speed limit. She would have to go into a tree or off a bridge if she wanted to have a convenient accident. And even her own driving was steadier than usual, bringing her safely toward Allison Street and her appointment. She thought: I probably won't die. It's really silly and theatrical to think about dying. But just in case of a freak series of mishaps, she should leave Robin some word, shouldn't she? Tell her where the money is and wish her good luck with the rest of her life. At least advise her not to get pregnant when she didn't mean to. Pregnant. The word was fat and hollow; it filled up quickly with Linda's terror. In the printed material accompanying the pregnancy-test kit, none of the pictured models seemed unhappy with their positive results. They were all smiling, and eagerly sharing the terrific news with loved ones. It could have been an ad for the telephone company.

She hoped the pickets would be gone when she got there this time, away on a coffee break or something. It was a private matter, strictly a personal decision, and they were turning it into some kind of public extravaganza. Yesterday, after she'd passed through them on the way back to the car, she had felt physically assaulted, although no one had actually touched her. Those voices. And the faces, so fierce with judgment.

Last night, soon after she and Robin turned off the lights and went to bed, the telephone rang. Neither of them made a move to answer it. Then, inexplicably, and with a fool's rush of hope, Linda thought of Wolfie. But he didn't know where she was, nobody did, except for the receptionist at the clinic. She could be calling to confirm Linda's appointment, or to cancel it because of a sudden outbreak of illness on their staff, because of overbooking, or even a negative urine test!

When Linda finally picked up the phone and said hello, there was nothing from the other end but heavy breathing. Supercreep! she thought, astonished. Had he followed her all the way *here?* She waited in dread for that weird humming to begin, but instead a muffled voice said, "Open your Bible, sister. Isaiah 33."

"Who is it?" Robin whispered.

The voice spoke intimately into Linda's ear. "Woe to you, destroyer, who yourself have not been destroyed," it said. "You treacherous one, with whom none has dealt treacherously! When you have ceased to destroy, you will be destroyed; and when you have made an end of dealing treacherously, you will be dealt with treacherously." *Click.*

Linda had difficulty breathing. Her hand went to her breast, to her throat. "Hello?" she croaked into the silence of the wires. "Hello?"

"Who *is* it?" Robin asked again, sounding cross.

"Nobody. It was a wrong number. They must have rung the wrong room." Linda put the light on and rum-

HEARTS

maged in the drawer. She found the Bible under the local telephone book and the room-service menu.

Robin groaned. "I can't sleep with the light on," she said.

"I'll shut it off in a minute," Linda told her.

Robin pulled the pillow over her face.

Linda opened the Bible to the first page of Genesis. *In the beginning God created the heaven and the earth. And the earth was without form, and void; and darkness was upon the face of the deep. And the Spirit of God moved upon the face of the waters.* She felt moved, and awed by all those powers outside herself. Then she turned the pages quickly, but couldn't remember the number in Isaiah, couldn't find the quoted passage. She didn't know why she was looking for it, anyway. Nobody has the right to play God, to tell other people what to do. Cowards who call you up in the middle of the night and put hankies over the mouthpiece so you can never identify them. Who would probably argue in favor of war and the electric chair and nuclear plants sending out death rays everywhere. And who beat the living joy out of born children who were never wanted in the first place. Her father would have been against legalized abortion, too, if he had lived long enough to see it.

"Shut off the *light*," Robin whined from under her pillow. Linda did and of course the darkness was biblical. She lay there stiffly until the telephone rang again. This time she didn't say hello, or even listen. She put the receiver under her bed, where it wound out its message like the thrown voice of a ventriloquist.

The pickets were there, walking zealously, chanting. The counterpickets likewise. Linda drove around the block twice before she parked close to the place she had parked the day before. The same cops were on duty, the weather was still gorgeous, hot and clear; everything was the same, except this was the day she was having it done.

There was a minimum of harassment. She was crowded briefly again and one marcher said, "You murderer," but in a tone that was almost conversational. The law of the land is in my favor, Linda said to herself as she walked into the building, and she was aware of her lips moving.

A different receptionist was on duty today, someone older, and wearing wire-rimmed bifocals, which Linda found oddly comforting. This woman was as brisk and professional as a dental hygienist. Linda would not have been surprised if she'd been led to a reclining chair and asked to open wide. Just last month she'd read somewhere that a legal abortion is no more complicated than a tooth extraction.

She paid the fee, using traveler's checks for a crisis American Express had probably never considered. The receptionist told her to take a seat with the others; she would be called shortly. The others were the adolescent girl from yesterday, still under her parents' armed guard, a woman whose face was mostly hidden by large sunglasses and a wide-brimmed hat (was she somebody famous?), and the young man who'd held his girlfriend's hand. This time he was alone, and his empty hands ran back and forth across his knees and then up and down the buttons of his shirt. She was probably inside already, Linda decided, and listened, but there were no sounds at all from that part of the clinic. Painless dentistry. The woman in the sunglasses slouched in her seat and kept her face averted from the light. She began to look familiar. Around the mouth a little, and the chin. A few dark strands of hair escaped from under the hat. Who had cheekbones like that? Linda gasped. Jackie Onassis! That's who she looked like! But what would she be doing in Iowa? She could *buy* a whole clinic someplace, in New York, or Switzerland, if she wanted to, and staff it with secret-service men who would send those pickets flying. Besides, Jackie was Catholic. And this woman had legs like tree stumps. I'm going crazy, Linda thought.

She knew she needed to talk to someone, to make inane conversation about the weather, or serious, pointed conversation about what they were all here for. She looked around the room, but none of the other faces opened to receive her.

She picked up a magazine. *Newsweek*; it was a month old. She read the same sentence three times. *The black citizens of Rhodesia have voted for the first time on the basis of a universal franchise (one person, one vote).* What did that mean? It didn't seem to make any sense. It didn't even seem like a real sentence. And now Linda had cramps. Was it possible to miss your turn by going to the bathroom? She'd just tell the receptionist where she was going and that she'd be right back. But before she could stand, the cramps had passed. Well, this is only nerves, she told herself. Even the real Jackie Onassis would be nervous here, now.

Then Linda's name was called and she stood up. A nurse took her to a cubicle, where she removed her clothes and put on a paper gown, a white one this time. "Dentures?" the nurse asked. "Removable bridges?" Linda shook her head and the nurse hurried out.

"Help me," Linda whispered when she was alone.

A few minutes later the nurse returned and walked with Linda to the operating room. Dr. Lamb came in, said good morning in her no-nonsense manner, and immediately began to explain the procedure again. There was to be an injection to induce sleep, but not a deep or lasting sleep. Linda would feel very relaxed and would not experience pain during the surgery. A suctioning process would be used to extract the uterine tissue. Afterward, Linda might feel mildly crampy—this varied with different women—and there would be some bleeding, but it was not expected to be excessive. Was she ready? Any questions? No? Good. Then why didn't she climb up onto the table and they'd get started.

"Help me," Linda said, and the nurse laughed and said, "Why, just step on that little stool and then lie down. That's right." She eased Linda's bare feet into the stirrups.

The doctor wore a mask now, and gloves, like a Sunday gardener. Linda tried to think of Wright before this mortal bond with him was severed. Suctioned. When had it all begun?

When Linda was very young she believed you conceived a baby by kissing someone. Not just a friendly peck on the lips, but extraordinary kissing, powerful as commercial vacuum cleaners, hard as matches struck against stone. And when she was older, old enough to know better, she believed it happened only during the high moments of sexual feeling and love. Which would leave children born in loveless marriages, and pregnancies due to rape, completely unaccounted for. And what about this one? As she reached for sexual memory, it quickly evaporated. It was impossible to imagine the simplest embrace.

HEARTS

Two other masked figures came into the room. They spoke to one another in what sounded like a foreign language, but probably wasn't. One of them lifted Linda's arm in a gentle grasp and placed it on a narrow board, like the one her mother had used for ironing sleeves. He raised a hypodermic. "Okay, Sleeping Beauty," he said. "Soon you will be in my power."

Linda shut her eyes, inviting, willing, nothingness. She felt the prick of the needle and then the room lifted with a violent noise, and there were alternate spasms of blackness and brilliance. She sat up and clutched the edges of the trembling table. "Don't begin!" she shouted. "I'm not asleep yet!" Then there was another bang, louder than the first one. She fell back and felt a sudden, blunt pain in her belly, as if she'd been elbowed there. "Ow!" Linda cried, but no one paid any attention. It seemed to be raining, and the room was filling with clouds through which the masked figures disappeared. She heard screaming in the distance and in her own throat. "Bastards!" a woman yelled. "Oh, God, evacuate the building! Get them out!"

Footsteps thundered and glass shattered and came ringing down. Linda slid off the table, pitching with vertigo. Someone emerged from the clouds and took her arm. "Let's go!" he commanded.

"Is it over?" Linda asked. "Was that it?"

"Yeah, yeah," he said. "Come on!"

"My clothes," she said, resisting. "My keys."

"The hell with them! Move! Let's got *out* of here!"

But Linda broke away and found herself in the smaller room where she'd undressed. There was less smoke in here, but still she gagged and coughed as she struggled to put her things back on. Now there were sirens outscreaming the human screamers. She didn't buckle her shoes, but shuffled away in them, the ankle straps flapping and tripping her every few steps. There was an open door through which she saw an amazing rectangle of sky. She stepped toward it and then wandered until she came to a small patch of lawn. All the chaos was behind her. This was somebody's back yard, orderly and domestic. Three plastic garbage pails with the number 18 painted on their lids. Sheets and towels dangling from a nylon clothesline. A small herd of people who didn't appear to notice her ran past, in the direction of the clinic. Linda went the opposite way, cutting down a narrow path, between two houses, that led to the sidewalk. She walked a few blocks, in a circle maybe, to the street where the Maverick was parked. She wept when she recognized it.

Robin took what was left of the started joint from the foil packet hidden in her blue sock. She lit it and drew in twice, then a third time, reducing it to a tiny roach. As soon as it was cool, she rehid it in the sock. The sunburn was terrible, worse than it had been outside. Robin took off her bathing suit, moaning a little, and sprinkled talc over the tightening redness, but it didn't soothe her. She couldn't stop shaking. Linda seemed to be gone forever. What was she always shopping for, anyway?

Robin tried to put her bathrobe on and couldn't bear it against her skin. She turned the air conditioner all the way up, although she realized that her heat had become internal, and the blasting chill only caused her to shiver harder. She closed the green drapes, making the room green-shadowed, turned on the television set, and got into bed. There was a little kids' program on—cartoons—and it squealed with frenzy.

The telephone rang. It was a woman's voice. She sounded funny, as if she had a bad cold. "Listen," she said. "Are you satisfied now? Suffer, as He suffers the little children to come unto Him. You only got what you deserve, bitch."

Robin was too stunned to speak. But it didn't matter. The woman had hung up already and now there was only the steady monotony of the dial tone. Robin hung up, too, slowly.

Was it that man's wife, talking about Debbie and their other children? What did she mean about suffering? Robin hadn't done anything. Maybe it was the man himself, disguising his voice. Was the sunburn what she deserved? Her father's death? This endless trip that didn't go anywhere? There were no reasonable answers to any of her questions. She thought about Steve and his family in their camper trailer on their way to Texas. They probably sang asshole rounds in the car, like Linda. Robin and Ginger and Ray would have laughed their heads off if a kid like Steve ever showed up in Newark, smiling all the time and saying "neat" and other words like that. He was probably a fag. When she got out of bed again, she would tear up his address and flush the pieces down the toilet. Meanwhile, she watched as Popeye rescued Olive Oyl one more time, and then she fell asleep.

Driving back, Linda caught a glimpse of her own disordered face in the rearview mirror, and immediately prepared a story about falling into a hole at a construction site. When she opened the door to number 24, she saw that Robin was lying on her bed in the darkened room. Linda was grateful for the pulled drapes, for the calming voice of the television set, for Robin's usual lack of interest. The kid seemed groggy, and Linda was able to tiptoe quickly past her into the bathroom and examine herself in fluorescent light. She looked terrible, as if somebody had tried to murder her. Somebody *had*. Her blouse was filthy and she had ripped it groping for the armhole that way. There was a black smear on her forehead, and another that looked like a painted mustache on her upper lip. Her hair was raised in a crown of spikes and it glittered with tiny fragments of glass. No wonder that man in the Marriott parking lot had turned to stare at her.

She tried to remember what had happened. The last thing was the needle, before the explosion, which she'd imagined at first to be a dream, a dreadful, punitive narcotic dream. Her teeth were still clacking and her heart had not quieted. She lifted her skirt, tentative and fearful, and saw that she had forgotten her underpants, and that there was some dried blood on the insides of her thighs. Then she remembered that significant pain in her belly. So it had been done, after all.

There would be a police investigation, of course, and her underpants would probably be found in the debris and taken as evidence. Against whom? She imagined them in the trouser pocket of one of those two lounging policemen. Maybe he'd forget to turn them in—they would be so slight in the depths of his uniform pocket—and he'd find them weeks later, a silken surprise to his callused hand. Or his wife would find them . . . Why was she having such strange and stupid thoughts? It must be because of the injection, and the trauma.

HEARTS

She bathed her face and the place where she had bled, and inserted a tampon. Her teeth still clattered like castanets, and her reflection in the basin mirror was blurred by all the trembling. She brushed her hair over the wastebasket until all the glass showered down. Then she took several deep breaths, urging herself to become tranquil before she went back into the bedroom.

Robin was sitting up in bed, like an invalid, watching an old movie. "What time is it?" she asked.

Linda looked at her watch, surprised to see that it was still intact on her wrist. "Eleven o'clock," she said. Was that all? She held it to her ear. "Eleven o'clock," she said again, disbelieving. Why wasn't that girl outside somewhere having fun? Linda pulled back the stubbornly tight covers on her bed and climbed into it. Her body was settling down a little now. It was all over. Everything was all right. There had hardly been any blood.

On screen, Glenda Farrell was lounging in white, fur-trimmed pajamas in a white room. The light was unnatural, dazzling. Linda had always loved movies like this one, and she wondered if Robin did, too, or just watched with the same dispassionate attention she gave the landscape when they drove. "You have a little sunburn," Linda said. At least she hadn't been in the room all morning.

"Uh-huh."

Glenda Farrell played with a white kitten and turned the pages of a magazine.

"What's this about?" Linda asked.

"I don't know," Robin said. "I was sleeping before, when you came in."

"Mmmmm," Linda said. "*That* sounds like a good idea." She moved further down between the sheets. They felt so clean and cool. She had not died, after all.

A newscaster appeared on the screen in startling color. "This just into the newsroom," he announced. "A Des Moines abortion clinic was heavily damaged by two firebombs a short time ago as three abortions were taking place inside. In the panic and confusion that followed the attack, patients, doctors, and nurses ran from the smoking building on South Allison Street. No one seems to have been severely injured, although two patients are as yet unaccounted for. It is believed they may have fled the scene. Many of the clinic's files were destroyed by the blasts, and property damage is estimated at over thirty thousand dollars. Placard-carrying demonstrators from a group called MAD, or Mothers Against Death, who have been picketing the site for more than three weeks now, have denied responsibility for the bombing. A young man, wearing a bathrobe and bedroom slippers, who shouted obscenities at the fleeing women, has been taken into custody for questioning. A police spokesman says that the subject appears to be incoherent. More on the six o'clock news."

Robin stared at the screen, apparently unmoved, disinterested. How could she be otherwise? There were bulletins like this one, and worse, all the time. The other day a man in Moline, Illinois, shot a gas-station attendant three times because the lines at the pumps were too long. The world was full of assorted lunacy and sorrow, most of it readied for instant publicity. God knows what else would show up on the six o'clock news.

Linda wondered if that was new blood pulsing down

HEARTS

there, or just an echo of her still erratic heartbeat. She lifted the covers to look and saw only the reassuring, pristine string of the tampon. "Did you have a nice morning?" she asked Robin.

"It was okay."

"What did you do?"

"Nothing. I went swimming. I hung around."

"Oh. Well, that sounds nice."

"Did you get anything?"

"Pardon?"

"When you went shopping. Did you buy anything?" Linda sighed. "No, I just looked. Walked around."

Someone knocked on Glenda Farrell's door. "Who is it?" she called, her voice sweet with expectancy.

THEY DIDN'T GET BACK ON THE ROAD AGAIN
for two days because Linda couldn't seem to
stay awake. Whenever she would rouse herself, she'd only go to the bathroom. Then she would pad
back to the bedroom, where she'd look down through
the window at the parking lot before collapsing into bed
again.

The weather had changed suddenly, due to a warm
front moving up from the Southwest, the man on television said, and it had been raining steadily for a day
and a half. Robin kept going out to the coffee shop to
bring in food for both of them.

Linda had turned the maid away at the door yesterday, and again today. "Sick," she'd said, without removing the chain.

"What's the matter with you?" Robin asked. "You're
sleeping an awful lot."

"Spinning wheel," Linda mumbled.

"What?"

"Nothing. I don't know. I think it's all that driving
we've done so far, all this rain. I'm just exhausted,
that's all. A few more hours and I'll probably be raring
to go."

"*Where?*" Robin asked. They still hadn't discussed
any possible plans.

But Linda was asleep again.

The two wastebaskets filled up with junk: half-eaten
hamburgers and limp fries, greasy paper bags, candy
wrappers, collapsed soft-drink cans. Robin ate and drank
twice as much as Linda. She licked ketchup, mustard,
chili sauce, salt, and chocolate from her fingers. Her
belly felt round and taut, and when she slapped it, it

sounded like a small drum. She could burp at will, and often did.

She hid under the hood of her slicker every time she ran out for new supplies, terrified that she would meet the man from the game room again. As she ran she made up things she would say to him if she did see him. She'd tell him that she was only thirteen years old, jailbait in *every* state, that her father was the chief of police and intended to kill him. She would burp in his face and then puncture the tires on his car with the fork from her father's house. She kept it ready in the right-hand pocket of her slicker.

The swimming pool was deserted. All the webbed lounges were folded and stacked in a corner of the deck. An abandoned towel lay near them, twisted and soaked. Watching the rain hit the surface of the blue water made Robin feel unaccountably anxious and she hurried back to the room. She was going crazy with boredom there. There was nothing to do but watch television, strip the translucent layers of skin from her shoulders where they had begun to peel, and wait for Linda to wake up for good.

Finally she did. When Robin opened her eyes the next morning, she found that Linda was dressed and packing. She was very cheerful. "Rise and shine, morning glory! The sun is out!" she announced, as if it were a phenomenon for which she was personally responsible. She urged Robin to get moving, to pack up her things so they could get an early start.

Again, Robin asked where. Linda didn't answer right away, and Robin said, "*You're* going to California. But what about me?"

Linda sat down on the bed, next to her suitcase. She picked at the lock with one fingernail. "Robin," she said softly. "Do you ever think about your mother?"

The southern route Wolfie had suggested seemed sensible and appealing, now that their destination was Arizona. In Des Moines they picked up I-35, which took them quickly in and out of Missouri. Linda remembered further information from those Presidential place mats in the Marriott. Missouri was called the "Show Me" state. It was the birthplace of Harry S. Truman. "Do you know who was born around here?" she asked Robin.

Robin leaned back and shut her eyes, but Linda suspected she was only pretending to sleep. After they crossed the border into Kansas, Robin sat up and began fiddling with the radio. On one station the Mamas and the Papas were singing that Golden Oldie, "California Dreamin'." "Oh, leave that!" Linda cried, and she began to hum along and move her shoulders to the music as she drove. She thought: By the time I get there, it will probably have fallen into the ocean.

There had been a discussion of natural disasters on a television show just last week, while they were still in Illinois. "The fault of the Fault," one panelist quipped, and a seismologist from UCLA predicted that a major earthquake would probably beat out any process of erosion. The moderator interrupted to ask why these two distinguished scientists continued to live in Southern California, considering their firsthand knowledge of predestined doom. The seismologist said cheerfully that there were all *kinds* of doom in the wings, everywhere. Tidal waves, drought, Halley's comet, tornadoes, plagues.

HEARTS

"Do you think you're going to be safe in Westport?" he asked. Killer bees and towering infernos were kids' stuff. He said that Hollywood apocalypse writers couldn't dream up some of the real disasters in store for us. Besides, he added, his wife wanted to live near her mother. Everyone had laughed and applauded.

By the time Linda got there, if it still *was* there, she wouldn't even know the latest dance steps. They changed every minute. John Travolta would be as old as Fred Astaire. Maybe she wouldn't even be able to get a job. Everything was changing. Gas prices had gone up five cents a gallon while she was sleeping off the effects of the abortion in Des Moines. The money was dwindling quickly, and she was still determined to give Robin half of everything left. It would only be fair to Miriam, too, after presenting her with a full-grown, money-eating child, without any warning. The woman was still at that same address in Glendale, Arizona, according to Information. Eight years later; as if time had completely halted. Linda had decided to call ahead and talk to Miriam, straightforwardly, so as not to make the same disastrous mistake she'd made with those people in Iowa.

But Robin had extracted Linda's promise, had made her swear not to announce their arrival beforehand. She was practically hysterical about it. And Linda had given in, crossed her heart, hoped to die, and all the rest, if she ever betrayed that promise. She did telephone, though, from a gas station in Bethany, Missouri, using a ton of change to get through, to make sure Miriam was really still there, still alive. The phone rang for a long time before she answered. As Linda fed nickels and quarters into the slot, she pictured a beautiful dark-haired woman in a white tennis dress, running in from the garden.

From the phone booth she could see Robin sitting on the hood of the Maverick parked in the shade, killing another Coke.

It may have been Linda's imagination, but Miriam's voice sounded eerily long-distance, like the voices of the dead in movies about zombies and ghosts. "Hell-ooo?" she said.

"Just one moment. That will be fifteen cents more, please," the operator said.

The telephone booth was like a furnace and Linda's hands were sweating, making the coins stick, but she finally found and separated a dime and a nickel and dropped them in.

"Go ahead. Here's your party," the operator said.

"Hell-*ooo?*" the ghost called again, impatiently this time.

"Miriam . . . Miriam . . . Hausner?" Linda asked. Robin was bouncing on the hood of the car, like a three-year-old. Why am I so nervous, Linda wondered. It's not *my* mother.

"Speaking."

Now what? It seemed rude to simply hang up. Linda had had her share of anonymous phone calls. They always left her feeling faintly anxious for days after. And she had just dumped more than two dollars into that telephone. "Mrs. Hausner? This is a survey," she said. "We were wondering if you're listening to your radio."

"Is this some kind of a *joke?*" Miriam asked.

And Linda lost heart. "Yes," she said, and hung up.

Now they were on their way. As she drove, she

HEARTS

glanced from time to time at Robin's profile. She had not meant to spring her plans on the poor girl like that, but Robin had asked with such persistence, and she certainly had a right to know. Linda never expected the reaction she got, though. Robin was usually so passive about everything, so secretive. And memories of her mother had to be baby-vague now, no matter how grave the loss must have felt, once.

Wright had told Linda that he'd worked very hard to make up to Robin for Miriam's disappearance, that he'd been mother and father all by himself. You name it: dollhouses, sports, handicrafts, school projects; he really got involved. They were as close as *that*. He'd held up knotted fingers. And Robin stopped asking for her mother in a very short time. Time had eased his own anguish, too, and he had prepared a generous, watered-down version of the truth, in case adolescence brought new curiosity. Linda thought he'd arranged to make Miriam sound like an innocent and suggestible kid, someone who fell in with bad companions, sort of a middle-class Patty Hearst. Luckily, Robin seemed to have forgotten all about her mother, and never mentioned her to him again.

Still, he was grateful for Linda's appearance in his daughter's life at this delicate period of growth and change. He may have been successful as a parental one-man band, but he was respectful, in awe of woman's special mysteries, among them her need for the company and confidence of other females, after a certain age. Linda and Robin were going to be close, too. Like *that*. He just knew it.

In the motel room that morning, when Linda said,

"Robin, do you ever think about your mother?" the girl had been stunned. Her mouth opened into a perfect cartoon O and her eyelids batted with shock. For once she was incapable of hiding behind her disguise of indifference, those trouble-shedding little shrugs. She actually staggered before she sat down on the other bed.

"You're not going to cry, are you?" Linda said, although Robin considered it a source of pride that she never did, and Linda believed it would be consoling if she could. "Oh, boy, I've really upset you, haven't I?" Linda continued. "I didn't mean to. I only thought . . . it seemed like the *natural* answer. I mean, I'm not even sure she's still there; I was going to check it all out first, but you kept asking . . . Robin?"

It was worse than when she had told her about Wright's dying, because it was so much easier now to gauge her pain. "Listen," Linda said. "You don't have to go. We'll figure something else out if we have to . . ."

"*No!*" Robin shrieked that one syllable. Then she said, more calmly, "I want to."

"You do?"

"Where is she?" Robin asked.

"Arizona. Glendale. It's near Phoenix. At least I think that's where she is."

"How do you know? How did you find . . . ?"

Linda contemplated the details of her discovery among Wright's things: the private investigation itself, the B-movie prose of the detective's report. It all made Wright seem mean-spirited and vindictive instead of the way he probably was—tortured and lonely. Robin wouldn't want to know all that junk, anyway. It would be like altering her history.

HEARTS

"Just by chance," Linda said. "I found a slip of paper with an old address. But I'll call first and be sure."

"Don't!" Robin said.

"What?"

"Don't tell her about me."

"Robin, I don't understand. A minute ago you said—"

The girl was pulling at her fingertips as if they were gloves she was having difficulty removing. "I—I want to surprise her," she said.

"It would be more like a shock than a surprise," Linda said. "She could have a heart atta—"

"*Please*," Robin begged, with more passion than Linda would have believed possible. "Linda, *please!* You have to swear!"

And Linda had given her foolish promise.

"There's Wolfie!" Robin yelled, and
Linda's heart lunged. She applied the brakes
so swiftly and hard that at least three cars
traveling at a safe distance behind them had to do the
same. And it wasn't Wolfie at all, of course. Just a
couple of wild-haired teenagers who ran up eagerly for
the ride. One of them wore a lavender satin jacket with
the word *Killer* embroidered across the right breast.

"Oh, *great*," Linda said, but she had to let them in,
and then endure the curses of the other drivers as they
went past in a fury of exhaust. "You two-headed cock-
sucking moron!" the last one yelled, as the teenagers
jumped into the back, slamming both doors.

"There's no need for that language!" Linda called
out her window.

"Home, James," one of the hitchhikers said, and the
other one jerked around, cackling with laughter.

Linda, after she'd suffered the first moments of utter
disappointment, thought of Bonnie and Clyde and those
other two, those men who murdered a whole family in
Kansas. *This* was Kansas.

She signaled cautiously before she reentered the highway. "I hope you guys aren't going too far," she told
them. "We'll be stopping for the night pretty soon
ourselves."

Robin gaped at her. It was not even one o'clock in
the afternoon, and they'd overslept and gotten a late
start that morning, besides.

The backseat passengers merely giggled. They were
high on something; Linda could see that right away.
They laughed at everything, even when she asked a civil
question about their ultimate destination. "Oh-ul-ulti-
mate!" one of them cried, and his partner sounded as if

he had swallowed his tongue and was choking to death. He finally stopped long enough to say, "We're going to Florida, man."

"Florida!" Linda said. "Why, that's the other w—," before she caught on and stopped herself. But it was too late. They were off again, and pummeling each other hard while they laughed.

Linda glared at Robin, who turned the other way. Linda took one hand from the wheel and pinched Robin's sleeve. "*Now* see what you've done," she whispered, hardly moving her lips.

Robin was outraged with innocence. "One of them looked like him," she said, not bothering to lower her voice. "It's not my fault. He even has the same kind of shirt."

How did she have the nerve to say that? Linda observed her passengers in the rearview mirror. They were nothing like Wolfie. They were only adolescents, at that strange midpoint of formation when boys becoming men appear strikingly awkward, when their hands, feet, noses, and ears develop suddenly, before the rest of them. Maybe, Linda thought, it should all take place in darkness and secrecy, like the transformation of caterpillars inside cocoons.

Robin had obviously wanted one of them to be Wolfie, and she'd bestowed his likeness on a mere kid. Linda understood the lure of such magical thinking, but knew they could have been killed, stopping like that. "We could have been killed," she said. "And look what we—" She had glanced again at Robin and saw the familiar eye-narrowing and jaw-clenching that usually preceded hostilities between them. The last thing she needed was a quarrel with Robin in the confinement of the car, with these two maniacs behind them.

Linda turned her attention back to the road. She would have liked to stop and let them out, but she had fallen into traffic again. The boys were so spacey they were liable to go tripping across the divider into the path of a trailer truck and get flattened like those poor dogs and chipmunks she kept passing. And they had to be *some* mothers' children. The moment Linda picked them up, responsibility for their safety had been subtly transferred to her hands, almost as if she'd agreed to adopt them.

She looked at the next green sign. There wasn't going to be another exit for eight miles. Maybe if she ignored them, they'd stop carrying on. How could anyone laugh like that, anyway, especially when nothing was actually funny? It occurred to her that she and Robin had not laughed together once during this entire trip. The closest was when Wolfie was with them and there had been a few rounds of smiling. But he had been the instigator, the ambassador of all that good will. How could Robin have mistaken these hopheaded babies for him?

Linda decided she wasn't going to say another word to set them off, but she didn't have to; there was plenty of other stimulation. Through the mirror she saw them point helplessly at something out the window—what? there were only road signs, cars, a few trees—and then collapse against each other in another seizure of hysterics.

Once in a while, gasping, slobbering spittle, they'd interject things like, "Oh, man. Oh, my side. Oh, oh!"

You could go crazy listening to them. She put on

HEARTS

the radio, hoping to drown them out with music. But it was exactly one o'clock and the news was on every station she tried. It was mostly bad news, as usual. And it seemed familiar, as if it was also *old* bad news being replayed. They were still talking about that leaking nuclear plant. It wasn't very far from Slatesville. Linda wondered if the Piners had been contaminated and were sitting now, glowing, in front of their glowing Zenith. That is, if the asbestos dust hadn't gotten them yet, or ordinary death. Mideast, blah, blah, blah, Rhodesia, Canada, gasoline supply, blah, blah, blah. An elephant had escaped from the zoo in Wichita and had not yet been located. More rain was predicted for the Central Plains area. Even the sports news was bad; all the local teams had been disgraced.

Linda shut off the radio and listened to the laughter behind her, which had not stopped for any of those bulletins of world crisis. She wondered what they were on.

She had smoked marijuana a few times with Iola and had had too much beer once or twice with Wright. But she hadn't ever been this way. Stimulants never brought her past a certain edge of promise. She *almost* relaxed fully, almost became giddy, but didn't quite cross the threshold to that other place. After alcohol, she slept, and usually woke later with a headache. Once, after smoking pot, she threw up, and then felt anxious for hours.

They'll probably be miserable later, she told herself, but without much conviction. She hoped their false gaiety would not influence Robin and give her any ideas about drugs, make her think you had to depend on artificial means to have a good time.

She glanced at Robin furtively to see how she was taking all this. The girl's silvery profile was as cool as a queen's struck onto a coin. "What's the matter with them?" Linda said. When Robin didn't answer, Linda raised her voice. "What's so funny back there?" she asked. "How can you laugh like that after hearing the news?" She was rewarded with stifled sputters, a few squeals. "Oh, boy," Linda told Robin. "They must be really stoned, or crazy. I mean, there's probably radiation everywhere, not just in Pennsylvania. We'd probably be better off if we just breathed *out* all the time. And who knows what's coming next? Tidal waves, maybe. Or killer bees!"

"Zzzzzzzz," buzzed one of the madmen in the back-seat.

"Raid! Raid!" his partner screamed in a Looney Tunes soprano. In the mirror, Linda saw them shrivel and die in each other's arms.

"Well, the Mideast crisis is no joke!" she shouted. Then she turned to Robin again, for confirmation, and was astonished. The girl's face was crumpled, like a glove, and her shoulders were shaking violently. A few tiny, anguished sounds escaped her distorted mouth. Why, she was crying! Those white lashes were spilling tears and her face was pink with emotion.

"Robin!" Linda said. "What is it?"

Robin's hands flew up like demented birds, and more noises escaped her. "*Hee,*" she said. "*Hee-hee!*" And Linda finally understood that she was laughing.

It was the strangest sound, one that she would never have associated with Robin. Linda could not have been more surprised if she had heard a cat barking.

HEARTS

The boys were still at it, too, and the three of them formed a rude chorus of whoops and howls and titters.

"Stop that!" Linda said. "Will you all just stop it! You're encouraging them!" she accused Robin.

But Linda knew she could hardly be heard now over the uproar. And not only that—a current of silliness was charging through her own chest. Oh, no. She tried to suppress it, tried to focus on personal problems, all the bizarre and awful things that had happened. Think of the abortion, she ordered herself, the firebombs. Think about Wright, his lost goodness, his poor homeless ashes sliding around in the trunk of the car. But she couldn't concentrate on anything serious. All that commotion. Robin's *face*. The escaped elephant lumbering madly across Wichita. "The elephant!" she cried, and there were answering trumpets from the backseat, jungle bird-calls, the shrieking of monkeys.

The craziness spread quickly through her, erupting in her throat like contained sneezes. What am I doing, she thought, and gave in to it wildly and all at once. The others were winding down by then, capable of only brief convulsions. Linda had just begun. Her nose ran, her eyes streamed. She could hardly see the road and had to steer off it finally, and roll onto the graveled shoulder.

Having started last, she kept at it longest. Robin and the two boys became more and more sober, wiped their eyes, let out a few irregular neighs and bleats, and grew still. Only Linda was laughing now, and wishing that she could stop, too. It was tiring, enervating. Maybe they really would have to look for a place for the night in the heart of the afternoon. And it was different when she was laughing by herself. The giddiness was rapidly evaporating. She felt her mood alter sharply even as she continued giggling and hiccuping like a fool. When she was able to gain some control, she wiped her eyes, too, and pulled slowly out onto the road again. She drove in fits and starts to the next exit, where she stopped to discharge her passengers.

By then everyone was quiet, each one drawn into private and reflective silence. All the familiar phrases about laughter came into Linda's head. Laugh and the world laughs with you. He who laughs last laughs best. Laugh, clown, laugh. The laughter of angels. They died laughing.

The boys walked away from the car, listing toward one another, and without looking back. Robin rested her cheek on the window ledge and watched them go. Linda let the motor idle until it failed. "Well," she said, feeling immeasurably saddened, "that was a good laugh, wasn't it?"

HEARTS

LINDA WOKE, DREAMING OF WOLFIE, AN **20**
erotic dream that made waking a frustration.
She had probably been stimulated by Robin's
wrong identification of yesterday's hitchhikers. The un-
deniable power of suggestion. Linda looked at the other
bed, where Robin, in sleep, managed to look powerless.
The promise of the dream and the seeming reality of
its pleasures were fading fast.

They were still in Kansas. Some mornings it was
hard to get her bearings. If she slept deeply enough, she
might be convinced she was anywhere upon waking:
Pennsylvania, Ohio, Indiana. That garage mechanic back
in Bayonne had warned that much of the country would
look like Jersey. It didn't, really. There was a distinct
geographical quality to each state, and even to separate
areas within the state. Iowa, for instance, was not as flat
as she had supposed. The flourishing cornfields were
stretched over a beautiful rolling terrain. Kansas *was*
flat, a place where it was possible to believe the earth
isn't round, after all, and that you could fall right off it
if you walked far enough into the horizon.

The highway's ribbon was the same, though, and the
motels and the fast-food shops and the diners. Linda
suspected that the same waitress had stood at their table,
pencil poised for their order while she dreamed her own
escape, in the last three successive states. Linda wondered why she was dumb enough to expect something
new all the time, not just during this trip, but in every
aspect of her daily life. Why did something like a snow-
fall out of season or a benevolent glance from a stranger
on a bus make her feel unreasonably hopeful? And why,
when that stranger, Wolfie, was only the star of an

X-rated dream, did she imagine he'd be very different from Wright, or from Barry King, the lover she'd had before Wright?

Linda met Barry shortly after moving to Bayonne. She had taken a bedroom in a walk-up apartment that was a short bus ride from the dance studio. It was convenient and very cheap, and although she valued privacy, Linda thought it might be cozier and safer to share a place. Gayleen Hayes, the other woman who lived there, was not consumed by a compulsion to be tidy. She bathed first in the morning, and when it was Linda's turn she found the floor puddled and all the towels drenched. Gayleen didn't bother to wash hair off the soap or from the basin and she often left a magazine on the edge of the tub, its colors running over the side.

The kitchen fared no better. She never wiped up stove spatters and crumbs, which served as an open invitation to neighborhood roaches. Food aged radically on her side of the refrigerator; it grew the fur of mold and developed the slime and odors of decay. Linda tried to speak to Gayleen about it, but found it difficult. She was an overweight, depressed person who kept all the shades down against whatever light they might have gleaned in their tiny, dark apartment, and she grew sullen and tearful at once when Linda brought up the subject of housekeeping. "I'm not the maid around here," Gayleen said.

"Of course not," Linda agreed.

"I get hassled by everybody," Gayleen continued. "My mother hassles me because I'm fat and because I don't date; my boss hassles me because I make typing errors. I don't need you to hassle me, too." Her lip trembled and she crumbled the piece of toast she was holding.

Linda wanted to put her arms around Gayleen and say that it was all right, *she* liked her just the way she was. But that wasn't true. Gayleen fit the old cliché about the fat girl with a nice face; if she lost weight her life would probably be drastically improved. And she wasn't someone you could hug spontaneously. There was something formidable about her quavering bulk.

Instead, Linda reasoned that cooking only for herself was a lonely and uninspiring chore. She began to shop for one meal at a time in a local delicatessen, where she bought prepared foods, cold cuts, and salads. That's where she met Barry, who was working behind the counter.

He was immediately friendly and advised Linda on her purchases. The sliced turkey breast was far better than the pressed and rolled variety, and well worth the difference in price. The German potato salad won hands down over the kind made with mayonnaise. If his boss was around, Barry would signal a warning when Linda tried to buy anything that wasn't absolutely fresh. He had such a pleasant air of authority that Linda gladly took his advice. He was also very handsome and reminded her of a movie star she couldn't quite place.

As a matter of fact, Barry was aiming for a career in show business, as a singer. He hummed thrillingly in a resonant baritone while he sliced ham and roast beef and cheese. He confided, as he gave Linda her change, squeezing her hand in the transaction, that this job was only a layover on the road to stardom. Was *she* interested in show business, too? She was awfully good-looking, had such a stunning walk; it knocked him out. He showed her a bandaged finger and explained that he had injured himself on the slicer the day before because he'd been thinking about her. If this kept up, he'd be reduced to human slaw pretty soon. She murmured sympathy and rushed away with the makings of her solitary meal, feeling aroused and expectant.

One evening, Barry came through. Another clerk was behind the counter with him when Linda entered the delicatessen. And Barry, without his apron, and handsomer than ever in a black turtleneck sweater, had a package ready for her. He announced that it was a picnic supper, for two. Linda laughed in surprise and delight, but pointed out that it was windy and drizzling, hardly the ideal conditions for a picnic. Barry said they could eat in his car if she liked and then go to a movie.

Of course she invited him home. Gayleen was visiting her mother overnight, and Linda and Barry could have some privacy. The condition of the apartment embarrassed her and she raced around wiping off sticky surfaces and stomping roaches as surreptitiously as possible. Barry made her feel relaxed very quickly by keeping up the illusion of a picnic. He said, "Listen, a few ants are inevitable—right?" Then he unpacked the delicate pink slices of Westphalian ham, the imported pâté Linda could never afford, and, for dessert, a selection of sparkling marzipan fruit. They drank beer from Germany, Czechoslovakia, and Japan. During supper he sang for her, and she was amused and touched by the fist he held near his face as a microphone. "I'd like to dedicate this next number to a lovely new lady in my life," he said.

HEARTS

She was in his arms after the last stirring note, and he smelled sweet and spicy, like the delicatessen. They never even got to the marzipan.

Linda found Barry so charming, so lovable, that she didn't acknowledge at first that he wasn't a total success in bed, and then she consoled herself by making excuses for him. He was tired, he was shy, he was new.

Their picnics continued. On evenings when Gayleen was there, Barry and Linda took their supplies to bed, where he would lick a last crumb from the corner of her mouth and whisper that he was now going to bang her ears off. He made lots of promises like that, exciting himself to a state of near-delirium by the time their clothes were flung across the room. Despite herself, Linda grew excited, too, and when Barry came too quickly she wondered if she was somehow to blame. She knew it sounded as if they were having a wonderful time, though: his singing and shouting, the crazed voice of the bed-springs. Linda hoped that Gayleen wasn't listening through the thin plasterboard walls of the apartment and feeling left out. It seemed unnecessarily brutal to make so many joyful noises when loveless people might be in earshot. She thought of asking Barry if he knew anyone to introduce to Gayleen.

He went into New York City from time to time to audition for plays, movies, and television commercials, and he often rehearsed at the foot of Linda's bed, singing advertising jingles for coffee, margarine, and drain cleaners, or bellowing lines from Stanley's role in A Streetcar Named Desire. Linda thought he was terrific, very talented, but he didn't land any jobs and only had occasional callbacks.

Iola hated Barry on first sight. He came to pick Linda

up at the studio and later Iola pointed out that he had looked in the mirror behind her the entire time they were being introduced. She said he was too much in love with himself to ever really care about a woman. Linda denied that, and began telling all the endearing and thoughtful things Barry did: the little love notes he tucked into sandwiches he brought, the songs he wrote and sang for her alone, the way he bothered to brighten Gayleen's day by offering her compliments when they passed each other in the hallway. Iola said she'd bet her last dollar that he was a dud in the sack, anyway. Linda blushed but didn't admit anything. Their relationship was still far too new for such damning conclusions. Barry said that himself. He had to get used to her. They had to get used to each other. *Performance* was his thing in and out of bed. And he was usually dynamite. The trouble was, she turned him on too much. They'd fall into a better rhythm when the heat died down a little.

Once, when Gayleen wasn't there, they took a shower together and Barry sang into the loofah mitt while Linda knelt in the tub and lathered him into a frenzy.

Back in the bedroom, he announced into his fist that this next number was for his favorite shut-in, a bedridden gal in Bayonne, who was in bed at that very moment waiting to be ridden. Then he laughed maniacally and pounced on her. "Ohhh," he moaned moments later. "Why do you have to *move* like that?"

But nothing changed, even when she simply lay there and played dead. This became the pattern of their lovemaking and Linda quickly grew tired of it, although she continued defending Barry to Iola.

"Here comes Narcissus," Iola would say when Barry

appeared at the studio. "Here comes God's gift to starving women."

The sad thing was that Barry thought she liked him. He'd pause in the doorway, put his fist under his chin, and say, "Ladies and Gentlemen, I'd like to dedicate this next beautiful song to a very beautiful and special girl." Then he'd start to sing a familiar old song, "Dolores," or "Tangerine," and substitute Iola's name in all the appropriate places. "How I love the kisses of Iola," Barry sang. "Ay-ay-ay-I-ola!"

It might have gone on like that forever. Linda was practicing how to say that she wasn't totally satisfied, but she couldn't find the right words to convey something so painful without inflicting any pain.

Barry took the matter out of her hands. One day she went home from the studio very early because she had a stomachache. She heard his voice as she walked up the three flights of stairs to the apartment, but told herself it was only the radio, that it just proved Barry was as good as anyone on the radio. And maybe after he had the success he truly deserved, his sexual energy would be recharged. She told herself all sorts of things as she went up the stairs and knew that her heart was thudding as much from terrible knowledge as it was from physical exertion. Outside the door to the apartment, she paused, holding the key in her shaking hand, and heard him say, "And this one is for gorgeous Gayleen of Bayonne, New Jersey, folks, who is out there in Radioland just waiting to be fucked to death."

Linda moved out the following week. A couple of months later she met Wright. And they were married. And he died. And she was in Kansas with Robin, who was just starting to wake up.

THERE WAS A FLEA MARKET IN EARLY PROG- ress on the outskirts of Homewood, a small farm community west of Olathe. Tables were spread across the roadside area of a vast meadow. In the far distance, animals were feeding and a yellow tractor moved slowly over the landscape.

It was only nine o'clock in the morning, and some of the vendors were still setting up from the backs of trucks and vans and station wagons, handing down cartons and pieces of furniture, shaking out oilcloth to cover the tables. There were a few customers walking around, and others stepped from their cars, drawn forward by leashed dogs and small children.

Linda pulled the Maverick in under a large elm tree and leaned back in its dappled shade, her arms folded behind her head.

"What are we stopping for now?" Robin asked.

"I have to rest sometime," Linda said. "And don't you want to stretch your legs? We can walk around and browse a little."

"I thought we were broke."

"Not broke. Far from broke. I only said that we have to be a little more frugal from now on. With money going out all the time and nothing coming in. No more fancy motels, for instance." No more abortions.

"So we shouldn't go shopping, either," Robin said. "We don't need anything."

Linda sighed. At the beginning of their trip, she'd suffered terribly from Robin's silence, and longed for the girl to speak to her, to say *anything*. Now Robin was finally loosening up a little, but it seemed that every time she spoke, she argued or complained about something. "This is not shopping," Linda said firmly. "I said we'll browse, that's all. We don't have to buy anything. It will still be fun."

Robin was doubtful. "It looks like a bunch of junk to me," she said, as they approached the first table. "I can drive for a while if you're getting tired," she offered in a more pleasant tone.

"No thank you. And besides, this is another good way of seeing the country, of getting the sense of a place." Linda had once read an article in a travel magazine that said something like that. "Just look at all these tools," she said, squatting at a display of heavily rusted farm implements. There were huge clippers, double-bladed axes, a mammoth scythe, and something she didn't recognize, with a broad, cracked wooden handle and jagged cutting teeth. She tried to lift it, but her wrist bent easily under its weight, and it dropped with a resounding clang across the other tools. "I'll bet you never saw anything like this in Newark," she told Robin.

"I wouldn't want to," Robin said.

The vendor, who looked like a farmer himself, in overalls and a weathered felt hat, realigned the tools. "Morning," he said. "Anything special in mind today, ma'am?"

"It's all so interesting," Linda said. "I was just telling my . . . I was just saying . . ." She glanced up and saw Robin walking away.

"Got some real nice barbed wire," he said.

"Pardon?"

"Got several good hard-to-find patterns here. Got some Nadelhoffer U-Shape, Scutt Double Clip, some Vosburgh Clinch."

Linda felt vaguely pleased. Did he think she was a farmer?

The vendor lifted a large frame from the back of his truck and placed it on the grass at her feet.

"Oh, my," she said, staring at it. A dozen two-foot-long strips of barbed wire were stapled to a Masonite board, and the whole thing was set crudely into the frame. The wire was as rusted as the tools had been. Each strip was different from the others and all of them looked thorny and lethal. Yet they were beautiful in a way; the spiral twist of one, the even plaiting of another. Perhaps *everything* had beauty, if someone put a frame around it and made you see it.

Who would actually buy this, though? She imagined an elderly farmer, retired, whose sons and grandsons have taken over the hard labor, sitting idle now in his farmhouse. He could hang this up and really look at it, something he couldn't ever take the time to do when he was busy tilling and reaping. Maybe gazing through the rows of wire, the way he had once gazed through them into the fields, he'd be able to see back into the scenes of his early life, with his own father, his grand-father . . .

"I can let you have this for seventy-five dollars," the vendor said. "That's a special price, for being such an early bird."

Linda stood up slowly, her knees stiff from crouching so long. "Thank you," she said. "I think we'll look around for a little while."

He didn't seem disappointed, or even annoyed with her for taking up his time for nothing. "Thank *you*," he said. "Come see us again."

She found Robin going through a pile of comic books nearby. Linda picked up a deep blue jar from a box of jars on the same table, and held it up so the sunlight

---

HEARTS

intensified its color. "Look at this," she said. "Beautifully simple, but simply beautiful." There was a $1.50 price tag glued to the bottom of the jar.

"It's from Vicks," Robin said.

"What?"

"It's a Vicks Vaporub jar. You could probably buy it filled with Vicks for a lot less than that."

"Oh, I don't think that's what it is," Linda said.

"Yes, it is. Daddy used to buy it all the time when I was little. I used to get lots of colds." She sounded as if she was bragging. "Smell it," she told Linda. "I'll bet it still smells."

Linda raised the jar to her nostrils and sniffed delicately. It *was* faintly medicinal. She smiled falsely. "Not really," she said. She replaced the jar in the box and wandered away.

I'm not going to let Robin spoil everything, she decided, fingering the engraved flower on a tiny gilt frame, and then opening the clasp on a jet-beaded evening bag. That smelled, too, like silver polish, and it reminded her instantly of kitchens. She didn't feel homesick or unhappy, though; no past home had been that good, and a better future one was always possible.

Linda went to another table, where she opened a huge album filled with old picture postcards set into transparent sleeves. At first she turned the pages quickly, glancing at the faded views of lakes and mountains, but then she began to read some of the messages on the backs, and was excited by the glimpse they allowed into small personal histories. *Please remember your devoted friend Alice Newman. We are having a nice visit with Mama and Uncle Robert. I will come to see you next*

Sunday. I must say goodbye now the doorbell is ringing.
The baby has been sick all winter. Linda looked at post-
marks. The baby would be seventy-five by now, or dead.
Did it even survive the winter? The card came from
Montana, where the winters were still hard. Who was
ringing the doorbell? She believed she could rummage
forever through these extraordinary artifacts of ordinary
life.

But, in spite of her intentions, she began to feel
weary after a while, and even a little bored. She couldn't
work up the energy to sift through another album of
postcards with their spidery accounts, or through another tray of monogrammed railroad spikes. The first few
batches had seemed wonderful. She'd even thought of
buying one with an R on it for Robin, as a memento
of their journey, as a truly historical souvenir. This whole
nation had flourished with the growth of its railroads.
Kansas alone seemed to have a million miles of track,
with hardly a train in motion on them. But Linda
couldn't face the prospect of Robin's disdain at such a
gift. She would never appreciate it, never see its modest
beauty.

If everything had a quantity of beauty, it also seemed
as if nothing was without monetary value, at least to
somebody. In Newark you would have had to pay a
private trash collector to cart away big ugly ruined things
like that pink sofa with the feathers flying out of it, and
the hanging springs. And there was a woman in a sun
hat that said *Olé! Olé! Olé!* all around its brim, trying
to plump up the sofa's dead pillows, stroking the scarred
wooden arms as if that would revive it.

And the little things on some of the tables: bottle

HEARTS

caps and old keys, fountain pens that didn't work any more, tarnished spoons with teeth marks in them, ordinary seashells you could pick up free in Atlantic City or Coney Island. There were headless dolls and disembodied china heads, lying around like victims of a train wreck, boxes of flattened dusty hats and curled shoes, and even empty soft-drink cans. Why, Robin had probably thrown out a fortune in those already! People used to throw a lot of this stuff away without a second thought. And now other people were bargaining to buy it. How was it possible to own someone else's nostalgia?

Linda thought she could just pull the Maverick over into this row of sellers, open the trunk, and take out some of the things they'd been dragging across the country: the flowered buttons she had been saving from an old discarded sweater, photographs of her mother, her own underwear and Robin's, combs, toothbrushes . . .

Finally, in this inventory, she came to Wright's ashes. She thought with wonder that there was probably a buyer for *them*, too, somewhere in the world. Everything else was negotiable, wasn't it? Empty Vicks jars, old barbed wire, RC Cola cans. There had even been one table where little mystery sacks containing "Trash or Treasure" were being sold for twenty-five cents each. Was this the place to leave Wright's ashes, among all the other lives' leavings? And how should it be done? She imagined dumping them surreptitiously, the way some people dumped loaded ashtrays in the parking lots of shopping centers, and was horrified. She would sooner keep them forever than abandon them with so little regard or ceremony. Linda had read once that if you owned someone's hair or nail clippings, you had uncanny control over him. Did possession of Wright's ashes include his history and the future of his freed soul? If so, she did not want the responsibility or the burden of such property. But this wasn't the right place to dispose of it.

Linda had a sudden desire to get away. She'd had enough, more than enough, of the survival of things. And she wanted to stay mobile, anyway, to keep moving toward her destination before California broke away from America and drifted off, before the other states followed, one by one, and Kansas became part of the new coast-line, and those distant grazing beasts found themselves staring out to sea.

HEARTS

THEY LAID OUT THE FEW THINGS THEY 22 would need for the night. The room at Applegate Arms was small, but clean, and with the kind of shabbiness Linda found appealing. The discreet white patches on the white bedspreads, for instance, and the dark streaks in the bureau mirror where the silver had worn away.

The bathroom was halfway down the hall, and there was evidence of other guests: a yellow, chewed toothbrush tilted in a cloudy glass, a flowered shower cap, still shedding water, and footprints in a trail of dusting powder.

Linda looked through the tiny window while Robin spit blue toothpaste into the basin. There was a funeral home next door with floodlights directed at its sign. *John J. Keneally and Sons.* This proximity of mortuaries to inns and smaller hotels was not unusual, nor did Linda believe it was an ironic statement on the nature of human rest. The zoning laws probably lumped them together. And there were many large houses fallen to small or disintegrating families. Funeral homes needed the space; it was simply a matter of supply and demand. She did not feel morbid about the people she could see visiting in their dark cars as she brushed her hair. That place was as much a part of things as this one. But she was grateful for the bed she would soon climb into, for the kind of sleep she was about to enter, its temporary darkness. "Isn't this nice?" Linda said. "And we're paying less than half what we did at the Marriott."

She had been worried about staying in a rooming house, afraid that once inside she would feel as if she were back at Mrs. Piner's, trapped again in her own childhood. There were definite similarities. This, too, was an older, rambling house with a circular porch. A front-yard pin oak cut off the late-afternoon sun, and a dog barked eagerly when they rang the bell.

But the woman who came to the door was young and energetic. And a few small children in pajamas peered at Linda and Robin shyly from the doorway of the kitchen.

Upstairs, Robin soon grew restless. She kept opening the bureau drawers and the closet door and closing them again. She peeked into a shallow curtained alcove in the corner, where she found a tall electric floor fan and a sealed carton marked *Lucy's Snowsuit, Carriage Blankets, Quilts.* "What's this?" Robin asked.

"That looks like hand-me-downs from the last baby."

Robin sat on the carton and pushed the fan back and forth with her feet. Its wheels screeched.

"They're probably saving them for the next one," Linda said. "Don't do that, Robin, please."

"Well, why are they keeping this stuff here?"

"Because they have no other place for it, probably. And it doesn't really matter; we're only going to be here one night. It's not in our way."

"There's no air conditioner," Robin said.

"No, thank God. We'll be able to hear ourselves think for once. And it's actually pretty cool in here, because of that big tree out there. It blocks the sun."

"It blocks the *air*," Robin said. She sniffed. "It stinks in here."

"That's your imagination. It's only a little damp."

Robin opened the closet door again. Its hinges needed oiling.

HEARTS

"What are you looking for, Robin?"

"There's no TV set, is there?"

"No, there isn't."

"It's Sunday. My best shows are on."

"You can do without television for one night, can't you?"

"What will I do?"

"Do? Why—why, you could read a book, couldn't you?" Linda pointed to a few matched brown volumes on a shelf near the closet, thinking that she had not read a book herself for a long time. It was certainly something she intended to do, once she got to California.

Robin picked up one of the brown books and opened it. "It's not in English," she said, triumphant.

"Let me see that. Oh, I guess you're right. It looks like German, doesn't it? The paper is so thin. I wonder who these belonged to." She read haltingly, " 'Man kann nicht . . . wissen wie es . . . ausfallen wird.' I wonder what it says."

Robin was pacing again, losing interest. "Could we go to the movies tonight, Linda?" she asked.

"No."

"Bowling?"

"Robin, I've been driving all day. I'm really looking forward to a long hot bath and just getting into bed and relaxing. That's why we stopped to eat dinner before we even looked for this place. So we wouldn't have to go out any more tonight. You know that. And I thought we were economizing."

"But what will I do? It's not even eight o'clock yet."

Linda considered the question. "We could always talk," she said.

Robin's eyes narrowed. "About what?"

"About . . . anything. We could tell each other things we remember from before we met. I mean, we've been together all this time and we hardly know each other." Robin continued to look sullen and suspicious, so Linda went on. "For instance," she said, "I grew up in a house very much like this one. I'll bet you didn't know that, did you?"

Robin shrugged.

"And my mother was a nurse."

There was a faint glimmer of interest. "Where is she?" Robin asked.

"She's dead. She died five years ago. She was a baby nurse. Sometimes she had to go away for a few weeks at a time to take care of a new baby in somebody's house. When I was little I used to go clomping around in her old shoes. The landlady always said I gave her a headache, and she made me stop. When my mother came home, we'd take a bath together." Linda remembered the bobbing motion, a lulling mist of steam.

"Who took care of you when she wasn't there? The landlady?"

"My father." He was reading a newspaper in the morning and rubbing his naked feet. He sat near the back window because the light was better there. Overnight, his face had darkened with new growth. Linda came up behind him and looked at the enormous black letters. There were pictures underneath, of two men shaking hands near a flag, of a smiling woman wearing a crown and waving. Linda leaned into him to see, her shadow crossing the page. He moved her aside with his elbow. "You're *breathing* on me," he said. "*You're standing in my light.*"

"Tell me about him," Robin said.

———

HEARTS

"Uh-uh. Now it's your turn," Linda told her.

"I can't think of anything."

"Sure you can, if you try. Just think about it for a minute."

"I don't want to do this, anyway. It's dumb."

"It's not dumb, Robin," Linda said. "And you can't keep saying that everything you don't like is dumb. *That's* dumb." She took her nightgown and bathrobe and went to the door. "I'm going to get ready for bed," she said.

The claw-footed tub was enormous. There was really room for two. Linda kept sliding forward, her chin going underwater. Her hair floated around her like seaweed. Her other hair curled the way her mother's used to, and gathered a nest of tiny bubbles. Every time the water began to cool, she opened the tap and let in a churning rush that was too hot at first and made her draw her feet away. Then gradually the water became only warm again, ideally so, and she stretched out, loosening, dreaming.

There was a sharp rapping at the door. Linda slid up, gripping the sides of the tub. "Robin?" she asked. "Is that you?"

A man's hoarse voice spoke. "You going to be out of there soon?"

Linda bounded from the tub, almost slipping, and dried herself quickly and haphazardly on a thin towel. Her hair was still dripping, and there were wet patches on her back when she left the bathroom. There was no sign of anyone in the hall. But as soon as she opened the bedroom door, she heard another one slam, nearby.

As she entered the room, her wet hair was whipped backward and her robe was blown open by a blast of air. The fan was in the center of the room, going full speed. It sounded like the engine of a small plane. Robin stood directly in front of it, her arms wide, her hair flying.

"Shut that thing off, for heaven's sake!" Linda cried. Robin either didn't hear her or pretended not to, and Linda had to walk further into the fan's hurricane to push the switch herself. "There!" she said, when the noise had died down and the blades became visible, turning slower and slower.

"It's *hot* in here," Robin said.

"No, it's not," Linda answered. "Once you've taken a nice cooling bath, you'll feel perfectly refreshed."

She thought she heard Robin repeat the word "refreshed," softly, between her teeth.

"Pardon?" Linda said.

"I didn't say anything."

"I thought you did."

"Well, I *didn't*."

"All right, you didn't. Now why don't you see if the bathroom is free. You'll really feel much better once you've lowered your body temperature," Linda said, getting into bed.

After Robin left, she lay back, trying to recapture the drowsy peacefulness she'd felt in the bath. The overhead light was still on and she was too lazy to get out of bed and turn it off. She stared into the yellow circle until a spectrum of yellow circles grew from its center and moved across the ceiling. Linda shut her eyes. Outside, voices called good night to one another, and then car

---

HEARTS

doors slammed. The visiting hours at John J. Keneally's were probably over.

Linda's mother had lain in a place like that for three days, until her brother in Florida could be located and brought up to Pennsylvania for the funeral. Linda had only seen this uncle twice before. He was a couple of years younger than her mother, who had referred to him as a drifter.

The Piners and a few other guests had come to the chapel and were gone. Linda and her Uncle William were the only ones there. He was thin and hard-looking, like those beaten farmers in photographs from the Depression. His suit didn't fit him and Linda guessed that it had been borrowed for the occasion. "Thanks for coming, Uncle William," she said, wondering if he had ever been called Bill, or Will, or Billy when he was a child. She had never had a nickname, either, and it occurred to her that it was a kind of deprivation.

"Alma looks real nice," he said, cracking his knuckles in the stillness of the room.

The undertaker had done the best job possible, with makeup and something stuffed into the cheeks to disguise the distortion the strokes had left. Still, there was a stubborn pull to one side of her mother's face, as if she had a splitting headache. It would not allow Linda to think in terms of eternal peace.

And her mother was wearing a blue dress. When the undertaker's office had called, asking for suitable clothing for the viewing, Linda had hesitated, thinking only her mother's uniforms were truly suitable. She pictured her in the quilted coffin that way, the black satchel against her feet, her shoes polished to a dazzling contrast of whiteness. Then Linda had brought them the blue dress, and the dark, moderate-heeled pumps her mother would have taken off before lying down anywhere.

Uncle William asked if his sister had had a good death. Linda still wasn't sure what that expression meant. Her mother had been in the hospital, recently returned from a coma, and was propped in bed, being given oral nourishment for the first time in weeks. The nurse spooned food in and it quickly dribbled out again. Linda looked questioningly at the nurse, who closed her eyes and shook her head, as if she were delivering a verdict. "Daughter's come to visit, Mother," she said. "Laura's here."

"Linda," Linda said, but the nurse was noisily gathering dishes and leaving.

Linda walked around the room, touching things, looking everywhere but at that odd and anguished face. She said, "It's still raining outside." The doctor had assured her that her mother could hear even if she was unable to respond. And there was another listener, Linda remembered, a neighboring patient behind her drawn curtain. Mrs. Palchik, the woman's name was. She was in and out of the hospital all the time because her lungs kept filling up with water. She often looked even worse than Linda's mother, but when Linda asked how she was feeling, she invariably answered, "Fine, honey, just fine," in a thin and watery voice. Her side of the room was always colorful with flowers and greeting cards, was usually busy with loud and cheerful guests insisting on life. The day before, Mrs. Palchik had offered Linda's mother a wilting bunch of roses.

Linda stood at the drawn curtain, her hand foolishly

HEARTS

raised, as if she planned to knock. "Hello?" she called in through the fabric. There was no answer, so she tiptoed around and looked in. The bed was empty, stripped. And everything else—flowers, cards—was gone.

"Mrs. Palchik's gone home again, I see," Linda said. "Maybe you will soon, too."

She thought her mother made a sound, some kind of reply. Linda looked up, hopeful, and noticed that the nurse had pulled back the sparse dry hair with a pink ribbon. A speck of food was still clinging to the corner of her mother's mouth. Linda took a Kleenex from the table and rubbed gently at the place until it was clean. "Did you say something, Ma?" she asked. *Would* you say something?

The first major stroke had made it difficult to name familiar objects. Wanting a mirror, her mother had drawled, "White flash," and then, not understood, had grown angry. "Ohhh, face box!" she cried. Linda ran around the room bringing the wrong things: comb, magazines, handkerchief, water, becoming as frantic as her mother, who was losing the names of the things in the world.

The second stroke had impaired her speech even further, and had paralyzed the entire right side of her body. Linda was relieved when she understood anything her mother said in that thick garble. She liked to imagine it was a foreign language in which her mother was fluent and Linda had only a few words.

That last day, no one kicked her out at the end of visiting hours. After the nurse lowered her mother's bed for sleep, Linda pulled up a chair and took her mother's hand. It was inanimate, unresponsive, and she put it back gently, hoping its new placement was not uncomfortable.

The hand looked rejected and helpless, so she picked it up once again. It was winter and by late afternoon the room had darkened. The rain was steady against the window. It was stuffy in there, a sealed place with too much heat rising from the radiator. The closeness made Linda groggy.

She woke to a definite sound, someone gargling. Mr. Botts? Her father? Was it a school day?

"Ma?" she said, coming to in instant recognition and terror.

"Yes," Linda told her Uncle William. "I guess you could say it was a good death."

After the funeral she accompanied him to the airport. He was going back to Florida, used to doing his drifting in a more compatible climate. Linda had paid for his air fare. On the way to the boarding gate, she bought a red carnation from an impeccably dressed teenaged Moonie, for two dollars. "Could you make it three?" he asked. "Come on, you can help us more if you want to. Can you make it two seventy-five?" He peered inside her purse. "You've got some loose change in there. Make it two and a quarter." Linda edged away and tucked the carnation into her uncle's lapel.

Is it a good death if someone else is watching? The worst thoughts always sneaked around at bedtime. Robin had been gone for ages. Linda was about to get up and see what had happened to her when she heard the bedroom door open.

"Linda?" The name was whispered, urgent.

She sat up and whispered back. "What's the matter?"

"Nothing. There's this old lady down the hall. She wants to tell my fortune."

"What?"

HEARTS

"She's a *palm* reader. She told me to come to her room when I was finished with my bath."

"Did you go?"

"I wanted to ask you."

"Well, she'll probably expect to be paid for it, Robin. And you don't believe in that kind of thing, do you?"

"I don't know. Do you?"

"Just think about it for a minute. What could those lines in your hand, that you were probably born with, have to do with some drunk that comes down the street one day and runs you over?" After she said it, she knew it wasn't the best example.

Robin was thoughtful. "Maybe it could have to do with the lines in *his* hand," she said.

"I guess you want to try it out, don't you?"

Robin shrugged.

"Do you want me to go with you?" Linda asked.

"Yeah."

Linda reached for her robe. "I'll be ready in a minute," she said.

The woman *was* old, and as small as a child. She was perched on the edge of a wicker chair and her feet did not quite touch the floor. She welcomed them both in a high, piping voice and said that her name was Effie Borden.

Linda looked around. The room seemed ordinary, as ordinary as the name, and not like the gypsy's den she had anticipated. No beaded curtains. No enormous poster of a sectioned palm, like the ones she used to see in downtown Newark, where the readers were always called Madame Esmeralda, or something like that. The curtains here were white and simple. A Big Ben alarm clock ticked loudly on the nightstand, next to a glass of water and a vial of blue capsules. There was a crowd of framed photographs on the bureau top. Effie Borden was probably a permanent guest.

After the introductions were over, Linda confessed that they were really quite closely budgeted and couldn't afford a reading for Robin, as much as they would dearly love to have one.

Effie waved her little hand. It would be a gift, she said. She didn't get that many opportunities to practice her science on people who still believed there *was* a future. She invited Robin and Linda to sit on the edge of her bed and she moved the wicker chair around to face them. "Linda," she said, "I said the word 'science' just now, and I experienced your unspoken skepticism." Before Linda could protest, she went on. "Chiromancy and chirognomy are very ancient practices. They were not unknown to the early Chinese. Assyrians and Hebrews, the Greeks and the Romans paid them great respect."

Linda cocked her head and nodded, hoping she looked pleasant and receptive.

Then Effie Borden asked to see Robin's left hand. It curled in her own, hiding its ragged, close-bitten nails. Effie smoothed it open. "You're right-handed, aren't you?" she asked.

Robin nodded.

"This is the one you started with," Effie said. "And this is the one you've developed. Just look at the difference between them."

Linda stared into Robin's pink palms. It was true; they weren't identical. The lines *were* different. But what did that mean?

"So," Effie Borden continued, "don't let anybody

HEARTS

tell you that you can't alter your own fate. You have already begun to do so."

Robin flashed a pleased, sly look at Linda, who made an effort to smile back.

"Now regard the thumb," Effie said. "The single digit that keeps man supreme among beasts in the universe. Notice the well-developed phalange. That indicates the presence of powerful will and determination."

"Oh, yes," Linda murmured.

Effie Borden went on, explaining the little padded mounts that were named for the planets. She called them out—"Jupiter! Venus! Mars!"—as if this were a planetarium and she were the guide. She traced the four great lines of Life, Head, Heart, and Fortune. She said that longevity was clearly indicated in Robin's hand. "Look at that line!" she commanded. "You'll live to be a hundred and twenty!"

Linda looked down at her own hand that was resting opened on her knee. The lifeline ended abruptly in the middle of the palm. Quickly, she closed her fingers over it.

"There is a predisposition for adventure," Effie was saying. "Travel, perhaps? In the recent past, and in the near future?"

Again, Robin glanced at Linda.

Linda wondered if the Maverick with its Jersey plates was visible from Effie's windows. It didn't really matter, though. The old woman was telling Robin the usual harmless things, the ones people most wanted to hear, about good health and love, about long voyages. She mentioned a light-haired man and a dark one. Then she said, "There's been a death. Yes?"

"Yes," Robin answered, almost inaudibly.

"And long ago, a mystery, a disappearance! You are still concerned with its solution . . ." She hesitated. "There is a possibility of violence here. I see a shining weapon. Turmoil. Confusion. But . . ." And now she paused dramatically. "But it will all end well."

Linda was reminded of the Nancy Drew books she'd read and loved when she was Robin's age. Someone was always talking about mysterious disappearances, about impending danger. And of course it always ended well. Linda was getting sleepy at last, and had difficulty suppressing a yawn.

Robin looked more awake than ever, truly animated. She leaned forward and breathed raspily through her mouth.

"I see water in your future, vast and blue. I see mountains."

That could be almost anywhere, except Kansas maybe, Linda thought. But she couldn't help being moved by Robin's intensity. She was only a little kid, really. Linda tended to lose sight of that. And thank goodness, Effie was winding up. There was the usual again: health, friendship, romance, family happiness, finis.

Effie Borden went to the nightstand. She took one of the capsules with some water and threw back her head to swallow it, like a bird.

Robin thanked her. Linda stood up and added her thanks, not without sincerity. It had certainly been a distraction, a nice little evening's entertainment. And the tension that had been strung between Robin and herself all day was eased.

———————

HEARTS

Back in their own room, Linda considered what would be an appropriate response to the whole business, a kind of summing up, to give Robin the right perspective. The girl seemed to have taken it all very seriously. It wouldn't be fair to just smash that innocent faith. On the other hand, it wouldn't be very responsible of Linda to encourage it. "That was fun, wasn't it?" she said, turning off the light.

"Some of the things she said were true," Robin answered from her bed.

"Well," Linda said. "You know that stuff could be true about almost everybody."

"No, it couldn't," Robin said.

Linda didn't want to quarrel. She wanted to sleep, was almost there. But a sudden flow of logic came into her head and she needed to share it. "About the death, for instance," she said. "That could be about me, too, couldn't it? And the travel?"

Robin was silent.

"You sleeping?" Linda asked.

In response, Robin turned sharply in her bed, making it creak.

"And the dark man and the light man," Linda said. "They always say that. I mean, what other kinds are there?" She decided to end the matter there. She had made her point and there was no sense in arguing. Besides, all this chatter was waking her up.

Robin said, "That's dumb, and so are you. You don't know *anything*."

Linda sat up. "Now you're being rude, Robin. And I wish you wouldn't whine like that. You've been doing it all day."

"I have *not*."

"There! You just did it again."

"I *didn't.*"

"Robin, you did. You do quite a lot of it, and it is very nerve-racking. You are always whining and arguing."

"It's better than what you do," Robin muttered.

"Pardon?"

"Pardon?" Robin mimicked.

"Did I hear correctly?" Linda said.

"Did I hear correctly?" Her tone, her inflection were remarkably like Linda's.

"Stop that!" Linda demanded, swinging her legs over the side of the bed.

"Stop that!" Robin echoed.

"What are you doing!"

"I'm showing you how *you* sound. Always talking and talking at me, like a . . . like a machine!"

"Like a what?"

"Like a machine," Robin said, but her defiance was softening.

Linda had an instant image of expressionless robots moving across the room. Then she thought of all the vending machines Robin had punched to release Milky Ways and Mounds bars, Yodels and Orange Crush, and how, after the coins dropped into the slot, there was that mechanical whirring and then the dull thud of delivery. "How do you mean?" Linda asked in a hushed, serious voice.

Robin hesitated.

"No, go ahead," Linda urged. "I really want to know."

"You sound like you're always saying proverbs, or something," Robin said.

Linda groped for her slippers, and put on the light.

HEARTS

"You mean, basically, that I'm not . . . spontaneous, don't you?" she asked.

"I guess so. Shut off the light. I don't know what I mean. I was just mad before. And this is dumb."

Linda shut off the light. "It's not," she said. "Don't be embarrassed, Robin. Criticism can be extremely constructive, you know. Helpful." She swallowed deeply, and lay down again. "And there shouldn't be any hard feelings between us about things blurted out in the heat of anger. So let's forget everything we said to each other tonight, okay? And start all over again with a fresh new day tomorrow, okay?"

Robin mumbled something.

"Good night to you, too," Linda said. "And pleasant dreams."

Of course it would be some job to get to sleep now. Robin was quickly gone; Linda could hear that faint snoring, the grinding teeth. Wright was able to go off like that, too. It was a gift.

The dog was walking around above them, his toenails clicking on a bare floor. Somewhere else in the house, a man struggled to clear his throat. Then bedsprings moved and moved. Linda tried to concentrate on water, on floating, and it almost worked. She dozed off and then came back with a jolt, as if she'd been falling and had barely saved herself. She'd been dreaming about blood, she realized, something bloody. That was probably only natural. She had not bled at all after that first day, though, and had not suffered a sense of loss. She'd expected to and had braced herself for it.

She folded her pillow in half, and moved from her side to her back. If she could only relax, she would be able to go right back to sleep. Her quarrel with Robin wasn't keeping her awake anymore. What Robin had said could have come largely from hurt, from anger, or even fatigue. And it wasn't anything Linda didn't know about herself in the first place. It was just that confirmation from others always made things worse. But it was possible to change, to alter your life at any time. Effie Borden had said so, the one thing she'd said that was sensible and true.

Linda crossed her hands and cupped her breasts. In the bathtub this evening, they had seemed exceptionally white and full, really beautiful, with their pale tracing of veins. Now she brushed her nipples lightly with her fingertips. The nipples rose in idiot response. These were only her own fingers. She remembered married nights and lying against Wright's breathing. But it wasn't marriage she missed, or even Wright. She knew that the mindless body itself could experience loneliness, without memory, without thought. Even when she was a child, it had this same blind desire for touch. What if it never went away?

HEARTS

In the morning, Linda propped one of Wright's landscapes against Effie Borden's door, and tiptoed away. She and Robin were going to make an early start, before anyone else at Applegate Arms was up.

Linda had awakened with Robin's words of ridicule inside her head and the previous night's unhappiness was instantly revived. It was very disturbing to be told you were like a machine, an automatic dispenser of boring and useless words. She could not stop thinking about it, as they packed the car, as they drove away.

In an effort to become more interesting, she found herself pushed further and further into silence. Everything she intended to say seemed wrong before she said it, seemed self-conscious or silly. And how could you become a spontaneous person if you reviewed every thought and idea before you expressed it?

When they drove close to the airport in Emporia, and a low-flying plane threatened to skim off the roof of the Maverick, Linda ducked and her hand moved from the wheel to point out the window, and then lowered again, slowly. She realized she was always primed to indicate the obvious on the road. A sudden field of yellow flowers was hardly a private vision. And a vapor of skywriting to advertise cutworm killer could be seen for miles and miles. Even the cutworms probably saw it.

To make things more difficult, Robin had chosen to lie in the back again, a real regression in their shaky relationship. Now, once more, she was merely a passenger being sped to her destination; well, maybe not sped exactly, but getting there nonetheless. With all the windows open like this, Linda believed her voice would be carried right out and sail, unheard by anyone, over the flat landscape.

Still, she tried to think of something funny or original or necessary to say. Hey, Robin, did you hear the one about the midget and the new Pope?

Her own silence troubled Linda, not only because it stressed her inadequacy as a social being, but because human exchange was so essential to survival. That lovely volley of words across pillows, and into sleep. The first man she ever slept with had taken her to his room at his married brother's house and had held one hand over her mouth throughout the act, in case she cried out in pain and happiness and woke his niece and nephew. Later she learned that other people were often boisterous in bed, and even shouted, like storm-tossed sailors sighting land.

Robin understood that she had hurt Linda's feelings by what she'd said the night before. And now Linda was getting even by not speaking to her at all. If Robin spoke first, it would be a kind of apology, and she could not bring herself to do it. Anyway, Linda had started the whole thing, had picked on her first, said that about Robin whining. And then hadn't she made fun of everything important and serious that Effie Borden said? She *was* a real fortune-teller. She knew things she couldn't possibly know without secret and special powers. The light man and the dark man. About Robin's father. About traveling and a mysterious disappearance. She even knew about the fork and did not betray Robin to Linda by being more specific. And that was one of the

HEARTS

things Linda had criticized, that Effie Borden was vague, that what she said could mean anything.

Robin was lying on the backseat again, looking at some old comic books she'd read a million times. Reading in motion always made her feel sick, so she just looked at the pictures and watched the colors jump whenever the car hit a rut in the road. Archie and Jughead and Veronica and Betty, their words vibrating in blurred balloons.

Linda's big purse had been on the front passenger seat this morning when Robin got to the car. Well, she could take a hint. She didn't have to go where she wasn't wanted. And if Linda thought she could be broken down by silence, she picked the wrong person to break. Robin could go a thousand miles without speaking, a *million* miles. She would not speak to *anyone*, something Linda was unable to manage. "Fill it with regular, please. Am I close enough to the pump? I think we're in for another scorcher. Could I please have the key to the rest room?" She'd said all that already to the man at the gas station, her voice peculiar at first from disuse. If it had been Robin driving, she'd have stopped at a self-service island, and when the man came out and said, "Check your oil, lady?" or "Have a nice day," she would have simply stepped on the gas and zoomed away.

If you didn't use your voice for ten, or twenty years, could you lose it? What about those monks and nuns who take a vow of silence, and eat all their meals together without ever saying, "Pass the potatoes" or "This chicken needs salt"? What if one of them started choking on a fishbone? Or saw a mad strangler come up behind another monk?

Big deal, Linda told herself. Even the President of the United States is not a spontaneous person. Somebody else has to write all of his speeches. And the whole world listens, as if he were a great poet talking off the cuff and straight from the heart.

Robin was not speaking to her at all, that old punishment for unintentional crimes. The girl had not even shrugged for a long time; perhaps it was difficult to do effectively while lying down. When the gas-station attendant wiped the back window and said, "Hot enough for you in there, kid?" she had shut her eyes and pretended to sleep, with a comic book spread across her face.

Once, Linda read an article about a couple who had stayed married for fifty years without speaking. It had all started with an argument on their honeymoon about the wrong eggs ordered for breakfast. During the years that followed, they had children, bought a house and cars, took trips, without exchanging a word, and now they were having a golden wedding anniversary party. That's why they were in the newspaper. The caption, under the picture of a grim, white-haired couple holding champagne glasses, read: *Weehawken Pair Prove Silence Is Golden.* Maybe she should tell Robin about that. Or about the woman in an iron lung who had memorized the entire Bible. What made me think of that, Linda wondered. Anyway, Robin was really asleep now. The comic book had slipped off her face, leaving a small tattoo of color on her left cheek.

Robin woke and thought: What if the monastery caught on fire? But then they would have a special bell to ring, wouldn't they? She sat up and looked through the window. She wondered how long it was since she'd

HEARTS

last spoken. And what was the world's record? She didn't have a watch and she certainly wasn't going to ask Linda the time and spoil her own record, whatever it was. In the *Guinness Book*, she remembered, a man in Australia had showered non-stop for 336 hours.

Robin often dreamed that she could not speak in moments of crisis. Sometimes she was in danger; sometimes she recognized her mother in a huge crowd that pressed around her and wouldn't let Robin through. In the dream, she saw her own wordless mouth working, and would come awake, breathless and frightened.

She touched the fork in her pocket. At the Marriott in Iowa, she'd wrapped the tines in some of the free Kleenex they had in the bathroom wall, so that they wouldn't leave scratches across her hip any more. What if she said absolutely nothing when she saw her mother, became as mute as the dream Robin, except that her voicelessness then would be deliberate, controlled? What if she simply stared with burning eyes and took the fork from her pocket and plunged it in before her mother could speak, either, or scream? If Robin had had more time that day on the farm in Iowa, she would have stolen a real weapon, a sharp and shining knife. She thought of those three rifles on the wall of Linda's friend's house in Indiana. If they had been smaller, if they had been revolvers or pistols. If her father had really been the chief of police. The fork would have to do. She must remember to remove the Kleenex first, that's all.

An unspoken (ha!) contest had been started between them. Linda wasn't sure how, or even why. It was just that neither of them was speaking. If it came to it, she knew she could endure much longer than Robin. But she was the adult here, the one to set the proper tone for their behavior. And it was childish to continue this competition with a child. Her mouth began to shape Robin's name, and then shut again, with a defiance of its own. Anyway, what would she say?

They were going to have to stop soon for lunch. She thought, with a passing tremor of guilt, that it would be interesting to just drive and drive and see how long Robin could hold out without food or water or going to the bathroom. Linda had used the one at the Shell station while Robin pretended to sleep, and she had taken a long drink when she'd filled the thermos there. As far as hunger went, she could get by for hours on the Tropical Fruits Life Savers in the change tray on the dashboard. Linda saw with spiteful satisfaction that Robin's favorite, tangerine, was coming up next.

But the center line of the road was starting to have that hypnotic effect. At each rise, Linda worried that she would be carried over it into sleep, without warning. And using the radio to stay awake had to be a violation of the rules of whatever stupid game they were playing. How did this craziness begin? How would it end?

If you never spoke, would that increase your ability to send telepathic messages? In science last year, Oxhorn told them that the loss of one sense often led to the sharpening of another. Compensation, he called it. Robin sent a swift trial message to Linda, commanding her to shut the front window. It was blowing Robin's hair around, anyway. *Linda Close The Window.* She stared at the back of Linda's head. Nothing hap-

HEARTS

pened. It was probably Linda's fault. She was just a lousy receiver. You probably couldn't send a message through her brain with a poisoned dart.

Robin had ESP. She and Ginger tested themselves once with a deck of cards, according to instructions in a magazine, and Robin had come out Above Average in Telepathy and Clairvoyance. Sometimes she knew when the telephone was going to ring right before it happened. She'd get this tingling in her neck, and she would know. LINDA YOU DUMB ASSHOLE CLOSE THAT WINDOW.

There was a chartered bus at Howard Johnson's and another one pulling in. They were carrying a convention of insurance underwriters from the Plains states. Inside the restaurant, all the tables and counter stools were taken, and there was a considerable line of people waiting to be seated. They buzzed and trilled with conversation. The hostess occasionally held up three fingers or four. Feeling foolish, but enterprising, Linda raised two fingers herself when asked how many, and thought she perceived surprise on Robin's face. But the smaller tables had all been recently assigned, and Linda could see they weren't going to waste a whole booth on two diners. She was thinking of heading for the next Howard Johnson's, at least fifteen miles away on I-35, when a stranger spoke to her. He was a tall, handsome, elderly man who was holding an immaculate panama hat against his breast. Linda was so startled, and the conventioneers were making such a din, she didn't understand him. She almost said, "Pardon?" but checked herself in time. Instead, she moved her head inquiringly, and touched her ear, and the man obliged by repeating himself. He and his wife were wondering if she and the other young lady would mind sharing a table, so that they could all be seated sooner as a party of four.

Linda looked at Robin, who smirked, and then she nodded vigorously. The man informed the hostess of their new status and they were seated within a few minutes.

The man and his wife had the sweetest faces. They sat close to one another in the booth, sharing a menu.

Linda hardly had to look at hers. She knew most of the offerings by heart and could even predict the Daily Specials. But how was she going to convey her order to the waitress without speaking? This nice couple would think she was rude, or peculiar, if she didn't speak to them, either. The whole business was idiotic. Yet she said nothing and pretended to examine the Technicolor illustrations of fried clams and cheeseburgers.

Robin slid out of the booth to use the ladies' room. She glanced at Linda as if to say, *Dare* to speak while I'm gone! Linda stared back, intimating her outrage at such a suggestion.

The two strangers spoke to one another in gentle, considerate tones. "The ham salad looks good, dearest," he said. "What do you think?" She was thinking of the fish fillet on a bun. They decided to order one of each and share them. Their intimacy was so natural that Linda believed they shared everything. The mystery of love's beginning was nothing compared to the miracle of its endurance.

Inevitably, the couple turned their attention to Linda. "Have you decided yet, dear?" the woman asked.

HEARTS

And Linda nodded and pointed to the photograph of the grilled-cheese sandwich. It was a special that included potato salad and pickles, a choice of beverage, and one scoop of ice cream. The man and his wife exchanged a look of deep understanding and sympathy. Why, they think I *can't* speak, Linda realized, and was horrified.

"May I order for you?" the man asked. His eyes were watery with kindness. This was the appropriate time to end all this nonsense, and she would have, or would have cheated, whispering a fast explanation, if Robin hadn't come back to the table at that very moment.

"*Your sister is having the grilled-cheese special*," the woman said to Robin, after she was seated. Every word was enunciated with excruciating care. "*Would you like the same thing?*"

Robin shrugged, the international language that always worked for her.

"Good! Fine!" the man cried, in a jovial outburst. He snapped his fingers for the waitress, like a flamenco dancer, and she whirled to their table.

It all went like that. Even the choice of beverage was easy. The woman read them off until she was stopped by a show of hands. Linda thought: This is the worst thing I've ever done. When she was a child, she and a couple of friends liked to pretend they were blind. They would link arms and, with their eyes squeezed shut, walk downtown, careening into people and shop windows. Her father caught them once, and she was beaten for being disrespectful of the less fortunate. But she had not done it to ridicule anyone, only to test the terror of possibility. She remembered disabled beggars in Newark,

and Simonetti saying bitterly that they were all fakes;
the blind could see, the amputees were contortionists;
the world was full of phonies and crooks. Maybe he was
right. Her face flamed. She could barely chew her
sandwich. And it was much too late to undo this situation now, not without humiliating these strangers, too.
The man and his wife were overwhelmingly solicitous.
They discreetly asked questions that could be answered
easily with a gesture or a nod. They told about their
son, who was a plastic surgeon in Amarillo, and about
their daughter, who was a librarian and raised basenji
puppies, a rare breed that was barkless. After she said
this, the woman looked dismayed, and her husband
patted her hand to reassure her. Linda took some comfort from seeing that Robin was suffering as well, and
had let her ice cream melt into a soup in which she
drowned her spoon.

Of course the couple insisted on paying for everyone.
"It's a pleasure!" the woman shouted. Her voice had
doubled in volume since they sat down together. "And
a privilege!" her husband added. "We don't often get to
have lunch with such charming young ladies." They
both shook hands with Linda and Robin. Linda felt
hers being pressed fiercely. Courage, was the message,
courage.

In the parking lot she looked upward, feeling faintly
religious and expecting retribution. But the atmosphere
was cloudless and forgiving. The elderly couple waved
from their blue Pinto and drove away.

Robin climbed into the front seat next to Linda.
They went slowly down the service road and then merged
with the highway traffic. Still, neither of them spoke.

HEARTS

Maybe we can't any more, Linda thought, and put one hand against her own throat. It throbbed with contained language. Everywhere in the world, people were speaking civilly to one another. Good evening. Goodbye. It certainly looks like rain. Would you care for a cheese puff? In French, in Chinese, in that African click-talk that sounds like wooden beads being strung together across the vocal cords.

Robin's profile was cool and inscrutable. Her fine light hair blew wildly around it. I'll give in, Linda decided. *She* never will. "Is there too much of a draft for you?" she asked. "Shall I close my window?" Had her voice always been this musical? It was thrilling to speak again, like opening one's body willingly to love. Not really giving in at all.

Robin's eyes were astonished, and her skin blossomed with blood. "Yes!" she said. "Oh, yes!"

"SO NOW TELL ME ABOUT HIM," ROBIN ^24
said, as they were settling in for the night at
a place called Buddy's Siesta.

"Who?" Linda asked, already on guard. Robin often
didn't seem to listen to anything Linda said. And then
days later, without warning, she would gather up the
strings of a failed conversation, and begin again. It
startled Linda and made her feel uneasy, like a court-
room witness about to be caught in a lie.

"Your *father*," Robin said.

"What about him?" Linda was stalling for time in
which to invent history, or a further, convincing stall.

"*Anything*," Robin said, her voice stretched with
impatience, a cranky child demanding a new bedtime
story.

"Well," Linda said. "He was a mill worker and he
had a lung disease. It's called emphysema."

Robin nodded as if she had received the most pertinent facts.

Linda took that moment to shut the light and position herself for sleep. Maybe she could if Robin stopped
talking and she didn't start thinking. "Good night," she
called, with faint optimism and even less authority.

"What happened to him?" Robin asked.

"He died."

"Of what? The lung stuff?"

"No, not exactly . . . It was more of an accident."

"In a car?"

"No," Linda said. "I don't know about you, Robin,
but I'd better go to sleep before I drop." By now she
was as tightly coiled as a runner before a race.

"In a plane?"

HEARTS

"Uh-uh. It was a household accident. And I don't want to talk any more, okay?"

"That's the fourth biggest killer in America," Robin said. "After heart, cancer, and strokes. This insurance guy came to school last year and told us all this junk about not leaving your skates on the stairs and everything."

Linda was quiet, hoping that if she didn't answer, Robin would simply wind herself out.

"And not smoking in bed," Robin said. "Are you sleeping?"

Maybe never again, Linda thought.

"He came for career week," Robin said, yawning. "He was a real asshole."

"Mmmm," Linda dared, and then held her breath. She realized after a while that Robin had diverted herself, and that the inquiry was over, at least for now. Linda was grateful, if not quickly relaxed. Her father's death was something she was still unable to discuss with dispassionate calm. And everyone said it could never have happened exactly the way she remembered it, anyway. On a date last year with a rescue-squad paramedic, she'd tried to describe it, and he thought she was only kidding. He said she must have a terrific imagination and how about using a little of it on him? But she wasn't kidding and she didn't hold her imagination responsible, either. She believed, with valiant resolution, that it really had happened that way.

She'd had many fantasies about her father dying, before the actual event. Mostly they involved major catastrophes. What if the great maple out front finally collapsed under its burden of branches and fell on him? What about fire? Her chest would knock with alarm and excitement. She would have to go looking for him, then, to see that he was still alive, to reassure herself of her own impotence. And when she found him, it would all begin again—the abuse, the fantasies.

Linda would wonder sometimes about her mother and father together. Even before she knew about sex, or *knew* she knew, she'd try to think of them falling in love and agreeing to marry and have a child. She wished much later, too late, that she had asked her mother why she had chosen someone so darkly moody and cruel, and what she, Linda, had done right from the beginning to attract that cruelty. With others he was taciturn and gruff, but he seemed to reserve the center, the very eye, of his furious storm for her. One day, when Linda's mother came home from a job and found her crying in the sticky shade of the porch and rubbing the red places on her arms where he had gripped them, she didn't even ask what had happened. She knelt to embrace Linda, tried to erase those fingermarks with her own hands, and said, "He had a very hard life."

Linda thought she recalled some days of careless peace, herself in the doorway watching him asleep on the sofa, his afternoon snoring a steamboat's benign whistle. He didn't look so bad then, though she knew it had to do with the small charge of power she exerted by being the unseen observer. But maybe he'd once been a tamed and loving man, a daddy who played cards with her and carried her gently from an infant sickbed to the toilet. Or was that someone else with cool strong arms and a thundering heartbeat against hers? All the real witnesses were gone, and who could trust the unreliable witness of memory?

HEARTS

Yet she clearly remembered her parents walking up the stairs to the second floor, him following her like some large faithful dog, panting after the white stockings, almost nipping at the white hem. They'd go to their bed and Linda to hers, where she would count and hoard those latest miseries, all the prickly wounds of spirit and flesh. How he had locked her in her mother's closet for three hours because she had been found rummaging there, how he would not acknowledge her apologies after she was released, would not speak to her at all. How she had been awakened in the middle of the night to be held accountable for sins she was too confused to remember, but confessed to finally for the promised solace of bed. Where she would rock in a tight circle of herself until she gasped and could be delivered again to sleep.

It was early in March, about a month after her tenth birthday. Her mother had left for a new job, and Linda was instantly bereft. In those days her imagination ran to fear as much as it did to dreams of wish fulfillment. And she was always afraid her mother wouldn't come back. It was raining hard; Linda was positive of that detail. The rain fell through the trees with the noisy urgency of plumbing, and it intensified her bereavement. It also confined her to the house that Saturday, sealing her in with her father and Mrs. Piner and Mr. Botts and a new old lady who cried soundlessly most of the time, as if she were separated from them by a thick pane of glass. Linda couldn't remember the old lady's name now, but everything else was sharp and immediate—the way the rain sounded, the way the house smelled of trapped dampness and breath. Her mother was already miles away, powdering the newest baby, holding its little wrinkled legs up and patting on clouds of talc—the way she floured a chicken.

The game was to stay out of her father's notice for as much of the day as possible, to listen for his footsteps and his wheezing and to always go the other way. It was a large house, at least, with plenty of places to hide. She spent considerable time in the pantry, carefully examining the labels on cans. There was one for green peas, with a picture of a rainbow arcing over a sunny meadow. A chimney with a single spiral of smoke could be seen in the distance, and a giant pod, in which the pearly and perfect peas nestled, was superimposed across the scene. That label always filled Linda with an illogical surge of splendor and longing.

Sometimes she even hid upstairs in the more treacherous territory of her mother's closet, because there was consolation in the company of her clothes left behind, dresses and shoes that waited unmistakably for future days of celebration.

This time, though, Linda was downstairs, wandering. The radio played, with fitful bursts of static, in the kitchen. It was a religious program: God this and God that. She hated God that year and He hated her back. Elsewhere, the Hoover was droning, sucking up dust; Mrs. Piner always vacuumed when Mr. Botts was sleeping. Linda's father could be heard walking heavily overhead. The old lady was stationed in her wheelchair near the kitchen and, as usual, her face was wet. How did she manage to weep like that without bawling? Her eyes were squeezed shut, her mouth was stretched wide by despair. Linda wondered what sad thing she remem-

HEARTS

bered or what people she yearned after. Maybe her own family, lost somewhere beyond the front door. Couldn't she just get up if she wanted to and go after them? She was that close. And she had legs. They were supposed to be paralyzed. They were as thin as canes and covered with ulcerous sores, but still they were legs. Helpless herself, Linda could not bear to comprehend that much helplessness. Maybe it was only her loss of will the woman mourned. Linda went closer and watched the intricate passage of tears through the maze of wrinkles. "What?" she whispered. "What is it?" She was thrilled by the remote possibility of a response, but of course there wasn't any, only more of that silent crying. "Walk," Linda said, high-pitched, conspiratorial. "Go ahead. *Do* it." Her cheeks smoldered. She was much too old for such overwrought pretending, and even if the old lady didn't know what was going on, Linda suspected the savagery inside herself that wrestled with the desire to be good.

And then her father was coming down the stairs. As if he knew what she was up to in her Saturday boredom.

Linda went swiftly past the wheelchair, into the kitchen, and down the wooden steps to the basement, where the huge red heart of the furnace boomed. This was not her favorite place. She still kept an early belief that all her just punishments waited in its shadows for her descent. "They'll get you," her father had promised, and here she was, freshly stained with guilt, and making herself available.

But there were no visible demons lurking, only a sudden and shimmering field of water. The basement sometimes flooded like this during heavy rainstorms, despite her father's summer caulking around the small high windows. Other things he fixed failed to work soon after, also. Faucets with brand-new washers leaked. Radio voices came and went like ghosts after the replacement of tubes, and lamps he'd rewired flickered a few warnings and blinked out.

Linda sloshed around. There was more than an inch of water, maybe two inches, and her thin-soled shoes and cotton socks drank quickly and were soaked. She knew she had acted recklessly by plunging in like that. She knew she should go up and tell him about the flood, even at the risk of enraging him with such bad news. Mr. Piner was away, doing overtime at the mill. It would be her father's job to pump the water out, it would be his fault. The vacuum howled directly overhead. She could tell Mrs. Piner first, although that carried its own risks. Linda's wet feet would leave evidence of their passage across the clean floors, and Mrs. Piner would demand to know what she'd been doing down there in the first place.

Linda liked the water, despite the chilling discomfort. She pretended it was the ocean, which she had never seen, a gentle lapping ocean with France or China somewhere in the distance past the spot where Mr. Piner stored the snow tires for his pickup. It was difficult to pretend sunlight, but that was all right. It rained on oceans, too. There was a poem in one of her schoolbooks about it, by Robert Louis Stevenson. He had been sick when he was a child and spent lots of time in bed making up poems. In one of them he mentioned a counterpane. Linda wasn't sure what that was, but she liked the way it sounded. Now she waded through the shallow

---

HEARTS

water, her arms out like a tightrope walker's, saying the word "counterpane" over and over, almost to herself.

After a while she realized the house was unnaturally quiet. The furnace was quiet, its glow darkening. The vacuum was off and even the radio had stopped playing. Then her father shouted something and Mrs. Piner shouted back. Theirs were like voices calling across mountains. "Yes!" Mrs. Piner yelled. "All the lights! And the vacuum!" And Linda knew the electricity had gone off.

That and the flood! He'll be furious, she thought, with a wild shiver of pleasure. And then she remembered that this was where he would come, this was where he always came to investigate when things went wrong with the functions of the house.

There was no quick and comfortable place to hide. Her feet dragged in the water, their wetness now intolerable. She could have been pushing through mud and slush. Finally Linda realized that the snow tires made a low circular tower she could crouch behind. She worked her way toward it and got there just in time.

The weak, tri-circled beam of his flashlight preceded him, bouncing on the steps and then moving playfully up toward the ceiling. He stepped into the water before he saw it, and growled at the first splash. "What the—!" he cried, and the light danced jerkily across the room, passing just over Linda's head, like a bullet. "Flood!" he bellowed up the stairs and began to ford the ocean, in the direction of the furnace. "What?" Mrs. Piner shrieked from above. He didn't bother to answer her. Instead, he played the light along the walls, across the hanging shelves to the switches and outlets, to the fuse box and a coiling pipe above it; they all retained their mystery. "*What?*" Mrs. Piner insisted, and at the same moment the furnace rumbled to life, making him jump and curse. The vacuum started up again and the radio began to play music at a deafening volume. Someone must have fooled with the knobs when everything went off. It was a mad serenade of machinery, and Linda had an impulse to laugh with surprise and relief. He'd go away soon; she would not be discovered. Her father wasn't laughing, though, and was still in earshot, more than enough reason to contain that impulse. She watched as he poked around, doing useless things, hitting the furnace door with the side of the flashlight, patting the pipe above the fuse box, so that a small flurry of dust floated down and disappeared into the water. "*Fixed!*" Mrs. Piner screamed idiotically over the noise of the vacuum. If Mr. Botts could sleep through all that, Linda thought, he'd have to be dead. He must be up now, rushing his startled bladder to the bathroom, or to the kitchen if he was confused enough. Maybe he'd collide with the old lady in the hallway, astonishing them both. They were so far away from their own lives, as Linda's mother was far away with a nameless drowsing infant against her breast.

"*Linda!*" her father said. Had he seen or heard her? She was still in her hiding place, still silent. And she could see he was turned toward the stairs and looking up. He probably only wanted her to fetch some tool or bring a message to Mrs. Piner, who was vacuuming again. But there was no way to make the stairs without attracting his attention, no way to go up and then come down again, innocent and dry. He would know she was not

------

HEARTS

responsible for the flood, of course. The walls were black with dampness, and water seeped steadily through the windows. Could he blame her for the other thing, the lights going off? Not likely; he knew she was not the sort of child who arbitrarily touched things. Yet she felt strangely culpable and afraid she would confess everything, anything, under the slightest stress of inquisition.

"*Lin-daaa!*" His voice rolled out like drums and she was certain now that she would never answer him. Her shoes and socks were probably ruined. Why in the world had she jumped in with them on, just like a baby in a rain puddle? He would get her for that alone, and her feet ached with the cold that was rising like a tide up her bare legs and into her groin.

"Goddamn!" he muttered. "Goddamn!" And Linda said, "Counterpane, counterpane," but not really aloud. Her teeth skidded against each other.

He was coming toward her, splashing, stirring up a minor current. And then he stopped, as if he'd remembered something, and he turned around, reaching above him to take Mr. Piner's electric lantern from one of the shelves. Linda watched as her father slowly unwound the thick black cord until it was a long and restless serpent swaying at his side.

Of course he knew she was there. How could she think he wouldn't? He could sniff her out like those dogs the police used on television to find murderers. And now he only wanted more light by which to see her. He started moving again, toward the outlet next to the furnace, his left hand gripping the cord's neck just under its tiny dark head. Two silver tongues glinted in the dimness.

What was the use? Linda stood up, surrendering,

as his arm reached out. "I'm *here!*" she cried at the very moment of connection and met his astounded eyes with her own, and saw the crooked arrow of light as it entered his fingertips and sped directly to his heart. She saw the blazing outline of his heart, too, its last suspended pulse of blood like a ball of mercury. She saw right *through* him to the leaning mops and brooms against the wall. His entire frame lit up like a neon sign, and he danced and sizzled in a yellow circle of fire before he went out. He screamed, of course, or she did, and then the whole place reeked of smoke and cooked flesh.

Fifteen years later, the paramedic said, "God, you've got a lovely ass. And a terrific imagination, too. How about using a little of it on me, hmmmm?"

"But it's true!" Linda told him.

"Listen," he said. "You don't light up when you're electrocuted. That's first of all. Wait. And second of all, there is absolutely no fire. And I'm not even sure he'd get enough current that way to kill him, although the water must have been a perfect ground. I've seen people —a kid, once, who took maybe twenty thousand volts grabbing a kite from a live wire, and he lived to tell the tale. And another guy, taking a bath—"

"But it's *true!*" Linda said again, her voice rising dangerously.

"Okay, okay, so it's true," he agreed, in the soothing tone he probably used to reassure injured children or potential suicides teetering on ledges. "You got the smell right at least. It's the cannibal's dinner. Now why don't you lie back and relax a little." And his hands and mouth worked over her with the expertise of a rescue team.

But it really was true. Nothing anyone said could

HEARTS

make her doubt the stubborn memory she had of those events. The emergency crews showed up that day, sirens going like crazy: policemen, firemen, all the king's horses and men. By the time they got there it was over. His glow had darkened, like the furnace, and he was ordinary and harmless, a dead man deprived of influence, of venom, of everything.

She was still alive, her hands wildly gripping the tire treads. They had to pry them loose a finger at a time, and carry her like a drowned maiden up the wooden stairs and then to the second floor. The house swelled with neighbors and strangers, and Mr. Botts careened among them in his bathrobe. A policeman had his arm around the weeping old woman, trying vainly to comfort her.

Linda was placed in the center of her parents' bed. Her shoes and socks were removed, and someone rubbed her feet, which were even bluer than those of Jesus on the Lutheran Church calendar. Someone else tried to feed her golden, burning whiskey. She wailed, she screamed with previously untested operatic strength—"*Oh, no, oh, please!*"—and her mother, summoned away from the newest baby by Linda's need, materialized at bedside. Linda, in a sudden revival of piety and infancy, took her rightful place against her mother's breast, intoning, "Please, God, please." With the shocked outrage of the pious, she also heard an internal voice that said, "Thank you, thank you. Thine is the kingdom and the glory. Thank you, forever and always, amen."

LINDA RAN HER HANDS ONE MORE TIME under the beds in their room at Buddy's Siesta, searching for a possible stray sock or two. There was nothing there, though, except for the usual dust collection, and the paper band from a former tenant's cigar. *Te-Amo*, it said. She put the band on her wedding finger and pushed herself up again. Bending like this made her red-faced and dizzy. I need exercise, she thought. When I get to California, I'll swim and I'll jog. I'll jog along the beach, maybe. It would be her initiation into the real America. "Okay," she told Robin. "That's it. Let's hit the road."

When she looked up, Robin was slouched in the green armchair near the window, eating potato chips from a crackling bag. It was only seven o'clock in the morning. They'd shared an orange and intended to stop for a regular breakfast in an hour or two. And now Robin was inhaling junk food again.

Linda hesitated. She had decided, she had *promised* herself she wouldn't nag during this last segment of their trip. Things were easier between them. It would be possible to part soon with some feeling of friendship. She imagined them shaking hands warmly, perhaps even embracing, the way Begin and Sadat had done at the airport after the Mideast Peace Treaty was signed. In her mind, Miriam appeared, too, a blurred but benevolent background figure, like Rosalynn Carter.

But the potato chips looked so greasy; Robin's fingers glistened as she pushed them into her mouth. And she chewed with such noisy pleasure. Hadn't Wright bothered to teach the girl simple good manners? "You eat a lot of unhealthy snack food," Linda commented finally.

HEARTS

She couldn't help herself; the words flew out. "Sweets and stuff fried in rancid fat."

"Who cares?" Robin said, and licked salt from her fingers, one by one.

"*I* care," Linda said, wondering if she really did, or had only fallen into the habit of conflict. "I want to deliver you to your mother in the best of health. All these chips and cheese things and candy bars are terrible for you. Your teeth will rot in your mouth before you're sweet sixteen."

As a matter of fact, there was practically no silver in Robin's mouth. She had nearly perfect teeth, a lucky genetic handout, no doubt. Now she bared them to demonstrate. Golden flakes were wedged between them and Linda was revolted. "Mo cabities," Robin managed to say, still munching, and pointing inside.

Linda, who suffered fleeting toothaches on contact with any food that was either hot or cold, sweet or spicy, suspected that *she* had plenty of cavities. "You'll get fat, then," she said.

In answer, Robin smiled and held the loose waistband of her jeans away from her slender waist with the hook of one thumb. She hadn't lost any weight, certainly, not with her diet, but she must have grown a little since they'd started out, which gave the same favorable effect. She looked at Linda with that calculated stare and said, "If anybody's getting fat, it's *you*."

Linda had picked up her suitcase during this exchange and was ready to leave the room. As Robin spoke, she glanced behind her and saw her own reflection in the bureau mirror. It wasn't the best mirror in the world. When she stood directly in front of it, her forehead wavered and melted into her hairline. But there were no real distortions below that. And Linda did look fatter. Fatter than what? Fatter than *when?*

The waistband on her canvas skirt was made of soft elastic, so it offered no clue to possible change. She had two skirts in the same pattern, this dark red one and a navy blue, and she wore them frequently because they didn't show stains much and were comfortable for driving. The jeans she'd tried on yesterday had obviously shrunk in the last laundromat, and she had been thinking of offering them to Robin, and was trying to find an acceptable way of doing so.

"Why don't you put our stuff in the car, Robin," she said, holding out her suitcase and the keys. "I want to check the room one more time, in case we left anything."

"You did that already," Robin complained, and upended the bag of chips to shake the last crumbs into her open mouth. Linda marveled that anyone ever comes through childhood and adolescence still loved by anyone else. She almost shoved Robin through the door.

As soon as she was alone, Linda put the chain lock on and began pulling off her clothes. She threw them across the unmade beds. Breathing heavily, she faced the mirror again, that new accuser. She knew immediately that this was not her previously known self. This sleek fullness, this rosy roundness were surely new. She looked like a bowl of fruit.

"Oh, no," she whispered. She went closer to the mirror, dissolving her forehead until she became a Neanderthal.

Robin was waiting impatiently in the front seat, her bare feet on the padded steering wheel, her head hanging out the opposite window for air. All she could get on the radio was Country and Western, nothing good. She contemplated driving around the parking lot a few times to work up a breeze. Using the heel of one foot, she beeped the horn twice. What was Linda doing in there? Did she suspect something? Robin checked her treasures—the wrapped fork, the untouched joint, and the tiny roach, all still safely hidden—and felt better. She wished she had remembered to bring a roach clip, though. It was going to be hard to hold on to that little thing and get a decent toke. She'd have to look through Linda's junk and see if she had a pair of tweezers.

When Linda appeared at last, Robin said, "Hurry up, it's like a furnace in here."

Linda opened the door without answering. She looked very strange, very intense. "Move over," she said brusquely, and climbed in before Robin could actually do so.

"Ouch!" Robin yelled. "You sat on my foot!" What was she so mad about now? Just because Robin said she was fat? She didn't even get like this when Robin called her an asshole back in the Hidden River Motel.

It was like being in a getaway car, the squealing of brakes and everything. Robin, intimidated by their traveling speed, and by the new hardness of Linda's profile, groped for the ends of her seat belt and fastened them, something she hardly ever did. She looked at the speedometer and whistled weakly. For the first time, Linda was exceeding the speed limit. She was only doing about 70—Ray used to go way over that—but it felt like 100 after all those days at her usual creepy pace. Robin was thrilled and scared. She looked behind them frequently, wondering if a police car would appear, siren howling, if they would be involved in one of those chases they always have in the movies. Linda gripped the wheel as if she were going to throttle some sense into it. She passed other cars, slipping from lane to lane with nervy maneuvers. Robin saw startled faces at their windows as the Maverick picked up speed. Horns blared and faded in an instant. The Doppler effect, Wolfie had called that. Trees whizzed past, signs.

Linda kept it up for five or ten minutes. Then gradually she began to slow down. She moved to the right lane again. Other cars passed them. Their car hardly seemed to be moving at all.

The checkered seat-cover pattern was embossed deeply on Robin's palms, and she rubbed them together, trying to eradicate it. Whatever had possessed Linda was gone. Robin heard her groan once, softly, and knew intuitively not to ask any questions. She sure was weird.

Robin looked through the window and began to observe the landscape, now that it had stopped flashing by so fast. She read the road signs: *Rest Area 3 Miles Gas Food Comfort. Towanda Next Right*. There were hitchhikers at their posts and Robin waved to them, with small furtive flutters of her hand that Linda couldn't see. One of them waved back. It was Wolfie.

Robin shouted, "There's Wolfie! Stop, oh, stop!" and Linda said, "Robin, you can't keep doing that. I'm not *stupid*, you know."

Robin bounced in her seat, protesting. "But it *was* him. This time it really *was* him. Linda, I swear!" Linda kept driving and Robin leaned out the window, precari-

HEARTS

ously, her hips through the frame. "Hey, Wolfie!" she yelled. "Hey, it's us!"

Linda pumped the brakes and veered onto the shoulder while she gripped the back of Robin's shirt with one hand. "Are you crazy, Robin? Do you want to fall out and break your head? Don't you know the story of the boy who cried wolf . . . ?" Her voice trailed off when she recognized the unfortunate play on words, and then she looked through the rearview mirror and saw a small figure running desperately toward them, churning up a duststorm as he ran. It can't be, she told herself, and would not turn around, but kept watching in the mirror as the tiny figure grew and grew, becoming life-size. Watching the square tip of the backpack come into focus, and the khaki T-shirt, and the beard, and the sun dancing on something silver around his neck.

He was gasping when he came alongside the car and skidded to a stop in a billow of dust. He stood for a few moments, hands on hips, his chest working, and stared back at them. Then he opened the back door and threw his pack in, as casual as a commuter husband just off the 6:15. Robin, without being asked, climbed into the backseat, relinquishing her place to him.

"What took you so long?" he asked Linda as he got in beside her.

THEY HAD DINNER IN A SMALL CHINESE **26** restaurant in Guthrie, Oklahoma, called Ah Mee, where packaged rye bread and ketchup were served along with the duck sauce and hot mustard. When the waitress, a large Caucasian woman in a red dress, came to bring the menus, Wolfie asked her what she would recommend. "Not this place," she said darkly, and walked away. The mimeographed menus were stained and blurred, and the prices were suspiciously low. "I think we've fallen into a time warp," Wolfie said. "Look, isn't that Rod Serling over there?"

Robin actually spun around to look, and when she saw a bald man sucking on a sparerib at the next table, she only smiled at Wolfie, gently reproving.

"Do you want to leave, try some other place?" Wolfie asked Linda, who shook her head. She had been lost in reverie for a while, wondering if anyone there had perceived them as a kind of family. The place didn't matter. And it was too late, anyway. She'd already spread her paper napkin in her lap. They had been drinking the water, and Robin was eating the dry soup noodles, dipped in ketchup.

How decent that kid's behavior was now. Linda felt an urge to strangle her for such duplicity. At the same time she was pleased with the prospect of a pleasant meal, one in which the burden of conversation would not fall wholly on her.

The food was awful. They'd ordered chicken chow mein and it was an almost meatless mélange of limp onions and celery in a bland, watery sauce. Robin would certainly have made a first-class fuss if Wolfie hadn't been there. She would have said, accurately, that the chow mein had the consistency of worms in the rain. She would have discovered a long, dark hair in her soup and dangled it for Linda's benefit before disposing of it in the ashtray. But now she even attempted to eat with chopsticks, under Wolfie's patient instruction, and laughed—that unexpected exotic sound!—when food slipped past her open mouth and landed, slithering, in her lap.

Linda was like a parent who wishes it was her child's bedtime, who, if pressed, would confess she wishes she'd never had children in the first place. She willed Robin to be asleep, absent, anywhere but in this place where she now wanted to speak privately to Wolfie.

They'd driven for hours, taking equal turns at the wheel, and Robin had not once fallen into her customary doze. The first time that Linda did not long for her meager and grudging company, she was right there every minute, leaning forward so that her chin rested companionably on the back ledge of the driver's seat. She asked Wolfie reasonable questions about where he'd been since they had last seen him, questions Linda had intended to ask, herself, later. He said that the van in which he'd picked up a ride when he left them had broken down almost immediately. There were no more long-distance lifts in the offing, so Wolfie decided to visit some old friends, another silversmith and his wife, in western Ohio, and then a group of men and women who'd started a cooperative truck farm in Illinois. Seduced by good company, nostalgia, and the beauty of the countryside, he had stayed longer than he meant to. That's why he'd gotten only this far in all that time.

Silently, Linda blessed the disabled van, and those

unnamed friends for their delaying hospitality and goodness.

"How was Iowa and Grandpa's farm?" Wolfie asked.

Linda tried to warn him by shaking her head and
making faces as she drove, but Robin coolly answered
that it was all right. Then she told him about their
experience at the Hidden River Caverns, with an ironic
and witty style that amazed Linda. She even did a clever
imitation of the guide who'd led them underground.
Who asked *her* to get so charming?

"You married yet?" Robin had said to Wolfie as soon
as Linda had recovered from his presence in the car that
morning.

"Nope," he said. "How about you?"

Linda pretended he meant her—who knows? he
might have—and said, "I'm not, either," before Robin
could speak.

After dinner they opened their fortune cookies.
Linda's had one of those pseudo-Confucian sayings
about wisdom and laughter that she always got, and that
reinforced her doubts about a future worth predicting.
Robin's said, "A happy and romantic evening in store for
you." Wolfie read his aloud. "You will recover quickly
from ptomaine poisoning and will live a long and healthy
life with many beautiful children and—" Robin tried to
grab the little slip of paper from his hand, saying, "Hey,
let me see that," but he held it out of reach and continued, "—and several gerbils and horses and devoted
servants and—" Robin had succeeded in taking the
paper from him and squealed, "Oh, you dirty lying rat!"
obviously enchanted by his teasing.

It was a balmy evening. They walked in the small

HEARTS

shopping center that held the restaurant and looked into the windows of closed shops at clothing and hardware and furniture. Linda had reduced her worldly holdings to the few things in the Maverick's trunk, but she believed then that she did not desire anything but this particular evening and its charitable stillness. It was a false peace, she knew, in which dreadful problems were only suspended for a brief and illusory moment. She had a sudden intuition that there only *were* brief moments of this kind, and that they should be cherished even as their passing is mourned.

Later they looked for a place to spend the night. Wolfie said he would splurge on a room, too, if it wasn't too grand, and if they wouldn't mind his company again the next day.

They found a motel called Lincoln's Log Cabins a few miles from the restaurant. The logs were only a thin façade, and except for the motel office, there weren't any separate cabins—only one long building with twelve numbered doors.

"This gives me a weird feeling," Wolfie said. "When I was a kid, my favorite toy was a set of Lincoln Logs. I used to build cabins and forts that looked something like this. I'd put my soldiers inside and they'd shoot each other dead from the windows and doorways."

Linda was delighted to have this small bit of boyhood news. "I thought you were a pacifist," she said.

"Not in those days," Wolfie told her. "No kids really are, I think. Their little hearts are full of murder until they realize they're mortal, too. Oh, man, that's a terrible shock."

Lincoln's Log Cabins had some of the usual failings of motels in its class: dangerous proximity to a major highway, so that you had to dream of traffic noises to protect your sleep, and those soft mattresses into which you sank like so much boneless flesh.

It had an extra added attraction, a miniature golf course, just behind and adjacent to the rooms. At Robin's urging, they went to look at it. A Lincoln motif had been used, so that each of the nine holes represented another fact or accomplishment in the life of the sixteenth President. Hole number 1, for instance, was a tiny birthplace cabin, probably similar to the ones Wolfie had built as a child. The golf ball could be putted directly through its two parallel doorways and into the hole. Hole number 5 was protected by crossed rifles topped by military hats, one for the Union, one for the Confederacy. Number 9 was a replica of Ford's Theater, complete with a little marquee announcing a showing of *Our American Cousin*. The hole was inside the structure, a small hidden grave through which the ball would sink, and then travel down a pipe tunnel that ended in the motel office. They probably didn't lose too many balls that way. The whole place was lighted like a used-car lot and was that startling painted green of frozen peas. "Jesus," Wolfie said softly. "America. Love it or leave it."

There were a few players, like actors under the lights. Of course, Robin wanted to play, too. "Please?" she said, still aiming to be congenial. "One tiny little game?"

Linda was exhausted and she had not had a minute alone with Wolfie. She was afraid she would not be able to stay awake long enough to tell him anything. But she was also afraid to unleash the real Robin by not letting her have her way.

"Tomorrow, first thing in the morning," Wolfie said.

H E A R T S

"I'll challenge you to the first annual John Wilkes Booth Open. Okay? Now we've got to hit the sack."

Robin gave in easily. She was probably growing tired, too, at last.

They were given rooms next door to each other, and stood for an awkward moment examining their keys. Linda felt lonely and hopeful, erotic and sleepy.

Robin was losing the tenuous control of her new, pleasant personality. When Linda opened the door to number 8, Robin said, "It's so *small*. I want the bed near the window. Why are these places always green?"

Linda and Wolfie exchanged smiles as she shut the door to her room and Robin's. She wondered if she was supposed to say something, to give a signal of some kind that she was not finished with him or with the evening.

While Robin was using the bathroom, Linda could hear Wolfie moving around next door in number 9. She pressed her ear to the wall and listened hard. A drawer opened and closed. She thought she heard the thump of a dropped shoe and the twang of bedsprings accepting weight. "Don't go to sleep yet," she whispered. "Wait. Please wait."

"Who are you talking to?" Robin asked. She was wearing pink shortie pajamas and carrying her discarded clothing in a crushed heap. A sock wafted to the floor as she crossed the room. Linda retrieved it and put it on top of the pile in Robin's arms as Robin let it all fall and scatter between the beds. "*Who?*" she insisted.

"Nobody," Linda said. "I'm just thinking out loud."

"You can't think out loud," Robin told her. "There's no such thing. If it's out loud, it's talking. If it's thinking, it's inside your head and it's quiet. Otherwise, they wouldn't have two different words for it, would they?"

"Oh, be still," Linda said, and miraculously, she soon was. Oh, faithful and glorious sleep.

Linda took off her own clothes and folded them neatly across the chair. She did not have the courage to look in the mirror again. Instead, she showered quickly and put on her favorite nightgown, the white cotton one with chains of embroidered violets as straps.

She pulled back the covers on the other bed and climbed into it. The traffic moved steadily and an abbreviated cheer came from the miniature golf course. A hole in one at Gettysburg, maybe. But there was no sound from the room next door.

Linda was oppressed by all her contained secrets. She had looked forward so much to being alone with Wolfie, and yet she hardly knew him, and had no reasonable claim on his attention. It wasn't fair for her to expect an urgent response to her own urgency on such short acquaintance.

She told herself it was only because he was another adult, after all this claustrophobic time with Robin, that he was merely someone she could tell things to who would not judge her, who would not whine or shrug or argue. There was no reason in the world why she couldn't just get up now while it was still early and knock on his door and say casually that she felt like talking—did he?

Except that he might give her the same gentle brush-off he'd given Robin. See you first thing in the morning, kid. We'll have a nice little talk at breakfast, okay? And she couldn't bear that, not the disappointment or the humiliation. So she lay there until she gave in to the heaviness that was drawing her eyelids down.

She didn't sleep long. It was the kind of doze you fall into on buses and trains, from which you can always wake yourself in time for your stop. She had dreamed knocking and knew quickly that it *had* been a dream. Still, she listened for a moment to be sure. Then she rose from the bed and put on her robe. Robin was sprawled in sleep, looking as if she'd been mugged.

Linda opened the door with infinite care, and stepped outside. The Maverick was parked right in front of their room. For a moment she indulged in the childhood fantasy that allowed nocturnal life to inanimate objects. She felt affection for the car, and gratitude for having been taken this far in safety on her journey. She imagined a giant map of the United States, and the yellow state of Oklahoma as a vast moonlit area on which she and the Maverick stood absolutely alone.

Then she heard the other door open, and Wolfie, still in the clothes he'd worn all day, came outside, too.

"I couldn't sleep," Linda said, positive as she said it that it was a line from a famous movie, one that everyone else has heard and would instantly recognize.

Wolfie only said, "I know. Me, too." He had a drink in his hand.

Linda shivered with nervousness and tried to remember the way she had spoken to men on the job at Fred Astaire's. What had she ever said to all those strangers in whose damp embrace she'd moved so easily across the dance floor? What does anyone ever say?

"Cold?" Wolfie asked, and when she nodded, teeth chattering, he opened his door and she went inside. She sat down in the chair near the window and Wolfie sat on the edge of his bed. He looked at her without speaking and Linda glanced away and said, "You have a very nice room." It was exactly like hers, dismal and tiny.

Wolfie smiled, relentlessly engaging her eyes.

"So," Linda said. "What are you going to do? Love it or leave it?"

"What? Oh, love it, I guess. The way you love Robin. Hoping all the time it will change."

Did she love Robin?

"As soon as I crossed the border, I felt friendly toward the country again," Wolfie said. "Once, in Montreal, a Yugoslavian poet showed up to visit a guy I knew. He'd been a really well-known poet in Europe and then I guess he got too political. First there was a little censorship, and then they started shoving him around, and his books disappeared from the stores, from the libraries. He was even arrested, and they only released him because some bigwig American poets started making noises. Yet he was going back. We couldn't believe it. But he laughed. He said, 'Well, you know, I *live* there. It's my country.'"

And what about your woman, the one you were so happy with up there? Linda wanted to ask, but didn't.

"Now," Wolfie said. "Tell me about you."

Linda began her story. She told him about Wright, their first meeting, the marriage, his death. She realized that she now remembered Wright longer than she had known him.

Wolfie listened with an intensity that matched her telling, and he passed the glass to her. It was a sweetish wine, but as she drank from it, she felt like an obedient child taking medicine at bedtime because she has faith that it will make her well.

She told him about Robin, about the small, ongoing war that was their relationship, about finding her grand-

HEARTS

father's address and the private detective's report, and how they had been received in Iowa, and had fled. As she spoke, she thought about the pregnancy, and the abortion-clinic bombing, and her recent rediscovery, in their chronological sequence. Without fully understanding why, she withheld all of that from him. By the time she got to her plans to look for Robin's mother in Glendale and go on to California alone, they had passed the glass back and forth several times, and Linda had stopped shivering.

"You've had a very rough time, haven't you?" Wolfie said.

"It feels better, just talking about it," Linda told him. "Thank you for listening."

"I like listening to you," Wolfie said. "You have such a sweet voice, Linda. It's like being read to."

"You do? It is? I always worry. Robin says I'm not, you know . . . spontaneous. Maybe the wine helped. I feel kind of . . . light."

"It's a nice feeling, isn't it?"

"Yes. Do you know, before? I did sleep a little and I dreamed you knocked on my door." Linda was dazzled by her own boldness and poise.

Then Wolfie stood up and she felt a rush of despair. Was he going to dismiss her now? Maybe she had gone too far, had been *too* spontaneous.

She stood up, too, trying to look as if it had been her idea as well to call it a night. She even managed a queer little yawn. "Well!" she exclaimed, leaving herself breathless.

"I wanted to knock," Wolfie said slowly, and Linda started trembling again. It's only the wine, she thought, or the fatigue. Or longing. Or lust.

"But I couldn't take that chance," he continued. "Miss Teenage America might have been waiting right behind the door with her putting iron. Instead of you." He unstrapped his watch and laid it on the table next to one of the beds.

"Oh, no," Linda said, and she had to lean against the wall. "She's a very good sleeper. Her father was like th . . ."

Wolfie turned back the covers on the bed.

So this was it, the excitement before touching that was better than any touching she had known so far. "I mean she could sleep through anything, once she's out. Through an earthquake, even."

He came toward her across the room and there was a splendid spasm in her chest and belly. "Oh, babe. Oh, babe, come on," he said. His voice was gruffly, gravely sweet.

"And other natural disasters," Linda whispered, going into his arms. They reached the bed and lay down on it still in the violence of that first embrace, still clothed. The struggle to release themselves from their clothing was like some mad competition in which they had to do so without ever letting go of one another. At last they were victors, skin to burning skin, and when he entered her she became a vessel, a room, a house!—in which all the lights came on at once.

They slept, woke, talked, and made love again, a few times. *Five* times, to be exact. Why should she deny she kept this exultant mental record? She remembered a woman she'd known who carried around a written diary of all her sexual statistics: duration of orgasm, partner's birthstone, color of sheets, time of day, phase of moon.

When they were awake, she lay with her ear to

HEARTS

Wolfie's chest, and listened to the impressive drumbeat of his heart. When he fell asleep before her, she was forlorn, and when they woke and moved together again, she was rowdy with happiness.

Someone had once told Linda that there are still primitive cultures in which the men assure their pregnant women that lovemaking is what nourishes the fetus. Oh, that's what they *all* say, she thought, realizing immediately that she had made a spontaneous, if silent, joke. She laughed out loud and Wolfie said, sleepily, "Hey, what's so funny?"

"Me," Linda answered. She acknowledged, not without wonder, that it was possible to be articulate with passion. It was as if she had finally been released from some long and terrible enchantment.

Just before dawn she said she'd better get back to her room before Robin woke up. Wolfie staggered into his jeans while Linda watched from the nest of blankets and pillows. "I'll walk you home, babe," he said, and they went lockstepped to her door.

They lingered there, draped against one another, kissing, kissing. It was like a prelude to the evening rather than its conclusion. "I have to go," Linda whispered, without real conviction. "Good night." "Good night," Wolfie answered, and then they kissed some more before they let their arms drop, their bodies fall away.

Wolfie went to his door. "Good night," he called again.

"Good night," Linda said, and went inside. As advertised, Robin had slept through everything. Linda covered her and then collapsed into bed. She had decided not to sleep, though, not to allow this to become one of those transient ecstatic moments she'd thought about earlier, in the shopping center. If she reviewed and re-played what had happened as if it were a filmed histor-ical event, she could prevent its untimely passing.

The physical memory was easy; her body still hoarded every nuance of touch. She tried to remember some of the things they had said to each other. He had been concerned at the last minute about birth control, and asked, "Is it all right?" Linda had said, "Oh, yes, it's fine, it's wonderful," her answer layered with meaning. The word "love" had come up, but only in the worshipful naming of parts, of acts. During one period of rest there had been a short exchange of history. His father was dead; his mother now lived in Oregon. What was it he'd said? You'd like my mother? *You'll* like my mother? Something. And hadn't he rerouted her trip himself, and then shown up on that very route? The effort at recollec-tion was making her drowsy against her will. But it didn't matter. She had kept the resonance of experience, if not every detail, and could afford to rest her guard now and sleep.

When she woke, she was alone in the room. The pink shortie pajamas were on the floor between the beds. From the bathroom window she looked out onto the miniature golf course. Robin and Wolfie were just teeing off.

HEARTS

ROBIN DIDN'T MAKE A HOLE-IN-ONE, BUT
she beat Wolfie by two points, anyway. That
was close enough to make his loss legitimate,
and she didn't suspect him of throwing the game, the
way her father always did. It took her years to figure it
out, to understand why she consistently won, no matter
what they played (miniature golf, Go Fish, Ghost, Mo-
nopoly), why her pile of play money seemed to increase
mysteriously whenever she went to the bathroom. He
must have dealt himself *bad* cards from the bottom of
the deck, must have kept Boardwalk and Park Place as
undeveloped property on purpose. She guessed now that
he'd probably done those things to help build up her
self-confidence, to make the small areas of her life within
his control pleasant and even victorious. But she felt
cheated by the deception and knew that because of it
she had never learned to be a cheerful loser.

When she made the fifth hole in two under par,
Wolfie whistled appreciatively. "Did you stay up all
night to practice?" he asked. But he was the one who
kept yawning.

It was a beautiful day; some of the cool night air still
lingered, and there was real dew on the artificial grass
at their feet. Robin thought it was especially nice to
have Wolfie all to herself for once. Maybe after she was
completely on her own she would get in touch with him.
Maybe the two of them could travel somewhere together, taking turns driving, the way he did with Linda.
If Linda didn't screw everything up first by acting so
wimpy he'd never want to see either of them again. As if
on cue, she appeared in the doorway of their room, waving and smiling, as Robin and Wolfie walked back from
the golf course.

They drove slowly on side roads, stopping from time to time to examine something more closely, a cluster of wildflowers or a herd of cows. Robin wouldn't admit this to anyone, but she was actually afraid of cows. Seen close up, with only a few strands of wire separating her from them, they were enormous, and truly exotic, with their cartoon eyes and shivering flesh. Those udders, as pink and stretched as bubble gum, seemed like remarkable sexual baggage, and she glanced around nervously, wondering if there were any bulls in the neighborhood, too. Robin had always been afraid of animals, but it was a fear she had been able to dismiss or disguise pretty easily in Newark, except for an occasional encounter with a stray dog. Now she tried to appear casual, even indifferent. She stood back from the barbed wire with her hands in her pockets. "Moo, yourself," she said.

When they'd first stepped out of the car at the edge of the meadow, Linda brushed away the flies that dive-bombed them, then inhaled deeply. "Smell this air!" she shouted. "Will you tell me why people live in crowded, polluted cities when there's all this glorious air to breathe?"

It was another one of those million dumb questions she was always asking that didn't require an answer. When Robin looked at Wolfie, he winked at her, and she felt the thrill of collusion.

But soon he and Linda were off to one side, sitting in the sparse grass, and whispering together the way Ginger and Ray sometimes did, shutting Robin out. Wolfie and Linda were pulling up pieces of grass and tossing them at each other. They acted as dumb as the dumb cows, who stared mindlessly while they chewed and made deep lowing sounds in their throats. Robin

HEARTS

felt she had been rudely excluded from all levels of society. "Are we going to hang around here all day?" she demanded.

Linda looked up as if she was startled to see Robin there, and then she stood, brushing the grass from her skirt, pulling a whole handful of it from the neck of her blouse. Wolfie made her stand still while he picked a few more blades from her hair. Well, at least Linda wasn't bugging him yet.

They drove a few miles to a general store, like the one on *The Waltons*. It was jam-packed with every kind of item: food, tools, cigarettes, magazines, patent medicines, and even a few articles of clothing. Linda tried on a couple of sun hats, bending to look at her skewed reflection in a giant-sized cracker tin. Dolly Parton was singing "Here You Come Again" on a radio behind the counter and a man wearing a cowboy hat and a string tie waited on them. Wolfie said he was starving, and they bought bread and cheese and peanut butter and ham and fruit and beer. As they were paying for everything, there was a booming sound nearby, and Linda jumped.

"What was that, a gun?" Robin asked.

"Don't you know what today is?" Wolfie said. "It's the Fourth of July. Somebody's just celebrating early in the day, that's all." He asked the man in the cowboy hat if he had any fireworks for sale, and added half a dozen sparklers to their package.

They took their picnic to a wooded spot near a stream. As soon as they parked, two huge dogs came bounding out from somewhere, barking furiously and circling the car. Robin quickly rolled up her window and shut her eyes. She felt herself grow rigid, the way she used to when her father would drag some reluctant dog up to her and say, "Look, he *likes* you, he wants to make friends. He wants to lick your hand, Bobolink. Daddy wouldn't let him hurt you. Feel how soft his fur is."

Now she heard the car doors slam and Wolfie said, "Hello, boys. You the welcoming committee?" And Linda cooed, "Good doggies. You're so glad to see us, aren't you? Aren't you?"

Robin was almost afraid to look, but when she did, she saw Linda and Wolfie heading in the direction of the stream, carrying their supplies and a blanket, and the two dogs walking courteously behind them, their heads down. Linda stopped to pet one of them, and she looked like what's-his-name, that saint in Robin's old Bible picture book, who was always hanging around with animals, and had birds and squirrels sitting on his shoulders and on top of his head.

Robin opened her door and stepped out, too. Immediately the dogs turned and approached her. She stood completely still while they sniffed around her legs, their tags jangling and their tails churning. She was faint with terror and yet she had a mad impulse to touch their large silvery heads. But she listened to their frantic panting, observed the fangs set into the dark jagged gums, and dismissed the impulse. Her ankles glistened with saliva. How was she ever going to get past them?

"You okay, Robin?" Linda called.

"Sure," she said, hoarsely.

"Well, then come on!" Wolfie yelled.

The dogs must have thought he meant them, because they leaped away toward Wolfie, and then past him, into the woods, liberating Robin.

Linda had spread the blanket in a cleared space and

HEARTS

she and Wolfie laid out the food. They all ate piggishly, as if they were breaking a long fast. Over Linda's protests, Wolfie let Robin sip some of his beer. "I'm only giving her a little," he said. "It's a holiday. And nobody's going to card her out here."

The beer was deliciously cold and a little bitter, but it tasted nicer than gin. She took a deep swig, then another, and Wolfie said, "Hey!" and took the can back. Robin wanted to light the sparklers, but he said they had to wait until dark.

After lunch they lay three abreast on the blanket to take a nap. Robin kept sitting up, thinking she'd heard something, the dogs returning maybe, or other animals, but finally she lay back and slept, too.

Later they got onto a major highway and drove steadily until sundown. The towers of oil wells were black against the rosy sky. They stopped at a motel called The Western Star, and took the last two available rooms, at opposite ends of the place.

When it was dark, Robin reminded Wolfie about the sparklers. He brought them from the car and gave one to each of them. A little boy, barefoot and wearing pajamas, came to the door of his room and watched them with shy interest. Wolfie handed him a sparkler, too, and then he set a match to all of them. They hissed and flared, illuminating each face in turn. Linda said, "Ooooh!" and held hers solemnly at arm's length. Robin ran around the parking lot, waving hers over her head, so that brief sparks rained down and disappeared in her hair.

Someone took the little boy back inside his room. Wolfie and Robin lit the two remaining sparklers, joining them for maximum effect, and after those went out they heard the boom! boom! of fireworks somewhere else, and then the answering yelps of dogs at a safe distance.

H E A R T S

WITH WOLFIE DRIVING AGAIN, THEY WOULD **28**
probably reach Albuquerque by late morning,
one day before his friend's wedding. That was
where she and Robin would leave him before going on
to Glendale. Linda tried frantically not to think ahead
to their separation. Riding next to him in the flying
landscape, she distracted herself with silly and secret
games. Predicted red cars or white ones. While they
were still in farm and ranch country, she made God-
bargains that would change the inevitable outcome of
events if a barn would appear next instead of a silo.
Realizing that barns usually outnumbered silos, and
that she wasn't sure she believed in God.

The changes in the landscape were gradual and then
dramatic. The vegetation in New Mexico was sparser
than it had been a little further east, in Texas. And what
did grow was tougher-looking, spiky and aggressive, de-
fiant of the dry, penetrating heat. Linda pulled down
the sun visor and looked at herself in the little mirror
to see if she, too, was toughening to accommodate the
altering climate of her life.

Last night she had gone again, shy and audacious,
to his room. As they began to make love, she fleetingly
considered the risks. They were awesome, but that didn't
stop her, or make her cautiously decline in ardor or in
daring. "I love you!" she cried once, regretful to be first
in declaration, and maybe last as well.

"Ah," Wolfie said. "You don't even know me. This
is only my good side." Afterward he added, "*You* bring
out the good in me. It's your special gift, I think. I'm a
moody guy sometimes, Linda. And a little selfish."

She would not abandon him to the isolation of guilt.
"Oh, me, too!" she said. "Who isn't?"

No one had spoken for several miles. As he drove, Wolfie would remove one hand from the wheel, absently it seemed, and touch it to some part of Linda that was out of Robin's sight. Earlier, when Linda drove, she was so conscious of his closeness that her steering regressed. Horns bawled, larger cars bullied her into line. "What's everyone's hurry?" Linda asked. "Where are they all going?"

Wolfie said, "Listen, you must be tired, babe. Let me drive for a while." He paid for the gas when they stopped.

Robin, contributing to the silence, had apparently given up both her roles. She was neither difficult adolescent nor transformed charmer. Linda believed that Robin's quietude was like her own, was contemplative and sad.

After a sign indicating they were only fifty miles from Albuquerque, Wolfie said he had an idea. How would they like to go to his friend's wedding with him?

"*I* would," Robin said immediately. "I never went to a wedding."

Linda was astounded. "Why, Robin Reismann," she said. "How can you say that? You went to mine!"

Robin blinked and tossed her hair back and Linda didn't pursue the argument. What was the use? It was more of Robin's magical thinking at work. Without her approval or consent, Wright and Linda's wedding had never taken place. Even the groom, that staple of wedding evidence, was gone. She certainly managed to work up enthusiasm for the union of two complete strangers. And what had happened to her imperative need to get to her mother's?

"So, can we?" Robin persisted.

HEARTS

Linda didn't answer right away. She knew she had been indulging her own magical thinking. Because she had not acknowledged her pregnancy to Wolfie, she was able to put it aside for a few days. The logistics were fine. Dr. Lamb had said abortions were legal and safe until the twenty-fourth week. She had time. Except that the changes in her body continued with the dogged obstinancy of nature. She was blooming, or was her notice of it exaggerated? Wolfie hadn't remarked on it. Robin didn't either, not since the time in Buddy's Siesta when she said that Linda was getting fat. And she was probably inspired then by defensiveness and malice.

If Linda went with Wolfie now, it would only be a delaying tactic against the certainty of leaving him later. But so what? Wasn't living only a delaying tactic against death? Look what's happening, she marveled. Jokes! Philosophy!

"Well, *can* we?" Robin's voice had reached that treacherous pitch.

"Yes," Linda said. "I guess so. I mean, if you think it will be all right with your friend, Wolfie. He doesn't even know us."

"*She,*" Wolfie said. "And it will definitely be all right. It's not going to be a formal wedding. She's not even sure I'm going to show up. And any friends of mine . . ." He curled the fingers of his right hand around her unprepared left one, and Linda celebrated her decision.

Who did they think they were fooling? Did they suppose she was an idiot or a baby? She knew what was going on and she only grudgingly blessed it.

Last night Robin had dreamed of swimming in a

race through a dark, gelatinous fluid, and woke needing to pee. She sat up, disoriented. There had been so many different places, so many rooms. Then she noticed that Linda wasn't there, that her bed was empty and the pillow had slipped to the floor.

They had gone to bed at the same time. She remembered that Linda kept yawning, and she'd said, "I'm *so* tired, Robin, aren't you?" It wasn't that late yet. "Wolfie says we have to travel early in the desert, so we'd better get to sleep early, too. I can hardly keep my eyes open, anyway."

Thinking the bathroom was occupied made Robin's need to use it more urgent. She pressed her lower abdomen and it was tender and full. "Come on," she whispered at the closed bathroom door. "Hurry up." Gradually she became aware of the silence. What was she doing in there *now?*

While she waited, Robin's eyes adjusted to the room's dimness, and she saw that Linda's pocketbook was on the dresser, openmouthed. She tiptoed quickly across the room. There was so much junk inside: keys, a flashlight that was still on, burning faintly, tampons, tweezers, a paperback *Guide to Nature's Playgrounds, U.S.A.,* crushed and lip-printed tissues, a thick envelope stuffed with papers and secured with a red rubber band. Where was her stupid wallet?

It was at the very bottom, under everything else, and it was bulging. Maybe Robin's whole inheritance was in there. When she opened it, she found it was jammed with more papers, notes, scrawled addresses and telephone numbers, photos. One of these was an overexposed Polaroid shot of Linda and Wright and Robin.

HEARTS

Linda was wearing a drooping corsage and a broad-brimmed white hat that almost covered her eyes. She and Wright were smiling directly into the camera, and Robin, with a forkful of spaghetti halfway to her mouth, was scowling at them. How different and strange she looked, so chubby and babyish. A Chinese waiter could be seen in the background, clearing another table. Everyone was as pale as death. The spaghetti sauce was only slightly pink.

On one rumpled piece of paper it said, *Miriam Reismann? Hausner? 1418 Cornelia Street, Glendale, Arizona.* Robin thought she heard a sound from the bathroom and she dropped everything hastily back into the pocketbook and closed the clasp painfully over her fingers. She sucked on them, listening anxiously, and it was quiet. She opened the pocketbook again and looked at her mother's name. It was shocking to see it written out like that in Linda's familiar spastic script. And who was Hausner? Was that *him?* Robin had to pee so badly now that she pressed her thighs together and bit the inside of her mouth. There was hardly any money in the wallet. She counted the soft wrinkled bills and the handful of coins. Thirty-two dollars and sixty-three cents. Linda probably hid the rest of it somewhere else. Maybe she started doing that after Robin warned her about pickpockets, back in Des Moines.

She pulled the papers out of the envelope, breaking the rubber band, but there was no money, just some official-looking documents. A birth certificate from the Hall of Records in Slatesville, Pennsylvania, for Baby Camisko, Female, Feb. 13, 1953. There was a letter from an insurance company about an enclosed check. Robin shook the envelope, but no check fell out. What good would a check do her, anyway? No one would cash it for a kid, without proof.

There was a marriage license with what seemed like stern language in it, considering the occasion. It bound Wright Henry Reismann and Linda Marie Camisko in the eyes of the state of New Jersey, city of Jersey City, county of Hudson. The last paper was Robin's father's death certificate. What did they need something like that for? If you were dead, why did you have to prove it? You just weren't there any more. Robin could not pronounce the typed words after *Cause of Death*, but she believed she understood their code. She took the wedding photo out again. He looked peculiar, an impostor who only resembled her father. The headlights of a passing car scanned the ceiling and walls of the room. Maybe Linda had fainted in there. Maybe she had died. There were lots of singles in the wallet. Robin took three of them. It would have to be done like this, a little at a time. She wished she had started earlier.

Holding her legs together, she tottered to the bathroom door and knocked. "Hey," she said, "I have to go in." There was no answer. And the door had opened slightly under the pressure of her knocking. It was dark in there. "Linda?" Robin whispered, with an onset of dread. The bathroom was empty.

Gone! Robin thought, and grew dizzy. A few drops of urine ran down her leg. She sat on the toilet and released the rest of it in a downpour. Would Linda have left her pocketbook and everything? Robin ran to the window and saw that the Maverick was still right there where they'd parked it hours ago. Then she remembered Wolfie.

She went to the wall and pressed her ear against it.

HEARTS

She couldn't hear anything, except for a pounding like surf in her own head. A trick she'd once seen on television occurred to her. A detective had listened to gangsters plotting against him by holding a drinking glass between his ear and the wall. Robin went back to the bathroom and impatiently unwrapped the glass she found. There was nothing coming through the wall but the sound of someone snoring. But it was last night that Wolfie had the room next door. This time he was all the way down, at the far end of the motel. And that's where Linda was. And Robin knew what they were doing. Those assholes.

She borrowed Linda's tweezers to hold the tiny roach, and finished it, sitting on the closed toilet seat. Then she got back into bed, where she forced herself to stay awake, using mind control. It was almost morning when Linda came back. An edge of pink sky could be seen where the green drapes were not fully closed. Robin breathed like a sleeper, in, out, in, out.

Linda opened the door very slowly, with the expert caution of a thief. She was wearing her bathrobe. She walked across the room as if she were in agony, as if she were walking on broken glass or hot tar. Robin watched her through the white haze of her eyelashes and didn't move once. Not even when Linda came close to Robin's bed, looked down at her for a moment, and sighed. Then she got into her own bed, still wearing her bathrobe, still sighing.

THE BRIDE'S NAME WAS ELENA. SHE WAS about Linda's age, and she was gorgeous, with the kind of confident bearing and blond radiance Linda always wished she had.

Elena and the groom, Vincent, lived together in a two-bedroom, Spanish-style apartment near the University of New Mexico. The walls were stuccoed and decorated with many woven hangings.

Vincent was about ten years older than Elena. He was very tall and stooped, and had thin curly hair that he wore long and absentmindedly placed. The weavings were his work, and he used the second, smaller bedroom as his studio. He moved his loom against one wall and partway into a closet so that Wolfie could sleep there. They inflated an air mattress and put it between Wolfie's bedroll and a blanket on the terra-cotta floor. Linda and Robin were going to use a Simmons Hide-a-Bed in the living room.

The wedding would be held in the courtyard of the building complex very early in the morning, before it started to get hot. Elena, who took voice lessons at the university and worked as a waitress in a café, had taken a three-day leave from both places for the occasion. When Linda and Robin met her, she had just come off her last shift and was wearing a pink uniform with a tiny white apron. She changed into a trailing silk kimono that was embroidered with brilliant birds. She was delighted to see Wolfie and held his face in her hands for a long time, and said, "You came. You're really here. I can't believe it." If she was upset by his little entourage, she didn't show it.

Vincent was very emotional. He hugged Wolfie and

kissed him on both cheeks, as if he were a French military hero about to receive a decoration. Then he kissed Linda and Robin, too, crushing them in his embrace. His eyes were wet and he had to blow his nose several times.

Wolfie hadn't seen Elena and Vincent for almost a year, since they had left Montreal. While they all ate lunch, the three friends exchanged information about their own lives and about the lives of other, mutual friends who had married, separated, died, or fallen into industry. Linda didn't feel awkward in her role as outsider. She sipped strong coffee from an oversized mug and listened with the pleasure of an unbiased eavesdropper. Robin seemed content, too. Elena had asked her if she would be a bridal attendant and toss flowers during the ceremony. Linda was positive that Robin would be insulted and turn the offer down flat. Once again, the girl proved unpredictable. "Sure," she said amiably. "What should I wear?"

In the evening, two other out-of-town guests arrived, one at a time. The first was Tanya, an old friend of Vincent's from his undergraduate days at Alfred University's School of Ceramics. Again, Vincent's eyes grew wet and he hugged her so fiercely her glasses slipped to her chest and the frames snapped between them. "Forget it!" she cried gaily when Vincent tried to apologize, and she allowed him to repair them with black electrical tape. A rollaway cot was placed at the foot of the Hide-a-Bed for Tanya.

As everyone was preparing for sleep, the last houseguest showed up. He was Elena's younger brother, who had flown in from Seattle for the wedding. Montie was about sixteen, his body not yet synchronized with the towering promise of his hands and feet.

Vincent walked around for a while holding Montie's head in the curve of his elbow as if it were a football. "Look at this beautiful kid, will you?" Vincent kept saying, growing tearful again. "Will you look at this kid?" Linda thought she noticed a shift in Robin's attention after Montie's appearance.

He announced that he was going to sleep on three chairs in the kitchen. Everyone began to protest at once. Wolfie said that Montie could have the air mattress or the bedroll or both. Linda said she and Robin should give up the Hide-a-Bed, since they were intruders and actually strangers.

Montie thanked everyone and said nothing doing. If he didn't know it would make his sister hysterical, he would sleep directly on the terra-cotta floor. Man wasn't meant to sleep on soft surfaces, because they made his spine soft, too. Most people, he told them, have spines like Jell-O before they're twenty-five from sleeping on mattresses in regular beds. Linda put a casual hand to her own back and touched each hard vertebra she could reach. Montie put the chairs together and allowed Elena to arrange a couple of blankets over them to mask the joining. Poor immigrants, he announced, *had* to sleep this way, and were lucky if they had *two* chairs per person. He lay down across the construction immediately to show everyone how comfortable it was.

It took a long time for the household to settle down. There was the distribution of pillows and towels, the assignment of shifts for the bathroom, and the last-minute need for bedtime snacks. Montie's makeshift bed blocked the refrigerator door, but he was good-natured about getting up so that Tanya could rummage for apples and cheese and pickles before she tucked herself in. Vincent drank milk from a carton, his Adam's apple moving like a conveyor belt. The bride ate a salami sandwich and dripped mustard onto her nightgown. Linda stopped her from dabbing it with a dishcloth dipped in hot water, advising lukewarm instead, mixed with liquid detergent and a little vinegar, something she'd once heard her mother tell Mrs. Piner. When the stain came right out, Elena cried, "Where did you find this wonder?" Wolfie, who had been brushing his teeth at the kitchen sink, gave her a mad, frothing smile.

Linda waited patiently for her turn in the bathroom. As soon as she closed the door behind her, it opened again.

"Shhh," Wolfie warned, slipping quickly in and locking the door. He put his arms around her and kissed her face and neck and then her fingers when she put up her hands to stop him.

"Everyone will wonder what I'm doing in here," she whispered, before she began kissing him back. "Your friends . . . are so . . . nice," she said. "Elena is beautiful . . ."

"*You're* beautiful," he said. "You're delicious, do you know that?"

"You're using up my whole time in here," Linda said, her voice sliding on the last words.

"Linda, I want to be with you tonight."

"Oh, but we can't . . ." Linda told him. "There's Robin and Tanya . . ."

"I didn't have the women's dorm in mind," he said. "Come on over to my place. As usual."

"I don't know if I—" Linda began, and his hands and lips stopped her progress in midsentence. As her knees folded, she groped behind her and flushed the toilet, twice, in case anyone was listening and wondering what was going on.

Someone knocked on the door.

"Who is it?" Linda called, her voice high.

"Oh, are you still in there?" Montie said. "I wasn't sure."

"I'll be right out," she called.

"No, no. Take your time. I don't even have to do anything. Take your time."

When Wolfie left a few minutes later, Linda heard Montie say, "Oh. I thought Linda was in there."

"She is," Wolfie told him. "We were doubling up. You know, man, the water shortage, the energy crisis."

"I didn't mean to rush anybody," Montie said.

Robin and Tanya were both reading in bed. Linda got in on her side of the Hide-a-Bed and lay there in a tremor of anticipation. Tanya was reading a novel and Robin had a newspaper open across her lap. Every few minutes it rattled as she turned a page.

A chain of good nights started in the other end of the apartment. "Good night, kid!" Vincent called to Montie.

"Good night, sucker!" Montie yelled back. "And good night to you, too, Miss Pellegrini, for the last time."

"*Ms.* Pellegrini to you, brat," Elena returned.

"Listen to my horoscope for tomorrow," Robin said. " 'Financial problems eased by nightfall. But martial tensions increase. Be patient. Hold your temper.' "

"Let me see that," Linda said, grabbing the paper. "That's *marital* tensions, Robin, not martial."

H E A R T S

"Same difference, if you ask me," Tanya said. "I've been around twice myself. How about you?"

"Once," Linda answered.

"Splitsville?"

"Dead."

"Oh, really? What are you, Pisces?"

"Uh-uh."

"Sagittarius?"

"No, Aquarius."

"Yeah, that figures."

Linda didn't think it would be polite to mention that she wasn't a believer, and she didn't want to say anything that might promote further conversation.

"I'm Taurus," Robin said, and no one else spoke for a while.

When Linda looked at her again, she saw that Robin had fallen asleep, the newspaper covering her chest. Linda picked it up carefully and let it slide to the floor. "Poor kid's out like a light," she said. "It's really been a long day for all of us. Funny, she usually can't go off like that with the light on in the room."

"You don't mind, do you?" Tanya asked. "I'm one of those crazy night people. I have to read myself to sleep or I'll be up all night. I was probably a nocturnal animal in my last incarnation—like a bat, or an opossum. How about you?"

"Oh, I don't think I was ever here before," Linda said.

"How do you know?" Tanya asked.

"Well, I don't know, really," Linda answered. "It's just that everything seems so new."

Tanya considered this, closing her novel, using her finger as a bookmark. "*Jamais vous déjà vu?*" she asked.

"Pardon?"

"Haven't you ever thought you've had exactly the same experience twice?"

"I don't think so," Linda said. "No, actually I haven't." Worrying that she might seem merely disagreeable, she added, "Maybe I was a very low form of life then, like an insect or a germ, without any memory."

Tanya nodded and went back to her book. After a few minutes she said, "Did you ever think Elena and Vincent were going to make it?"

"I don't really know them," Linda confessed. "Robin and I came here with Wolfie."

"You know him very long?"

"No, not very," she said truthfully, marveling once more at the realization.

Robin had moved in her sleep, hogging the mattress, practically forcing Linda to the opposite edge. A strand of the girl's hair fell across Linda's shoulder and she had a longing to touch it, the way one wants to touch the tame fur of a sleeping wild beast. She didn't dare, for fear of waking her. One down, and one to go.

"So you didn't know him when he was in Canada with Elena?"

"No," Linda managed. "Since then."

Tanya began reading again and Linda was grateful for the silence in which to compose herself. So Elena was the woman in Canada. And Wolfie had come all this distance to give her away, ceremonially, to Vincent. It was over between them, Linda knew, or she would have perceived it herself. Wouldn't she? The pain was radical and quick. She wished she could pick up the burning lamp and club Tanya into unconsciousness for being the

HEARTS

bearer of such news and for staying awake once she had delivered it.

This was going to be Linda's last night with Wolfie, no matter what his history, and she knew she wanted to spend it with reckless extravagance. She hoped she would remember which door was his. She hoped she would be able to put aside sorrow and jealousy in favor of joy.

Tanya closed her book. "What bullshit," she said. She took off her taped eyeglasses and put them on the table before she turned off the lamp.

The apartment was humming with sleepers. Linda rose from the bed without disturbing Robin, a maneuver as tricky as the first one in a game of pick up sticks.

"Bathroom?" Tanya asked groggily.

Oh, God. "Yes," Linda said, still walking.

It was the right room and he was awake, waiting. The air mattress was like a life raft. It trembled under their weight and then floated. "Hello, love, my love," Wolfie said into her skin.

"Will it hold us both?" she asked. Will we drown?

Later she decided, I've never been here before. I would surely have remembered. Then she thought about Iola and her plans to retire one day with a vibrator and some mood-inducing music. "I'll always want the real thing," Linda said aloud.

"What?" Wolfie sounded drowsy.

She told him what Iola had said.

"What song do you think she had in mind?" he asked. " 'It Had to Be You'?"

Linda giggled, and then she said, " 'I Want to Hold Your Hand'?"

Wolfie sang, "He's just my Bill, an or-di-nary guy . . ."

They hugged, hushing each other, until they lapsed into seriousness again. The mattress had a slow hissing leak she kept confusing with their breathing. "I'd better go back," she told Wolfie. "I think I'm falling asleep."

"No, not yet," he said.

"We're sinking," Linda murmured.

"Let's get up for a minute," Wolfie said. "I'll fix it."

While he was blowing up the mattress, absurdly and handsomely naked, she put her arms around him and whispered into his ear, "How about 'Short People'?"

He sputtered and began to laugh loudly, dropping the mattress, and she had to keep one hand over his mouth and the other over her own. "Oh, shhh," she said. "You'll wake everybody."

Then they lay back on the deflating mattress. "Look, it's getting light," she said. "I really have to go."

"I wish you could stay forever," Wolfie said.

If wishes were horses, Linda thought. As she was leaving, she accidentally brushed against the loom, and something metal moved and rustled. "Shhh," she said, and tiptoed out.

When she climbed in beside Robin, Tanya's head appeared near their feet. "Cramps?" she asked sympathetically, and fell back again.

Linda had hardly slept at all when there was an enormous crash, followed by cursing. Montie had fallen between the chairs.

HEARTS

30

ROBIN DIDN'T HAVE A SUITABLE COSTUME for strewing flowers, and Elena offered to lend her something. Robin suggested the silk kimono with the birds all over it, but the women talked her out of it. She settled for a long, deep-pink jersey gown. An enormous basket was looped over her arm, and carnations, daisies, and irises were heaped inside.

Linda had been the first one up in the apartment that morning. She had awakened with an unfocused sadness that quickly identified itself. This was the last day. She looked at the sleeping Robin and Tanya, grabbed her clothes, and raced to the bathroom to use it first.

The dress she'd taken with her was her favorite, a pale floral print that seemed perfect for an outdoor wedding. After her bath, Linda stepped out of the tub and turned the shower tap to hot, hoping the steam would erase some of the wrinkles in the dress. It had not been out of the suitcase since she left Newark. The fabric was gauzy and cool and settled around her weightlessly. She couldn't zip it up, though. Every time she tried, she caught the same tender patch of flesh in the zipper teeth, and she screamed softly. The steam had fogged the mirror, so she shut the shower tap and rubbed the mirror with a towel. She saw that her breasts were straining the bodice of the dress, making her look both uncomfortable and pornographic. Even if she could zip it up, it would never do.

When she went back inside to look for something else in her suitcase, the others were waking, and a line soon formed for the bathroom. Linda dressed in the living room, putting on the blue skirt with the elastic waistband and a blousy white shirt. It looked like an outfit for a school assembly.

Robin came in, dragging pink jersey, and laden with her flower basket. She was barefoot, and someone had put a trace of green eyeshadow on her translucent lids. "Is *that* what you're going to wear?" she asked Linda, who wanted to cry.

"Yes," Linda said. "It's not *my* wedding."

Montie went by in his pajamas, smiling shyly, guarding an erection with a box of Cheerios.

"Here," Robin said, and she tucked a daisy's stem through Linda's damp hair.

Tanya said, "Does anyone have some lipstick that won't clash with lavender? Mine has too much orange in it." Linda wondered why she cared: her eyeglasses were still snarled in black tape.

They squeezed in around the kitchen table. Wolfie came in last and had to sit between Elena and Robin, facing Linda. She believed he was evading her glance, or was it she who kept looking away first, in a fluttering panic?

Montie surrendered the Cheerios for their quickie breakfast. "Where's my favorite new brother-in-law?" he asked, and was told that Vincent had decided not to look at the bride until the ceremony. Linda didn't blame him. Elena's beauty was almost unbearable today. As if on cue, the sun came crashing into the kitchen, spilling golden light onto her golden hair, onto her white-organza Victorian dress.

Remembering the mustard stain from the night before, Linda asked, "Shouldn't you be wearing an apron?" suspicious that her real motive was to extinguish some of that splendor. She saw her own reflection in the toaster and in the black glass door of the wall oven and decided that, even with the daisy in her hair, she looked

---

H E A R T S

like a school-crossing guard or like a nun in one of those new progressive orders.

"I'll only eat white things," Elena said dreamily, spooning sour cream over her cottage cheese.

The minister arrived on a bicycle at eight o'clock. He was from a local Unitarian Universalist church. His bicycle had an unoccupied baby seat on its rear, and a *No Nukes* banner. Other guests, thirty in all, gathered in the shaded area of the courtyard, where assorted chairs had been arranged, and they were ready to begin by 8:45.

The music was provided by a student string quartet from the university. They tuned up and began to play a medley of sprightly love songs as if it were the overture to a musical comedy. Wolfie and Vincent and the minister stood together waiting, all looking in the same direction, like men at a bus stop.

The door leading from the building to the courtyard was stuck. The knob rattled and spun impatiently and then the door flew open and Robin stepped out. Earlier, Linda had thought that Robin looked like a child dressed up in her mother's clothing and makeup. From this short distance, Linda had a new perspective. She now recognized the girl's exquisite potential and was suffused with pride, as if she had raised her from infancy and not just brought her these two thousand miles.

Robin went forward in half-time to a zingy rendition of "Ain't She Sweet," dropping flowers on either side of her like the leaves from a deciduous tree in a strong autumn wind. They were almost all gone before she was halfway there. The last carnation was sent like a hand grenade into the audience, and it struck Montie beneath his left ear. Linda saw him rub the place in astonishment and then bend to retrieve the flower.

The quartet began to play "If Ever I Should Leave You," to announce the bride's entrance. Linda thought it was an odd alternative to the more conventional Wedding March. The various kitchen, folding, and upholstered chairs scraped in the gravel as the door opened again. Still, Vincent could be heard moaning when Elena appeared. Behind her a telephone started ringing in one of the apartments. It rang on and off throughout the ceremony.

Vincent wept, of course. Wolfie turned over a fresh handkerchief along with the matching rings. Tanya, seated in front of Linda, tipped her chair back precariously. "For my money," she whispered, "I'll take a sentimental man any time."

Unwatched, Linda watched Wolfie watching Elena.

It was a fairly traditional wedding service, except toward the end, when the minister spoke about Vincent and Elena as people who had grown to know one another in every way, mingling like the beautiful threads in a weaving, and whose solemn choice today was based on that knowledge. He wished them a peaceful world in which to live and love, and an end to loneliness forever, amen.

The real wedding breakfast was held in a small local restaurant. Linda found that she was famished and yet unable to eat. She drank too much champagne, which made her feel giddy and desperate. When the string quartet fell to their omelets, someone played a disco number on the jukebox, and Linda, who was just returning from the ladies' room, moved in time to the music on the way back to her table. Montie intercepted her and they began to dance together.

The kid was terrific. Any inhibitions imposed by his

HEARTS

youth dropped away. He knew all the steps Linda used to teach at Fred Astaire's and a few she'd never seen. She caught on fast, and some of the wedding guests left their seats and stood in a circle around them, applauding. It was like a scene in one of those carefree college movies of the forties. Except Montie was only sixteen. And Linda was three and a half months pregnant.

She was out of breath when she was passed to Vincent, a stoop-shouldered twirler, and then to another man, with sweaty hands and long muscular arms, who propelled her with the determination of a forklift.

At last the number ended and another, slower one began. Montie took Robin from her seat, and other dancing couples wandered into the small space that wasn't really a dance floor. Linda turned and Wolfie had his arms out. She had just been considering how soon she could leave without being discourteous, and now she began to wonder how long you had to love someone before the sexual shock diminished. It did diminish eventually, she was sure of that, or almost everyone would die in the prime of their lives.

Dancing was something she knew, and could do without premeditation or fear. Even touching like this, which aroused the memory of more intimate touching, didn't make her falter. She was a good dancer. At the studio she used to listen to the stories of men whose wives, mothers, and girlfriends had just died or left them, who thought the fox-trot or the frug would be a first step on their road to recovery. The men breathed hard and she could smell fear and lust and whiskey and Old Spice after-shave without ever losing a beat.

Wolfie did not speak, as if the true business between

them was this slow dancing. At least I'm getting out while the getting's good, Linda thought, but it was hardly a comfort. It was something like dying in the prime of your life.

As soon as the wedding cake was served and eaten, she signaled to Robin that it was time to leave. They had to go back to the apartment to return Elena's dress and pick up their own belongings. Vincent lent Linda a key and kissed her wetly. Elena, Tanya, and Montie were affectionate in their farewell also, as if they had all passed a dangerous night together, binding them forever.

Wolfie said he would go back with them and keep them company until they were ready to leave. She wished he wouldn't, but didn't know how to say so.

As she entered the apartment, Linda imagined a matinee burglar might feel like this, entering strange homes in midday, when the people who live there are away. Maybe that's why they really did it, not for the loot but for the vicarious sense of family, for the evidence of meals shared and books left open to certain passages, for the tumble of unmade beds and the minutiae of shaved hairs in the washbasin.

She and Robin were not taking anything that didn't belong to them. They folded the Hide-a-Bed and left one of Wright's paintings propped against it as a wedding present. Linda's arms ached from the slight exertion of folding and repacking her flowered dress.

Robin removed the pink jersey and was reduced to cinders in the shorts and T-shirt Linda handed her. She lay down on the cot and began to read Tanya's novel, while Linda finished gathering their things.

There was something hard in the pocket of Robin's

jeans. Linda put her hand inside and withdrew a fork, its tines neatly bound in Kleenex. She glanced over at Robin, who read and twirled a strand of blond hair around and around one finger.

Where in the world did this fork come from, and why was she keeping it? With drugs, wasn't it a bent *spoon* they used? Linda imagined a long history of kleptomania. If she searched through Robin's things, would she find the other useless items those people took, for their own dark and unfathomable reasons? One earring. Gloves in the wrong size. A pair of left-handed pinking shears. The fork was definitely not a souvenir of their apartment in Newark. The silver-plated flatware they'd used there was the remains of one of Wright and Miriam's wedding gifts, Community's Morning Star pattern, service for eight. Wright had told Linda that she could discard or replace anything from that first marriage that made her feel uncomfortable in any way. The only thing that came to mind then was Robin.

Now she replaced the fork in the pocket of Robin's jeans, deciding not to say anything, that she was probably exaggerating its significance. It could be some new teenage craze, for all she knew.

Linda went into the bathroom to get their toothbrushes. Wolfie followed her. "I'm getting good at this," she said.

"At what?" He lifted her hair and kissed the back of her neck as his hands defined the outer curves of her breasts.

She slipped out of his reach. "At finding all our junk, not forgetting a toothbrush, or sunglasses, or anything."

"What about me?"

"Pardon?"

He smiled. "You're forgetting me, babe." When she didn't answer, he said, "I want to go with you, Linda. I want to stay with you."

"Oh."

"Now, how am I supposed to read *that?*" Wolfie asked.

Linda sat down on the edge of the bathtub. "There's something I have to tell you," she said, and didn't continue.

"So serious," Wolfie said, touching her chin. And then he leaned against the wall and waited. He was not going to lead her all the way into confession.

"We're always in the bathroom together, aren't we?" Linda said, remembering the sweeter time the night before and envying it. "The thing is, I'm pregnant."

"Hey!" he said. "You can't be. How . . . ?"

"It's not yours. You don't have to worry about that."

"Well, then whose?"

"Mine," she said.

"Now it's my turn. Oh."

"It's all right. You don't have to say anything else. I just figured you'd want to know."

"How long have *you* known, Linda?"

"A long time. Since Pennsylvania."

"Why didn't you say anything before this?"

Linda shrugged, her first dividend from all this time with Robin.

"What are you going to do?"

"I'm going to have it."

"I sort of figured that. But why, Linda?"

"I don't know." He waited and she laughed, to

HEARTS

quickly plug up the hole of silence. "Because I'm a little crazy, I guess. Because I've decided I want to."

"You didn't want to all along?"

"No, never. I tried to have an abortion in Des Moines, and it was foiled by someone even crazier than me. Somebody who was willing to *murder* me and a few other people, in the name of life. That has nothing to do with my decision, though. If I could go back to that time, to the way I was then, I'd still have it, the abortion, I mean."

"So what changed your mind?"

She realized that he expected her to say that it was because of him—he *needed* to hear it—but she could not. "I don't know," she said. "Maybe partly because of the wedding ceremony today. You know, when the minister said about an end to loneliness? And after we were together last night and I went back to bed, I thought about how lovely it was, but how *random*, I mean our ever meeting in the first place. In the second place. Do you remember those trees you told me about, coming up by themselves through sidewalk cracks? And this whole planet from a broken piece of sun, imagine!" Linda inhaled deeply, and she shuddered. "And the sperm and the egg getting together like that, by total chance, like two nervous strangers in a singles bar. I started to wish them well . . ." She lifted her hands. "I don't even know what I'm saying any more. And I have to go." She pushed away from the tub and stood up.

"I still want to go with you," he said, his voice cleared of seduction, his hands to himself.

"Wolfie, you don't," Linda said. Why was it always up to her to declare the truth? Now she could stand here for a hundred years before he'd deny it. She waited, anyway, in the beating silence.

Then Wolfie said, "This morning, before I was even awake, I reached for you. It was like we'd been together for a long, long time."

"Yes."

"And I kept thinking how much I wanted to find you there, every morning."

"But this changes everything, doesn't it?"

"Well, it makes it harder, that's all. More complicated." Wolfie sighed. "I wish . . ." he began.

"Oh, don't!" she said. "Wishing never does any good."

They looked at one another until the fervor of Wolfie's gaze softened. "No," he conceded then. "I guess it doesn't."

"So, I'd better go now," Linda said, not moving.

"But how will you take care of yourself?" he asked.

"I have a little money. I can still work for a while now, and after . . ."

"At what? Will you dance?"

Linda considered the question thoughtfully. "No," she answered. "No, only for myself." She saw his face change and before he could construct a new case, she said, "I'm healthy, and willing. There are other things I can learn to do."

"What about the baby?"

"I don't know. A day-care center, I guess."

"You're such a good person, Linda. But you're very romantic. And with everything that's happened to you, you're still kind of . . . inexperienced. What I'm trying to say is that it won't be easy."

HEARTS

"I know that. I never thought it would be easy."

"Have you ever really *thought?*"

Linda went past him in the narrow doorway, managing not to make contact. It will go away, she promised herself. Eventually it will go away.

"Are you sure you'll be okay? I want to know," Wolfie said. "I *care* about you."

She kept moving and didn't answer him.

"And Robin?" he said, following her. "Are you going to keep her, too?"

"No, I'll take her to her mother, the way we planned."

"Oh, Jesus," he said. "I can't help this right now, babe. It's this particular time."

He walked outside with them to the car. "You can reach me here, through Vincent and Elena," he said. "I'll be in touch with them. I really want to know about you. Linda?"

Linda had turned on the ignition. The windows of the Maverick were open, and they were sitting there, inhaling the exhaust.

Wolfie leaned in, the way he had that first time at the gas station in Ohio. His hand grazed her face. "Hey, Robin," he said. "Don't get married or anything. Wait for me, okay?"

What was making him stay like this? Guilt? Confusion? Relief? They would all be asphyxiated. Robin didn't give him any encouragement. She had reverted to her former self, and was crouched in the backseat like a stowaway.

"Goodbye," Linda said. She released the emergency brake and put the car into drive.

"Goodbye," Wolfie agreed finally, and withdrew his head. He said other things she couldn't hear over the motor's thunder. He waved, shouted, ran after the car for a few yards, and then disappeared.

HEARTS

31

MIRIAM REISMANN HAUSNER PLACED THE
last rose in the arrangement she was fixing in
the large crystal bowl on the piano. "Oh!" *she*
said. "You startled me. I didn't hear the door chime.
Did Parker let you in? Are you here about the maid's
job?"

The blond young girl in the doorway did not answer.
Miriam, whose eyesight had grown worse this year, put
on her glasses and stepped closer. The girl came into
focus, and Miriam could see they looked exactly alike,
except for the color of their hair. And except for their
clothing, of course. The girl was poorly dressed, in denim
shorts with a raveled edge, and a T-shirt with permanent
chocolate stains on the front.

She, Miriam, was wearing a pure-silk hostess gown
and suitable jewelry. She put one perfectly manicured
hand against her breast and murmured, "It's you, isn't
it?" She could hardly see because of the tears that were
gathering in her eyes and fogging up her eyeglasses.
"Why, you're beautiful!" she exclaimed.

Miriam Taylor-Harding (her pen name) put the
final page of her new novel into the typewriter. It had
the same kind of plot she always used. This time, the
mother and daughter are separated during the war, each
one going on with her own life, each one believing the
other has been killed by the enemy. Sometimes they are
separated by a mistake in the hospital where the girl is
born. Sometimes there is a kidnapping. In TV interviews
Ms. Taylor-Harding admits that she cries while she
writes.

She began to type. She heard the French doors open
behind her, and she felt a little chill on the back of her

neck, but she didn't turn around. This was always the most difficult scene to get down on paper—the reunion. She was so incredibly moved. And yet her fingers flew, as if the story had come to life by itself. She sobbed as she typed The End, and she shut off the electric typewriter.

"Nicky, darling," she said. "Pour me a Manhattan, will you? I'm emotionally drained." And then she turned around.

The distinguished, but ailing, man closed the trunk of the white Mercedes 450SL.

The once beautiful, dark-haired woman said, "That's it, I guess. Well, goodbye Arizona, hello New Jersey!"

"Are you sure you know what you're doing, Mimi?" he asked. "Giving up all this, to go back to that life?" His rings flashed in the sunlight as he waved his hand at the huge mansion behind them, at the gardens and the pool and the tennis courts.

She laughed bitterly. "Oh, yes, I know what I'm doing, all right," she said. "I only hope to God it's not too late."

They climbed into the Mercedes, put on the air conditioner and the tape deck. The motor roared as they pulled away from the curb. Neither of them looked back. Neither of them saw the other, small green car pulling up to the curb near the mansion, and the lovely blond girl opening the door and stepping out.

A man came to the door. He said, "You don't have to tell me who you are. The resemblance is uncanny."

———————————

HEARTS

The girl stepped into the drawing room. She kept one hand in her pocket.

The man said, "Was the trip difficult? Have you had lunch? You'll want to freshen up before you go in. You'll want to prepare yourself. It's not a pretty sight."

The girl shook her head and he noticed how lovely her hair was when it moved like that, sort of in ripples. It looked freshly shampooed.

He led the way up the spiral staircase. "I must warn you," he said, "she does not recognize anyone anymore. And even the latest wonder drugs cannot calm her."

Their footsteps were silent in the carpeted corridor. As he opened the heavily carved doors leading to the bedroom, the girl could hear the clinking of chains—and then the horrifying cackle . . .

Linda sneezed and Robin was jerked from her reverie. She had forgotten that Linda was there, that both of them were in the car again, being borne away from the last place. That happened occasionally, allowing Robin to feel cozily alone, free to daydream or remember things. For most of their trip, Linda hadn't let her be for more than a minute at a time. She was always butting in, always asking questions, her voice as carefully polite as a guidance counselor's. It was hard to even think.

But since they'd left Albuquerque, and Wolfie, Linda had become quiet, even withdrawn. Robin knew it was unhappiness that was keeping her to herself. It wasn't a difficult deduction to make. Wolfie had run after them like one of those mad dogs that chase cars. He yelled at Linda to wait, that he cared, that he wanted something or wanted to tell her something. It was impossible to hear him over the noise of the car. She had sped away like she did after that time they stayed in Buddy's Siesta. When she was really upset, Linda became a driving fiend, a maniac who made everyone else on the road get out of her way.

She and Wolfie were in love. That wasn't difficult to figure out, either. All that dumb, love-struck whispering and touching that had gone on in the car and back at Elena's, and before that at the motels. Robin guessed that this was only a lovers' quarrel, a necessary ritual in love affairs, and a passing thing. Any minute now, Linda would come to a skidding stop in her daredevil driving, and turn the car around and head back toward Albuquerque at the same breakneck speed. Or she would keep driving like this, blindly forward, while Wolfie took a faster car or a helicopter to get ahead of them, and would show up all out of breath, but playing it cool, after the next curve in the road. Then Linda would let him in again and that whole craziness between them would start once more. All the time and energy they wasted in fighting and making up; Robin would never understand it.

For a couple of hours after their getaway, she looked out the window, waiting for the reunion, and when it didn't happen, and when Linda's driving reduced to its old normal creepy speed, Robin gave up her first theory and wondered if Linda and Wolfie were simply star-crossed lovers like Tony and Maria in *West Side Story*. Though she couldn't see what was stopping *them*. And why did she care anyway? Why did their separation interest her so much and sadden her? She was never

---

HEARTS

going to see either of them again, anyway. And she had her own future to think about. But her concern for them stayed, a peculiar ache that resisted the comfort of reason. They were like characters she had been cheering on in a movie, for whom she wanted a satisfying ending, and they were also heroes in her real life. Even while she made private fun of them, she had enjoyed the protective atmosphere of their loving, and felt betrayed and lonely in its absence, the way she'd felt after her father's death. It was the scariest thing to consider, that you might always have to depend on other people for your happiness. It meant *you* had no control at all, and who else in the world could be trusted?

Robin decided not to think about that, or about them, if she could help it. Grateful for Linda's simultaneous retreat, she leaned back against the seat cushions and dozed and woke, dreaming and planning.

Later in the day, Linda pulled off the highway at some exit, without a word to Robin, who said, "Where are we going now?" She hoped Linda didn't have some more asshole friends from high school to visit, and that they were only going to stop for lunch. Linda didn't say.

It was a little hick town, and they drove slowly up the narrow main street in the broiling sun, past old ladies in white shoes and straw hats, past Indian men clustered in the shade of doorways and awnings, past shimmering parked cars that appeared to be dissolving in the heat.

Linda parked near a storefront movie in the center of town. She got out of the car and went to the cashier's window without even glancing up at the marquee to see what was playing, or back at Robin, who followed her without being told to. When Linda was in one of her schizo moods, it was no use asking her why they were doing anything, why they were going to the movies now, in this particular place. Robin knew she'd never get a straight answer. She walked quickly behind her, catching a glimpse of the advertised program—two thrillers—and the blue plastic icicles over the door that promised air-conditioned comfort inside.

It *was* cool, a little cold even, and neither of them had taken sweaters from the car. Robin was wearing a tiny stretch of puckered elastic that left her arms and shoulders and midriff bare. She had broken out in goose bumps before they even sat down. The theater was almost empty. There were only some little kids sitting in the front row and a few others running up and down the aisle.

Linda and Robin had come in right in the middle of one feature. It was an old murder mystery with a shaky sound track that made all the actors sound as if they were gargling when they spoke. There were already a few dead bodies lying around, and a million suspects. Robin couldn't make head or tail of it. She turned to ask if Linda knew what was going on, and to complain about the cold, and saw that Linda was staring straight ahead without seeing anything, tears streaming down her face, and her whole body shaking.

They stayed for both features, Linda crying soundlessly the entire time. When the show ended and the lights came on, they left the theater, got back into the car, and out onto the road again.

HEARTS

"Where are we?" Robin asked as she came awake. The car was pulling in somewhere and the sky was brilliant with stars.

"Motel," Linda said. Then she opened her door and staggered out, past the lit *Vacancy* sign, toward the motel office.

Robin imagined they'd driven pretty far. They usually stopped before it was this dark. Her stomach whined with hunger and she wondered if there was a place open around there where they could get supper. As far as she could tell, Linda had not eaten since the wedding breakfast, and Robin had only had some sweet rolls she'd filched from the restaurant that morning, and the taco chips and Coke she'd bought at the movie theater in the afternoon. Linda looked exhausted, as if she just wanted to fall into the nearest bed and sleep for a few weeks.

Robin was wide awake and buzzing with need. She had to eat, to drink some water, to pee, to move her cramped legs, even to talk. She left the car, too. Her right foot had fallen asleep and it began to tingle with moving blood as she stamped on it and did a little dance in the parking lot of the Carioca Motel, which boasted *Color TV, Telephones, and In-Room Coffee*. The ones that bragged about having telephones were usually as bad as the ones that didn't have them. And In-Room Coffee, which sounded like an interesting phenomenon the first time they saw it advertised, in Indiana, turned out to be a little water-stained Pyrex beaker sitting on an electric coil, with two Styrofoam cups and two packets of instant coffee nearby. Linda had acted as if some handsome stranger had sent champagne to their room. "Isn't this nice!" she exclaimed. "Isn't this lovely!" And even though neither of them was particularly fond of coffee, she'd filled the little beaker in the bathroom and made some. It tasted peculiar, as if the water had come from a fish tank or something.

Linda came out of the Carioca office carrying a key, and she was still lurching around in that dopey, drunken way. "Come on, it's all the way down the other end," she said to Robin, and got back into the car.

"I'm hungry," Robin complained. "Aren't we going to have any supper? We didn't even have lunch."

"I cannot drive another inch beyond that room," Linda said. "But I saw a machine in the office. You can go get yourself something if you want to."

Robin held out her hand for money. She wasn't going to dip into the small store of funds she'd been accumulating from her forays into Linda's purse. The night before, Robin had woken up and found herself alone in the Hide-a-Bed. Tanya was snoring away on the cot, and Linda was gone, probably with Wolfie somewhere, climbing all over each other. Robin took five dollars. In the morning, in desperate daring, and because Linda looked so preoccupied, she took three more. By the time Linda noticed her loss, if she ever noticed it, she'd have to consider other suspects: Tanya, maybe, or Montie. It was Robin's own money she was taking, anyway, kind of like withdrawing it from a bank. There was no actual question of theft, and she'd probably still come out way behind unless she found the real stash before they parted.

Now Linda gave her a handful of change, told her it was room 14, and drove away.

Robin hoped she wasn't going to find one of those

HEARTS

machines with nothing but Life Savers and gum in it. Linda was so beat she might not have even noticed if it was a Dispenz-All, like they had in the bus station in Newark, a machine that coughed up combs, pocket packs of Kleenex, lipstick, little magnetic scottie dogs, and emergency vials of lilac perfume.

Robin opened the door to the office and there was nobody there. A bell above the door had tinkled, though, and soon a further door opened and a man in a bathrobe stumbled out. He didn't even look at her. "Twelve-fifty single," he said. "Fifteen double. TV, phone, and In-Room Coffee."

"I'm already checked in," Robin said. "I just came out to get something to eat."

"Oh, good Christ," he said, and went back behind the door, slamming it.

She was glad to be alone in the office. Sometimes it took her a while to make up her mind about the food in vending machines, and she didn't like anyone looking over her shoulder, offering advice or rushing her. This was a sandwich dispenser, the kind with a glass front and the cut ends of the sandwiches facing the customer. There was a choice of ham, turkey, chicken, or tuna. The last three appeared indistinguishable from one another, and Robin knew that they would all taste pretty much the same, too, slick with mayonnaise and a little fishy. Still, she hesitated, trying to make up her mind. Linda had given her plenty of change. She spread it across the registration desk to count it. Two dollars and ninety-five cents. The sandwiches were seventy-five each. She could eat at least two of them, probably three, and still have a few cents left over for her fund. Linda would be too wiped out to remember to ask for her change.

Robin pushed the money into the slot and pressed the selection buttons for one turkey, one chicken, and one tuna. She could amuse herself later by trying to guess which was which. And she knew from experience that the ham, cut into see-through slices, would be salty and dry. Each time a sandwich dropped into place, the machine rang and there was a muffled answering curse from behind the inner door.

Number 14 was at the very end of the L-shaped building. It had to be pretty late, Robin thought. There were a few other cars pulled up to other numbered doors, but all those room windows were dark, and except for some crickets singing in the black distance, it was quiet, too. Nobody in there reading, or groping somebody else, or making cut-rate long-distance phone calls or lousy In-Room Coffee.

Linda was asleep already. She'd left the lock off so that Robin could get in without a key. All the lights were on in the room, but those dusty, 40-watt bulbs didn't illuminate the place beyond a frustrating dimness. Robin, feeling lively and curious despite her hunger and other discomforts, looked around. It was one of the ugliest rooms they'd had so far. The two narrow beds didn't even match. One had a cracked tufted headboard, and the other one was metal and severe. It looked as if it had been used previously in a hospital or an orphanage. Linda lay on the metal bed, corpselike in her pallor, arms folded across her chest. She always claimed to be such a light sleeper, but she didn't make a move now as Robin clattered around, dropping one shoe and then the other, rattling wire hangers in the closet, and flushing the toilet.

There was a sheet of paper taped to a wall in the

HEARTS

bathroom, just to the left of the light switch. It was a child's broad-handed drawing of clouds, and it was signed, in tall, careful letters, *Maureen W*. A kid who stayed here once had probably done it, maybe the daughter of a widowed traveling salesman, who went everywhere with him. Robin had a sudden image of a small, serious girl sitting cross-legged on the bed, frowning with concentration, replacing each crayon in the box after she used it. The father was in the bathroom, shaving. When he came out, he made a big fuss over the picture and insisted they hang it right up, the way her mother used to do on the door of the refrigerator at home.

It was a familiar drawing—the clouds were like cotton balls against the Crayola blue of the sky; a traditional yellow sun emerged from a corner of the page—but Robin kept staring at it as if it were extraordinary graffiti, and contained a special heavenly message. The ordinary kind was pretty much the same in every state they'd visited: *Bobbi and Pete fucked here. If you sprinkle when you tinkle, please be neat and wipe the seat. Remember God loves you.*

Robin wondered again where they were. They must have crossed into Arizona while she slept. She wished she hadn't slept that long. It was going to be hard to fall asleep now, and even harder to stay awake alone in this crummy place. She got into the bed with the tufted headboard, still dressed, taking the sandwiches with her. The silence was going to drive her crazy. Everything she didn't want to think about would fly into her head. Glancing at Linda once more, she got out of bed and put the television set on, careful to move the volume button to its lowest position first. There were three working channels. One of them had nothing but a test pattern, accompanied by that irritating signal hum. The second channel was showing the kind of movie Robin hated, a war picture in which the heroes took a couple of years to die after they were shot. The third one was signing off with a film of a flapping flag and a recording of "The Star-Spangled Banner," barely audible with the volume down, as if it were being played by an orchestra of mice. Robin shut off the set. "Linda?" she said, softly at first, and then in a louder, more conversational tone.

Linda didn't budge either time. Maybe she'd OD'd on something because of what happened between her and Wolfie. Lots of high-school girls did that after they split up with somebody. One of them at Newark High even died, without meaning to probably, because she'd signed up that same day for cheerleader tryouts. But what would Linda OD on? Tylenol? Vitamin C? That's all she had in the way of drugs, as far as Robin could see.

The second time Robin went through Linda's purse, she searched in every pocket and crevice, even cased the lining, looking first for money and then, with a kind of dumb desperation, for pot. She had only that one joint of her own left and she was saving it, thinking she would need it for the encounter with her mother. How could she deal with that if she wasn't stoned?

When Robin and Montie had danced together at the wedding reception, she had wanted to ask him if he had any grass. But he beat her to it, asking her first, and she'd lied. Robin had been appalled when he practically dragged her from her chair and out onto the floor like that, in front of everybody. She didn't like dancing in a public place, away from her known friends, who would not judge her, who would hardly even notice her. Robin secretly believed she was a terrible dancer, that she moved like a gorilla. After a few agonizing moments, she realized that no one was looking at her; they were all watching Linda, who was better than anyone Robin had ever seen, even on *American Bandstand*. Linda's dancing was the only thing Robin admired about her, or envied.

When Robin told Montie that she didn't have any grass, he seemed vaguely disappointed, but he didn't hold her any less tightly in that slow touch-dance number, and something—his hardness, probably—pressed against her with a mind of its own. Even that was not unpleasant. She thought now that Montie would have been someone good to get high with. Ginger and Ray were like remote babies from her long-abandoned childhood.

"Linda!" she said, louder than she'd intended, and Linda sat up, clutching one hand to her breast. "Oh, God, what is it?" she cried, before her eyes were open.

"It's nothing," Robin said. "Hey, it's only me, Robin. I just wanted to talk to you."

Linda tilted onto one elbow, dazed. Then she said, "Where are we, anyway?"

"How should I know?" Robin answered. "We're in this sleazy place somewhere."

Linda brought her alarm clock close to her swollen eyes and she forced them open. "Ohhh," she moaned. "I just want to sleep. I wish I could sleep forever. Why did you wake me up?" She fell back against the pillow, with her hands over her eyes as if she were shutting out the blinding glare of a searchlight.

Robin considered the question. "I don't know," she

said, fumbling for an idea. She certainly wasn't going to admit to a dread of loneliness, or to that stupid vision of straight Linda wasted on drugs. Then her own eyes found the sandwiches, still untouched, on the other bed. "I thought maybe you were getting hungry," she said, and congratulated herself on such fast thinking. This excuse sounded reasonable, and generous, besides. She watched as Linda came awake in slow stages.

"What do you have?" Linda asked finally.

"Huh?"

"To *eat*. What did you get to eat?"

"Oh. Tuna fish. Chicken. Turkey. Which do you want?"

"Chicken, I guess, if you don't want it. Now that I'm up, I'm starving. Did you get anything to drink?"

"They didn't have anything."

"I guess we could have water, or some of that coffee."

Robin went to the other bed and examined the sandwiches and sniffed them, but they withheld the secret of their contents. She chose one at random and brought it back to Linda. Then she went to the bathroom and filled the two Styrofoam cups with water. It looked suspiciously foamy.

Linda bit into her sandwich. "This tastes like tuna," she said.

"They all do," Robin allowed, chewing on the white soggy paste of what might have been the turkey. She wondered if she'd be able to tell the difference if she bit off a piece of the cardboard underneath the bread, by accident. Still, she ate the two remaining sandwiches with a real and demanding appetite. Linda had quickly declined half of the second one.

———————

HEARTS

Then they were both thoroughly awake, with nothing to do.

"Maybe there's something on television," Linda suggested. "We could keep the sound low."

"There isn't," Robin said. "I tried while you were sleeping."

"Well, try it again," Linda urged.

Robin clicked the tuner impatiently from channel to channel.

"Wait!" Linda cried. "Leave that, Robin!"

"What, this? It's only a commercial. And there's a jerky movie on this channel."

"No, look! That man in the commercial. It's Barry King, someone I used to know back in Bayonne."

On screen, one man in a locker room was telling another that his trouble was that his smile was too dim.

"*That's* not his trouble," Linda murmured.

"What?"

"He's still handsome, though, isn't he?"

The guy in the commercial brushed his teeth with some crap and was smiling again. Now his teeth shone like the brights of an oncoming car, and two girls were hanging around his neck. "He looks like a fag to me," Robin said.

"Maybe that was it," Linda said.

"Maybe that was *what?*"

"Nothing," Linda said. The commercial was over and the movie came on again. People were still killing each other all over the place.

"You can shut it off now," Linda said, and Robin did.

After a moment, Linda moaned. "Now what? And I don't even have anything to *read*," she said. She sounded desperate. "How will I ever be able to get back to sleep? I'll have to take a couple of Tylenol and see what happens. Maybe they'll relax me a little."

Robin snorted. "Why don't you try Vitamin C while you're at it?"

"What?"

"Nothing."

"You said *something*, Robin, don't deny it. You woke me up in the middle of the night to eat a sandwich that I'll probably get botulism from, after I drove all day and am half dead. And I don't want to be *conscious*, much less fully awake, so there is to be no muttering, no sarcasm, and no back talk! Do you understand me? Oh, God, what am I going to *do*?" She flung herself face down into the pillow as she said these last words, so that they came up muffled and indistinct.

"I know something you could do," Robin said.

Linda turned over. "What?"

"I mean to relax you, to make you sleepy again."

"What is it, meditation? I can't do things like that, Robin. If a car went by on a highway three miles away, I'd hear it and lose my concentration. I'm too easily distracted."

"I didn't mean meditation," Robin said. "I was thinking maybe you . . . maybe we could smoke."

Linda stared at her. "You don't mean regular cigarettes, like Viceroy and Marlboro, do you?"

"No."

"Well, where are you going to get . . . ?" Linda's voice faded. Robin saw that she understood at last what was being offered. And Robin was reflecting on the mad impulsiveness of her offer. She'd been saving that last

HEARTS

joint for an important purpose, and now she'd practically promised it for no good reason. She wanted to back out, but something in Linda's face held her. It was genuine grief, and the fevered desire to escape from it. Robin knew about that. Maybe they could only smoke half the joint tonight, just enough to ease them both into sleep. Robin would still have the rest for the time she'd really need it.

"You're not a pothead or anything, are you?" Linda asked.

Robin didn't even deign to answer that one. Where did Linda think she would get the money for a full-time habit? She took out the blue sock and removed the foil packet from the toe as Linda watched, fascinated. "I only have this one joint," Robin said, "and I don't want to use it all up this time, okay?"

"Okay," Linda said. She paused and added, "But I don't think I should really be doing this, Robin. I think it may be something like impairing the morals of a minor. Or vice versa."

"Look," Robin said. "Do you want to relax? Do you want to feel better or don't you?"

"Yes. Yes, I do."

"Well, so there," Robin said. She sat down on the edge of the metal bed and tried to light matches from the Des Moines Marriott. They had gotten a little wet somehow and she had to strike three of them before one took.

"Robin?" Linda said. "This isn't my first time, you know. I once had what you'd probably call a bad trip. What if that happens again?"

"Don't worry. It won't. This is good stuff." She inhaled deeply, holding her breath in and shutting her eyes. Then she opened them and passed the joint to Linda, who took it delicately between her second and third fingers and looked at it.

"Don't let it burn down like that!" Robin said. "You're wasting it. You have to take a hit right away."

Linda did, and let the smoke out again almost immediately, through her nostrils.

"No, no!" Robin said, regretting everything. "*Swallow* the smoke. Hold it *in!*" she ordered.

Linda obeyed, eyes bulging with the effort, and she coughed and retched a little. "Sorry," she gasped.

Robin grabbed the joint and toked again. She wasn't high yet, of course, but she felt fine, in command and hopeful, as if she had just absorbed a secret that was going to change her life. She let her own nostrils flare, smokeless, and noted Linda's admiring observation.

The next time, Linda did it right, too, although Robin didn't offer approval. She took the joint back and examined it. It was considerably smaller. Maybe neither of them would get high and there wouldn't be enough left for Glendale, either. "I'm going to put it out soon," she warned, and Linda nodded, accepting with ease their reversal of roles. Robin felt gloriously powerful, and that sense of power led to a reckless generosity. Instead of putting the roach out, she drew on it once again and then gave it back to Linda. I'll think of something later, she told herself.

In the meantime, old Linda was becoming a pro, doing everything in careful mimicry of Robin: narrowing her eyes, shaking her hair back, sucking the smoke in hard and holding it.

HEARTS

Robin went to Linda's purse and reached into the bottom for the tweezers to use as a roach holder. She expected Linda to say something about this casual invasion of her property, but Linda only smiled. Robin smiled back.

"It's so quiet in here," Linda said. "Quieter than before, I think. Is that part of it?"

"We need music," Robin told her. "You're supposed to have music." She took the keys from the dressertop and went outside to get her portable radio from the trunk of the car. She carried it carefully, with a rare sensation of sentimental possession. This was one of the last gifts from her father. How glad she was now that she had not given it to Ginger that day.

Robin didn't feel like going back into the room yet. The air was cool and fragrant with summer. She turned the radio on and lingered in the parking lot, in the meager traffic of fireflies, listening to music.

While Robin was gone, Linda took a last drag in front of the mirror, thinking she looked quite natural, and then she dropped the crumbling, sparking stub, and the tweezers, into the ashtray next to her bed. Well, she thought as she lay down, I must be pretty desperate to be doing this. I *am* desperate. She was beginning to feel cautiously different, not relaxed exactly, but removed from the immediacy of her despair. Thoughts of Wolfie wandered in and out, and when they did, she longed for him with a good imitation of the pain she'd felt on leaving. She even said his name aloud once, testing her threatened tolerance further.

Robin came back with the radio playing. She was

hugging it close to her and the disco tune seemed to be emanating from her chest.

"Shhh," Linda said, and she giggled.

Robin laughed, too, companionably, and she lowered the volume. "So," she said, as if she were continuing an interrupted conversation. "What's been happening?"

Linda shrugged. "Nothing, I guess. What's been happening with you?"

"Nothing. What's been happening with you?"

"Hey, you just asked me th— Oh, *I* get it."

"You do? You must be getting real cool, Linda."

Linda got out of bed and started moving around the room in time to the music. How she loved to dance. Whenever she heard music, she readied herself like an orchestra at the conductor's warning tap. Maybe it began in her blood, a simmering, a kind of dancing there. Then the message spilled quickly over to nerves, bone, muscles, everywhere. Sometimes she heard nothing; her body, needing to dance, invented music, the baton's strike only her own heart.

Linda learned to walk early, her mother once confided, way before she learned to talk, and had never had that typical flat-footed baby's lurch. From the beginning she went forward on toe, arms out and fluttering for balance. Linda couldn't actually remember that far back, but as she snapped her fingers and danced loosely in her long white nightgown, she sensed an echo of that first joyous venture into space.

Robin leaned against the door and watched. "You're really a good dancer," she said.

"I know," Linda admitted. "It's the only thing I'm good at."

HEARTS

"I'm a rotten dancer," Robin said.

"No, you're not. I mean, you have such a nice body and everything. You *should* be good. Come on, I'll teach you. I'll give you a free trial lesson."

"What? With those dumb footprints you have to follow?"

"No, silly. Of course not. Come on, just come here."

She held out her arms and Robin took a few steps toward her and then stopped. When she was still a couple of feet away, she began dancing, too, clearly attempting to repeat Linda's gestures. Robin's were too broad, though, and jerkily nervous.

"Wow!" Linda said. "See? But don't move your shoulders so much. And let your joints loosen up. That's right. That's *good*."

Linda circled Robin, dancing nearer and nearer until she was able to reach out and put her arm around the girl's waist. Then she began to guide her, using the old studio trick of gentle force that always made the client feel *he* was the terrific dancer, *he* was the one responsible for all that smooth, synchronized motion.

Robin was so serious about it, so earnest. Linda grabbed her and spun her swiftly out.

"Ohhhh," Robin said, looking flushed and dizzy. When she was reeled in again, she leaned heavily against Linda, who welcomed her weight. They danced slowly then, Robin's breath against Linda's throat. That blond hair smelled oddly sweet, with its mingling of perspiration and smoke and the scent of strawberry shampoo. The flesh of her narrow waist was solid under Linda's right hand. The left hand held Robin's, and steered her easily around the furniture.

They had not been this physically close before and it was thrilling in a way that Linda had never experienced. I have tamed the beast, she thought. Her eyes filled with tears as they turned and turned in the feeble light of the room.

When the music ended, they were next to Linda's bed. If they had been lovers, they would surely have lain down together then to extend the pleasure of their contact. Instead, they went to separate beds and lay on their sides, facing one another. Linda could still feel the heat of Robin's hand in hers, and the pulse of music that had caused them to converge. She was stung with happiness.

HEARTS

THE NEXT DAY LINDA ACKNOWLEDGED THAT **32**
one more proverbial truth was really a lie.
Things *didn't* look brighter in the morning.
She felt physically well when she woke, but faintly embarrassed and no less burdened with misery than she'd been the day before.

While Robin slept on, burrowed so deep under the covers it looked as though she might suffocate, Linda recalled the events of the previous night with astonishment. There was no way to hold the marijuana accountable for everything. Wolfie was right; she did love Robin. Maybe the resemblance he'd claimed to see in their eyes that first time was there, too, and she and Robin were kindred in more ways than their limited chance relationship allowed.

Oh, fine. One by one, she was being severed from each connection that mattered, almost as soon as it began to matter. Except, of course, for the one she kept inside her body, the one who was still a total and untried stranger. And why did she think that would work out? Aside from everything else, there was the practical business of food, clothing, and shelter. The confidence she had demonstrated with such bravado yesterday—day care! job training!—faded now. She had invented it on the spot to ward off the hurt of Wolfie's qualified love for her. It cost a fortune to raise a child nowadays. There had been an article in the paper about it recently. They all seemed to require corrective dentistry, ten-speed Italian bicycles, and a college education. The final figure was staggering, more like the National Debt than the living expenses for one measly human being.

Who's in there, she wondered, with more curiosity than she had felt so far. Would the baby be fair like

Wright and Robin, or would it look like her? She could not imagine her own genes as dominant, although she thought she remembered from high-school biology that dark hair and eyes were. Would it be a good dancer, or inherit Wright's ability to draw and paint? Would it be secure or uncertain? Cheerful or morose? Imagining the baby in its earnest work of formation, Linda felt great tenderness. But was this only another hormonal trick? Perhaps she, Linda, had inherited her father's compulsion to be cruel, and it would lay dormant in her until the first moment of parenting. Maybe there is no antidote once you've had a wounding, poisonous childhood, only the desire to make it up to, or inflict the same horror on, a new child. It was truly scary and yet this pregnancy was an undying commitment, one she could not simply drive away from if it didn't seem to be working out. She had decided to give this unknown person life. At the same time she'd also bequested death. How is it possible that we keep doing it, knowing what we know? And why aren't all the sane and conscious people in the world busy dashing their brains out against rocks because of that knowledge, instead of locking themselves in rooms, two by torrid two, to make frantic love and new creatures in their own perishable image?

"My God," Linda said aloud, and Robin wriggled and stretched, showing her sleep-closed face in the other bed.

"What time is it?" she asked.

"It's late. It's almost ten o'clock. I don't know why I'm lying here like a bump on a log. How are you today?"

"All right, I guess." She turned over and started to crawl under the covers again.

"Robin, wait. Don't go back to sleep."

HEARTS

"Why not?"

"Because we're going to have to get moving soon. Checkout time is eleven o'clock."

"So? I could get ready in two minutes. And nobody's lined up waiting for rooms in this dump, anyway."

"And I wanted to talk."

"About what?"

"Well, about things. Do you know we're in Arizona already? Before you know it, we'll be parting company, today probably. There are things we should say to each other."

"Like *what?*" Robin sounded exasperated.

"Like about the baby I'm going to have." Linda was sure she had not intended to say that a moment before. It was because of Robin's surliness and out of a need to have her absolute attention for once.

She'd certainly accomplished that. Robin was sitting up in bed staring at Linda, all the sleep gone from her eyes. "What?" she said. "*What* baby?"

"This one," Linda said, touching her blanketed belly with both hands.

"Oh, boy. So why did you . . . ?" She stopped, flustered and pink.

"You mean, why did I leave Wolfie? It's not his baby, Robin. It was started before I even knew him. It's your father's."

Robin lay back again, felled by the news, and Linda continued. "I didn't realize it myself when we started out. Maybe I really believe it today for the first time. I mean, I've been thinking about it since I woke up this morning, about how it would look and everything."

Robin was silent.

"So, *say* something," Linda urged her.

"Congratulations," Robin said, tonelessly.

It was not what Linda wanted to hear. She felt grave disappointment. First Wolfie, now Robin. She would have to be her child's only enthusiast, a one-woman welcoming committee to the world. Yet crossing that border into being was such a daring act. A brass band and skyrockets would not be too much to expect. Linda got out of bed, slowly and laboriously, as if she were already at full term. She began to put things into the suitcase.

"So *that's* why you got fat," Robin said.

"Uh-huh. Not actually *fat*, though."

"And you threw up a couple of times, didn't you?" The girl sounded like a ruthless D.A., determined to get all the facts.

"Yes, I suppose so. In the beginning." Was she looking for clinical proof or something? Linda shut the suitcase and practically flung it to the floor. She started to walk toward the bathroom.

"I won't be an only child any more, will I?" Robin said, her voice altered by emotion, and Linda stood still.

"No, you won't," she said, after a while. "And neither will I." She turned and looked at Robin, who was standing now, too. Linda saw that she had never undressed for the night.

"It will be like a sister or a brother. A stepsister," Robin said.

"*Half* sister, I think. But definitely related. It could even look like you, you know."

"By the time it's my age, I'll be old."

Linda did some fast calculations in her head. "No,"

she said, "only twenty-six. Hey, like you and me!" Robin seemed doubtful, even disconsolate, so Linda added, "That's not so old, you know. I've hardly done anything yet."

"I won't ever see it, anyway," Robin said, "so it doesn't matter."

"Of course it matters," Linda insisted. "We'll keep in touch. How far do you think California is from Arizona, anyway? It's practically next door. And we'll write to each other and call." Her argument was only burdening her own heart, and Robin looked so forlorn, standing there in her rumpled clothes. How could her mother have left her forever? Linda put her hands to her belly again, that new, easy gesture, and contemplated the first separation. "Come on," she said. "Let's go."

LINDA COULD DANCE, BUT SHE CERTAINLY *33*
couldn't sing. Her voice traveled aimlessly
from key to key and broke like an adolescent
boy's on the high notes. She went for them, anyway,
bravely, or as if she couldn't hear the noise she made.
And got the words all wrong, too. "Blackbirds singing
in the dead of light . . ." They had listened to a two-hour
program of Beatles numbers and this was the payoff. It
was terrible to be stuck in the car with her when she
sang, but Robin, who didn't want to speak or be spoken
to, accepted Linda's singing as a lesser irritation.

They were finally on their way to Glendale, the last
stage in Robin's journey toward her mother. Thoughts
of her mother occupied her entirely now, driving out the
still-fresh news of Linda's pregnancy. She tried to concentrate on that, but couldn't. And couldn't work up
the fantasies she had found so comforting only yesterday.
All she was left with were the grim probabilities of
reality, and the fork in her pocket that drew her hand
to it again and again. That woman who had gone away
eight years before would be a stranger because eight
years had happened and because she had chosen to go.
But she would still be, with the stubbornness of fact,
Robin's mother, the one who had given birth to her
and, before that, carried her everywhere in the sheltering
ark of her body. There were these two separate people
who became one, who merged into the image you finally
see when you adjust the focus on binoculars. Robin, who
was set now to reject *her*, to turn away a belated appeal
of love with violence, wondered if she would get the
chance. To be rejected twice was unthinkable. In all her
dreams of their reunion, it was her mother who experienced joy, and Robin who closed in on that joy with the

deadliness of her resolve. But what if there was no welcome, if absence only made the heart grow colder, if it
forgot in ways the brain did not?

Robin closed her eyes and reviewed some of her
own behavior, long past and recent, for which she might
have invited punishment. Once, she stood on the
dropped dime of a bereft classmate and pretended to
help him look for it while the day darkened and his
mother called him home. There was that other time
when she was small and pinched the finger of someone
much smaller until it was shocked into bloodlessness.
And the waking dreams in which she foretold her own
father's death. Didn't she deserve retribution for that,
and for flushing a Modess and its cardboard container
down a motel toilet in Pennsylvania? A polite sign had
urged her to use the provided receptacle. And for writing
on the walls of ladies' rooms everywhere that *Linda
Reismann sucks/does it for a nickel/writes on walls*. If
she'd only admit it, Robin was guilty of a thousand secret
crimes, even those against harmless strangers, whom she
imagined squashed by cars as they crossed the street,
obliterated by sudden outbreaks of war, by hostile inter-
planetary invasion. Teachers she had hated were de-
tained forever in the rooms of torture behind her eyes.
Even friends. Bad thoughts about good friends in the
very act of friendship. She loved no one, then, was incapable of loving, thereby earning with justice her status
of being unloved.

Next to Linda, Robin was asleep again, sitting
up, her body vibrating as the Maverick rode the rough-
textured streets. On other occasions, Linda had observed

the girl's talent for making herself smaller or larger at will. In times of stubborn perversity, she blew up with argument and righteousness. She took up too much room in motels or in the car. When she did not want to speak at all, when she was melancholy, she retreated into the private smallness of her bones and could not be reached. Now, when they were almost there, Linda saw that Robin was growing smaller again. What if she disappeared completely before she could be delivered to her mother? Linda saw herself pulling up to Miriam's house and running inside breathlessly to explain that she meant well, had almost brought off this family reunion, had traveled 2,804 miles by the speedometer. There was proof of her good intentions in the car—look!—that puddle of clothing on the front seat, those long strands of blond hair still clinging to the headrest, the impression in the cushion where Robin had recently been sleeping, warm as life. She knew she was being sentimental, the quality that Robin found most disgusting in her, but she couldn't help it. It was her own loss she contemplated. Where was Cornelia Street anyway? They could *both* melt in this heat.

Linda pulled into a gas station to ask directions and Robin came awake drenched, and with rubbery limbs. She banged her helpless hands against each other and grunted. "What's this?" she demanded in a troll's voice.

"I'm only stopping for directions. Do you want to use the bathroom?"

Robin shook her head.

"I mean, to freshen up or something. You're not going to wear that, are you?" She gestured at Robin's creased and stained T-shirt and shorts.

HEARTS

Robin made a growling noise and threw herself back against the hot plastic.

"All right, all right," Linda said. "I was only asking." She pulled her own wet shirt away from her body and went to speak to the attendant. She learned that Cornelia Street was only a few blocks east of the station. Linda looked at her watch. "Good," she announced after she got back into the car. "Perfect timing."

Someone was home, Robin guessed, because a sleek yellow sportscar slouched in the shade of the carport. It was exactly two o'clock in the afternoon, and it was Sunday. Linda had calculated their appearance carefully, explaining to Robin that the most important thing was not to start off on the wrong foot, psychologically speaking, by showing up at the wrong time. It would be no good to arrive during breakfast, for instance, or dinner, or after Miriam and Anthony had gone to sleep. She called them that—Miriam and Anthony—as if suggestion of intimacy creates intimacy.

They parked on the street and walked to the front door. After Linda rang the bell, they waited in the clamoring of chimes for a response. Robin closed her eyes but her lids trembled open again. There was a chance she would be blinded by the first sight of her mother, and that her mother would make some move toward her against which she would have no defense. Her hand went automatically to the pocketed fork, and it comforted her. Thy rod and thy fork.

The man who came to the door was wearing a short bathrobe, hastily tied. There was a tangle of chains in the gray springy hairs of his chest, and several turquoise rings on his fingers. He looked sweaty and confused, as if he'd just been awakened from a nap. "I hope we didn't interrupt . . . disturb you," Linda said.

Robin stared hard at the man. This was probably *him*. She was surprised, even disappointed, by her own cool assessment. He looked like an actor she had seen in an old movie on TV, the one who played a gangster in love with the cop's sister.

He eyed them, pushing his rumpled hair back with one hand and squinting at the intrusion of sunlight. "Forget it, sisters," he said. "We're already saved." He started to close the door.

"Oh, no," Linda told him. "We're not here to save anybody or anything like that. This is a personal call, Mr. Hausner."

Robin tried to look past him into the house, where her mother was surely waiting, maybe hiding. But the man's broad shoulders blocked most of her view, and the dimness in there made it difficult to see much of anything. But she could hear distant music; amazingly, the same music that she and Linda had been listening to a few minutes ago on the car radio.

"I don't know you, do I?" the man said.

"No, you don't," Linda admitted. "It's Miri— It's your wife."

The sun on Robin's back and neck was fiery. She shook her hair to loosen it into a protective veil, while the man hesitated and looked them over. "Who should I say?" he asked finally.

"I think I should say myself," Linda told him. She spoke with astonishing confidence, even nerve, like a door-to-door salesman of encyclopedias who knows that only aggression will get you anywhere in this world.

And it worked. The man stepped back to let them in. As Robin went past him, she noticed that he was barefoot and that he emitted a strange perfume. Then she was inside her mother's house.

There were no dogs or cats or children here. All the shades were down against the midday heat, and the dark, cool quiet seemed religious to Robin, who had not been to church for years. She remembered that it felt something like this, though. Or maybe it was because of what he'd said when he opened the door. She had the giddy notion that she and Linda *had* come to save the sinners who lived here.

Two facing sofas in the living room were white, ghostlike. No one had sat recently on the smooth, plump cushions, and the polished floors bore no witness to human traffic. The heavy outer door clanged shut behind them, like the door of a safe.

"Who was *that*, Tony?" a woman's voice called. "Come on back to bed."

The man smiled nervously at Linda. He shifted on his silly, naked legs. "You'd better come out, Mim," he called back. "We've got company."

They were *both* napping, Robin thought. So much for Linda's great strategy. And then she understood, in an avalanche of knowledge and memory, that that wasn't what they had been doing at all. The smell on the man was the smell of her mother, an ancient clue from childhood, from bedclothes, from the first intimation of adult conspiracy. It made her dizzy now as it had made her manic then. The whole place stinks of it, she thought, I can hardly breathe, and then footsteps came from the back of the house.

Robin looked and looked at the woman, at her mother, who came into the room like an ordinary person entering a room. Oh, she was beautiful and terrible at once. How could she be shorter than Robin, look so old and so young, so familiar and so unknown? Her bathrobe matched the man's, and she was wearing glasses. Glasses!

Robin had meant to go right for the fork, to be

HEARTS

ready for anything, but instead her hands came together in a kind of involuntary applause, and then clutched one another.

If this was actually her mother, then maybe *she* was actually a lost Robin, someone reduced to early needs, to early speech and gestures. If she could move, if she were not stuck in place like this, she might pitch around the room in some old attention-getting dance, and then lie on the floor to be small, to be at the feet of grownups, under a table, worshipping feet, smelling shoes and dust and the cheesy scent of speckled linoleum. She felt a mad thrill of hunger, real belly-hunger for milk and bread, and eggs fixed a special way on a special blue-rimmed plate. If she could speak, she would say, "Feed me!" or something else crazy like that.

But Robin was as voiceless as she had been on that day when she and Linda had their contest of silence. Maybe Linda was stricken again, too, because her mouth was open in a kind of dumb declaration. And she was tilted toward Miriam, as if the two women would soon meet in an embrace. They were all frozen that way for a moment, and then Robin's mother glanced at the man for an explanation. Who *are* these people? He only raised his eyebrows and shoulders at the same time. Nobody *he* knew would come out of the blue like this at two o'clock on a Sunday afternoon when people are in bed together doing it. Miriam exhaled, exasperated, her heart's action visible under the yellow velour of the robe.

Robin, her power of movement restored, reached into her pocket for the fork. With one hand, she deftly removed the rubber band, the soft layers of Kleenex, until the cold metal of the tines burned her fingers. But it was

Linda she most wanted to stab now, in the arm or the leg, so that she would find her voice again and speak for both of them.

Linda's enchantment seemed to lift at the same moment. "Maybe we should all sit down," she said. "I have news. I have something important to tell you."

Robin looked at the impeccable white furniture.

"Are you sure you have the right place?" Miriam asked.

"Yes," Linda said. "I think I would know you anywhere. I'm Linda Reismann. I was married to Wright after you were. And this . . . and this is Robin."

Before she even said this last, though, Miriam had already turned to gawk at Robin, not as if she knew her, but as if she were someone famous, a movie star seen for the first time off the silver screen. "Robin," Miriam said faintly, and Robin believed she was being named then, being christened in this cool desert house a million miles from home. "Robin," Miriam said again, in absolute wonder.

"Maybe we should sit down," Linda urged once more, and they moved in a cautious ballet to the white sofas. Robin and Linda sat together, and the single cushion they shared sighed gently under their combined weight and took them in. Miriam and Anthony faced them. The seats were too wide and deep for this tense encounter. There was no way to sit on edge and lean forward, and they all sank into false attitudes of relaxation.

"This is my . . . this is *Robin*," Miriam said to Anthony, and she laughed excitedly.

He took her hand in his. "Maybe you should have

called," he told Linda, and clutched the bathrobe over his knees with the other hand.

"I tried to," Linda said, and looked to Robin as if to measure her own sin of betrayal.

But Robin didn't feel betrayed, at least not by Linda.

"And Wright?" Miriam asked.

"Gone," Linda told her. "I mean dead. He died."

"Died? How?"

"Heart attack."

"Oh," Miriam said.

"Mim, Mim," Anthony murmured, squeezing her hand, pumping it, the way Robin's father used to squeeze the Test-Your-Grip handles at the penny arcade. She remembered how the machine registered his strength in ascending lights: Puny, 90-Pound Weakling, Getting There, Strong Man, Musclebound, Popeye! Her mother's hand fell back lifelessly into her lap when Anthony let go, and it registered nothing.

"I'll make some coffee," he said, and still modestly holding his bathrobe shut, he stood.

Miriam was looking at Robin and didn't reply.

"I'll help you," Linda said, and after one backward glance, she followed him across the shadowed tile floor and out of the room.

Linda imagined that leaving a child in school for the first time would be something like this. Knowing how good education was for the child would not diminish the pain of parting.

In the kitchen she watched as Anthony set the table with thoughtful care. He folded a yellow paper napkin neatly at each place. There was a large bakery box on the table, and when he cut the string the box fell open to reveal four golden and sugared pastries. Linda guessed that this was the celebratory snack they'd planned to share after making love. It was probably a ritual. She imagined Anthony, still naked and flushed, bounding inside with the pastries on a tray, and how Miriam would smooth a place in the bed for him, and how their sticky fingers would sparkle later with crumbs. The nude photos of Miriam flickered through her head. That over-exposed pallor and the dark lipstick. Wright's triumphant and breathless smile, his arm circling her waist. It should be easier to separate people into heroes and villains. But Linda pitied everyone. And then, without warning, Wolfie entered her thoughts, and she grieved for all their forfeited greedy Sundays like this one.

Anthony plugged in the coffee maker and sacrificed the pastries to a communal platter. He seemed distressed that there was nothing else to do. "You really should have called," he told Linda again.

"It's hard to discuss certain things over the phone," Linda said, thinking briefly of Supercreep, his impassioned and wordless messages.

"Yeah," he said. "But this is quite a shock."

"What happened to your family?" she asked, surprised that she really wanted to know. She remembered the postcard he had written to his son, the picture of the giant saguaro cactus. It was like catching up with the lives of the characters in a soap opera she had not seen in years.

Anthony didn't question her curiosity or her right to know. "My wife got married again," he said. "The boy joined the army right after high school. He's married, too, to a Hawaiian girl. She's very nice, religious. My daughter's still at home. She does ceramics." They both

HEARTS

pondered this synopsis, and then, as if he had just come to his senses, Anthony asked, "What does she want? To come live with us?"

"I guess," Linda said. "It's between them."

In the living room, Robin and her mother had remained in a silent tableau for a few moments. Then, surprisingly, Miriam laughed, a short, anxious trill of laughter. She said, "You're thirteen now, aren't you?"

The laughter and the question both startled Robin, and she found herself recalling bitterly the missed birthdays. Her own birthdays and her father's, the imposed solitude of all their celebrations. On New Year's Eve, he always woke her at midnight and brought her, in her pajamas, to the living room, where they both donned silly hats and blew a short discordant duet through tin horns.

"Yes," she said.

Miriam's hands raised, opened. "Your hair . . . You look exactly like your father. *Exactly.*" Her tone was slightly accusing, as if Robin had chosen to look like Wright or he had used undue influence over her in Miriam's absence.

"It's hard to know . . . what to say," Miriam said. "I suppose you hate me." She paused expectantly.

But Robin didn't answer. Hate. Love. They were such puny, useless words. She touched the fork, counted the tines.

Miriam moved from her sofa to Robin's. "I was only twenty-one when you were born," she said. "I guess that seems old to you, but it wasn't. Girls were different then, more innocent. I didn't know up from down." She sighed. "Wright was older, like Tony. My fatal weakness." She laughed again. "Did he ever tell you I called? *Twice?*"

Robin shook her head, disbelieving.

"Well, I did. The first time right after we came here. I offered to take you, but he said no."

Offered. Take. One by one the words were losing meaning, slipping away.

"The second time was about a year later. *You* answered the phone."

Robin searched frantically for the event and couldn't find it.

"I didn't say who I was," Miriam said. "You couldn't possibly know." She touched her brow, pushed her fingers through her hair. "He acted crazy that time. He said he'd *kill* me if I ever called again, if I ever tried to contact you. I wrote a couple of letters to him, to you, and then I tore them up. Time went by, like it does." That laugh again. Then she leaned forward, clutching her own arms. "Listen, I *thought* about you. Every time I saw a little girl in the street . . . God, the *nights* . . . Tony wanted to have you kidnapped and brought here. Can you imagine?"

Robin could barely pay attention. She was much too busy trying to remember that phone call, her father's murderous impulse. She imagined him hanging up, beating his fists against the wall, and then going to look for her, Robin. What was she doing? Watching television? Getting ready for bed? She pictured one of those suffocating embraces, Wright's passion, her own wriggling impatience to be free.

"You believe me, don't you?" Miriam asked.

Robin attempted a shrug, but couldn't bring it off. One shoulder kept twitching involuntarily.

HEARTS

"I know I'm not the best mother in the world, but I'm not the worst, either," Miriam said. "When I was there, we were very close. You probably don't remember it, but I used to brush your hair all the time." She laughed.

Robin thought that if her mother had never left she would have grown up listening to that laugh, that it would have become as casual and familiar as language. But now she despised its sound, its inappropriate punctuation of Miriam's narrative. Robin knew it was an evasive technique, that it replaced the truth that could only be told through language. Unreasonably, she was disturbed in the same way by the eyeglasses. They seemed to make it impossible for their eyes to be engaged for more than a glance. They were a disguise, another evasion, and Robin could kill her mother for that alone. Her hand crept into her pocket and held the fork.

"Talk about mothers. *My* mother was the worst," Miriam continued. "She stayed home and made everybody miserable and guilty. She didn't believe in normal feelings. Since she missed her chance in life, she wanted everybody else to miss theirs. I wasn't even allowed to *talk* to men until I was eighteen. And do you know what she used to do, Robin? She used to *smell* me when I came home. She pretended it was to see if I'd been smoking or drinking, but it wasn't, take my word for it. She wanted to see if . . . well . . . if I had *experienced* anything she didn't want me to experience. Do you wonder I took off with your father when I was only nineteen? And you know what *he* was like."

Robin's whole body prickled, and her grip tightened on the fork's handle. "His heart . . ." she began.

"I know," Miriam said. "I know. It's hard to believe. He was so healthy. He bowled and he worked out. But what I meant to say was, he was so *nice*. At first I really liked it. Everything I did pleased him. I could burn the roast and he'd say he liked it that way. He'd chew on it until he choked. No roast and he'd say he wasn't hungry anyway." Miriam laughed. "He used to say he wanted to make it up to me, that I had this unhappy childhood, that my mother was so strict. He said he wanted me to feel *free*. But he was always asking me if I was happy, he was always hugging me." She hesitated. "And I didn't feel certain things for him that I wanted to, that a wife is supposed to feel for her husband. In some ways I might as well have been back with my mother; you know, trapped, and being *good*."

Robin began to draw the fork from her pocket. She was furious that Miriam had spoken against her dead father, and that what she had said was undeniably true. She was furious that she had understood all the other implications when she wasn't ready to understand them. This woman who had eloped with Robin's childhood was forcing her now into sudden adult knowledge she didn't want.

Miriam slid nearer to Robin. "Then there was Tony," she said softly, earnestly. "Sometimes you don't meet the right people at the right time. It's not always *convenient*." She was close to Robin, leaning closer. Robin felt as rigid and tense as she had that day when the beautiful silver dogs had circled her feet, panted against her skin. She half closed her eyes and tried not to inhale her mother's scent.

Miriam's hand reached out in the milky light to

HEARTS

touch Robin's hair. "You *loved* when I brushed it," she said. "You used to close your eyes just like that. Your hair was like corn silk. It still is. I thought it would be so much darker by now." She stroked Robin's head and Robin grew sleepy. She had to force herself to stay awake, not to lose her fierce and precious guard. Her hand relaxed and almost released the fork, the way it let go of the pillow at night the moment before sleep.

Miriam whispered, "I would dream about the old apartment in Newark and wake up, hearing you. Once or twice it was really Nicky, Tony's son. He came to stay with us for a while because he didn't get along with his stepfather. But he got into trouble here. Fights at school, and he set little fires."

Robin came awake abruptly, gripping the fork. "You could have taken me," she said, meaning to sound condemning, rather than the way she did, pleading and sad.

Miriam withdrew her stroking hand. "But I *couldn't*," she said. "Not then. When you run away like that, you're a little *crazy*. I hardly took anything, clothes, anything. I don't know, I thought he'd let me have you later . . . I didn't think . . ." Her hand rose up again.

Robin moved away, out of reach, and saw that Anthony had come back into the room. Miriam didn't seem to notice him. "But you're here now," she told Robin. "It's sort of like a miracle. You can stay and we can make up for it . . . ?"

"Coffee, Mim," Anthony announced in his firm baritone.

Linda looked closely at Robin's face to see if she could figure out what had taken place in the other room. Robin looked back at her with that old warring expression, as if nothing had changed, nothing was about to change.

They all took their places around the table. Miriam sat next to Anthony. She gave some signal in the shorthand of habit, and he proceeded to pour the coffee.

Linda put cream and sugar in hers, even as her throat closed against the possibility of food or drink or speech. She looked politely, brightly at Anthony, the other minor player in this drama, who might provide some necessary comic relief.

But he didn't. With serious attention he served the coffee and passed the plate of pastries to Linda, who simply took it from him and held it. Then he got up and stood behind his wife and gripped her shoulders with his large beringed hands. In their plush matching robes, Miriam and Anthony reminded Linda of pictures she'd seen of the Duke and Duchess of Windsor, exiled forever from the kingdom of real privilege.

Miriam tried to laugh, but achieved only a small, failed sound. "I'd like Robin to stay," she said, "to live with us?" It was definitely a question.

Linda saw Anthony flinch at this threat to their obsessive privacy. "Well, sure," he managed. "If that's what you—"

"Why, that's wonderful!" Linda interjected. "It's exactly what we'd hoped." She turned to smile or grimace at Miriam, who was holding her teaspoon up, seeking her own tiny inverted reflection in its bowl. Then Linda looked at Robin and saw that she had risen in her place, clutching a fork in her hand. It was an elaborate, heavy, old-fashioned fork, very different from the severe stainless steel flatware that Anthony had arranged in perfect symmetry. Linda had seen that fork somewhere before.

HEARTS

Robin held it as if it were a weapon, and she looked from one of them to the other, taking deep, desperate breaths like a silent-film vamp simulating ecstasy.

"Arizona," Linda said, standing, too, still holding the platter. "The climate alone—"

"*Shut up!*" Robin bellowed, and she raised the blanched fist that held the fork, over her head. "Shut up," she said again, this time to her mother and Anthony, who had not spoken or moved at all. Her face was deeply flushed and her hair was a crackling halo of light. "Why don't you ask *me*?" she demanded. "Why don't you ask *me* if I want to stay?"

"I'm asking you, Robin," Miriam said weakly.

"No, you're not! You're asking *him*. You never asked me *anything!* And you never called up! You're a liar and a murderer!"

"Hey, *hey*," Tony warned.

Linda was mesmerized. Never in all their time together, during vocal battles or battling silences, had the girl looked quite like this, so violent, so thrillingly beautiful. "Oh, Robin honey," Linda said, and she stepped back from the table and walked slowly toward her.

"I don't want to stay here," Robin said in a calm, even a reasonable, voice. "I wouldn't stay here for a hundred million dollars." Her back was curved like an archer's extended bow. Her eyes were clear and brilliant with intention. As Linda reached her side, the hand holding the fork came down in one swift and stabbing plunge.

Miriam screamed and Robin pulled her hand back. She looked in wonderment at the fork, and at the quivering, crumbling pastry impaled on its points.

35
Glendale and Robin had not cried yet, or
spoken one unsolicited word.

Linda ventured careful questions. "Shall I put the
radio on? Should we stop soon to have something to
eat?"

And Robin said yes automatically, without delibera-
tion or affect.

Even back in Miriam's house, after the stabbing of
the pastry, Robin had moved in a kind of trance, and
displayed almost no emotion. Linda had quickly taken
charge. Miriam and Anthony were still frozen in their
royal pose, obviously too stunned or confused to act.
"It's all right," Linda told Robin. She took the girl's
arm and led her into the living room. Robin was like the
victim of a street accident, a hit-and-run. There was no
blood or other evidence of injury, but she seemed to be
in shock, and who knew what damage was unseen.

Linda spoke clearly and loudly, as if she had to pene-
trate an invisible barrier. "It's all right," she repeated.
"Nobody will make you stay. I'll take you with me."

"You don't have to," Robin muttered.

"I know that, Robin," Linda said. "I want to." Then
she went back to the kitchen, where Anthony and
Miriam huddled in their robes. "I'm sorry," Linda said,
trying to avoid Miriam's stricken glance. "I really
thought it would work out. But I guess it's just too late.
Or maybe it's too early."

"Could I ask you . . . Would you please . . ." Miriam
began. And Linda said she would write and let her know
how Robin was getting along. Then she and Robin left
the house.

HEARTS

As she drove, Linda glanced at the girl from time to time and saw the same pale, impassive face. She was convinced now that Robin had to cry in order to avoid the greater consequences of denied grief. Linda felt a responsibility to make her cry, if necessary. But first she had to get her attention. "Robin?" she said. "Remember when you asked about my father? About how he died?"

There was no answer.

"And remember I said he died in a household accident? Well, it wasn't because I left my skates on the stairs. And he wasn't smoking in bed, either. He was electrocuted."

Robin turned to look at her for the first time. "You mean in the electric chair?"

"Oh, no, no. It really *was* a household accident. Bad wiring, and he was standing in a lot of water. The basement was flooded. And I saw it happen."

Robin was facing forward again, staring ahead at the road.

"I hated my father," Linda said. "He used to hurt me when I was a child, and I used to wish that he would die. I *prayed* for it. But still I cried when he did."

Robin had turned completely away, was curling up, for an escape into sleep, probably.

Linda kept driving and she began to see signs for cities in California, even though they were pretty far from the border. And there were more and more California license plates. Many of them had names or phrases instead of random letters and numbers. NICE GUY, CLASSY, LOVER, CINDI B. Well, at least they seemed to know who they were.

Robin hadn't moved for an hour or more. She was

remarkably stubborn, but Linda was, too, and would not be swayed from her mission. Everyone has to be a mourner sometime. The very nature of human life demands that. Why did Robin think she could escape it?

Linda saw a sign for a rest area ahead, and she signaled and slowed down. It was one of those wooded places, with a few redwood tables and benches, a couple of telephones, and toilets. After so many miles of open, sun-bleached landscape, it was a real oasis. There was only one other car there, a station wagon with bicycles and a baby stroller tied to the roof rack. As Linda pulled in and parked, the family sitting at one of the tables gathered their belongings and started to leave. The children distributed their garbage among the four trash baskets, each labeled with a sign: *Thank You For Not Littering*. A beautiful and lively Irish setter was called from its hideout in the woods. When they were gone, Linda touched Robin's shoulder. "Robin, wake up," she said.

"Are we in California?" She rubbed her eyes.

"No, almost. I needed to rest for a while. And I wanted to show you something."

"What?"

"Come out." Linda opened the door and walked to the rear of the Maverick, where she waited for Robin.

"What?" Robin said again. "I don't see anything."

Linda opened the trunk of the car and took out the plastic mortuary box. It seemed heavier than she remembered.

"What's that?" Robin asked.

Linda hesitated for a moment, and then she said, "It's your father's ashes, Robin."

H E A R T S

"But he didn't smoke!" Robin said, and then her face swiftly changed and Linda knew that she understood.

"I brought them all the way from Jersey," Linda said. "I didn't tell you about them because . . . well, because I thought you were too young, that it was too morbid. But now I think it's your right to know, to help me to scatter them."

Robin was staring at the box. Linda might have been holding a live cobra.

"For a while I thought the location was most important, you know, somewhere peaceful and beautiful. I thought I would have to find a cliff somewhere, or a running stream. No place seemed exactly right, and I couldn't bring myself to just leave him . . . them anywhere. Maybe that's because it was wrong to keep this from you in the first place. Maybe I was waiting for an opportunity to do this with you. Should we walk into the woods a little?"

Robin was unable to answer. It was as if she were being confronted with her father's death for the first time. The idea of ashes horrified her, although she had understood about the cremation, and clearly remembered the rush of air from the oven. Maybe you are never done with dead people. If there are ashes, perhaps there are also ghosts.

Linda was walking away, going through the trees carrying the box. Robin paused and then followed her, quickly catching up. It was sharply cooler in this shaded place, and really quiet. Robin didn't want to think about anything, least of all what they were about to do. Maybe

Linda was lying. Maybe there were cigars in that box, or candy. It was shaped something like a book, and it could contain anything.

Linda stopped walking suddenly, and Robin almost collided with her. "This is a good place, isn't it?" Linda asked. "I mean, it's cool and still here. He painted trees a lot, too." She put her right hand on the lid of the box and tugged, but it didn't open. She held the box in the crook of her elbow and pulled harder, but still nothing happened. She smiled at Robin. "It's stuck, I think," she said. She tapped the box lightly with her fist, still smiling, and then tapped it a little harder. Her mouth formed a firm, determined line as she pulled at the lid once more. "I don't understand it," she said. "There doesn't seem to be any reason . . . There's no tape on it or anything. Maybe I'm just doing it wrong."

Robin leaned against a tree and waited. She scratched off little flakes of bark and crumbled them, and she watched as Linda bent to pick up a small rock.

"This is awful," Linda said. "The terrible thing is that *he* was so good at opening things: olive jars, peanuts, sardine cans, anything." She clenched her teeth and hammered at the box with the rock. She looked as if she was trying to kill something.

Robin blinked at each blow. She thought of all the nicknames her father had used for her: Bobolink, Redbird, Roblet. Nobody would call her those names any more.

Linda put the box on the ground. She picked up a bigger rock and held it over her head, grunting. "Oh, God," she said, and brought it down with force. There was a large crack in the lid's surface now, but the box

HEARTS

was still closed. Linda was sweating. She sat down and leaned against a tree, holding the box in her lap. "I can't seem to do anything right," she said. "I'm so sorry." She stroked the lid with her fingertips and it sprang open.

"Oh," Robin said. She leaned forward and peered inside. There was a thick, rolled plastic bag there.

"It's like a Chinese puzzle," Linda said. "Or a desk with a secret compartment. It just opened—like that!— when I touched it a certain way. I thought I'd have to get a screwdriver from the car, or something." She, too, was staring at the plastic bag. Then she stood, unsteadily, taking the bag from the box. Something rattled, like beads.

Linda unrolled the bag slowly and looked into it. Robin had leaned backward and was averting her face, but not her eyes. Linda wasn't sure what she had expected to see. She'd thought of the fat, substantial ashes left by cigars, and of the ashes in a fireplace after a good fire, the residue that can be swept with a broom until it disappears. But the contents of the bag hardly looked like ashes at all. They were a grayish yellow, and were like pieces of fallen plaster or chipped paint. And they clattered against each other, making an unexpected noise. For the briefest moment she imagined that she had been given the wrong box—through some incredible mix-up or hoax. Then she knew what it was she was holding. These were bits of bone, of *Wright's* bones, mortal relics impervious even to fire. The knowledge seemed to travel through her own marrow and then explode into her bloodstream. Robin—she had almost forgotten her— was hugging the tree, and waiting. There were no tears, only an expression of genuine terror.

Linda felt light, as if she had entered another atmosphere in which she'd become weightless. She cleared her throat. "I guess we should begin," she said. "I'll say something first, a kind of prayer or eulogy, you know, to mark the occasion. Then you can, too, if you want to." She cleared her throat again. "We have stopped here in the woods in . . . *near* Quartzsite, Arizona, to say farewell to Wright Henry Reismann, dear husband and father, who has left this life . . . He was a good man . . . and we will remember him." Linda tipped the plastic bag and began to shake out its contents. She was grateful for the soft floor of pine needles that took the ashes so quietly. "Robin?" she said.

But Robin still held the tree and did not say anything.

Linda walked around a little, shaking the bag gently until it was empty. Then she put her arm around Robin's shoulders and drew her away. They walked back through the woods to the rest area, where two other families had now stopped to eat at the picnic tables. A little girl held a sandwich in one hand and waved with the other. Linda waved back. She realized she was still holding the plastic bag. "Just a minute," she said to Robin, and she walked to one of the trash baskets and threw it in.

HEARTS

36

A CANDLE FLICKERED BETWEEN THEM ON the table, while the waitress intoned the specialties of the day. "Chicken Cordon Bleu, Sole Amandine, Veal Marsala." She might have been a train conductor in a foreign country, calling out the strange names of the stations.

They ordered steak. After the waitress left, Linda said, "I felt we should splurge tonight, the last night, so to speak, in our old life."

Robin sipped water and crushed an ice cube between her teeth.

"We're practically there, you know, and I'm so excited. Can you imagine the pioneers? Although they couldn't tell when they crossed into another state, could they? I think the land ought to look more like it does on the map. When I was a child, Robin, I actually thought it did, the colors and all, and the little broken lines."

"Could I have a Seven-Up?" Robin asked.

"Sure. Of course. You can have anything you like. Should we go all out and order the onion rings? And the garlic bread?"

By the time the waitress came with their steaks, Robin had finished all the bread in the basket, and the water and ice in both glasses. She'd been to the salad bar twice, once illegally. She seemed to be eating with the same manic appetite that was driving Linda to talk.

"Here we go," the waitress said. "Green flag's for medium, blue one's well-done. Sour cream for the potatoes, and ketchup if you need it. Enjoy your dinner, ladies."

"Everything looks lovely," Linda told her. "Thank you very much." She pulled the green paper flag from her steak and picked up her knife and fork. Then she put them down again. "Before we left New Jersey," she said, "I did a little research. I went to the library and looked California up in the encyclopedia. And there were some books and magazine articles, too. Do you know what I found out?"

Robin was putting both butter and sour cream on her baked potato. Her steak was covered with ketchup. She had washed her hands before dinner, but Linda saw that she still wore little wristlets of dirt. In the candlelight, she could have been twelve or thirty-seven.

"Well, for one thing," Linda said, "there are more cars per capita in Los Angeles than in any other large American city. And the supermarkets are open twenty-four hours a day. If you feel like having a snack in the middle of the night, you just go out and get it. And they have drive-in churches! There was a picture in one of the magazines. They put these little speakers in your car, the way they do at a drive-in movie, and you can listen to the sermon without getting out. And Disneyland! It's the most popular tourist attraction in the whole country!"

Linda was winded, and Robin didn't seem to be paying any attention to her. The girl was attacking her steak, chewing steadily and hard. Her mouth was rimmed with ketchup, and the very ends of her hair were frosted with sour cream.

Why am I talking so much, Linda wondered, and decided it was to avoid speaking the unspeakable. It was because she could not say aloud that she was *bound* to Robin, that you can become a family by the grace of accident and will, that we have a duty to console one another as best we can. Iola used to tell Linda that she

HEARTS

was too soft for this life. Wolfie said she was romantic. And Robin had called her an asshole, which is more or less the same thing. Linda thought that she had outgrown some of that despised sentimentality, and would become tougher and more disenchanted as she went along. Finally she would be old and tired of everything, and ready to face death with resignation, if not courage. But then someone would probably come in at the last minute, wearing a coat that still held the scent of cold air. And Linda would want more, the way she did now.

She realized she had stopped talking, and that during her silence Robin had stopped eating. The ruins of dinner cluttered the table. Linda looked up and found Robin looking back, her eyes alive with tears.

"We're here!" Robin said, and they were.

There had to be some scientific explanation for the blueness of the air: smog, the onset of evening, some simple chemical balance of heat and moisture and light. Linda's right foot pressed the accelerator and her left one was braced against the floor of the Maverick, but she believed she was dancing.

HEARTS

Hilma Wolitzer

A Conversation with Hilma Wolitzer

Q: What inspired you to write the story of *Hearts*? Was it one particular character? One particular scene?

A: Linda and Robin had been living in the back of my mind, like squatters, for a long time, so I'd have to say that *Hearts* was character-inspired. I knew vaguely that they were two vastly different young women who'd come together by chance. But I didn't really begin to know their story until I wrote the first sentence of the book.

Q: When you first conceived of the story, what did you want it to be about? Did you imagine it as a mother-daughter story? A love story? Something else entirely?

A: All of the above! I'd been thinking a lot about domestic life and the particular struggles of single-parent households. I wondered what truly binds people together for good, and if you can form a solid family without a blood relationship.

Q: Did you have a sense of how the story would unfold as you started writing? Did any section or character in particular present a challenge to write? Were there any surprises in the writing?

_____

A: It's a road book, so it had a built-in geographical destination. Linda was going to drive (however haphazardly) from New Jersey to California, and she'd try to drop Robin off with suitable relatives on the way. What I wasn't sure of was the characters' emotional destination. You can't force people to love each other; that has to evolve from their experiences and their deepest feelings. The biggest challenge was to make the trip interesting from a tourist's point of view, without losing sight of the interior story. My characters surprise me all the time. In a way, that keeps me writing, so I can find out what happens to them.

Q: The novel is titled *Hearts*, and the heart—both physical and emotional—proves to be a unifying and pivotal concept throughout. Was there something in particular about the human heart that you wanted to write about? Was *Hearts* always the title?

A: *Hearts* was always the title, because all of its meanings and connotations were so important to the book, especially the amazing connections the human heart is capable of making. I tried to explore that in several different ways, including Robin's feelings about the mother who abandoned her, Linda's relationships with Wright and then with Wolfie, and finally, in the ways that Robin and Linda and the expected baby might create a lasting attachment.

Q: How did you decide to structure *Hearts* in sections that alternate between Linda and Robin's points of view? Did you find this structure at all limiting?

Did you identify more with one character as you were writing?

A: I began writing from Linda's point of view in a very limited third-person. But Robin (right in character) insisted on having her say, and it would have been a lopsided narrative if I didn't let her speak for herself. Actually, I found the alternating-voices structure freeing, because I identified strongly with both Linda and Robin at different times, so I always got to speak my mind, too.

Q: Many readers will be able to identify with the relationship between Robin and Linda—that of a difficult teenager and her frustrated stepmother. Was your relationship with your own children in some way reflected in the story?

A: I never write directly about myself or my family and friends. It's more fun to make everyone up, and you avoid hard feelings and lawsuits that way. But my own experience as a mother of two daughters (adolescents are *hard*!) and as the daughter (one of three, and once a hellish adolescent myself) of a harried mother, definitely informed the writing of *Hearts*.

Q: Have you ever taken a road trip like Linda and Robin's? Or visited any of the places they do? If not, how did you choose their fictional route?

A: I don't think my family would have survived the trip Robin and Linda take, and I wasn't going to test them.

A READER'S GUIDE

I've done short teaching stints in various parts of the country, so I used my own vision of the American landscape. As for Robin and Linda's route, I did what most travelers do—I consulted a map, and I had AAA figure out a TripTik for them.

Q: *Hearts* was originally published in 1980, more than twenty-five years ago. Is there anything that strikes you about the characters or the text differently now, as you're reexamining it? Do you think, if you were writing the story today, that the characters or the plot would need to change for any reason?

A: Certain elements of the larger world have changed, naturally; Linda might be driving a Hyundai Elantra instead of a Ford Maverick if I wrote the book today. But I'm surprised by how much is really unchanged, like the controversy over abortion, and young people having to deal with a war they may not necessarily support. I believe my characters would remain the same no matter when the book was written—true to themselves in any given situation.

Q: You wrote about abortion at a time when the topic was perhaps even more controversial than it is today. Was it something you wanted to address specifically in your writing? Did you ever imagine a story line where Linda's abortion is performed successfully?

A: Novels are stories about people within a social context. The people always come first with me, before any subject matter (no matter what my personal opinion may be), so I didn't intend to specifically address abortion in a polemical fashion. What happens to Linda at the clinic is part of her story, what might have really happened to her in those circumstances, and the choice she makes later to keep the pregnancy comes from her own character and from what she experiences.

Q: At times *Hearts* is tragically comic, even laugh-out-loud funny. Do you see humor as an essential author tool?

A: I'm glad you thought the book was funny without losing its tragic edge. A sense of humor is absolutely essential, I think, in life and in art. It really helps you get through.

Q: Linda and Robin are so close in age, yet often Robin seems more worldly and aware than Linda, who some might describe as naively optimistic. Robin, as we eventually learn, is even a better driver! Did you intend for their roles to almost switch back and forth throughout? Why?

A: That was intentional, because it seems true. Nobody is one-dimensional; as naive and tentative as Linda is, she has to make nervy choices and moves, and at heart Robin is not always as confident and surly as she appears. We all shift roles constantly, especially parents and children, who take turns caring for each other.

Q: Who are your favorite novelists? Have any writers in particular influenced your own work?

A: That's always the hardest question, because there are so many writers, living and dead, whom I admire, and no matter how many I mention I'll keep thinking of others long after this is in print. But Jane Austen comes to mind first and has the most relevance for me. She's so wryly funny and demonstrates how one can paint the world on a small, domestic canvas. Above all, I admire and am influenced by novels and stories that say that what happens in bedrooms and kitchens matters as much as what happens in boardrooms and war rooms.

Q: What can your readers look forward to next? Is there anything in particular you're working on now?

A: Well, *The Doctor's Daughter*—a father-and-daughter story this time—is about to come out. And I've just begun a new novel, about three women of different social classes, whose lives intersect in surprising ways.

Reading Group Questions and Topics for Discussion

1. Linda and Robin become reluctant relatives after Wright and Linda marry. What effect did Wright's death have on their relationship? What might have happened to Linda and Robin's relationship if Wright had survived, or if they'd simply stayed on in New Jersey?

2. How does Linda and Robin's cross-country trip contribute to their hostilities and to their rare moments of détente? Is a lengthy car ride the acid test of any friendship?

3. Stepmother and stepdaughter are close in age but markedly different. Sometimes they don't even seem to speak the same language. But in what crucial ways are they alike? And what aspects of their respective histories connect them?

4. How is the motif of "hearts" woven throughout the novel? What are the key secrets that Linda and Robin keep from each other, and what finally compels them to open their hearts?

5. How do you imagine Linda at the Robin's age—a teenager—and Robin at twenty-six? Are there times when they seem to trade ages and roles?

6. Hilma Wolitzer uses humor and pathos to tell Robin and Linda's story, sometimes on the same page, as in their stubborn silence at the Howard Johnson's in chapter 23, and when they spread Wright's ashes at a rest stop in chapter 35. Have you experienced a desire to both laugh and cry on similar occasions in your own life? Does a comic vision help to leaven the pain of tragedy?

7. How important are the minor characters and a tourist's view of the American landscape to the novel's progress and the heroines' emotional destination? Did the references to pop culture help to orient you in time and to place?

8. What role does Wolfie play in Robin and Linda's relationship?

9. In what ways might *Hearts* be considered a feminist novel?

10. Linda's dancing is the only thing she can do "without premeditation or fear." She is physically graceful even when she's socially awkward. Does Robin have a similar saving grace?

11. Did you feel as though the author had equal affection and regard for Linda and Robin? Did you sympa-

thize or identify with one more than the other? How does your own status as parent or child affect your attitude toward the characters?

12. Robin has fantasies about her missing mother. What role do these dreams play for Robin? How does Linda help her to cope with her shattered illusions? And how does Linda use fantasy to deal with her own disappointments and losses?

13. Is Robin really "cured" of her longing for her mother by their failed reunion, or is she simply unable now to deny the reality of her abandonment? Does she carry another, unspoken, even unconscious fantasy about forming a new family with Linda? If so, what part does the news of Linda's pregnancy play? How do you envision the future for Linda and Robin and the baby?

Read on for a preview of

THE
DOCTOR'S DAUGHTER

by Hilma Wolitzer

Coming in March 2006

from Ballantine Books

I

The moment I awoke I knew that something was terribly wrong. I could feel it in that place behind my breastbone, where bad news always slides in like junk mail through a slot. It was there that I first acknowledged my parents would die someday ("Oh, sweetheart, but not for such a long, long time!"); where I knew I was ugly and would never be loved; where I suffered spasms of regret about my marriage and my children, and fear of their deaths and of my own. God knows there were plenty of things wrong in the larger world I could easily have named, and that aroused a similar sense of dread, but whatever was lodged in my chest that April morning was personal, not global. I knew that much, at least.

Was it something I'd done, or forgotten to do? There was a vague suggestion of amnesia, of loss, but when I tried to pin down its source, it proved to be elusive, a dream dissolving in daylight. In fact, I'd had a dream just before waking, but the content was obscured by a kind of white scrim. The only thing I could remember was the whiteness. And I couldn't discuss any of this with Everett—we'd quarreled again the night before and were being stonily polite. And what if my awful feeling turned out to be about him?

So I put it all aside while we ate breakfast, chaperoned by CNN and the *Times*, and chatted about Iraq and the weather and the eggs on our plates. I told myself that this was what long-married people do, even when things are good between them. Then I had a flash of my parents in their nightclothes, slow-dancing to the radio in their Riverdale kitchen.

After Ev left for work, I grabbed my bag and left the apartment, too. I had to go to the bank, and then I was going to buy a sandwich and sit near the East River to read manuscripts. Maybe the bank would be my last stop—it wasn't safe to walk around this crazy city with that much money.

Our doorman and the doorman from the building next door were outside in the sunlight, taking a breather from the bell jars of their lobbies. It must have rained the night before; the drying pavement gave off that sour-sweet musk I love, and up and down York Avenue, the ginkgo and honey locusts were suddenly, lushly budding. At fifty-one and with everything I knew, I was still such a sucker for spring. I probed for that sensitive spot in my chest as I walked, almost jogged, along in my jeans and Reeboks, outpacing kids in business suits, and it seemed diminished by then, practically gone. It probably really was only the residue of a bad dream.

Outside Sloan-Kettering, patients tethered to their

scured by a kind of white scrim. The only thing I could remember was the whiteness. And I couldn't discuss any of this with Everett—we'd quarreled again the night before and were being stonily polite. And what if my awful feeling turned out to be about him?

So I put it all aside while we ate breakfast, chaperoned by CNN and the *Times*, and chatted about Iraq and the weather and the eggs on our plates. I told myself that this was what long-married people do, even when things are good between them. Then I had a flash of my parents in their nightclothes, slow-dancing to the radio in their Riverdale kitchen.

After Ev left for work, I grabbed my bag and left the apartment, too. I had to go to the bank, and then I was going to buy a sandwich and sit near the East River to read manuscripts. Maybe the bank would be my last stop—it wasn't safe to walk around this crazy city with that much money.

Our doorman and the doorman from the building next door were outside in the sunlight, taking a breather from the bell jars of their lobbies. It must have rained the night before; the drying pavement gave off that sour-sweet musk I love, and up and down York Avenue, the ginkgo and honey locusts were suddenly, lushly budding. At fifty-one and with everything I knew, I was still such a sucker for spring. I probed for that sensitive spot in my chest as I walked, almost jogged, along in my jeans and Reeboks, outpacing kids in business suits, and it seemed diminished by then, practically gone. It probably really was only the residue of a bad dream.

Outside Sloan-Kettering, patients tethered to their

which she often read to me at bedtime. I'm still haunted by its recurring lament:

> *Alas! Queen's daughter, there thou gangest.*
> *If thy mother knew thy fate,*
> *Her heart would break with grief so great.*

As a child, I didn't really get all that archaic usage, or other words in the story, like *cambric* and *knacker*. But listening to my mother read "The Goose Girl" aloud as she lay next to me at night initiated my life-long romance with language. The plot was electrifying, with its drama of switched identities, talking drops of blood, and a decapitated horse's head (also verbal), more than a century before Mario Puzo. And the message, that children, especially girls, are responsible for their mothers' happiness, was profound and unsettling. I became determined never to break my mother's heart, any more than I would break her back by inadvertently stepping on a sidewalk crack. And I meant to keep my promise to my father about not smoking again.

Passing the Mary Manning Walsh home at 71st Street, I thought of him, imprisoned since early winter in that other place, the one he'd always called, with a theatrical shudder, the "Cadillac" of nursing homes. "I'd rather be dead, Alice," he once said, pointedly, as if he were extracting another, unspoken promise. The Hebrew Home for the Aged isn't very far from the house where we once lived, although since his confinement my father didn't remember that proximity or appreciate the sad irony of it. He didn't remember a lot of things, including me most of the time, a likely source of misery in any grown child's breast. But somehow I knew it wasn't the source of mine. Maybe that was because I'd had several months to deal with the gradual death of my father's personality, a dress rehearsal for the big event.

Occasionally, he would still ask after my mother. "And how is Helen?" was the way he'd put it, a ghostlike version of his old courtly self. The first time he asked, I was so dismayed I couldn't speak. After that, I tried telling him the truth, but he always received it as fresh, agonizing news, and he'd grieve for a few awful moments before he went blank again. I couldn't keep putting him, and myself, through that, so I began to simply say, "She's fine." But once I saw him flinch when I said it, and I amended my lie to reflect his absence from home. "Getting along as best she can, Daddy," I said.

"But who's taking care of her?" he asked, with the perseverance of demented logic.

The worms, I thought, but I said, "Why, I am. And Faye, of course." And he finally sank back in his wheelchair, assuaged. Faye had been our family's housekeeper during my childhood—if he could bend time, well, then so could I. As I crossed East End Avenue to enter Carl Schurz Park, I realized that I hadn't visited my father in almost two weeks. I had to go and see him soon, but not on such a perfect day.

There was the usual pedestrian parade in the park. Runners went by wearing wristbands and earphones. Babies were being pushed in their strollers and the elderly in their wheelchairs, like a fast-forwarded film on the human life cycle. The pigeons paced, as if they'd forgotten they could fly, and dogs circled and sniffed one another while their owners, in a tangle of leashes, exchanged shy, indulgent smiles.

The homeless man who screamed was quietly sunning himself on my favorite bench, so I sat a few benches away, next to a woman absorbed in a paperback. I glanced at the cover, expecting a bodice ripper or a whodunit, but she was reading Proust, in French. *Touché*. The river glittered and flowed on the periphery of my vision as I took the manuscripts out of my bag. I was sure they would distract me from whatever was worrying me; they always did, even when I knew what was on my mind. There were four new submissions that day, three nonfiction proposals and a few chapters of a novel in progress. I began to read, and quickly set aside, the first three submissions. After all this time, I can usually tell before the end of the first paragraph if a writer has any talent.

My training began in 1974 at the literary publishing house of Grace & Findlay, where I mostly answered the phones, typed and filed for the editors, and read through the slush pile. It was only a summer internship, between Swarthmore and an MFA, and before I knew it some lowly reader at another publisher was going to discover *my* novel in their slush pile and make me rich and famous. That never happened, though. All I ever received were standard letters of rejection, the ones that say "Thank you for thinking of us, but your manuscript doesn't meet our needs right now," with the hidden subtext: *This is precisely what we hate. Do try us again when hell freezes over.*

A few years later, I joined the enemy, becoming an assistant editor at G&F, and I was still there, in a senior position, last June, when they merged with a multinational communications group and let me go. I understood that my firing was merely a fiscal matter, and I saw it coming, like a storm darkening a radar screen. But I felt shocked and betrayed anyway, even with the generous severance package.

At first I missed everything about my job—the physical place, my colleagues, my daily sense of purpose, and especially the work itself—with an ache akin to mourning. I decided that this was what it would be like to be dead, but still hovering restlessly at the edges of the living world. There were a few job offers at less prestigious houses, with lower pay and reduced status, and I swiftly, scornfully declined them. Ev says that I went nuts for a while, and I suppose he's right, if crying jags and episodes of misplaced rage are valid clinical signs. "Al," he reasoned one night, "you'll do something else, something new." What did he have in mind—tap dancing? Brain surgery? Part of the trouble was that I believed he was secretly pleased.

He had been in competition with me ever since graduate school in Iowa, where we'd met in a fiction workshop. Even his strapping good looks seemed like a weapon then. To be fair, I was pretty critical of his work, too, a defensive response, really. Everyone there was madly competitive and ambitious, despite the caveats of our instructor, Phil Santo, a mild-tempered, mid-list novelist who kept reiterating that he wasn't running a writing contest—there would be no winners or losers—and that we only had to compete with the most recent drafts of our own stories. "Make it new!" he exhorted us. "Make it better!"

Of course there were winners; soon after graduation two of the men in our workshop went on to capture the fame and fortune we had all craved. And the rest of us, accordingly, became losers. Ev never published anything, either, but I think we both knew that I had come out ahead. At least I'd become a handmaiden in heaven, while he ended up at his family's printing firm, Carroll Graphics—brochures, letterheads, that sort of thing.

So, right after my dismissal, which my friend Violet Steinhorn wryly referred to as my "fall from Grace and Findlay," I read all of Ev's unexpected kindnesses to me, like the freshly squeezed orange juice and impromptu foot massages, as condescending and, at heart, unkind. In return, I withheld my sexual favors for a while, or gave them robotically, until I was proved to be right.

At Violet's urging I went into therapy for a few months, where I mostly wept while the psychologist, Andrea Stern, passed a box of Kleenex to me and crossed and uncrossed her legs. I stopped seeing her soon after she pointed out, and I agreed, that I was avoiding any reference to anything else in my current or past life besides my job. "I can't right now," I said. "Everything hurts too much." And she invited me to come back whenever I was ready.

Then, slowly, I began to recover on my own, to actually enjoy my newfound freedom to read just for pleasure, and go to museums or the movies in the middle of the afternoon. One day I made a lunch date with

Lucy Seo, a book designer at G&F I'd stayed in touch with. She was full of industry chatter, and she kept looking at her watch because she had to get back to work. I guess it was contagious or still in my blood, because I became just as restive. I had to work, too. That's when I came up with my brainstorm, and placed ads in *The New York Review of Books* and *Poets and Writers.* "The book doctor is in. Seasoned editor will help you to make your manuscript better."

The response was immediate and enormous. Some of the letters, of course, were from the kinds of crazies and lonely souls I used to hear from when I was a reader at G&F: people burning to write about their abductions to other planets, or paeans in verse to their departed pets. But there were serious, interesting proposals, too—more than I could handle—and the recovered satisfaction of doing something I liked that was also worthwhile.

The ad was a little precious, and I couldn't help thinking how disdainful my father would have been if he'd seen it. He didn't believe even PhDs had the right to call themselves doctors. Violet, another physician's daughter, teased me about practicing without a license. And she was right, it did seem slightly illicit. But as the more open-minded Lucy pointed out, editing is actually analogous to medicine, with its orderly process of diagnosis, prognosis, and treatment.

I never made any promises to my clients about publication, but most of the projects I took on seemed to have a decent shot, and by choosing carefully I still allowed myself lots of time for personal pursuits and for my family. After I left the park that April day, I was going to go up the street to the ATM at Chase and withdraw five hundred dollars from my private money market account. In a day or two I would give it all to my son Scott, who had asked me for a loan.

He'd said that it was just a temporary cash-flow problem, but he hadn't paid back the other, smaller "loans" I'd made to him in recent months. "This isn't for drugs, Scotty, is it?" I asked, and he held both hands up as if to halt oncoming traffic. "Hey, whoa!" he said. And then he explained that he'd just gone overboard on some things he needed, clothes and CDs, stuff like that.

If Ev knew what I was up to, he would probably have killed me. Our quarrel the night before had been another version of the usual one about Scott, with Ev accusing me again of spoiling him stupid, of encouraging his dependency. "Someone has to make up for your coldness," I said, already weary of our Ping-Pong game of blaming. Which one of us should take the credit for the two children who had turned out so well? Then Ev said, "Don't try to throw this onto me, Alice. You're the enabler here." God, *that* psychobabble again—no wonder he couldn't get published. The money I was about to squander was mine, some of it inherited and some of it earned. I didn't need Everett's or anyone else's permission to help my own child.

It was soothing to sit on a bench in my new, vast outdoor office, with a roasted vegetable sandwich in my hand and the sun beating down like a blessing on my scalp and eyelids. That uneasiness I'd felt since awakening was definitely gone. A Circle Line boat glided by in the distance, for good measure, its passengers waving gaily to those of us on shore, and I waved back. The pages fluttering on my lap were by a first-time novelist, a thirty-six-year-old machinist in Pontiac, Michigan, whose cover letter had simply stated, "I really need help with this." But the opening paragraphs were exceptionally good.

The woman next to me reserved her place in her book with one finger and glanced surreptitiously sideways, as I often do on buses and the subway when I want to see what my seatmate is reading. I imagined that she'd sensed my pleasure in the manuscript and was merely curious about it. She caught me catching her and smiled. "Are you an agent?" she asked, and her smile became wolfish. She probably had her own unpublished six-hundred-page novel stashed behind the gin in the cupboard.

No, I wanted to say, *I'm a doctor.* Or, *I'm a writer, like you, only better.* But that would have been unreasonably mean, and a lie, besides. "An editor," I finally answered, a half-truth, tilting the manuscript out of her line of vision, like a grind hiding the answers to a test, and she nodded brusquely and went back to Combray.

I resumed reading, too, and as I turned the ninth or tenth page I was suddenly infused with joy and envy, the way I used to be in Iowa when someone presented a wonderful piece in the workshop. I hadn't even finished the first chapter and the voice of this writer—this Michael Doyle—was singing in my head. The story line, written in the first person about a young man's search for his missing sister, was fairly simple, even familiar, but the telling was unexpectedly vivid and complex. And it was funny, in a dark, yet sympathetic, way.

Who did he remind me of—Salinger? Grace Paley? No, no one at all—that was the thing.

Now I wanted to thrust the manuscript on the woman sitting next to me and say, *Here, you have to read this!* Of course I didn't; I just kept on reading it myself, wondering why this naturally gifted writer thought he needed anyone's help. By the middle of the third chapter, though, his narrative began to flag and flatten, as if he'd lost his way in the story, or maybe just his nerve. I felt deflated for a moment or two before the old excitement took over—this was where I came in, wasn't it?

Then the homeless man began to howl his familiar aria of despair, and that disturbance in my chest came back, full force—*something is wrong*—and I wondered if it was only the renewable pain of failure, in art and in life. Hastily, I gathered the pages and the sandwich wrapper and shoved them into my bag. As I walked away from the bench, the Proust woman called after me, like someone having the last, triumphant word in an argument, "Have a nice day!"

ABOUT THE AUTHOR

HILMA WOLITZER is the author of several novels, including *Ending*, *Silver*, and *The Doctor's Daughter*, as well as the nonfiction book *The Company of Writers*. She is a recipient of Guggenheim and NEA fellowships, and an Award in Literature from the American Academy and Institute of Arts and Letters. She has taught writing at the University of Iowa, New York University, and Columbia University. Hilma Wolitzer lives in New York City.